INCLUDES
AN ALL-NEW
LORD

D0036739

· ED

GEORGE R. R. MARTIN
& GARDNER DOZOIS

WARRIORS 3

All-new tales of war and warriors—in worlds of old,
worlds to come, and worlds that never were

DIANA GABALDON
ROBIN HOBB
LAWRENCE BLOCK
CARRIE VAUGHN
DAVID MORRELL
JAMES ROLLINS
JOE R. LANSDALE

TOR®
fantasy

$7.99
($9.99 CAN)

ISBN 978-0-7653-6028-1

9 780765 360281

50799

EAN

"You will find warriors of every shape, size, and color in these pages, warriors from every epoch of human history, from yesterday and today and tomorrow, and from worlds that never were. Some of the stories will make you sad, some will make you laugh, and many will keep you on the edge of your seat."

—George R. R. Martin,
from his introduction to *Warriors*

PRAISE FOR *WARRIORS*

WARRIORS 3

EDITED BY

GEORGE R. R. MARTIN

AND

GARDNER DOZOIS

TOR®
fantasy

A TOM DOHERTY ASSOCIATES BOOK
NEW YORK

This is a work of fiction. All of the characters, organizations, and events portrayed in these stories are either products of the authors' imaginations or are used fictitiously.

WARRIORS 3

Copyright © 2010 by George R. R. Martin and Gardner Dozois

A Tor Book
Published by Tom Doherty Associates, LLC
175 Fifth Avenue
New York, NY 10010

www.tor-forge.com

Tor® is a registered trademark of Tom Doherty Associates, LLC.

ISBN 978-0-7653-6028-1

First Edition: March 2010
First Mass Market Edition: August 2011

Printed in the United States of America

0 9 8 7 6 5 4 3 2 1

Copyright Acknowledgments

To Lauren and Jeff,
to Tyler and Isabella,
to Sean and Dean,

may you be strangers to war

Contents

Introduction

Stories from the Spinner Rack
by George R. R. Martin

There were no bookstores in Bayonne, New Jersey, when I was a kid.

Which is not to say there was no place to buy a book. There were plenty of places to buy books, so long as what you wanted was a paperback. (If you wanted a hardcover, you could take the bus into New York City.) Most of those places were what we called "candy stores" back then, but Hershey bars and Milky Ways and penny candy were the least of what they sold. Every candy store was a little different from every other. Some carried groceries and some didn't, some had soda fountains and some didn't, some offered fresh baked goods in the morning and would make you a deli sandwich all day long, some sold squirt guns and hula hoops and those pink rubber balls we used for our stickball games . . . but all of them sold newspapers, magazines, comic books, and paperbacks.

When I was growing up in Bayonne's projects, my local candy store was a little place on the corner of

First Street and Kelly Parkway, across the street from the waters of the Kill Van Kull. The "book section" was a wire spinner rack, taller than I was, that stood right next to the comics . . . perfect placement for me, once my reading had expanded beyond funny books. My allowance was a dollar a week, and figuring out how I was going to split that up between ten-cent comic books (when the price went up to twelve cents, it really blew the hell out of my budget), thirty-five-cent paperbacks, a candy bar or two, the infrequent quarter malt or ice cream soda, and an occasional game of Skee-Ball at Uncle Milty's down the block was always one of the more agonizing decisions of the week, and honed my math skills to the utmost.

The comic book racks and the paperback spinner had more in common than mere proximity. Neither one recognized the existence of genre. In those days, the superheroes had not yet reached the same level of dominance in comics that they presently enjoy. Oh, we had Superman and Batman and the JLA, of course, and later on Spider-Man and the Fantastic Four came along to join them, but there were all sorts of other comic books as well—war comics, crime comics, western comics, romance comics for the girls, movie and television tie-ins, strange hybrids like *Turok, Son of Stone* (Indians meet dinosaurs, and call them "honkers"). You had Archie and Betty and Veronica and *Cosmo the Merry Martian* for laughs, you had Casper the Friendly Ghost and Baby Huey for littler kids (I was much too sophisticated for those), you had Carl Barks drawing Donald Duck and Uncle Scrooge. You had hot rod comics, you had comics about models complete with cut-out clothes, and, of course, you had *Classics Illustrated*, whose literary adaptations served as my first introduction to everyone from Robert Louis Stevenson to Herman Melville. *And all these different comics were mixed together.*

The same was true of the paperbacks in the adjacent spinner rack. There was only the one spinner, and it had only so many pockets, so there were never more than one or two copies of any particular title. I had been a science fiction fan since a friend of my mother's had given me a copy of Robert A. Heinlein's *Have Space Suit—Will Travel* one year for Christmas (for the better part of the decade, it was the only hardcover I owned), so I was always looking for more Heinlein, and more SF, but with the way all the books were mixed together, the only way to be sure of finding them was to flip through every book in every pocket, even if it meant getting down on your knees to check the titles in the back of the bottom level. Paperbacks were thinner then, so each pocket might hold four or five books, and every one was different. You'd find an Ace Double SF title cheek-by-jowl with a mass market reprint of *The Brothers Karamazov*, sandwiched in between a nurse novel and the latest Mike Hammer yarn from Mickey Spillane. Dorothy Parker and Dorothy Sayers shared rack space with Ralph Ellison and J. D. Salinger. Max Brand rubbed up against Barbara Cartland. (Barbara would have been mortified.) A. E. van Vogt, P. G. Wodehouse, and H. P. Lovecraft were crammed in together with F. Scott Fitzgerald. Mysteries, westerns, gothics, ghost stories, classics of English literature, the latest contemporary "literary" novels, and, of course, SF and fantasy and horror—you could find it all on that spinner rack in the little candy store at First Street and Kelly Parkway.

Looking back now, almost half a century later, I can see that that wire spinner rack had a profound impact on my later development as a writer. All writers are readers first, and all of us write the sort of books we want to read. I started out loving science fiction and I still love science fiction . . . but inevitably, digging through those paperbacks, I found myself intrigued by other sorts of books as well. I started reading horror when a book with Boris Karloff on the cover caught my attention. Robert E. Howard and L. Sprague de Camp hooked me on fantasy, just in time for J. R. R. Tolkien and *The Lord of the Rings*. The historical epics of Dumas and Thomas B. Costain featured sword fights too, so I soon started reading those as well, and that led me to other epochs of history and other authors. When I came upon Charles Dickens and Mark Twain and Rudyard Kipling on the spinner rack, I grabbed them up too, to read the original versions of some of my favorite stories, and to see how they differed from the *Classics Illustrated* versions. Some of the mysteries I found on the rack had cover art so salacious that I had to smuggle them into the apartment and read them when my mother wasn't watching, but I sampled those as well, and have been reading mysteries ever since. Ian Fleming and James Bond led me into the world of thrillers and espionage novels, and Jack Schaefer's

Shane into westerns. (Okay, I confess, I never did get into romances or nurse novels.) Sure, I knew the differences between a space opera and a hard-boiled detective story and a historical novel . . . but I never *cared* about such differences. It seemed to me, then as now, that there were good stories and bad stories, and that was the only distinction that truly mattered.

My views on that have not changed much in the half century since, but the world of publishing and bookselling certainly has. I don't doubt that there are still some old spinner racks out there, with all the books jumbled up together, but these days most people buy their reading material in chain superstores, where genre is king. SF and fantasy over here, mystery over there, romance back of that, bestsellers up front. No mixing and no mingling, please, keep to your own kind. "Literature" has its own section, now that the so-called "literary novel" has become a genre itself. Children's books and YAs are segregated.

It's good for selling books, I guess. It's convenient. Easy to find the sort of books you like. No one has to get down on their knees in hopes of finding Jack Vance's *Big Planet* behind that copy of *How to Win Friends and Influence People*.

But it's not good for readers, I suspect, and it's definitely not good for writers. Books should broaden us, take us to places we have never been and show us things we've never seen, expand our horizons and our way of looking at the world. Limiting your reading to a single genre defeats that. It limits us, makes us smaller.

Yet genre walls are hardening. During my own career, I have written science fiction, fantasy, and horror, and occasionally a few hybrids that were part this and part that, sometimes with elements of the murder mystery and the literary novel blended in. But younger writers starting out today are actively discouraged from doing the same by their editors and publishers. New fantasists are told that they had best adopt a pseudonym if they want to do a science fiction novel . . . and god help them if they want to try a mystery.

It's all in the name of selling more books, and I suppose it does.

But I say it's spinach, and I say to hell with it.

Bayonne may not have had any bookstores when I was growing up, but it did have a lot of pizza parlors, and a bar pie from Bayonne is among the best pizza anywhere. Small wonder that pizza is my favorite food. That doesn't mean I want to eat it every day, and to the exclusion of every other food in the world.

Which brings me to the book you hold in your hands.

These days I am best known as a fantasy writer, but *Warriors* is not a fantasy anthology . . . though it does have some good fantasy in it. My co-editor, Gardner Dozois, edited a science fiction magazine for a couple of decades, but *Warriors* is not a science fiction anthology either . . . though it does feature some SF stories as good as anything you'll find in *Analog* or *Asimov's*. It also features a western, and some mystery stories, a lot of fine historical fiction, some mainstream, and a couple of pieces that I won't even begin to try to label. *Warriors* is our own spinner rack.

People have been telling stories about warriors for as long as they have been telling stories. Since Homer first sang the wrath of Achilles and the ancient Sumerians set down their tales of Gilgamesh, warriors, soldiers, and fighters have fascinated us; they are a part of every culture, every literary tradition, every genre. *All Quiet on the Western Front, From Here to Eternity,* and *The Red Badge of Courage* have become part of our literary canons, taught in classrooms all around the country and the world. Fantasy has given us such memorable warriors as Conan the Barbarian, Elric of Melnibone, and Aragorn son of Arathorn. Science fiction offers us glimpses of the wars and warriors of the future, in books like Robert A. Heinlein's *Starship Troopers,* Joe W. Haldeman's *Forever War,* and the space operas of David Weber, Lois McMaster Bujold, and Walter Jon Williams. The gunslinger of the classic western is a warrior. The mystery genre has made an archetype of the urban warrior, be he a cop, a hit man, a wiseguy, or one of those private eyes who walks the mean streets of Chandler and Hammett. Women warriors, child soldiers, warriors of the gridiron and the cricket pitch, the Greek hoplite and Roman legionary, Viking, musketeer, crusader, and doughboy, the GI of World War II and the grunt of Vietnam . . . all of them are warriors, and you'll find many in these pages.

Our contributors make up an all-star lineup of award-winning and bestselling writers, representing a dozen different publishers and as many genres. We asked each of them for the same thing—a story about a warrior. Some chose to write in the genre for which they're best known. Some decided to try something different. You will find warriors of every shape, size, and color in these pages, warriors from every epoch of human history, from yesterday and today and tomorrow, and worlds that never were. Some of the stories will make you sad, some will make you laugh, many will keep you on the edge of your seat.

But you won't know which until you've read them, for Gardner and I, in the tradition of that old wire spinner rack, have mixed them all up. There's no science fiction section here, no shelves reserved just for historical novels, no romance rack, no walls or labels of any sort. Just stories. Some are by your favorite writers, we hope; others, by writers you may never have heard of (yet). It's our hope that by the time you finish this book, a few of the latter may have become the former.

So spin the rack and turn the page. We have some stories to tell you.

WARRIORS 3

Robin Hobb

New York Times bestseller Robin Hobb is one of the most popular writers in fantasy today, having sold more than one million copies of her work in paperback. She's perhaps best known for her epic fantasy Farseer series, including *Assassin's Apprentice, Royal Assassin,* and *Assassin's Quest,* as well as the two fantasy series related to it, the Liveship Traders series, consisting of *Ship of Magic, The Mad Ship,* and *Ship of Destiny,* and the Tawny Man series, made up of *Fool's Errand, Golden Fool,* and *Fool's Fate.* Recently, she's started a new fantasy series, the Soldier Son series, composed of *Shaman's Crossing, Forest Mage,* and her most recently published novel, *Renegade's Magic.* Her early novels, published under the name Megan Lindholm, include the fantasy novels *Wizard of the Pigeons, Harpy's Flight, The Windsingers, The Limbreth Gate, Luck of the Wheels, The Reindeer People, Wolf's Brother,* and *Cloven Hooves,* the science fiction novel *Alien Earth,* and, with Steven Brust, the collaborative novel *The Gypsy.*

Here she takes us to the edge of human endurance and considerably beyond, for a harrowing study of the ultimate meaning of loyalty, when everything else has been lost.

The Triumph

The evening winds swept across the plains to the city and pushed on the iron-barred cage hung in the arch of the gate. The man in the cage braced himself against the bite of the inward-facing spikes and stared into the westering sun. He had small choice in that. Before they'd hoisted his cage into position, they'd cut away his eyelids and lashed his wrists to the bars, so that he could not turn away from the fiery gaze of the Carthaginian sun.

The dust-laden wind was drying his bared eyes, and his vision was dwindling. Tears, the tears of his body rather than the tears of his heart, ran unchecked down his cheeks. The severed muscles that had once worked his eyelids twitched in helpless reflex; they could not moisten his eyeballs and renew his vision. Just as well; there was little out there he wished to see.

Earlier in the day, there had been a crowd below him. They'd lined the street to watch the laughing, mocking soldiers roll him along inside the spiked barrel of his cage. Despite the earlier torture he had endured, he'd still had a bit of defiance in him then. He'd seized the bars of the cage and braced himself, fighting the momentum of the bumping, bouncing cage as they tumbled him along. He hadn't been completely successful. The spikes inside the cage were too long for that. They'd scored his body in a dozen places. Still, he'd avoided any immediately mortal wounds. He now doubted the wisdom of that.

At the bottom of the hill, beneath the arch of the city gates, the crowd had roared with avid approval when his guards dragged him out and sliced the eyelids from his face. "Face the sunset, Regulus! It's the last one you'll see, dog of a Roman! You'll die with the sun today!" Then they'd forced him back into his spiked prison, lashing his wrists to the bars before they hoisted him up high so that all might have a good view of the Roman consul's slow death.

His torment had drawn a sizable crowd. The Carthaginians hated him, and with good reason. Very good reason. They'd never forgive him for the many defeats he'd dealt them, or forget the impossible treaty terms he'd offered them after the battle at Adys. He bared what remained of his broken teeth in a grin. He still had that to be proud of. His gallery had pelted his cage with rocks and rotten vegetables and offal. Some of the missiles had ricocheted off the iron bars that confined him, a shield wall that flung their insults back into their upturned faces. Others had found their mark. Well, that was to be expected. No defense was completely impenetrable. Even the Carthaginians could hit a target sometimes. He had tucked his chin to his chest to offer his eyes what shelter he could from the dazzling African sun and looked down at the crowd.

They'd been both exultant and furious. They had him caged, Marcus Atillius Regulus, and their torturers had wreaked on him all that for so long they had desired to do, but feared. His final defiance of them had pressured them to do their worst. And now they would watch him die in a cage hung from the city gates of Carthage.

His cracked lips pulled wide in a smile as he looked down at the hazy crowd. A film obscured his vision, but it seemed to him that there were not so many of them as there had been. Watching a man die painfully offered an hour or two of amusement to vary their tepid lives, but Regulus had prolonged their voyeurism too long, and they had wearied of it. Most had returned to the routine tasks of their ordinary lives. He gripped the bars firmly, and with all his will he bade his fingers to hold fast and his trembling legs braced him upright. It would be his last victory, to deny them any spectacle at his passing. He willed himself to take another breath.

Flavius looked up at the man in the cage. He swallowed. Marcus appeared to be looking straight at him. He resisted the temptation to look aside and tried to meet his old friend's gaze. Either Marcus could not see Flavius or knew that if he recognized him and reacted to him in any way, his old friend would pay with his life. Or perhaps more than four years of slavery in Carthage had changed Flavius so much that even his childhood friend could not recognize him. He had never been a fleshy man, and the hardships of slavery had leaned even his soldier's muscles from his frame. He was a bone man now, skeletal and ravaged by the harsh African sun. He was ragged and he stank, not just his unwashed body but also the dirty sodden bandage that wrapped the still-oozing injury on his left thigh.

He'd "escaped" from his master a scant month ago; it had not required much subterfuge. The overseer was a sot, more intent on drinking each day than on wringing work out of slaves that were no longer capable of real labor. One night, as the slaves made their weary way in from the grain fields, Flavius had lagged behind. He had limped more and more slowly and finally, while the overseer was haranguing another slave, he had dropped down amongst the rustling stalks and lain still. The grain was tall enough to conceal his supine body; they would not locate him without a search, and even so, in the failing light, they might miss him. But the old sot had not seemed to notice even that he was one slave short. When the moonless night had deepened, Flavius had crawled to the far edge of the field and then tottered to his feet and limped away. The old injury to his leg had already been suppurating. He had known then that the broken dragon tooth inside it had begun to move again. The pain had awakened memories of how he'd taken the injury, and made him think of Marcus and wonder about his friend's fate.

How long had it been since he'd last seen him?

Time slipped around when a man was a slave. Days seemed longer when someone else owned every minute of your time. A summer of forced labor in Carthage could seem a lifetime with the sun beating down on a man's head and back. He counted the harvests he could recall and then decided that it had been over four years since he'd seen Marcus. Over four years since that disastrous battle where everything went wrong. On the plains of the Bagradas, not far from the cursed river of the same name, Consul Marcus Atillius Regulus had gone down in defeat. Flavius had been one of the five hundred soldiers taken prisoner. Some of those who had survived had pointed out that being captured alive was one step above being one of the twelve thousand Roman dead who littered the bloody battlefield. On the longest days of his slavery, Flavius had doubted that.

His eyes were drawn again to his friend and commander. The spikes had pierced him in a dozen places, but blood no longer trickled from the injuries. The dust-laden summer wind had crusted them over. His chest and belly looked like a map of a river system where the red trickles had dried to brown. Stripped of armor and garments, naked as a slave, Marcus' body still showed the musculature and bearing of a Roman soldier. They had tortured him and hung him up to die, but they still hadn't managed to break him. The Carthaginians never would.

After all, it had not been the Carthaginians who managed to defeat Consul Regulus, but a hired general, one Xanthippus, a Spartan, a man who led his troops not out of love for his country but for cold coin. The Carthaginians had hired him when their own Hamilcar had been unable to deliver the victories they needed. If Marcus had been fully cognizant of what that change in command would mean, perhaps he would not have pressed his men so hard toward their last encounter. That fateful day, the sun had beat down on them as fiercely as if it were a Carthaginian ally. Dust and heat had tormented the troops as Marcus had marched his forces round a lake. Toward evening, the weary soldiers approached the river Bagradas. On the other side, their enemy awaited them. Everyone had expected that their leader would order them to strike a camp, to fortify it with a wall and a ditch. They'd counted on a meal and a night of rest before they engaged in battle. But Marcus had promptly ordered his forces to cross the river and confront the waiting army, thinking to confound the Carthaginian force with his bravado.

Had Hamilcar been the Carthaginian general, the tactic might have worked. Everyone knew that Carthaginians avoided fighting in the open, for they dared not stand against the organized might of a Roman army. But Xanthippus was a Spartan and not to be taken in by show. Nor did he allow his men to fight like Carthaginians. Marcus had drawn his force confidently into their standard formation, infantry in the middle and their cavalry flanking them on both sides, and moved boldly forward. But Xanthippus had not drawn back. Instead, he sent his elephants crashing squarely into the middle of the infantry formation. Even so, the beleaguered square of infantry had held. Flavius had been there. They had fought like Romans, and the lines had held. But then Xanthippus had split his cavalry, a tactic that Flavius had never seen in such a situation. When the horses thundered down on them from both sides, their own outnumbered cavalry had gone down, and then the flanks of the infantry formation had caved in and given way. It had been chaos and bloody slaughter the like of which he'd never seen. Some men, he had heard, had escaped, to flee to Aspis and be rescued later by the Roman fleet. Those soldiers had gone home. Flavius and close to five hundred others had not.

Consul Marcus Atillius Regulus had been a prized captive and a valuable hostage and was treated as such. But Flavius had been only a soldier, and not even one from a wealthy family. His body and the work he could do had been his only worth to the victors. As a spoil of war, he'd been sold for labor. He'd taken a blow to the head in the course of the defeat; he'd never know if it had been from a horse's hoof or a random slingstone. But for a time, he'd seen rings around torches at night and staggered to the left whenever he tried to walk. He'd been sold cheap, and his new master put him to work in his grain fields. And there he had toiled for the last four years. Some seasons he plowed and some he planted, and in the heat of the summer as the grain began to ripen, he'd moved through the field, shouting and flapping his arms to keep the greedy birds at bay. Rome and his soldiering days, his wife and his children, and even Marcus, the boyhood friend who had gotten him into this situation, all had begun to fade from his thoughts. Sometimes he'd felt that he had been a slave always.

And then one night he'd awakened to a familiar pain, and known that the dragon's tooth was once more moving inside his flesh. And within a handful of days, he'd limped away from his overseer.

Had the shifting tooth in the old wound been an omen, a warning from the gods of what was to come? Flavius had given small thought to such things in recent years. The gods of his youth had forsaken him; why should he care any longer to give them honor or even regard? Yet it seemed to him now that the tooth's stirring on the final leg of its journey through his flesh might have come close to the time when Marcus was making his final appearance before the Chief Magistrates of Rome. In the days that followed, the old wound had swollen, turned scarlet, and then began to crust and ooze. And on those same days, he heard the gossip that even Carthaginian slaves would repeat. "The war will soon be over. They paroled the Consul to Rome, to present their treaty terms for them. Consul Regulus is to meet with the Roman magistrates and convince them that it's useless to defy us. He gave his word that if Rome did not accept the terms, he'd return to Carthage."

Flavius had shaken his head and turned wordlessly away from their rumors. Marcus had gone home without him? Marcus had gone home, abandoning the five hundred men who had once served him? Marcus would present Carthaginian terms of surrender to Rome and urge them to accept them? That did not seem like Marcus. For three days, he had mulled it over as he limped through a grain field, flapping his arms at black birds. Then he had decided that the moving tooth inside his flesh was a message. That very day, he had made his escape and begun his slow journey back toward the city of Carthage.

It was a long and weary way for a man half-crippled, without a coin or a purse to put it in. He'd traveled by night, stealing what he could from fields and outlying farmsteads. He avoided speaking to anyone, for although he had learned Punic during his servitude, his Roman accent was strong and would betray him. As the miles between him and his former owner had increased, he'd become a bit more bold. He'd stolen worn garments from a ragpicker's cart that were much more serviceable than the twist of cloth his owner had given him. He'd begged, too, sitting at a village gate and showing his oozing wound and bony body, and a few fools had taken pity on him. And so he had made his slow way, step by step, toward Carthage.

Two nights ago, he had camped in sight of the city walls. As evening fell, he'd found a place to sleep in the dubious shelter of a leafless grove of trees. In the night, he'd wakened to the fever of his wound. In the feeble light of a full moon, he had mustered his courage, set his teeth, and bore down on the swollen tissue. He'd gripped his thigh's hot flesh in both hands and squeezed, pushing up and away from the bone.

The dragon's tooth had emerged slickly, jabbing its way out of his body just as bloodily as it had gone in. It had passed through his entire leg, from back to front. He'd pulled it from his flesh, his wet fingers slipping on the gleaming white tooth's smooth surface. When he'd finally tugged it from its hiding place, a gush of foul liquid and pus had followed it. And for the first time in over six years, he finally felt alone in his body, freed of the dragon's tooth and its presence in his life. For a short time, he had held the tooth in his hands, sick with marvel at how long he had carried it. It was sharper than any arrow, and longer than his forefinger. The snapped-off stump where it had broken from the monster's jaw was still sharp-edged. He clutched it in his hand and slept well that night, despite hunger and a bed that was no more than dirt and tree roots.

The next morning, he had risen, bound his old injury afresh, and limped off in search of Marcus. Midway through his first day of walking, he found a likely stick along the roadside and made it his staff. At dusk that day, he came to a sluggish flow of water in a sunken stream. He'd followed it upstream, into a farmer's field, and found a quiet place to bathe his wound and wash out his scant clothing and his bandaging. He'd stolen handfuls of underripe grain from the field, filling his belly with the milky, chewy kernels. When he lay down that night to sleep, he'd dreamed of home, but not of his wife and his sons. No. He'd dreamed of a time before them.

His father's small acreage had been adjacent to

that of Marcus' family. Neither parent was a wealthy man, but while Flavius' father was a farmer who had been to war, Marcus' father had risen to the rank of Consul and never forgotten it. His family holding had been twelve acres, while Marcus' father could claim only a scanty seven, yet when Marcus was recounting his father's heroism, Flavius had always felt he was the poorer of the two boys. He smiled bitterly to himself. When Marcus' father had died, Marcus had been devastated, not just by the man's death but also by the thought that his days as a warrior were finished. Marcus had gone to the Roman Senate and reluctantly requested to be freed from his military duty, so that he might return home to till his seven acres and support his wife and children and mother, for with his father gone, there was no one else to shoulder that task. Yet even in that early flush of his career, the Senate had recognized his military worth. They'd taken from taxes the funds to hire a man to till the lands of Marcus Atillius Regulus and sent him forth yet again to serve Rome where he functioned best, at the bloody forefront of the war.

Marcus had gone joyfully. Flavius had shaken his head over it then even as he did now. War and its glory were all Marcus had ever wanted. When they were boys, in the green of their youth, they had both dreamed of escaping their chores for the adventure of soldiering. They'd counted down the musterings until they reached an age when they, too, could stand with the other eligible men in the town square and await a chance to be chosen to serve. They'd both been seventeen years tall and of a like height at that first dilectus, and it had been Marcus who had contrived that they must find a way to stand four men apart. "For we shall be called forward four at a time, for the tribunes to have the pick of us. If we go up together, one will choose me and another you, and then we shall certainly be separated. So, see that you come up after me, for if I can at all, I shall whisper to the tribune that chooses me that although you may not have the muscle I show, there is no one like to you for an arrow well shot or a spear flung straight. I'll see that so long as we march to war, we always march together. That I promise you."

"And what of our marching home? Do you promise we shall always be together then?"

Marcus had stared at him, affronted. "Of course we shall! In triumph!"

Small matter to Marcus that, if Flavius had had his way after his first stint of soldiering, he might have stayed at home, well away from the gore and boredom of a soldier's life. But of course, he had no choice; no son of a Roman citizen did. And so at that first muster he stood, knees slightly bent to blend in with three shorter youths, and watched Marcus being chosen. He saw his frantic whispering and pointing, and he saw the stony-faced tribune who waved an angry hand at him to silence him. But when the time came for the tribune to choose from the four men offered him, he had chosen Flavius. And thus the two boyhood friends had marched off together for their first foray into a soldier's life.

Marcus thrived on a military life. As Marcus' talent for strategy had blossomed, he had risen in rank. Although Marcus was his commander on the battlefield each year, when they returned home, they resumed being friends and neighbors. As the years had passed, and especially after the dragon had damn near taken his leg off, Flavius had answered the muster more reluctantly each year. He had begun to hope that the tribunes would see that the injury to his leg had made him an old man before his time. But every year when he presented himself for the dilectus, Marcus contrived that Flavius was chosen to serve in his legion. And at the end of each campaign, when they returned home together, always they slipped comfortably back into their old friendship.

Had Marcus ever wanted to be anything but a soldier? Even now, as Flavius looked up at him in his cage, he doubted it. When they were boys, after their chores, Marcus had always wanted to be fighting with staves or staging ambushes on the neighbor's goats. Flavius had preferred the hunt to a battle, and on the evenings when he persuaded Marcus to follow him on his quests, his friend had been unstinting in his amazement and praise of Flavius' skills. He excelled at stealth and marksmanship. Flavius well remembered the sweetness of the long evenings of late summer, when the two boys had lounged by a small fire, savoring the smell of plundered apples baking by the embers and a small game bird sizzling over the last of the flames. Flavius' thoughts would wander to whether he might persuade his father to let him range farther in search of larger game, but for Marcus, the dream was always the same.

"I know my destiny," he had confided to Flavius, more than once. "I've seen it in my dreams. I shall rise through the ranks, to be a praetor or a consul, just as my father did before me. And then I shall lead my troops forth into war."

"To kill a thousand of the enemy?" Flavius would ask, grinning.

"A thousand? No! Five thousand, ten thousand will fall to my strategy. And I shall be summoned back to Rome and awarded a Triumph. I shall be paraded through the streets, with wagons full of my plunder, and my captives walking barefoot behind me. My army will follow me, of course, and you, Flavius, you I promise will be in the first rank. My wife and my grown sons will be honored with me. And I, I shall be stained as red as this apple, and my toga whiter than snow. At Jupiter's temple, I will sacrifice six white bulls to him. All of Rome will line the streets to cheer me. This I know, Flavius. I've seen it."

He'd smiled at his friend's posturing. "Don't forget the best part of it, Marcus. There will be a slave in the chariot with you, standing just back of your shoulder and leaning forward to whisper into your ear the words that remind you that every hero is mortal. And thus you will be kept humble." He grinned. "Perhaps, instead of a slave, they will let me do that!"

"Mortal? The body perhaps is mortal, Flavius. But once a man has had a Triumph, once he is an imperator, then his legend is immortal and will be passed on through all the generations of soldiers that will ever spill blood on the earth."

One of the stolen apples had popped on the fire, spitting out a tiny missile of pulp and then draining a sweet stream of hot juice into the embers. Flavius had speared it with the small stick he was using to tend their meal and drawn it back from the fire's edge. He held it up gravely on its skewer. "Memento mori!" he had toasted it gravely, and then blown on it before scalding his mouth with an incautious bite of it.

Regulus tried to decide if the evening was as chill as it seemed. The day had been hot enough to bake him. But now, as the sunlight that jabbed through his hazed vision turned the world to a bloody red, he felt chilled.

His eyeballs were too dried to see clearly, but he could still perceive that the light was fading. So the cooler evening was finally coming. Or death. Blindness would make the light fade, and blood loss could make a man cold. He well knew that. He'd lost count of the times when he'd lent his cloak to wrap a dying man. Flavius, he suddenly thought. He'd knelt by Flavius and tucked his cloak around him as he shivered. But Flavius hadn't died, had he? Had he? No, not then. Not then, but now? Was Flavius alive now? Or had he left him dead on that last battlefield?

Men always complained of the cold when they were dying, if they had breath left to speak. The cold and the enveloping darkness troubled them, or they expressed regrets in a muttered word or a sigh as he knelt beside the fallen man. As if the cold or the dark were what a man should worry about when his entrails were spilled in the dust next to him, or half his body's blood was congealing in a pool beneath him. Still, it was a small comfort to offer, the lending of a cloak for the usually brief time it took a man to bleed out from a battle wound. A small comfort he would have welcomed just now. The touch of one friendly hand, one word from a friend to send him on his way. But he was alone.

No one would come to wrap him in a cloak, or to take his hand, or even to speak his name. No one would crouch down beside him and say, "Regulus, you died well. You were a fine consul, a loyal centurion, and a good citizen. Rome will remember you. You died a hero's death." No. His parched tongue tried to wet his cracked lips. Another stupid reflex of the body. Tongue, lips, teeth. Silly, useless words now. None of them applied to him. As stupid as his mind, going on thinking, thinking, thinking while his body spiraled down into death.

Something landed on the top of his suspended cage. A bird, it would have to be a bird up here. Not a serpent, not a dragon. It was not heavy, he didn't think, but it was enough to make the cage rock a tiny bit.

And enough to make the spikes bite just that much deeper. He held his breath and waited. Soon, they'd reach something vital, and he would die. But not just yet. No. Not just yet. He tightened his grip on the bars of his cage, or tried to. They'd shackled his hands higher than his heart, and they were numb now. It made no sense to cling to life when his body was already ruined. They'd broken so many parts of him that he could no longer catalog them. He did remember the moment when he suddenly knew that they weren't going to stop. He'd known that before they began, of course. They'd promised him that. The Carthaginians had sent him forth, bound doubly by his word and their promise. They'd made him promise to return. In turn, the Carthaginians had promised that if he did not convince the Roman magistrates to accept the terms of the treaty, they would kill him on his return.

He recalled standing among slaves as the Carthaginian envoys presented their terms. He had not shouted out that he was a Roman citizen, had not announced that he was Consul Marcus Atillius Regulus. No. He was ashamed to return to Rome in such a way and he had no intention of being a tool for the Carthaginians. They had had to bring him forward and announce him to the Magistrates themselves. And then he had done the only thing he could do. He denounced the treaty and its harsh terms, and advised the Magistrates to refuse it.

And they had.

And then he had kept his honor by keeping his word to his captors. He returned to Carthage with them.

So, he'd known all along that the Carthaginians would kill him. Known with his mind. But that was different from knowing with his body. His body hadn't known. His body had believed that somehow, he'd be able to go on living. If his body hadn't believed that, his torturers would not have been able to wring scream after scream from him.

He'd tried not to scream, of course. All men tried, at first, not to scream under torture. But sooner or later, they all did. And sooner or later, they all stopped even pretending to try not to scream. He could command one hundred men and they'd obeyed him in his days as a centurion, and as a general and as a consul he could command thousands. When he had told the Magistrates that they should refuse the terms of the treaty, they had listened. But when he had commanded his own body not to scream, it hadn't listened to him. It had screamed and screamed, as if somehow that would mitigate the pain. It didn't. And then, at some crucial point, when they had broken so many parts of him that he could no longer keep count, when really, no part of him was left whole, even his body had known that he was going to die. And then it had stopped screaming.

A very long time after that, or perhaps only a short time that seemed like a long time, they'd stopped actively torturing him. Was it hours or days ago that they'd rolled him down to the city gates inside his spiked cage? Did it matter?

He listened to the sounds of the city below him. Earlier, there had been crowd noises. Exclamations, shouts of disgust and ridicule, mocking laughter and the stupid shouts of triumph from men who had never fought, never even tortured, but somehow thought they could claim his death as their victory. *By virtue of what?* he'd wanted to ask them. *That you were whelped on a piece of dirt somewhere near the place where my torturer was born? Does that make seeing me dangle in a cage over your city gate a victory for you? You have no victory here. I told the Magistrates to refuse the treaty. Rome will not go down on its knees before you. I saw to that. If I could not give my country the victory it deserved, at least I have preserved it from accepting a defeat.*

He hadn't said any such words to his gallery, of course. His mouth, tongue, and teeth were no longer useful for talking. He'd almost wished, at one point, that his torturers were pretending to wring information from him. If that had been their pretense, they'd have left him a mouth to babble with when they'd hurt him badly enough. But they'd been freed from any need to pretend they were doing anything other than hurting him as much as they could without killing him. And so they had done their worst, or perhaps they thought of it as their best. Torturers, he knew from employing them, were not interested in information or confessions. They weren't even interested in reforming the wicked or making them sorry for their misdeeds. Torturers were interested in hurting people. That was all. He'd seen how it aroused them, how their eyes glittered and their mouths grew wet. It was in how lovingly they handled their tools and the great thought they gave to how they applied them. Torture, he thought, was sex for the sexless. Not a one of them ever worked for anything except his own joy in hurting. They were not warriors, not soldiers; perhaps they were not men at all. They were torturers. Consumers of pain, and they'd fed off his screams, just as the carrion birds waited to consume his flesh. The torturers were tools, servants of the ones who commanded them. And in his case, the men who had commanded the torturers were simply keeping a promise to him.

His thoughts were jumping around like fleas evacuating the carcass of a dead animal. The mental image pleased him for a moment, and then it vanished from his mind. He cast his thoughts wider, tried to find an image or an idea to cling to, anything that would distract him from the slow pain of dying. There was his wife to think of, Julia. She would mourn and miss him. How many soldiers could say that of women left behind and know that it was true? And his sons, Marcus and Gaius. They would hear of their father's death, and it would stiffen their resolution to defend Rome. They'd realize more clearly just what evil dogs these Carthaginians were. They would not feel shamed that he had been defeated and captured. They would take pride in how he had not scrabbled for a chance at life by betraying his country. No. He'd defied Carthage. If he could not leave his boys a Triumph to remember him by, at least he would leave them his honorable death as a loyal Roman.

They'd hear how he died. He had no doubt of that. The Senate would noise it about. It would put some fire in their bellies, to think of Marcus Atillius Regulus, once a proud consul of the Roman legions, tormented and hung up to die like fresh meat hung to bleed in a butcher's stall. The Senate would make certain that everyone heard of how he died.

It would be the last use they'd make of him. He knew that and didn't resent it. But gods, gods, how much longer must it take him to die?

Flavius realized that he had been standing and staring too long. The stream of people moving into the city had parted to go around him. Earlier, he was sure, there had been a standing audience for Marcus' last moments. But the stubborn soldier had defeated those gawkers. He'd refused to die for them.

Flavius crossed the street to a merchant hawking slabs of flat bread. It smelled wonderful. He had a few coins from a purse he'd cut last week. At one time, he would have been shamed to resort to common thievery, but he had learned to justify it to himself. Even if he no longer wore the armor of a Roman soldier, soldier he was, and every Carthaginian remained his enemy. Stealing from them, even killing one if the opportunity were offered, was no different from hunting any other sort of prey. It had been a good pouch he'd cut, a leather one with woven throngs, and inside it was half a dozen coins, a small knife, a man's ring, and a slab of wax. He took out his smallest coin and held it up for the bread merchant to see, scowling darkly all the while. The merchant shook his head disdainfully. Flavius let his scowl darken as he brought another small coin from the twisted rag at his hip and offered it as well. The merchant muttered, "You will beggar me!" but picked up one of his smaller loaves and offered it. Flavius handed over the two bits of metal and took the bread without thanks. Today he would take no chance of his accent betraying him.

He broke the bread into small pieces and ate it dry, casting furtive glances up at Marcus as he did so. It felt traitorous to eat while his friend was dying, but he was hungry, and the activity gave him an excuse to loiter where he was. Marcus held steady. He gripped the bars of his cage and stared down at the passing folk. Some still looked up at him as they passed, but others scarcely noticed the dying man in the cage. Perhaps it was because he did not look as if he were dying. Yet Flavius looked up at him and knew. His boyhood friend was past saving. Even if a Roman legion had miraculously appeared to rescue him, Marcus would still die. There was a dusky color to his hands and feet that spoke of blood settling. The attentions of the torturers had left streaks of blood that had dried as brown stripes on his face and his chest and thighs. Yet Marcus stood and waited and Flavius stood and watched and waited, even though he could not say why.

It seemed only fitting. After all, Marcus had once kept a death watch for him.

It had been years ago. Six years? Seven? And it had not been that far from this dusty, evil city. They had been trying to cross the Bagradas River at a place where it ran through thick brush and verdant reeds that grew higher than a man's head. The Bagradas Valley was a rich and fertile swath of ground that received the waters from the Tells on either side of it. On the flanks of the Tells, cork and oak and pine forests grew. The banks of the wide river were thick with both vegetation and stinging insects. Marcus had been a general then, but not yet risen to the rank of consul. That title he would earn by cutting a swath of destruction across Carthage. It had been a summer of conquest for him. That day, Marcus pushed infantry, horse, and archers to move swiftly as he sought for the best place to ford the Bagradas. He had chosen a prime spot for his evening camp, on a rise that overlooked a river. The troops settled in to create the standard fortification, a ditch and a wall made from the upflung dirt. Marcus had sent his scouts ahead to survey the fording place. They had returned too soon, to report unusual activity by the water's edge.

"We saw a snake, sir. A huge snake. By the river."

Flavius had been in earshot of that first report. Sometimes of an evening, after the boundaries were set for the night, he'd go by Marcus' tent. If the general was not too busy, he'd find time for some talk with his old friend. But that evening, as he approached, he was blocked by a huddle of men clustered around the tent. Marcus stood scowling, while the two velites reporting to him looked at the ground and shifted sheepishly. Flavius had seen Marcus' consternation that they had even dared to return to report such a thing. "Amazing," he had responded, his voice dripping sarcasm. "That we should encounter a snake on an African riverbank. Is that why you fled back here before determining if we can ford there tomorrow?"

The velites had exchanged glances. They were among the poorest of the soldiers that were recruited, often without enough money to equip themselves well and accorded little status by their fellows. In battle, they were skirmishers and javelin throwers, not recognized as formally belonging to any group. They had been sent to scout precisely because they were expendable. They knew it and did not like it. Flavius could scarcely blame them for retreating from whatever they had seen. They had to watch out for their own backs. One of the men was wet to the waist. The other man spoke. "We couldn't see all of it, sir. But what we saw was, well, immense. We saw a piece of its side moving past us through the tall river grass. It was the diameter of a hogshead, sir, and that was close to the end of it. We aren't cowards. We went toward it, for a better look. And then, close to a hundred feet away, this head reared up from the reeds."

"Glowing eyes!" broke in the other scout. "On my word, sir, big glowing eyes. And it hissed at us, but the hiss was more like whistling. I had to cover my ears. It kept to the water, and the reeds hid most of it from us, but what we could see was immense. From the size of its eyes and head, it had to be—"

"That's twice now that you've admitted coming

back to report to me on something that you haven't completely seen," Marcus had observed coldly. "It is the function of a scout, is it not, to see things and then come back to report? Rather than to come back to report what he has *not* seen?"

The first man scowled and looked at his feet. The second scout flushed a deep red. He didn't meet Marcus' gaze, but there was no shame in his voice as he said, "Some things are so strange that even a glimpse of one should be reported. That is no ordinary snake, sir. And I'm not just speaking of its size, though it dwarfs any other snake I've ever seen. Its eyes glowed when it looked at us. And it more whistled than hissed. It didn't flee at the sight of us, as most snakes would. No. It challenged us. And so we came back to report it to you."

"River dragon," someone said into the silence that followed the scout's words.

Marcus' eyes snapped to the men clustered at the edge of the firelight's reach. Perhaps he knew who had spoken, but Flavius didn't. In any event, he didn't single out anyone. "Ridiculous," he said scathingly.

"You didn't see it," the first scout said abruptly, but before he could continue, Marcus cut in with, "And neither did you! You saw something. Probably a glimpse of a hippo, and then a glimpse of a snake, and in the reeds and the evening light, you thought they were one and the same." He pointed a finger at the one scout and demanded, "How did you get wet?"

The man drew himself up. "If I could finish my

report, sir. That head came up out of the reeds. It lifted its head higher than I'm tall, and it looked down on us. Then it whistled. Startled us both, and I shouted back at it. Big as it was, I still thought it would turn aside and go its way. Instead, it came at us. It darted its head at me, mouth open, and all I could see was row after row of teeth, in a maw the size of a cart. Carus shouted at him and threw his javelin. It stuck in him, made him angry. He roared again and went for me. I jumped to one side and ran. I thought it was solid riverbank, but it wasn't and I went right over the edge and into the water. Lucky for me, because it lost sight of me."

The other man took up the tale. "That's when it turned on me and came after me, but I was already moving by then. It stopped to rub my javelin off. I heard the shaft snap, like it was nothing. I'd run up the bank and I think it was reluctant to come out of the reeds and cattails. I thought Tullus was dead. When he came out of the reeds and joined me, we decided we'd best come back to report this."

Marcus had crossed his arms on his chest. "And the light is almost gone. And no doubt by the time we reach the river tomorrow, your giant snake will be gone as well. Go about your duties, both of you. Glowing eyes!"

And with that sharp remark, he dismissed not only the two scouts but all of the men as well. Just before he turned away, his eyes met Flavius' and he gave a small toss of his head. He knew that he was summoned, but privately. In the dark and almost quiet hours of the restive camp, he went to Marcus' tent.

"I need to know what they saw. Can you go out, before dawn, and then come back to me? If anyone can read the ground and let me know what is out there, you can. I need to get our troops across the river, Flavius. I'd like to cross here, at first light. But if there are hippos and crocodiles, then I need to know before we enter the water, not when we're halfway across."

"Or giant snakes?" Flavius asked him.

Marcus gave a dismissive laugh. "They're young and poorly armed. I don't blame them for running back here, but they have to learn that what I need is information, not rumors. I'll have them here to hear your report in the morning. And that's when they'll face their discipline as well."

Flavius had nodded, and gone off to take what sleep he could.

A Roman camp stirs early, but he was the first to arise that morning. He took with him not the arms of a warrior but the tools of a hunter. It did not take a lot of modification to turn a pike into a pole sling. It had greater range and could launch a heavier weapon than his small sling. If there were an irritable hippo or basking crocodiles, he wished to turn them away before they got too close to him. The gladius at his side was for closer occasions. The short blade was good for both stabbing and slashing. Flavius hoped it came to neither.

The banks of the Bagradas River teemed with life. Brush edged it and deep reed beds lined it. He followed the same well-trodden game trail that the scouts had investigated the day before. Animals knew the best places to water and the safest places to cross. That this path was so well trodden made him suspect he'd find a safe fording for the troops. Closer to the river, the brush to either side grew thicker and the reeds and cattails before him loomed taller. He was reassured by the plentiful birdsong and the darting of the busy feathered creatures. Off to one side, he heard some larger creature startle out of its wallow and then crash off into deep brush. It was a four-legged beast, he was sure of that. It increased his wariness, and he went more slowly. The ground began to become bog. He reached the edge of the reed bed and looked down a clear channel, almost a tunnel of a path that led out into the open moving waters of the river. On the far side, a similar muddy track led up the opposite bank. So. A place to cross. He decided to wade out and check the strength of the current and the footing. He was knee-deep in the water when suddenly all the bird noises stopped.

Flavius halted and stood still, listening. His eyes sought not color or shape but motion. He heard only the lapping rush of the water, saw only the normal movement of the reeds in harmony with the water's flow.

Then, a sling's shot away from him, the tops of the cattails moved *against* the current. He remained as he was, breathing slowly. A bank of the cattails bowed in unison, and then, a distance from that motion, a group of reeds bowed in the opposite direction. The next motion of the reeds was closer to him, and suddenly he realized that he was hearing a sound, one that had blended with the water noises when it was distant. But now it was closer. Something scraped through the reeds. The tall standing grasses rubbed against a creature's hide in a long, smooth chorus. Flavius parted his lips, took a silent breath. He'd find out what it was now, before it came any closer. His pole sling was loaded. In a motion so practiced and natural that he gave it no thought, he tipped the pole and snapped it forward.

The missile was one of his own devising, heavier than he would have launched from a hand sling and with one end pointed. Sometimes it tumbled and struck blunt end first. Other times, the sharpened end bit. He cared little what happened this time; his intent was to startle whatever it was into betraying itself. His missile flew silently but when it struck, all silence ended.

The creature's whistle was like a shriek of wind. Much closer than he had expected, a head reared up from the reeds. It turned its outraged gaze from its own body to see what had dared to attack it. Flavius was already backing up before it turned its boxy head and fixed its eyes on him. Even in the clear morning light, they burned orange. It took in breath with a sound like cold water hitting hot stone, its slit nostrils flaring as it did so. Then it opened wide its mouth and he saw, just as the scout had reported, a maw the size of a cart, lined with rows of inward-leaning teeth. He stumbled backwards, then spun and fled. The massive head struck the ground a pike's length behind him. The shock of the impact traveled through the wet soil; he felt the weight of the creature's head through the soles of his feet, and abruptly he was running as he had never run before. He risked one glance back when he gained the top of the bank. He saw nothing.

Then, just as he dared to take a breath, the immense head on its thick neck rose again from the reeds and rushes. It stared at him, and a long forked tongue emerged from its blunt snout, flickering and tasting the air. It regarded him with nothing of fear, only malevolence, with lidless orange eyes. It opened its maw and again that whistling shriek shattered the air around him. Then it came on, moving much faster than any legless creature had a right to. Flavius turned and fled. He ran and heard the gruesome sounds of an immense footless creature coming after him. His terror put the spring of a boy in his man's legs and his heart thundered in his ears. When he finally mustered the courage to glance back, the snake was gone, but still he ran, unable to stop, almost to the outskirts of the camp.

He hurried through a camp that had begun to stir, pausing to speak to no one. He would start no rumors until Marcus had heard his news and decided how to deal with it. His mouth was dry; his heart still shaking when he stood before Regulus to make his report. It was to his commander, not to his old friend that he said, "They told you true, sir. It's an immense snake, the likes of which no one has ever seen. I'd estimate it at one hundred feet long. And it's aggressive. I hit it with a sling stone, and it came after me."

He watched his friend absorb the news. He peered at him and perhaps a smile threatened as he challenged him quietly, "One hundred feet long, Flavius? A snake one hundred feet long?"

He swallowed in a dry throat. "My best estimate, sir. From the size of the head and how high he lifted it, and from how far away the reeds were stirred by his tail." He cleared his throat. "I'm serious."

He watched Marcus rethink his words, his face growing still, and then his jaw setting. He saw his commander announce his decision. "Regardless of its size, it's still just a snake. A wolf or a bear may stand and face one man, or even half a dozen, but no creature will take a stand against a legion. We'll form up and march down there. Doubtless the noise and activity will scare it off. What did you think of the river? Are the baggage train carts going to have any problems crossing there?"

Before Flavius could reply, they heard wild yells, and then a sound that stood all the hair up on Flavius' back. A shrill whistle split the air. It was followed by shouts of "Dragon! Dragon!" The whistling shriek of the creature was repeated, more loudly. It was followed by screams, very human screams that abruptly stopped. More shouting, panicky, wordless yells.

Marcus had been half-dressed when Flavius arrived. Now he hastily buckled his breastplate and snatched up his helm. "Let's go," he said, and though a dozen men fell in at his heels, Flavius felt the words had been meant for him. They went at a dogtrot through the camp and toward the river. Flavius drew his shortsword as he ran, hoping he'd never be near enough to use it. All around him, other men in various stages of dress joined the hurrying throng. "Archers to me!" Marcus shouted, and within a score of strides, he was flanked by bowmen. Flavius doggedly held his place just behind Marcus' left shoulder.

They did not reach the edge of camp before a tide of shouting men met them. They carried one man, and though he was still roaring with pain, Flavius knew him for a dead man. His left leg had been shorn away at the hip.

"It's a dragon!"

"Snake got two of them right way. They just went to fetch water."

"Eyes the size of cartwheels!"

"Knocked down six men and crushed them. Just crushed them!"

"It ate them. Gods help us, it ate them!"

"It's a demon, a Carthaginian demon!"

"They've set a dragon on us!"

"It's coming! It's coming!"

Behind the fleeing men, Flavius saw the great head rise. Up it went and up, higher and higher. It looked down on all of them, eyes gleaming, forked tongue long as a bullwhip flickering in and out of its mouth. Flavius felt cold, as if evil had looked directly at him. The creature, dragon or snake, whistled then, a high powerful gust of sound. Some men cried out and others clapped their hands to their ears.

"Archers!" shouted Regulus, and a score of flights took wing, their hiss lost in the snake's long whistle. Some arrows missed; others skipped over the creature's scaled back. Some struck, stuck briefly, and then fell as the snake shook itself. Perhaps six hit and sank into the creature. If it felt any pain, it did not show it. Instead, it struck, the immense head, mouth open wide, darting down to seize two soldiers. The men shrieked as it lifted them into the air. It threw back its head and gulped, and their comrades were suddenly visible lumps moving down the snake's throat. Flavius felt cold. The snake had seized them so quickly, they could not be dead. They had been swallowed alive.

Flavius had not heard the command given to fire again, but another phalanx of arrows was arching toward the beast. It had come closer and they struck more true. Of those that hit, most stuck well. This time, the snake gave a whistle of fury. It flung itself flat and wallowed, trying to dislodge the arrows. Its whipping tail cleared brush from the riverside.

"Fall back!" Regulus shouted, and in a matter of moments they were in full retreat from the creature. It was not the most orderly withdrawal that Flavius had ever participated in, but it achieved its goal. The ranks of men reformed defensively as they put distance between themselves and the Carthaginian monster. Flavius' knees felt rubbery and his mind still reeled from that one revealing glimpse of the full extent of the creature. It was more than a hundred feet long; of that, he was sure. How much longer, he had no desire to know.

"It's not following!" someone shouted.

"Keep moving!" Regulus ordered. "Back to the camp and man the fortifications." Then he cast a sideways look at Flavius. "Go see," he said quietly. Heart in his throat, Flavius turned and began to walk back through the crowd of oncoming men. When he had passed the last stragglers, he pushed on, ears strained and his sling at the ready. He knew it would not do much, but it was his oldest and most familiar weapon. And, he thought to himself, it had a lot more range than a gladius. He grinned, surprising himself, and walked on.

When he could see the bodies of the fallen, he stopped. He scanned the surrounding brush and saw no sign of the immense creature. It had wallowed out a section of brush and grasses where it rolled to dislodge the arrows. He stood a time longer, surveying the scene. When first one carrion bird and then another swept in and landed near the bodies, he judged that the serpent was truly gone. Still, his advance was cautious.

All the downed men were dead. One breathed a little still, air rasping in and out of his slack mouth, but his torso was crushed and there was no light in his eyes. Sometimes the body took a little time to know it was dead. He stood from appraising the man and forced himself to walk on. The serpent had cut a large swath through the brush in its retreat. He found no blood or any sign that they had dealt it significant injuries. He followed it until he could see the river and the crushed reeds where the creature had returned to the water. Down there, it could conceal itself. He would go no farther. There was no need of it.

When he reported back to Marcus, he realized how shaken his friend was. He listened gravely to what Flavius told him, then shook his head. "We are here to fight Carthaginians, not deal with a giant snake. The idea that it is some kind of demon or dragon set on us by the Carthaginians has shaken them. I don't intend to challenge it again. I'll send a burial detail for the fallen, but I've decided to move downriver. I've already sent the scouts ahead, looking for a place to cross. We can't linger here. We'll move on."

Flavius had felt relief but also surprise that Marcus would follow so sensible a course. He had expected his friend to dig in and do battle with it. Marcus' next words cleared away the mystery. "It's big, but it's only a snake. It's not worth our time."

Flavius nodded to that and withdrew. Marcus had always been about being a soldier. The stalking that a hunter did and the necessity of trying to think like his prey in order to hunt it had never appealed to him. War he saw as a challenge between men, demanding an understanding of strategy. He had never seen animals as complex and unpredictable, as Flavius did. He had never seen animals as worthy opponents, never understood Flavius' fascination with hunting.

Now, as Flavius looked up at his friend in his cage, he saw too clearly the animal that Marcus had always lived inside. The man's mind was slowly giving way to the beast that enclosed him. Pain wracked him and demanded his attention. He saw the tremors that had begun to run over Marcus' body. His knees shook, and a trickle of blood-tinged urine ran down his leg and dripped onto the street and the passersby below him. A shout of outrage greeted this, and the market crowd that had almost forgotten the dying man above them once more turned their eyes upward.

The woman who had been spattered tore her scarf from her shoulders and threw it to the ground. She looked up at Marcus and shook her fist and shouted obscenities at him. A wave of mocking laughter followed her words, along with pointing gestures and other mocking shouts. A few onlookers stooped to pick up stones.

The pain, for a time, had come in waves that threatened to sweep his consciousness away. Through each engulfing surge, he had held tight to the bars of his cage as a drowning sailor might cling to a bit of floating wreckage. He knew it offered him no safety, but he would not release his grip. He'd die standing, and not just because a fall would mean being impaled on one of the coarse spikes sticking up from the bottom of his cage. He'd die upright, a Roman citizen, a consul, a soldier, not curled like a speared dog.

The pain had not abated, but it had turned into something else. Just as the crash of storm waves can eventually lull a man to sleep, so it was with the pain now. It was there, and so constant that his thoughts floated on top of it, only disconnecting when an especially sharp jab penetrated his mind. The pain seemed to provoke his memories, waking the sharpest and most potent of them. His triumph at Aspis; he had seized the whole city with scarcely a blow. That had been a summer! Hamilcar had avoided him, and his army had virtually had the run of Carthage. The plunder had been rich, and he'd lost count of how many captured Roman soldiers he had regained. Oh, he had been the Senate's darling then. Then, the prospect of being granted a Triumph and paraded through Rome had loomed large and fresh before him, as keenly imagined as when he had been a boy. It would be his. He would be acknowledged as a hero by cheering, adoring crowds.

But then Manlius, his fellow consul, had decided to sail back to Rome, taking the best of their plunder home. And Hamilcar, general for the Carthaginians, had perhaps decided that gave him some sort of advantage. He had brought his army to an encampment on high wooded ground on the far side of the Bagradas River. Regulus had not been daunted. He'd set out to meet and challenge him, taking infantry, cavalry, and a good force of ballistae.

But then they had come to the river. And that damn African snake. Some of his men had believed it a Carthaginian demon, sent by Hamilcar to attack them. When he had seen it for himself, he hadn't been able to comprehend the creature. Flavius had tried to tell him; that was the first and last time he'd ever doubted his friend's evaluation of an animal. He'd lost thirteen men in his first encounter with the creature, too big a loss against such an adversary. He'd been intent on Hamilcar and fearful of losing his element of surprise. And so, he'd withdrawn his men, surrendering the riverbank to the immense snake, as he never would have conceded it to any human opponent. He'd marched his men downriver, looking for a good place to ford, while his baggage train and the heavier wheeled artillery had followed on the higher, firmer ground.

A few hours of marching and he'd found a good fording place. He'd congratulated himself on losing so little time. Mounted on his horse, he'd led his men to the river and halted there on the bank to watch the crossing of his troops. He'd posted archers on what little higher ground there was, a standard precaution he took whenever he committed that many troops to a river crossing. The Bagradas was wide, shallow at the edges and mucky, with muddy banks forested with reeds and cattails taller than a man on horseback. The front ranks of his soldiers pushed their way forward through them. He watched them go, the leading men disappearing into the green ranks of river plants, pushing a narrow path that those who followed would soon trample into a wide swath.

He hoped the bottom would be more gravel than muck as they got closer to the middle of the river. He wanted to get across quickly and out onto the other side, and then up onto firmer ground. Fording a river was always a vulnerable time for any military force. A man chest-deep in moving water presents a good target without being capable of defending himself. Anxiously, he scanned the far side of the river through the fence of reeds and grasses. He saw no sign of the enemy. He would not relax until his first ranks were on the other side of the river and posting more archers there to guard the crossing place.

But he was not looking in the right place, or for the right opponent.

Flavius had been standing near his horse. He heard his friend gasp and turned his head. For a moment, his eyes could make no sense of what he saw. And then he realized that he was staring at a wall of snakeskin, a pattern of animal hide that was sliding through the tall bank of reeds, headed directly for his vulnerable troops.

Who could ever have imagined that a snake of that size could move so swiftly, let alone so quietly? Who could ever have imagined that any animal would have anticipated that they would move downriver and attempt another crossing? It might have been a coincidence. It might have been that the creature was hungry and had followed the noise of the troops on the march.

Or it might truly be a Carthaginian demon, some ancient evil summoned by them to put an end to his domination of their lands. The creature slid near soundlessly through the water and the bowing reeds. For a moment, he was stunned again at the size of it. It seemed impossible that such a long movement of grasses could be caused by a single creature. He saw it raise its blunt-nosed head, saw its jaws gape wide.

"Ware serpent!" he shouted, the first to give the warning, and then a hundred voices took up his cry. "Serpent!" Now there was an inadequate word to describe the nightmare that attacked them! A serpent was a creature that a man might tread underfoot. At its worst, here in Africa one might encounter a boa crushing a goat in its coils. *Serpent* was not a word that could apply to a creature the length of a city wall and almost the height of one.

It moved like a wish, like a sigh, like a gleaming scythe, newly sharpened, mowing down grain. He glimpsed it as a moving wall seen between the vertical spikes of the upright reeds. Scales glittered when the sun touched them and gleamed in the gentle shade of the reeds. It moved in a relentless, remorseless way that seemed more like a wave or a landslide than like a living creature as it sliced through the ranked men in the water. Some it caught up in its jaws. It swallowed them whole, the great muscles on the sides of its throat working as it crushed the men down its throat. Others were pushed down into the water, if not by the creature's own body, then by the wave that its undulating motion created. It moved swiftly through the formation, and then, with a lash of its gigantic tail, it slashed again at the struggling men who either swam or tried to regain their footing in the current.

"Archers!" Regulus had shouted, but their arrows were already bouncing off the snake's smooth hide or sticking like wobbly pins, barely penetrating its armor.

The missiles did no good and much harm, for the snake doubled back on itself. A rank reptilian stench suddenly filled the air as the creature lashed like a massive whip through the struggling men in the water. It caught some of them in its jaws, crushed them, and flung the bodies aside in a fury. One man in the water, brave or foolish, most likely both, tried to plunge his pike into the creature. The sharp point skittered along the snake's scales to no effect. An instant later, the snake bent its head and engulfed the man in its mouth. A shake sent his pike flying. A convulsive swallow, and its enemy was gone. Whistling scream after scream split the air. The few bodies it snapped up and swallowed seemed afterthoughts to its wrath.

Regulus fought his mount. Battle-trained, nonetheless, she reared, screaming in terror, and when he tightened his reins, she backed and fought for her head. Was that struggle what turned the snake's attention to him? Perhaps it was only that a man mounted on a horse was a larger creature than the frantic men drowning in the river. Whatever it was, the snake's gleaming gaze fell on him, and suddenly it came straight for him. The lashing tail that drove it whipped the river to brown froth. The snake turned its immense head sideways, jaws gaping wide, plainly intending to seize both man and horse in its jaws.

Useless to flee. He'd never escape the snake's speed. Might as well stand his ground and die a hero, as flee and be remembered as a coward. Strange. Even now, he recalled clearly that he had not been afraid. Surprised, a bit, that he would die in battle against a snake rather than against the Carthaginians. He re-called thinking clearly that men would remember his death. His sword was already in his hand, though he could not recall drawing it. Foolish weapon for an encounter such as this, and yet he would draw blood if he could. The snake whistled as it came, a sky-splitting sound that made thought impossible. He felt stunned by the impact against his ears, his skin.

Around him, he was dimly aware of his men scattering. The mare reared and he held her in with sheer strength. The snake's gaping mouth came at him; the stench was overpowering. Then, as the creature's jaws were all around him, he felt a sudden slam of a body against his. "Marcus!" the man might have shouted, but that smaller sound was lost in the snake's whistle.

He didn't recognize Flavius when he tackled him from the horse. He only knew him as he hit the muddy bank of the river, and looked up, to see the snake lifting both horse and Flavius from the ground. The creature's jaws had closed on the horse's chest. Flavius' flying dive to drive Marcus from the horse meant that one of his legs had been caught in the snake's jaws as it gripped his unfortunate mare. Flavius dangled, head down, roaring with terror and pain as the mare struggled wildly in the snake's mouth.

Marcus had rolled as he struck the ground. He came instinctively back to his feet and then leaped upward and caught his friend round the chest. His added weight literally tore Flavius from the serpent's jaws. Lightened of Flavius' weight, the snake was content to continue its battle to engulf the wildly kicking horse. He scarcely noticed the men who fell back to the ground. That time, Marcus had landed heavily with Flavius' weight on top of him. Gasping for air, he rolled out from under his friend, then seized him under the arms and dragged him back, away from the open riverbank and into the protective brush.

They both stank of serpent, and Flavius was bleeding profusely. His thigh was scored deeply in several long gashes where the serpent's teeth had gripped him. He fought Marcus as Marcus tried to bind his leg firmly to stop the bleeding. Only as he tied the last knot did he realize that his friend was not fighting him, but was convulsing. The snake's bite was toxic. Flavius was going to die. He'd taken Marcus' death as his own.

A shiver shook Marcus and he came a little back to himself. He still gripped the bars of his cage. The sun and wind had dried his eyes to uselessness. He could sense there still was light; that was all. How many days had he stood here, he wondered, and how many more must he endure until death took him? His cracked lips parted, snarl or smile, he did not know. His mind shaped words his mouth could no longer form. *Flavius, you took my hero's death from me. And left me to find this one. It was no favor, my friend. No favor at all to me.*

Flavius saw him shudder. So did the rest of the crowd. Like jackals attracted to an injured beast, they fixed their eyes on him. Flavius glanced from face to face.

Flared nostrils, parted lips, shining eyes. They wagged their head knowingly to one another and readied their dirty little missiles. They would see that Marcus' last moments were full of torment and mockery. With flung stones and vile words, they would claim his dog's death as a bizarre victory for themselves.

Anger swept through him, and he longed for a sword. He had no weapon, only the pole sling he'd manufactured from the stolen purse and his walking staff. Last night, he'd used it to kill a bird perched in a tree. It had been a small meal, but he'd been pleased to discover that he hadn't lost his skill. But it was a hunter's or a marksman's weapon, not something to turn against a mob.

He could turn his walking staff against them, perhaps, but there would not be the satisfaction of teaching them anything. Even if he'd had a gladius, he could not kill them all, but he could teach them the difference between tormenting a man in a cage and dying in a battle against a bared blade. Not that it would save Marcus. There would still be the rattle of stones against the iron bars of his prison and the small batterings of the ones that reached him. He would still hear their insults and mockery hurled along with the stones. His friend had stood strong all day, but now he would go down ignominiously. Flavius looked around him, sick with knowledge. He could not save Marcus.

He could not save Marcus from death. But, perhaps, he could save him from this particular death. He stooped for a stone, picked up a likely one, and retreated to the edge of the street. He'd have to work quickly. The crowd was already winging stones at Marcus. Most of them fell short, and even the missiles that struck had little power. He was satisfied to see that they fell back into the gathering crowd, striking some of the gawkers' upturned faces.

In the shelter of a doorway, he considered the stone he'd chosen. Then he groped in the knotted rag at his waist, and found the wad of wax from the stolen purse. He jabbed himself on the serpent's tooth as he took it out. The damnable thing was still sharp as ever, despite all the time it had festered inside his body.

He remembered too well the day he'd acquired it. He'd leaped, intending only to knock Marcus out of the way. He could still recall, in ghastly detail, how the serpent's jaws had closed on his leg. He'd dangled, upside down, the pain from the stabbing teeth as sharp as the toxin from the creature's mouth. Instantly, he'd felt the hot acid kiss of it and known he was poisoned. He'd been saved by the horse's harness. The serpent's teeth had passed completely through his leg; they grated on something, perhaps a buckle or bronze plate. He'd felt the snake's fury as it clenched its teeth all the tighter. And then, as teeth ground against metal, he'd felt one break.

The snake had briefly loosened its grip just as Marcus leaped for him and seized him. He'd literally been torn from the jaws of death by his friend. "Leave me!" he'd gasped, knowing that he was dying, and he'd sunk into blackness.

When next he'd found light, all had changed. His

leg was tightly bandaged, his swollen flesh rippling next to the wrapping, and fever burned him. Marcus had been crouched beside him. He looked up at the leaves of an oak tree against the evening sky and smelled pine needles. So Marcus had withdrawn from the snake. Had he given up his river crossing, then? He'd blinked dully, knowing that, for him, the fight was done. Whatever became of him now was in the hands of his friend and commander. Marcus had grinned at him, a wolf's smile. "You're awake then? Good. I want you to see, my friend. If you should die this night, I want you to know that I did not suffer your enemy to outlive you.

"Sit him up," Marcus commanded someone, and, with a fine disregard for Flavius' wishes, two men did just that. He realized dizzily that he was on a slight rise scarcely worthy to be called a foothill, looking down on the river valley. They were not, then, that far away from the snake's territory. He felt queasy, and not just from the poison. Fear could do that to a man.

"What?" he managed, and with the word, felt that it was not just his leg, but his entire body that swelled with the venom.

"Give him water," Marcus directed one of the men, but he didn't even look toward Flavius. He was watching the river. Watching and waiting. "There," he breathed. "There you are. We see you now." He turned and shouted to someone behind them, "Do you mark him now? You can't miss him. He's as big as a city wall, and so shall we treat him. Take your best aim and let fly."

One of the men held water in a cup to his mouth. Flavius tried to drink. His lips, his tongue, all parts of his mouth were stupid and swollen. He wet his tongue, choked, gasped in air, gulped water, and then managed to pull his face away from the offered cup. Someone, somewhere was beating a drum, a slow thwacking noise. It made no sense. As he pulled his face away from the cup, he heard the familiar thud and then deep vibration as a ballista launched a shot. Four others followed in succession. He knew them now, knew the deep *thock-thock-thock* as the bowstring was racheted back, and then the release, followed by the deep hum of vibrating leather. They were using shot, not bolts, and the men on the rise were shouting and leaping in excitement as each missile was launched. "That's a hit!" someone shouted, and "Look at him thrash! Look at him thrash!" another replied.

Flavius forced his eyes wider and managed to focus them on the scene. Marcus had chosen to attack the snake with ballistae. The men on the weapons were working frantically, loading and cranking and adjusting each launch to target the writhing snake. Below, each heavy shot of stone either sent up a plume of brown water as it missed, or thudded harshly against the scaled back of the snake before splashing into the river. The snake was in the deep reeds, but from his vantage, Marcus could look down on him. He had glimpses of the broad scaled back and his lashing tail, but even when no part of the snake was visible, they could track him by the way he parted the reeds and sent brown tendrils of mud unfurling into the tan waters of the river.

"Can't kill him," Flavius said, but it came out as a muted mumble and no one paid him any heed. He caught only glimpses of the battle, for the men in front of him shouted and leaped and pounded one another with each successful hit on the snake. But Flavius knew snakes. He'd held them in his hands when he was a boy and knew how supple they were, how flexible their ribs. "Head," he suggested, and then, from swollen lips, he shouted at Marcus, "Head. Skull!"

Had he heard him, or had he figured it out for himself? "Aim for his head. All of you. Focus your missiles on his head! Quickly, before he finds better cover or goes back deep into the river."

His men complied, ratcheting and loading and raining a hail of rocks down on the snake below. Battered and confused, the creature turned first one way and then another, trying to elude its mysterious enemy. Its tail, Flavius saw, did not thrash so wildly as it had; perhaps one of the missiles had done some damage to its spine after all. Another hit, this one closer to the snake's wedge-shaped head, and suddenly its movements slowed and became more labored. It more twisted than thrashed now; Flavius caught a glimpse of pale belly scales as the creature rolled in agony.

And then, the hit. Flavius knew the death blow when he saw it. The rock struck the snake's head and stuck there, wedged into the animal's skull. The twitches became ever slower; undeterred, the men on the ballistae continued to rain stone after stone down on the creature. Even after it was still, they assaulted it, pelting its yielding body over and over.

"Enough!" Marcus shouted at last, long after Flavius knew the snake was dead. He turned to someone, spoke over Flavius' head. "Send two men down to be sure of it. And when they are sure it's dead, I want them to measure it."

"It's a hundred foot if it's one," someone observed.

"Closer to a hundred and twenty," someone else opined.

"No one's going to believe us," someone else laughed sourly.

Flavius saw Marcus stiffen. The poison was working in him, and his vision wavered before him. He had a glimpse of Marcus' set jaw and grim eyes. Then, as he gave in and closed his own eyes, he heard Marcus say, "They'll believe us. This is no wild tale from Africa, no braggart's boast. They'll believe because we'll send them the hide. And the head. We'll skin it out and send it back to Rome. They'll believe."

And they had. Flavius had ridden in the oxcart alongside the salted and stinking hide. The severed head, missing a number of souvenir teeth, had been at the end of the wagon. The sight and the smell of it baking under the hot African sun had sickened him almost as much as the poison and infection coursing through his body. He had leaned against the side of the wagon, his bandaged leg propped up before him and stared at it blearily. He could see the broken tooth in the snake's jaw, and knew where the rest of it was. Up against the bone in his thigh, snugged in tight. The healer had judged it safest to leave it where it was. "You'll heal up around it, never know it's there," the man had lied to Flavius. And Flavius, too sick and weary to consider the idea of letting him dig in the wound for it, had nodded and accepted the lie.

Marcus had come to bid him farewell. "You know I'd keep you by my side if I could, but it's for the best that you go home. You can tell my tale better than anyone else. And no one will doubt you when you've got both skull and hide to back you up. I'm sorry to send you home like this. But I promise that at the next muster, you'll join me again. I hope you don't think I'm breaking my promise."

They both knew to what he referred. Flavius had sighed. Even if he had told Marcus that he never wanted to go soldiering again, his friend would not have believed it. So he summoned a smile and said, "As I recall, you only promised that you'd never go to war without me. And I don't recall that I ever said I wouldn't go home without you!"

"That's true, old friend. The promise was mine, not yours. Well, travel well. And send me word of my family, and tell my boys of our deeds. I'll be home again soon enough. And next time we form up, be sure that you will march with me again."

And he *was* home again soon. That time. Flavius squeezed his eyes shut for a moment, wishing he could shut out the sounds of the crowd as well. The catcalls were getting louder. Marcus had never grasped that for Flavius, war was a duty, not a call to glory. So the next time there had been a muster, as Flavius limped forward on the leg that had never fully healed, Marcus kept his word. Flavius was once more chosen to march with him.

And he'd ended up here. An escaped slave in Carthage.

He looked at what he had fashioned from the serpent's tooth. He balanced it in his hand, considering. A pole sling worked best with a rounded stone. This missile might well tumble. The bars of the cage might deflect it. It was a stupid plan, a hopeless gesture. He looked up at his friend, and what he saw decided him.

Some flung object had struck Marcus' brow. Bright blood trickled from the split. But more than that, the setting sun cast a red light on him. His bared skin looked scarlet in the dying light. Red painted him, just as if he were riding in a chariot through Rome, riding to have his Triumph recognized. He stood upright, trembling with the effort of remaining so. His ruined eyes stared to the west.

Flavius stepped out into the street, walked determinedly to the best vantage point. He'd have one chance, and the pole sling demanded space. Marcus was visibly failing as petty stones and flung insults filled the air and his ears. Flavius considered well. Then he took a deep breath.

"Ware serpent!" he shouted.

Marcus did not turn toward him. Perhaps, his grip on the bars tightened. Perhaps not. He might never know that his friend was there to witness him die, might never know what Flavius risked in raising his voice. A few people had turned to stare at him, hearing his foreign words. He busied himself, settling his missile in his sling, testing the swing of it. He fixed his eyes and his heart on his friend. He nodded a farewell Marcus could not see. Then he launched the tooth. It flew true. He saw it strike Marcus' chest, saw it sink into his heart. Marcus jerked with the impact.

"Memento mori!" he shouted, and at those words, his friend did, for the last time, turn toward him. Then he sank, dead but never relinquishing his grip on the bars, onto the spikes that had so long awaited him. The crowd roared in triumph, but he was past hearing them. Consul Marcus Atillius Regulus was dead, slain by a serpent. It no longer mattered that fools continued to hurl stones and offal at him. He was gone.

Flavius stood but a moment longer. A few people had marked what he had done, but they marked also that he gripped his staff tightly, and that he did not avoid their stares. They turned away from him and continued to pick up stones and hurl them at Marcus' body. Like soldiers hurling rocks at a dead serpent. Better to taunt a dead lion than a live jackal, Flavius thought to himself.

Then he turned and walked away. Home was a long way from here, but he knew he would make it.

He had never promised Marcus that he wouldn't go home without him. He would. He spoke a new promise to the gathering evening. "I'll never go to war again, Marcus. Not without you."

Joe R. Lansdale

Prolific Texas writer Joe R. Lansdale has won the Edgar Award, the British Fantasy Award, the American Horror Award, the American Mystery Award, the International Crime Writer's Award, and seven Bram Stoker Awards. Although perhaps best known for horror/thrillers such as *The Nightrunners, Bubba Ho-Tep, The Bottoms, The God of the Razor,* and *The Drive-In,* he also writes the popular Hap Collins and Leonard Pine mystery series—*Savage Season, Mucho Mojo, The Two-Bear Mambo, Bad Chili, Rumble Tumble, Captains Outrageous*—as well as western novels such as *A Fine Dark Line* and *Blood Dance,* and totally unclassifiable cross-genre novels such as *Zeppelins West, Magic Wagon,* and *Flaming London.* His other novels include *Dead in the West, The Big Blow, Sunset and Sawdust, Act of Love, Freezer Burn, Waltz of Shadows,* and *The Drive-In 2: Not Just One of Them Sequels.* He has also contributed novels to series such as Batman and Tarzan. His many short stories have been collected in *By Bizarre Hands, Tight Little Stitches in a Dead Man's Back; The Shadows, Kith and Kin; The Long Ones; Stories by Mama Lansdale's Youngest Boy; Bestsellers Guaranteed;*

On the Far Side of the Cadillac Desert with Dead Folks; Electric Gumbo; Writer of the Purple Rage; A Fist Full of Stories (and Articles); Steppin' Out, Summer '68; Bumper Crop; The Good, the Bad, and the Indifferent; For a Few Stories More; Mad Dog Summer and Other Stories; The King and Other Stories; and *High Cotton: Selected Stories of Joe R. Lansdale.* As editor, he has produced the anthologies *The Best of the West, Retro-Pulp Tales, Razored Saddles* (with Pat LoBrutto), *Dark at Heart* (with wife Karen Lansdale), and the Robert E. Howard tribute anthology, *Cross Plains Universe* (with Scott A. Cupp). An anthology in tribute to Lansdale's work is *Lords of the Razor.* His most recent books are *Leather Maiden* and a novel written with John Lansdale, *Hell's Bounty.* The newest anthology, *Son of Retro Pulp Tales,* was published in 2009. He lives with his family in Nacogdoches, Texas.

Here's a funny and sizzlingly fast-paced look at two men who do what Huck and Tom only dream about doing and actually do "light out for the territories"—and run into a lot more trouble there than they bargained for.

Soldierin'

They said if you went out West and joined up with the colored soldiers, they'd pay you in real Yankee dollars, thirteen of them a month, feed and clothe you, and it seemed like a right smart idea since I was wanted for a lynchin'. It wasn't that I was invited to hold the rope or sing a little spiritual. I was the guest of honor on this one. They was plannin' to stretch my neck like a goozle-wrung chicken at Sunday dinner.

Thing I'd done was nothin' on purpose, but in a moment of eyeballin' while walkin' along the road on my way to cut some firewood for a nickel and a jar of jam, a white girl who was hangin' out wash bent over and pressed some serious butt up against her gingham, and a white fella, her brother, seen me take a look, and that just crawled all up in his ass and died, and he couldn't stand the stink.

Next thing I know, I'm wanted for being bold with a white girl, like maybe I'd broke into her yard and jammed my arm up her ass, but I hadn't done nothin' but what's natural, which is glance at a nice butt when it was available to me.

Now, in the livin' of my life, I've killed men and animals and made love to three Chinese women on the same night in the same bed and one of them with only one leg, and part of it wood, and I even ate some of a dead fella once when I was crossin' the mountains, though I want to rush in here and make it clear I didn't know him all that well, and we damn sure wasn't kinfolks. Another thing I did was I won me a shootin' contest up Colorady way against some pretty damn famous shooters, all white boys, but them's different stories and not even akin to the one I want to tell, and I'd like to add, just like them other events, this time I'm talking about is as true as the sunset.

Pardon me. Now that I've gotten older, sometimes I find I start out to tell one story and end up tellin' another. But to get back to the one I was talkin' about . . . So, havin' been invited to a lynchin', I took my daddy's horse and big ole loaded six-gun he kept wrapped up in an oilcloth from under the floorboards of our shack, and took off like someone had set my ass on fire. I rode that poor old horse till he was slap worn out. I had to stop over in a little place just outside of Nacogdoches and steal another one, not on account of I was a thief, but on account of I didn't want to get caught by the posse and hung and maybe have my pecker cut off and stuck in my mouth. Oh. I also took a chicken. He's no longer with me, of course, as I ate him out there on the trail.

Anyway, I left my horse for the fella I took the fresh horse and the chicken from, and I left him a busted pocket watch on top of the railing post, and then I rode out to West Texas. It took a long time for me to get there, and I had to stop and steal food and drink from creeks and make sure the horse got fed with corn I stole. After a few days, I figured I'd lost them that was after me, and I changed my name as I rode along. It had been Wiliford P. Thomas, the *P* not standing for a thing other than *P*. I chose the name Nat Wiliford for myself, and practiced on saying it while I rode along. When I said it, I wanted it to come out of my mouth like it wasn't a lie.

Before I got to where I was goin', I run up against this colored fella taking a dump in the bushes, wiping his ass on leaves. If I had been a desperado, I could have shot him out from over his pile and taken his horse, 'cause he was deeply involved in the event—so much, in fact, that I could see his eyes were crossed from where I rode up on a hill, and that was some distance.

I was glad I was downwind, and hated to interrupt, so I sat on my stolen horse until he was leaf wiping, and then I called out. "Hello, the shitter."

He looked up and grinned at me, touched his rifle lying on the ground beside him, said, "You ain't plannin' on shootin' me, are you?"

"No. I thought about stealin' your horse, but it's sway back and so ugly in the face it hurts my feelings."

"Yeah, and it's blind in one eye and has a knot on its back comes right through the saddle. When I left the plantation, I took that horse. Wasn't much then, and it's a lot less now."

He stood up and fastened his pants and I seen then that he was a pretty big fellow, all decked out in fresh-looking overalls and a big black hat with a feather in it. He came walkin' up the hill toward me, his wipin' hand stuck out for a shake, but I politely passed, because I thought his fingers looked a little brown.

Anyway, we struck it up pretty good, and by nightfall we found a creek, and he washed his hands in the water with some soap from his saddlebag, which made me feel a mite better. We sat and had coffee and some of his biscuits. All I could offer was some conversation, and he had plenty to give back. His name was Cullen, but he kept referrin' to himself as The Former House Nigger, as if it were a rank akin to general. He told a long story about how he got the feather for his hat, but it mostly just came down to he snuck up on a hawk sittin' on a low limb and jerked it out of its tail.

"When my master went to war against them Yankees," he said, "I went with him. I fought with him and wore me a butternut coat and pants, and I shot me at least a half dozen of them Yankees."

"Are you leaking brains out of your gourd?" I said. "Them rebels was holdin' us down."

"I was a house nigger, and I grew up with Mr. Gerald, and I didn't mind going to war with him. Me and him was friends. There was lots of us like that."

"Y'all must have got dropped on your head when you was young'ns."

"The Master and the older Master was all right."

" 'Cept they owned you," I said.

"Maybe I was born to be owned. They always quoted somethin' like that out of the Bible."

"That ought to have been your clue, fella. My daddy always said that book has caused more misery than chains, an ill-tempered woman, and a nervous dog."

"I loved Young Master like a brother, truth be known. He got shot in the war, right 'tween the eyes by a musket ball, killed him deader than a goddamn tree stump. I sopped up his blood in a piece of his shirt I cut off, mailed it back home with a note on what happened. When the war was over, I stayed around the plantation for a while, but everything come apart then, the old man and the old lady died, and I buried them out back of the place a good distance from the privy and uphill, I might add. That just left me and the Old Gentleman's dog.

"The dog was as old as death and couldn't eat so good, so I shot it, and went on out into what Young Master called The Big Wide World. Then, like you, I heard the guv'ment was signing up coloreds for its man's army. I ain't no good on my own. I figured the army was for me."

"I don't like being told nothin' by nobody," I said, "but I surely love to get paid." I didn't mention I also didn't want to get killed by angry crackers and the army seemed like a good place to hide.

About three days later, we rode up on the place we was looking for. Fort McKavett, between the Colorady and the Pecos rivers. It was a sight, that fort. It was big and it didn't look like nothin' I'd ever seen before. Out front was colored fellas in army blue drilling on horseback, looking sharp in the sunlight, which there was plenty of. It was hot where I come from, sticky even, but you could find a tree to get under. Out here, all you could get under was your hat, or maybe some dark cloud sailing across the face of the sun, and that might last only as long as it takes a bird to fly over.

But there I was. Fort McKavett. Full of dreams and crotch itch from long riding, me and my new friend sat on our horses, lookin' the fort over, watchin' them horse soldiers drill, and it was prideful thing to see. We rode on down in that direction.

In the Commanding Officer's quarters, me and The Former House Nigger stood before a big desk with a white man behind it, name of Colonel Hatch. He had a caterpillar mustache and big sweat circles like wet moons under his arms. His eyes were aimed on a fly sitting on some papers on his desk. Way he was watchin' it, you'd have thought he was beading down on a hostile. He said, "So you boys want to sign up for the colored army. I figured that, you both being colored."

He was a sharp one, this Hatch.

I said, "I've come to sign up and be a horse rider in the Ninth Cavalry."

Hatch studied me for a moment, said, "Well, we got plenty of ridin' niggers. What we need is walkin' niggers for the goddamn infantry, and I can get you set in the right direction to hitch up with them."

I figured anything that was referred to with *goddamn* in front of it wasn't the place for me.

"I reckon ain't a man here can ride better'n me," I said, "and that would be even you, Colonel, and I'm sure you are one ridin' sonofabitch, and I mean that in as fine a way as I can say it."

Hatch raised an eyebrow. "That so?"

"Yes, sir. No brag, just fact. I can ride on a horse's back, under his belly, make him lay down and make him jump, and at the end of the day, I take a likin' to him, I can diddle that horse in the ass and make him enjoy it enough to brew my coffee and bring my slippers, provided I had any. That last part about the diddlin' is just talkin', but the first part is serious."

"I figured as much," Hatch said.

"I ain't diddlin' no horses," The Former House Nigger said. "I can cook and lay out silverware. Mostly, as a Former House Nigger, I drove the buggy."

At that moment, Hatch come down on that fly with his hand, and he got him too. He peeled it off his palm and flicked it on the floor. There was this colored soldier standing nearby, very stiff and alert, and he bent over, picked the fly up by a bent wing, threw it out the door and came back. Hatch wiped his palm on his pants leg. "Well," he said, "let's see how much of what you got is fact, and how much is wind."

They had a corral nearby, and inside it, seeming to fill it up, was a big black horse that looked like he ate men and shitted out saddlebags made of their skin and bones. He put his eye right on me when I came out to the corral, and when I walked around on the other side, he spun around to keep a gander on me. Oh, he knew what I was about, all right.

Hatch took hold of one corner of his mustache and played with it, turned and looked at me. "You ride that horse well as you say you can, I'll take both of you into the cavalry, and The Former House Nigger can be our cook."

"I said I could cook," The Former House Nigger said. "Didn't say I was any good."

"Well," Hatch said, "what we got now ain't even cookin'. There's just a couple fellas that boil water and put stuff in it. Mostly turnips."

I climbed up on the railing, and by this time, four colored cavalry men had caught up the horse for me. That old black beast had knocked them left and right, and it took them a full twenty minutes to get a bridle and a saddle on him, and when they come off the field, so to speak, two was limpin' like they had one foot in a ditch. One was holding his head where he had been kicked, and the other looked amazed he was alive. They had tied the mount next to the railin', and he was hoppin' up and down like a little girl with a jump rope, only a mite more vigorous.

"Go ahead and get on," Hatch said.

Having bragged myself into a hole, I had no choice.

I wasn't lyin' when I said I was a horse rider. I was. I could buck them and make them go down on their bellies and roll on their sides, make them strut and do whatever, but this horse was as mean as homemade sin, and I could tell he had it in for me.

Soon as I was on him, he jerked his head and them reins snapped off the railing and I was clutchin' at what was left of it. The sky came down on my head as that horse leaped. Ain't no horse could leap like that, and soon me and him was trying to climb the clouds. I couldn't tell earth from heaven, 'cause we bucked all over that goddamn lot, and ever time that horse come down, it jarred my bones from butt to skull. I come out of the saddle a few times, nearly went off the back of him, but I hung in there, tight as a tick on a dog's nuts. Finally he jumped himself out and started to roll. He went down on one side, mashing my leg in the dirt, and rolled on over. Had that dirt in the corral not been tamped down and soft, giving with me, there wouldn't been nothing left of me but a sack of blood and broken bones.

Finally the horse humped a couple of sad bucks and gave out, started to trot and snort. I leaned over close to his ear and said, "You call that buckin'?" He seemed to take offense at that, and run me straight to the corral and hit the rails there with his chest. I went sailin' off his back and landed on top of some soldiers, scatterin' them like quail.

Hatch come over and looked down on me, said, "Well, you ain't smarter than the horse, but you can ride well enough. You and The Former House Nigger are in with the rest of the ridin' niggers. Trainin' starts in the morning."

We drilled with the rest of the recruits up and down that lot, and finally outside and around the fort until we was looking pretty smart. The horse they give me was that black devil I had ridden. I named him Satan. He really wasn't as bad as I first thought. He was worse, and you had to be at your best every time you got on him, 'cause deep down in his bones, he was always thinking about killing you, and if you didn't watch it, he'd kind of act casual, like he was watching a cloud or somethin', and quickly turn his head and take a nip out of your leg, if he could bend far enough to get to it.

Anyway, the months passed, and we drilled, and my buddy cooked, and though what he cooked wasn't any good, it was better than nothin'. It was a good life as compared to being hung, and there was some real freedom to it and some respect. I wore my uniform proud, set my horse like I thought I was somethin' special with a stick up its ass.

We mostly did a little patrollin', and wasn't much to it except ridin' around lookin' for wild Indians we never did see, collectin' our thirteen dollars at the end of the month, which was just so much paper 'cause there wasn't no place to spend it. And then, one mornin', things changed, and wasn't none of it for the better, except The Former House Nigger managed to cook a pretty good breakfast with perfect fat biscuits and eggs with the yolks not broke and some bacon that wasn't burned and nobody got sick this time.

On that day, Hatch mostly rode around with us, 'cause at the bottom of it all, I reckon the government figured we was just a bunch of ignorant niggers who might at any moment have a watermelon relapse and take to gettin' drunk and shootin' each other and maybe trying to sing a spiritual while we diddled the horses, though I had sort of been responsible for spreadin' the last part of that rumor on my first day at the fort. We was all itchin' to show we had somethin' to us that didn't have nothin' to do with no white fella ridin' around in front of us, though I'll say right up front, Hatch was a good soldier who led and didn't follow, and he was polite too. I had seen him leave the circle of the fire to walk off in the dark to fart. You can't say that about just anyone. Manners out on the frontier was rare.

You'll hear from the army how we was all a crack team, but this wasn't so, at least not when they was first sayin' it. Most of the army at any time, bein' they the ridin' kind or the walkin' kind, ain't all that crack. Some of them fellas didn't know a horse's ass end from the front end, and this was pretty certain when you seen how they mounted, swinging into the stir-rups, finding themselves looking at the horse's tail instead of his ears. But in time everyone got better, though I'd like to toss in, without too much immod-esty, that I was the best rider of the whole damn lot. Since he'd had a good bit of experience, The Former House Nigger was the second. Hell, he'd done been in war and all, so in ways, he had more experience than any of us, and he cut a fine figure on a horse, being tall and always alert, like he might have to bring somebody a plate of something or hold a coat.

Only action we'd seen was when one of the men, named Rutherford, got into it with Prickly Pear—I didn't name him, that come from his mother—and they fought over a biscuit. While they was fightin', Colonel Hatch come over and ate it, so it was a wasted bout.

But this time I'm tellin' you about, we rode out lookin' for Indians to scare, and not seein' any, we quit lookin' for what we couldn't find, and come to a little place down by a creek where it was wooded and there was a shade from a whole bunch of trees that in that part of the country was thought of as being big, and in my part of the country would have been considered scrubby. I was glad when we stopped to water the horses and take a little time to just wait. Colonel Hatch, I think truth be told, was glad to get out of that sun much as the rest of us. I don't know how he felt, being a white man and having to command a bunch of colored, but he didn't seem bothered by it a'tall, and seemed proud of us and himself, which, of course, made us all feel mighty good.

So we waited out there on the creek, and Hatch, he come over to where me and The Former House Nigger were sitting by the water, and we jumped to attention, and he said, "There's a patch of scrub oaks off the creek, scattering out there across the grass, and they ain't growin' worth a damn. Them's gonna be your concern. I'm gonna take the rest of the troop out across the ground there, see if we can pick up some deer trails. I figure ain't no one gonna mind if we pot a few and bring them back to camp. And besides, I'm bored. But we could use some firewood, and I was wantin' you fellas to get them scrubs cut down and sawed up and ready to take back to the fort. Stack them in here amongst the trees, and I'll send out some men with a wagon when we get back, and have that wood hauled back before it's good and dark. I thought we could use some oak to smoke the meat I'm plannin' on gettin'. That's why I'm the goddamn colonel. Always thinkin'."

"What if you don't get no meat?" one of the men with us said.

"Then you did some work for nothin', and I went huntin' for nothin'. But, hell, I seen them deer with my binoculars no less than five minutes ago. Big fat deer, about a half dozen of them running along. They went over the hill. I'm gonna take the rest of the troops with me in case I run into hostiles, and because I don't like to do no skinnin' of dead deer myself."

"I like to hunt," I said.

"That's some disappointin' shit for you," Colonel Hatch said. "I need you here. In fact, I put you in charge. You get bit by a snake and die, then, you, The Former House Nigger, take over. I'm also gonna put Rutherford, Bill, and Rice in your charge . . . some others. I'll take the rest of them. You get that wood cut up, you start on back to the fort and we'll send out a wagon."

"What about Indians?" Rutherford, who was nearby, said.

"You seen any Indians since you been here?" Hatch said.

"No, sir."

"Then there ain't no Indians."

"You ever see any?" Rutherford asked Hatch.

"Oh, hell yeah. Been attacked by them, and I've attacked them. There's every kind of Indian you can imagine out here from time to time. Kiowa. Apache. Comanche. And there ain't nothin' they'd like better than to have your prickly black scalps on their belts, 'cause they find your hair funny. They think it's like the buffalo. They call you buffalo soldiers on account of it."

"I thought it was because they thought we was brave like the buffalo," I said.

"That figures," Hatch said. "You ain't seen no action for nobody to have no opinion of you. But, we ain't seen an Indian in ages, and ain't seen no sign of them today. I'm startin' to think they've done run out of this area. But, I've thought that before. And Indian, especially a Comanche or an Apache, they're hard to get a handle on. They'll get after somethin' or someone like it matters more than anything in the world, and then they'll wander off if a bird flies over and they make an omen of it."

Leaving us with them mixed thoughts on Indians and buffalo, Hatch and the rest of the men rode off, left us standing in the shade, which wasn't no bad place to be. First thing we did when they was out of sight was throw off our boots and get in the water. I finally just took all my clothes off and cleaned up pretty good with a bar of lye soap and got dressed. Then leaving the horses tied up in the trees near the creek, we took the mule and the equipment strapped on his back, carried our rifles, and went out to where them scrubs was. On the way, we cut down a couple of saplings and trimmed some limbs, and made us a kind of pull that we could fasten on to the mule. We figured we'd fill it up with wood and get the mule to drag it back to the creek, pile it and have it ready for the wagon.

Rigged up, we went to work, taking turns with the saw, two other men working hacking off limbs, one man axing the trimmed wood up so it fit good enough to load. We talked while we worked, and Rutherford said, "Them Indians, some of them is as mean as snakes. They do all kind of things to folks. Cut their eyelids off, cook them over fires, cut off their nut sacks and such. They're just awful."

"Sounds like some Southerners I know," I said.

"My master and his family was darn good to me," The Former House Nigger said.

"They might have been good to you," Rice said, pausing at the saw, "but that still don't make you no horse, no piece of property. You a man been treated like a horse, and you too dumb to know it."

The Former House Nigger bowed up like he was about to fight. I said, "Now, don't do it. He's just talkin'. I'm in charge here, and you two get into it, I'll get it from Hatch, and I don't want that, and won't have it."

Rice tilted his hat back. His face looked dark as coffee. "I'm gonna tell you true. When I was sixteen, I cut my master's throat and raped his wife and run off to the North."

"My God," The Former House Nigger said. "That's awful."

"And I made the dog suck my dick," Rice said.

"What?" The Former House Nigger said.

"He's funnin' you," I said.

"That part about the master's throat," Rice said, "and runnin' off to the North. I really did that. I would have raped his wife, but there wasn't any time. His dog didn't excite me none."

"You are disgustin'," The Former House Nigger said, pausing from his job of trimming limbs with a hatchet.

"Agreed," I said.

Rice chuckled, and went back to sawin' with Rutherford. He had his shirt off, and the muscles in his back bunched up like prairie dogs tunnelin', and over them mounds was long, thick scars. I knew them scars. I had a few. They had been made with a whip.

Bill, who was stackin' wood, said, "Them Indians. Ain't no use hatin' them. Hatin' them for bein' what they is, is like hatin' a bush 'cause it's got thorns on it. Hatin' a snake 'cause it'll bite you. They is what they is just like we is what we is."

"And what is we?" The Former House Nigger said.

"Ain't none of us human beings no 'count. The world is just one big mess of no 'counts, so there ain't no use pickin' one brand of man or woman over the other. Ain't none of them worth a whistlin' fart."

"Ain't had it so good, have you, Bill?" I asked.

"I was a slave."

"We all was," I said.

"Yeah, but I didn't take it so good. Better'n Rutherford, but not so good. I was in the northern army, right there at the end when they started lettin' colored in, and I killed and seen men killed. Ain't none of my life experience give me much of a glow about folks of any kind. I even killed buffalo just for the tongues rich folks wanted to have. We left hides and meat in the fields to rot. That was to punish the Indians. Damned ole buffalo. Ain't nothin' dumber, and I shot them for dollars and their tongues. What kind of human beings does that?"

We worked for about another hour, and then, Dog Den—again, I didn't name him—one of the other men Hatch left with us, said, "I think we got a problem."

On the other side of the creek, there was a split in the trees, and you could see through them out into the plains, and you could see the hill Hatch had gone over some hours ago, and comin' down it at a run was a white man. He was a good distance away, but it didn't take no eagle eye to see that he was naked as a skinned rabbit, and runnin' full out, and behind him, whoopin' and having a good time, were Indians. Apache, to be right on the money, nearly as naked as the runnin' man. Four of them was on horseback,

and there was six of them I could see on foot runnin'
after him. My guess was they had done been at him
and had set him loose to chase him like a deer for fun.
I guess livin' out on the plains like they did, with
nothin' but mesquite berries and what food they
could kill, you had to have your fun where you could
find it.

"They're funnin' him," Rutherford said, figurin'
same as me.

We stood there lookin' for a moment; then I remembered we was soldiers. I got my rifle and was
about to bead down, when Rutherford said, "Hell,
you can't hit them from here, and neither can they
shoot you. We're out of range, and Indians ain't no
shots to count for."

One of the runnin' Apaches had spotted us, and he
dropped to one knee and pointed his rifle at us, and
when he did, Rutherford spread his arms wide, and
said, "Go on, shoot, you heathen."

The Apache fired.

Rutherford was wrong. He got it right on the top
of the nose and fell over with his arms still spread.
When he hit the ground, The Former House Nigger
said, "I reckon they been practicin'."

We was up on a hill, so we left the mule and run
down to the creek where the horses was, and waded
across the little water and laid out between the trees
and took aim. We opened up and it sounded like a
bunch of mule skinners crackin' their whips. The air

filled with smoke and there was some shots fired back at us. I looked up and seen the runnin' man was makin' right smart time, his hair and johnson flappin' as he run. But then one of the horseback Apaches rode up on him, and with this heavy knotted-looking stick he was carrying, swung and clipped the white fella along the top of the head. I seen blood jump up and the man go down and I could hear the sound of the blow so well, I winced. The Apache let out a whoop and rode on past, right toward us. He stopped to beat his chest with his free hand, and when he did, I took a shot at him. I aimed for his chest, but I hit the horse square in the head and brought him down. At least I had the heathen on foot.

Now, you can say what you want about an Apache, but he is about the bravest thing there is short of a badger. This'n come runnin' right at us, all of us firin' away, and I figure he thought he had him some big magic, 'cause not a one of our shots hit him. It was like he come haint-like right through a wall of bullets. As he got closer, I could see he had some kind of mud paint on his chest and face, and he was whoopin' and carryin' on somethin' horrible. And then he stepped in a hole and went down. Though he was still a goodly distance from us, I could hear his ankle snap like a yanked suspender. Without meaning to, we all went, "Oooooh." It hurt us, it was so nasty soundin'.

That fall must have caused his magic to fly out of his ass, 'cause we all started firing at him, and this time he collected all our bullets, and was deader than a guv'ment promise before the smoke cleared.

This gave the rest of them Apache pause, and I'm sure, brave warriors or not, a few assholes puckered out there.

Them ridin' Apaches stopped their horses and rode back until they was up on the hill, and the runnin' Indians dropped to the ground and lay there. We popped off a few more shots, but didn't hit nothin', and then I remembered I was in charge. I said, "Hold your fire. Don't waste your bullets."

The Former House Nigger crawled over by me, said, "We showed them."

"They ain't showed yet," I said. "Them's Apache warriors. They ain't known as slackers."

"Maybe Colonel Hatch heard all the shootin'," he said.

"They've had time to get a good distance away. They figured on us cuttin' the wood and leavin' it and goin' back to the fort. So maybe they ain't missin' us yet and didn't hear a thing."

"Dang it," The Former House Nigger said.

I thought we might just mount up and try to ride off. We had more horses than they did, but three of them ridin' after us could still turn out bad. We had a pretty good place as we was, amongst the trees with water to drink. I decided best thing we could do was hold our position. Then that white man who had been clubbed in the head started moaning. That wasn't enough, a couple of the braves come up out of the grass and ran at his spot. We fired at them, but them Spencer single shots didn't reload as fast as them Indians could run. They come down in the tall grass where the white man had gone down, and we seen one of his legs jump up like a snake, and go back down, and the next moment came the screaming.

It went on and on. Rice crawled over to me and said, "I can't stand it. I'm gonna go out there and get him."

"No, you're not," I said. "I'll do it."

"Why you?" Rice said.

" 'Cause I'm in charge."

"I'm goin' with you," The Former House Nigger said.

"Naw, you ain't," I said. "I get rubbed out, you're the one in charge. That's what Colonel Hatch said. I get out there a ways, you open up on them other Apache, keep 'em busier than a bear with a hive of bees."

"Hell, we can't even see them, and the riders done gone on the other side of the hill."

"Shoot where you think they ought to be, just don't send a blue whistler up my ass."

I laid my rifle on the ground, made sure my pistol was loaded, put it back in the holster, pulled my knife, stuck it in my teeth, and crawled to my left along the side of that creek till I come to tall grass, then I worked my way in. I tried to go slow as to make the grass seem to be moved by the wind, which had picked up considerable and was helpin' my sneaky approach.

As I got closer to where the white man had gone down and the Apaches had gone after him, his yells grew somethin' terrible. I was maybe two or three feet from him. I parted the grass to take a look, seen he was lying on his side, and his throat was cut, and he was dead as he was gonna get.

Just a little beyond him, the two Apache was lying in the grass, and one of them was yellin' like he was the white man bein' tortured, and I thought, Well, if that don't beat all. I was right impressed.

Then the Apache saw me. They jumped up and come for me. I rose up quick, pulling the knife from my teeth. One of them hit me like a cannon ball, and away we went rollin'.

A shot popped off and the other Apache did a kind of dance, about four steps, and went down holdin' his throat. Blood was flying out of him like it was a fresh-tapped spring. Me and the other buck rolled in the grass and he tried to shoot me with a pistol he was totin', but only managed to singe my hair and give me a headache and make my left ear ring.

We rolled around like a couple of doodle bugs, and then I came up on top and stabbed at him. He caught my hand. I was holding his gun hand to the ground with my left, and he had hold of my knife hand.

"Jackass," I said, like this might so wound him to the quick, he'd let go. He didn't. We rolled over in the grass some more, and he got the pistol loose and put it to my head, but the cap and ball misfired, and all I got was burned some. I really called him names then. I jerked my legs up and wrapped them around his neck, yanked him down on his back, got on top of him and stabbed him in the groin and the belly, and still he wasn't finished.

I put the knife in his throat, and he gave me a look of disappointment, like he's just realized he'd left somethin' cookin' on the fire and ought to go get it; then he fell back.

I crawled over, rolled the white man on his back. They had cut his balls off and cut his stomach open and sliced his throat. He wasn't gonna come around.

I made it back to the creek bank and was shot at only a few times by the Apache. My return trip was a mite brisker than the earlier one. I only got a little bit of burn from a bullet that grazed the butt of my trousers.

When I was back at the creek bank, I said, "Who made that shot on the Apache?"

"That would be me," The Former House Nigger said.

"Listen here, I don't want you callin' yourself The Former House Nigger no more. I don't want no one else callin' you that. You're a buffalo soldier, and a good'n. Rest of you men hear that?"

The men was strung out along the creek, but they heard me, and grunted at me.

"This here is Cullen. He ain't nothing but Cullen or Private Cullen, or whatever his last name is. That's what we call him. You hear that, Cullen? You're a soldier, and a top soldier at that."

"That's good," Cullen said, not so moved about the event as I was. "But, thing worryin' me is the sun is goin' down."

"There's another thing," Bill said, crawlin' over

close to us. "There's smoke over that hill. My guess is it ain't no cookout."

I figured the source of that smoke would be where our white fella had come from, and it would be what was left of whoever he was with or the remains of a wagon or some such. The horse-ridin' Apache had gone back there either to finish them off and torture them with fire or to burn a wagon down. The Apache was regular little fire starters, and since they hadn't been able to get to all of us, they was takin' their misery out on what was within reach.

As that sun went down, I began to fret. I moved along the short line of our men and decided not to space them too much, but not bunch them up either. I put us about six feet apart and put a few at the rear as lookouts. Considerin' there weren't many of us, it was a short line, and them two in the back was an even shorter line. Hell, they wasn't no line at all. They was a couple of dots.

The night crawled on. A big frog began to bleat near me. Crickets was sawin' away. Upstairs, the black-as-sin heavens was lit up with stars and the half moon was way too bright.

Couple hours crawled on, and I went over to Cullen and told him to watch tight, 'cause I was goin' down the line and check the rear, make sure no one was sleepin' or pullin' their johnsons. I left my rifle and unsnapped my revolver holster flap, and went to check.

Bill was fine, but when I come to Rice, he was face-down in the dirt. I grabbed him by the back of his collar and hoisted him up, and his head fell near off.

His throat had been cut. I wheeled, snappin' my revolver into my hand. Wasn't nothin' there.

A horrible feelin' come over me. I went down the row. All them boys was dead. The Apache had been pickin' em off one at a time, and doin' it so careful like, the horses hadn't even noticed.

I went to the rear and found that the two back there was fine. I said, "You fellas best come with me."

We moved swiftly back to Cullen and Rice, and we hadn't no more than gone a few paces, when a burst of fire cut the night. I saw an Apache shape grasp at his chest and fall back. Runnin' over, we found Cullen holding his revolver, and Bill was up waving his rifle around. "Where are they? Where the hell are they?"

"They're all around. They've done killed the rest of the men." I said.

"Ghosts," Bill said. "They're ghosts."

"What they are is sneaky," I said. "It's what them fellas do for a livin'."

By now, I had what you might call some real goddamn misgivin's, figured I had reckoned right on things. I thought we'd have been safer here, but them Apache had plumb snuck up on us, wiped out three men without so much as leavin' a fart in the air. I said, "I think we better get on our horses and make a run for it."

But when we went over to get the horses, Satan, soon as I untied him, bolted and took off through the wood and disappeared. "Now, that's the shits," I said.

"We'll ride double," Cullen said.

The boys was gettin' their horses loose, and there was a whoop, and an Apache leap-frogged over the back of one of them horses and came down on his feet with one of our own hatchets in his hand. He stuck the blade of it deep in the head of a trooper, a fella whose name I don't remember, being now in my advanced years, and not really havin' known the fella that good in the first place. There was a scramble, like startled quail. There wasn't no military drill about it. It was every sonofabitch for himself. Me and Cullen and Bill tore up the hill, 'cause that was the way we was facin'. We was out of the wooded area now, and the half moon was bright, and when I looked back, I could see an Apache coming up after us with a knife in his teeth. He was climbin' that hill so fast, he was damn near runnin' on all fours.

I dropped to one knee and aimed and made a good shot that sent him tumbling back down the rise. Horrible thing was, we could hear the other men in the woods down there gettin' hacked and shot to pieces, screamin' and a pleadin', but we knew wasn't no use in tryin' to go back down there. We was outsmarted and outmanned and outfought.

Thing worked in our favor, was the poor old mule was still there wearing that makeshift harness and carry-along we had put him in, with the wood stacked on it. He had wandered a bit, but hadn't left the area.

Bill cut the log rig loose, and cut the packing off the mule's back; then he swung up on the beast and pulled Cullen up behind him, which showed a certain lack of respect for my leadership, which, frankly, was somethin' I could agree with.

I took hold of the mule's tail, and off we went, them

ridin', and me runnin' behind holdin' to my rifle with
one hand, holdin' on to the mule's tail with the other,
hopin' he didn't fart or shit or pause to kick. This was
an old Indian trick, one we had learned in the cavalry.
You can also run alongside, you got somethin' to hang
on to. Now, if the horse, or mule, decided to run full
out, well, you was gonna end up with a mouth full of
sod, but a rider and a horse and a fella hangin', sort of
lettin' himself be pulled along at a solid speed, doin'
big strides, can make surprisin' time and manage not
to wear too bad if his legs are strong.

When I finally chanced a look over my shoulder,
I seen the Apache were comin', and not in any Sunday
picnic stroll sort of way either. They was all on
horseback. They had our horses to go with theirs.
Except Satan. That bastard hadn't let me ride, but he
hadn't let no one else ride either, so I gained a kind of
respect for him.

A shot cut through the night air, and didn't nothin'
happen right off, but then Bill eased off the mule like a
candle meltin'. The shot had gone over Cullen's shoulder and hit Bill in the back of the head. We didn't stop
to check his wounds. Cullen slid forward, takin' the
reins, slowed the mule a bit and stuck out his hand. I
took it, and he helped me swing up behind him.
There's folks don't know a mule can run right swift, it
takes a mind to, but it can. They got a gait that shakes
your guts, but they're pretty good runners. And they
got wind and they're about three times smarter than a
horse.

What they don't got is spare legs for when they

step in a chuck hole, and that's what happened. It was quite a fall, and I had an idea then how that Apache had felt when his horse had gone out from under him. The fall chunked me and Cullen way off and out into the dirt, and it damn sure didn't do the mule any good.

On the ground, the poor old mule kept tryin' to get up, but couldn't. He had fallen so that his back was to the Apache, and we was tossed out in the dirt, squirmin'. We crawled around so we was between his legs, and I shot him in the head with my pistol and we made a fort of him. On came them Apache. I took my rifle and laid it over the mule's side and took me a careful bead, and down went one of them. I fired again, and another hit the dirt. Cullen scuttled out from behind the mule and got hold of his rifle where it had fallen, and crawled back. He fired off a couple of shots, but wasn't as lucky as me. The Apache backed off, and at a distance they squatted down beside their horses and took pot shots at us.

The mule was still warm and he stunk. Bullets were splatterin' into his body. None of them was comin' through, but they was lettin' out a lot of gas. Way I had it figured, them Indians would eventually surround us and we'd end up with our hair hangin' on their wickiups by mornin'. Thinkin' on this, I made an offer to shoot Cullen if it looked like we was gonna be overrun.

"Well, I'd rather shoot you then shoot myself," he said.

"I guess that's a deal, then," I said.

It was a bright night and they could see us good, but we could see them good too. The land was flat there, and there wasn't a whole lot of creepin' up they could do without us noticin', but they could still outflank us because they outnumbered us. There was more Apache now than we had seen in the daytime. They had reinforcements. It was like a gatherin' of ants.

The Apache had run their horses all out, and now they was no water for them, so they cut the horse's throats and lit a fire. After a while we could smell horse meat sizzlin'. The horses had been killed so that they made a ring of flesh they could hide behind, and the soft insides was a nice late supper.

"They ain't got no respect for guv'ment property," Cullen said.

I got out my knife and cut the mule's throat, and he was still fresh enough blood flowed, and we put our mouths on the cut and sucked out all we could. It tasted better than I would have figured, and it made us feel a mite better too, but with there just bein' the two of us, we didn't bother to start a fire and cook our fort.

We could hear them over there laughin' and a-cuttin' up, and I figure they had them some mescal, 'cause after a bit, they was actually singin' a white man song, "Row, row, row you boat," and we had to listen to that for a couple of hours.

"Goddamn missionaries," I said.

After a bit, one of them climbed over a dead horse and took his breechcloth down and turned his ass to us and it winked dead-white in the moonlight, white as any Irishman's ass. I got my rifle on him, but for some reason I couldn't let the hammer down. It just didn't seem right to shoot some drunk showin' me his ass. He turned around and peed, kind of pushin' his loins out, like he was doin' a squaw, and laughed, and that was enough. I shot that sonofabitch. I was aimin' for his pecker, but I think I got him in the belly. He fell over and a couple of Apache come out to get him. Cullen shot one of them, and the one was left jumped over the dead horses and disappeared behind them.

"Bad enough they're gonna kill us," Cullen said, "but they got to act nasty too."

We laid there for a while. Cullen said, "Maybe we ought to pray for deliverance."

"Pray in one hand, shit in the other, and see which one fills up first."

"I guess I won't pray," he said. "Or shit. Least not at the moment. You remember, that's how we met. I was—"

"I remember," I said.

Well, we was waitin' for them to surround us, but like Colonel Hatch said, you can never figure an Apache. We laid there all night, and nothin' happen. I'm ashamed to say, I nodded off, and when I awoke it was good and daylight and hadn't nobody cut our throats or taken our hair.

Cullen was sittin' with his legs crossed, lookin' in the direction of the Apache. I said, "Damn, Cullen. I'm sorry. I fell out."

"I let you. They're done gone."

I sat up and looked. There was the horses, buzzards lightin' on them, and there were a few of them big ole birds on the ground eyeballin' our mule, and us. I shooed them, said, "I'll be damn. They just packed up like a circus and left."

"Yep. Ain't no rhyme to it. They had us where they wanted us. Guess they figured they'd lost enough men over a couple of buffalo soldiers, or maybe they saw a bird like Colonel Hatch was talkin' about, and he told them to take themselves home."

"What I figure is they just too drunk to carry on, and woke up with hangovers and went somewhere cool and shaded to sleep it off."

"Reckon so," Cullen said. Then: "Hey, you mean what you said about me bein' a top soldier and all?"

"You know it."

"You ain't a colonel or nothin', but I appreciate it. Course, I don't feel all that top right now."

"We done all we could do. It was Hatch screwed the duck. He ought not have separated us from the troop like that."

"Don't reckon he'll see it that way," Cullen said.

"I figure not," I said.

We cut off chunks of meat from the mule and made a little fire and filled our bellies, then we started walkin'. It was blazin' hot, and still we walked. When nightfall come, I got nervous, thinkin' them Apache might be comin' back, and that in the long run they had just been funnin' us. But they didn't show, and we took turns sleepin' on the hard plains.

Next mornin' it was hot, and we started walkin'. My back hurt and my ass was draggin' and my feet felt like someone had cut them off. I wished we had brought some of that mule meat with us. I was so hungry, I could see cornbread walkin' on the ground. Just when I was startin' to imagine pools of water and troops of soldiers dancin' with each other, I seen somethin' that was a little more substantial.

Satan.

I said to Cullen, "Do you see a big black horse?"

"You mean, Satan?"

"Yep."

"I see him."

"Did you see some dancin' soldiers?"

"Nope."

"Do you still see the horse?"

"Yep, and he looks strong and rested. I figure he found a water hole and some grass, the sonofabitch."

Satan was trottin' along, not lookin' any worse for wear. He stopped when he seen us, and I tried to whistle to him, but my mouth was so dry, I might as well have been trying to whistle him up with my asshole.

I put my rifle down and started walkin' toward him, holdin' out my hand like I had a treat. I don't think he fell for that, but he dropped his head and let me walk up on him. He wasn't saddled, as we had taken all that off when we went to cut wood, but he still had his bridle and reins. I took hold of the bridle. I swung onto his back, and then he bucked. I went up and landed hard on the ground. My head was spinnin', and the next thing I know, that evil bastard was nuzzlin' me with his nose.

I got up and took the reins and led him over to where Cullen was leanin' on his rifle. "Down deep," he said, "I think he likes you."

We rode Satan double back to the fort, and when we got there, a cheer went up. Colonel Hatch come out and shook our hands and even hugged us. "We found what was left of you boys this mornin', and it wasn't a pretty picture. They're all missin' eyes and balls sacks and such. We figured you two had gone under with the rest of them. Was staked out on the plains somewhere with ants in your eyes. We got vengeful and started trailin' them Apache, and damn if we didn't meet them comin' back toward us, and there was a runnin' fight took us in the direction of the Pecos. We killed one, but the rest of them got away. We just come ridin' in a few minutes ahead of you."

"You'd have come straight on," Cullen said, "you'd have seen us. And we killed a lot more than one."

"That's good," Hatch said, "and we want to hear your story and Nate's soon as you get somethin' to eat and drink. We might even let you have a swallow of whiskey. Course, Former House Nigger here will have to do the cookin', ain't none of us any good."

"That there's fine," I said, "but, my compadre here, he ain't The Former House Nigger. He's Private Cullen."

Colonel Hatch eyeballed me. "You don't say?"

"Yes sir, I do, even if it hair lips the United States Army."

"Hell," Hatch said. "That alone is reason to say it."

There ain't much to tell now. We said how things was, and they did some investigatin', and damn if we wasn't put in for medals. We didn't never get them, 'cause they was slow about given coloreds awards, and frankly, I didn't think we deserved them, not with us breakin' and runnin' the way we did, like a bunch of little girls tryin' to get in out of the rain, leavin' them men behind. But we didn't stress that part when we was tellin' our story. It would have fouled it some, and I don't think we had much choice other than what we did. We was as brave as men could be without gettin' ourselves foolishly killed.

Still, we was put in for medals, and that was somethin'. In time, Cullen made the rank of Top Soldier. It wasn't just me tellin' him no more. It come true. He become a sergeant, and would have made a good one too, but he got roarin' drunk and set fire to a dead pig and got his stripes taken and spent some time in the stockade. But that's another story.

I liked the cavalry right smart myself, and stayed on there until my time run out and I was supposed to sign up again, and would have too, had it not been for them Chinese women I told you about at the first. But again, that ain't this story. This is the one happened to me in the year of 1870, out there on them hot West Texas plains. I will add a side note. The army let me keep Satan when I was mustered out, and I grew to like him, and he was the best horse I ever had, and me and him became friends of a sort, until 1872, when I had to shoot him and feed him to a dog and a woman I liked better.

Lawrence Block

New York Times bestseller Lawrence Block, one of the kings of the modern mystery genre, is a Grand Master of Mystery Writers of America, winner of four Edgar Awards and six Shamus Awards, and has also been the recipient of the Nero Wolfe Award, the Philip Marlowe Award, a Lifetime Achievement Award from the Private Eye Writers of America, and a Cartier Diamond Dagger for Life Achievement from the Crime Writers' Association. He's written more than fifty books and numerous short stories. Block is perhaps best known for his long-running series about alcoholic ex-cop Private Investigator Matthew Scudder, protagonist of novels such as *The Sins of the Fathers, In the Midst of Death, A Stab in the Dark,* and thirteen others, but he's also the author of the bestselling four-book series about the assassin Keller, including *Hit Man, Hit List,* and *Hit Parade,* the eight-book series about globe-trotting insomniac Evan Tanner, including *The Thief Who Couldn't Sleep* and *The Canceled Czech,* and the eleven-book series about burglar and antiquarian book dealer Bernie Rhodenbarr, including *Burglars Can't Be Choosers, The Burglar in the Closet,* and *The Burglar Who Liked to Quote Kipling.* He's also written stand-alone novels such as *Small Town, Death Pulls a Double Cross,* and sixteen others, as well as writing novels under the names Chip Harrison, Jill Emerson, and Paul Kavanagh. His many short stories have been collected in *Sometimes They Bite, Like a Lamb to Slaughter, Some Days You Get the Bear, By the Dawn's Early Light, One Night Stands, The Collected Mystery Stories, Death Wish and Other Stories,* and *Enough Rope: Collected Stories.* He's also edited twelve mystery anthologies, including *Murder on the Run, Blood on Their Hands,* and, with Otto Penzler, *The Best American Mystery Stories 2001,* and produced seven books of writing advice and nonfiction, including *Telling Lies for Fun & Profit.* His most recent books are *Hit and Run,* the new Keller novel, *One Night Stands and Lost Weekends,* a new collection, and, as editor, the anthology *Speaking of Wrath.* He lives in New York City.

In the terse and hard-edged story that follows, he shows us that obsession can take us down some curious paths indeed . . . and lead us to some very dark destinations.

Clean Slate

There was a Starbucks just across the street from the building where he had his office, and she settled in at a window table a little before five. She thought she might be in for a long wait. In New York, young associates at law firms typically worked until midnight and took lunch and dinner at their desks. Was it the same in Toledo?

Well, the cappuccino was the same. She sipped hers, making it last, and was about to go to the counter for another when she saw him.

But was it him? He was tall and slender, wearing a dark suit and a tie, clutching a briefcase, walking with purpose. His hair when she'd known him was long and shaggy, a match for the jeans and tee shirt that were his usual costume, and now it was cut to match the suit and the briefcase. And he wore glasses now, and they gave him a serious, studious look. He hadn't worn them then, and he'd certainly never looked studious.

But it was Douglas. No question, it was him.

She rose from her chair, hit the door, quickened her pace to catch up with him at the corner. She said, "Doug? Douglas Pratter?"

He turned, and she caught the puzzlement in his eyes. She helped him out. "It's Kit," she said. "Katherine Tolliver." She smiled softly. "A voice from the past. Well, a whole person from the past, actually."

"My God," he said. "It's really you."

"I was having a cup of coffee," she said, "and looking out the window and wishing I knew somebody in this town, and when I saw you I thought you were a mirage. Or that you were just somebody who looked the way Doug Pratter might look eight years later."

"Is that how long it's been?"

"Just about. I was fifteen and I'm twenty-three now. You were two years older."

"Still am. That much hasn't changed."

"And your family picked up and moved right in the middle of your junior year of high school."

"My dad got a job he couldn't say no to. He was going to send for us at the end of the term, but my mother wouldn't hear of it. We'd all be too lonely is what she said. It took me years before I realized she just didn't trust him on his own."

"Was he not to be trusted?"

"I don't know about that, but the marriage failed two years later anyway. He went a little nuts and wound up in California. He got it in his head that he wanted to be a surfer."

"Seriously? Well, good for him, I guess."

"Not all that good for him. He drowned."

"I'm sorry."

"Who knows? Maybe that's what he wanted, whether he knew it or not. Mom's still alive and well."

"In Toledo?"

"Bowling Green."

"*That's* it. I knew you'd moved to Ohio, and I couldn't remember the city, and I didn't think it was Toledo. Bowling Green."

"I've always thought of it as a color. Lime green, forest green, and bowling green."

"Same old Doug."

"You think? I wear a suit and go to an office. Christ, I wear glasses."

"And a wedding ring." And, before he could tell her about his wife and kiddies and adorable suburban house, she said, "But you've got to get home, and I've got plans of my own. I want to catch up, though. Have you got any time tomorrow?"

It's Kit. Katherine Tolliver.

Just saying her name had taken her back in time. She hadn't been Kit or Katherine or Tolliver in years. Names were like clothes; she'd put them on and wear them for a while and then let them go. The analogy went only so far, because you could wash clothes when you'd soiled them, but there was no dry cleaner for a name that had outlived its usefulness.

Katherine "Kit" Tolliver. That wasn't the name on the ID she was carrying, or the one she'd signed on the motel register. Once she'd identified herself to Doug Pratter, she'd become the person she'd proclaimed herself to be. She was Kit again—and, at the same time, she wasn't.

Interesting, the whole business.

Back in her motel room, she surfed her way around the TV channels, then switched off the set and took a shower. Afterwards she spent a few minutes studying her nude body and wondering how it would look to him. She was a little fuller in the breasts than she'd been eight years before, a little rounder in the butt, a little closer to ripeness overall. She had always been confident of her attractiveness, but she couldn't help wondering what she might look like to those eyes that had seen her years ago.

Of course, he hadn't needed glasses back in the day.

She had read somewhere that a man who has once had a particular woman somehow assumes he can have her again. She didn't know how true this might be, but it seemed to her that something similar applied to women. A woman who had once been with a particular man was ordained to doubt her ability to attract him a second time. And so she felt a little of that uncertainty, but willed herself to dismiss it.

He was married, and might well be in love with his wife. He was busy establishing himself in his profession, and settling into an orderly existence. Why would he want a meaningless fling with an old girlfriend, who'd had to say her name before he could even place her?

She smiled. *Lunch*, he'd said. *We'll have lunch tomorrow.*

———

Funny how it started.

She was at a table with six or seven others, a mix of men and women in their twenties. And one of the men mentioned a woman she didn't know, though she seemed to be known to most if not all of the others. And one of the women said, "That slut."

And the next thing she knew, the putative slut was forgotten while the whole table turned to the question of just what constituted sluttiness. Was it a matter of attitude? Of specific behavior? Was one born to slut-dom, or was the status acquired?

Was it solely a female province? Could you have male sluts?

That got nipped in the bud. "A man can take sex too casually," one of the men asserted, "and he can consequently be an asshole, and deserving of a certain measure of contempt. But as far as I'm concerned, the word *slut* is gender-linked. Nobody with a Y chromosome can qualify as a genuine slut."

And, finally, was there a numerical cutoff? Could an equation be drawn up? Did a certain number of partners within a certain number of years make one a slut?

"Suppose," one woman suggested, "suppose once a month you go out after work and have a couple—"

"A couple of men?"

"A couple of drinks, you idiot, and you start flirting, and one thing leads to another, and you drag somebody home with you."

"Once a month?"

"It could happen."

"So that's twelve men in a year."

"When you put it that way," the woman allowed, "it seems like a lot."

"It's also a hundred and twenty partners in ten years."

"Except you wouldn't keep it up for that long, because sooner or later one of those hookups would take."

"And you'd get married and live happily ever after?"

"Or at least live together more or less monogamously for a year or two, which would cut down on the frequency of hookups, wouldn't it?"

Throughout all of this, she barely said a word. Why bother? The conversation buzzed along quite well without her, and she was free to sit back and listen, and to wonder just what place she occupied in what someone had already labeled "the saint–slut continuum."

"With cats," one of the men said, "it's nice and clear-cut."

"Cats can be sluts?"

He shook his head. "With women and cats. A woman has one cat, or even two or three cats, she's an animal lover. Four or more cats, and she's a demented cat lady."

"That's how it works?"

"That's exactly how it works. With sluts, it looks to be more complicated."

Another thing that complicated it, someone said, was if the woman in question had a significant other, whether husband or boyfriend. If she didn't, and she hooked up half a dozen times a year, well, she certainly wasn't a slut. If she was married and still fit in that many hookups on the side, well, that changed things, didn't it?

"Let's get personal," one of the men said to one of the women. "How many partners have you had?"

"Me?"

"Well?"

"You mean in the past year?"

"Or lifetime. You decide."

"If I'm going to answer a question like that," she said, "I think we definitely need another round of drinks."

The drinks came, and the conversation slid into a game of truth, though it seemed to Jennifer—these people knew her as Jennifer, which had lately become her default name—it seemed to her that the actual veracity of the responses was moot.

And then it was her turn.

"Well, Jen? How many?"

Would she ever see any of these people again? Probably not. So it scarcely mattered what she said.

And what she said was, "Well, it depends. How do you decide what counts?"

"What do you mean? Like blow jobs don't count?"

"That's what Clinton said, remember?"

"As far as I'm concerned, blow jobs count."

"And hand jobs?"

"They don't count," one man said, and there seemed to be general agreement on that point. "Not that there's anything wrong with them," he added.

"So what's your criterion here, exactly? Something has to be inside of something?"

"As far as the nature of the act," one man said, "I think it has to be subjective. It counts if you think it counts. So, Jen? What's your count?"

"Suppose you passed out, and you know something happened, but you don't remember any of it?"

"Same answer. It counts if you think it counts."

The conversation kept going, but she was detached from it now, thinking, remembering, working it out in her mind. How many men, if gathered around a table or a campfire, could compare notes and tell each other about her? That, she thought, was the real criterion, not what part of her anatomy had been in contact with what portion of his. Who could tell stories? Who could bear witness?

And, when the table quieted down again, she said, "Five."

"Five? That's all? Just five?"

"Five."

She had arranged to meet Douglas Pratter at noon in the lobby of a downtown hotel not far from his office. She arrived early and sat where she could watch the entrance. He was five minutes early himself, and she saw him stop to remove his glasses, polishing their lenses with a breast-pocket handkerchief. Then he put them on again and stood there, his eyes scanning the room.

She got to her feet, and now he caught sight of her,

and she saw him smile. He'd always had a winning smile, optimistic and confident. Years ago, it had been one of the things she liked most about him.

She walked to meet him. Yesterday she'd been wearing a dark gray pantsuit; today she'd paired the jacket with a matching skirt. The effect was still business attire, but softer, more feminine. More accessible.

"I hope you don't mind a ride," he told her. "There are places we could walk to, but they're crowded and noisy and no place to have a conversation. Plus they rush you, and I don't want to be in a hurry. Unless you've got an early afternoon appointment?"

She shook her head. "I had a full morning," she said, "and there's a cocktail party this evening that I'm supposed to go to, but until then I'm free as the breeze."

"Then we can take our time. We've probably got a lot to talk about."

As they crossed the lobby, she took his arm.

The fellow's name was Lucas. She'd taken note of him early on, and his eyes had shown a certain degree of interest in her, but his interest mounted when she told the group how many sexual partners she'd had. It was he who'd said, "Five? That's all? Just five?" When she'd confirmed her count, his eyes grabbed hers and held on.

And now he'd taken her to another bar, a nice quiet place where they could really get to know each other. Just the two of them.

The lighting was soft, the décor soothing. A pianist played show tunes unobtrusively, and a waitress with an indeterminate accent took their order and brought their drinks. They touched glasses, sipped, and he said, "Five."

"That really did it for you," she said. "What, is it your lucky number?"

"Actually," he said, "my lucky number is six."

"I see."

"You were never married."

"No."

"Never lived with anybody."

"Only my parents."

"You don't still live with them?"

"No."

"You live alone?"

"I have a roommate."

"A woman, you mean."

"Right."

"Uh, the two of you aren't . . ."

"We have separate beds," she said, "in separate rooms, and we live separate lives."

"Right. Were you ever, uh, in a convent or anything?"

She gave him a look.

"Because you're remarkably attractive, you walk into a room and you light it up, and I can imagine the number of guys who must hit on you on a daily basis. And you're how old? Twenty-one, twenty-two?"

"Twenty-three."

"And you've only been with five guys? What, were you a late bloomer?"

"I wouldn't say so."

"I'm sorry, I'm pressing and I shouldn't. It's just that, well, I can't help being fascinated. But the last thing I want is to make you uncomfortable."

The conversation wasn't making her uncomfortable. It was merely boring her. Was there any reason to prolong it? Was there any reason not to cut to the chase?

She'd already slipped one foot out of its shoe, and now she raised it and rested it on his lap, massaging his groin with the ball of her foot. The expression on his face was worth the price of admission all by itself.

"My turn to ask questions," she said. "Do you live with your parents?"

"You're kidding, right? Of course not."

"Do you have a roommate?"

"Not since college, and that was a while ago."

"So," she said. "What are we waiting for?"

The restaurant Doug had chosen was on Detroit Avenue, just north of I-75. Walking across the parking lot, she noted a motel two doors down and another across the street.

Inside, it was dark and quiet, and the décor reminded her of the cocktail lounge where Lucas had taken her. She had a sudden memory of her foot in his lap, and the expression on his face. Further memories followed, but she let them glide on by. The present moment was a nice one, and she wanted to live in it while it was at hand.

She asked for a dry Rob Roy, and Doug hesitated, then ordered the same for himself. The cuisine on offer was Italian, and he started to order the scampi, then caught himself and selected a small steak instead. Scampi, she thought, was full of garlic, and he wanted to make sure he didn't have it on his breath.

The conversation started in the present, but she quickly steered it back to the past, where it properly belonged. "You always wanted to be a lawyer," she remembered.

"Right, I was going to be a criminal lawyer, a courtroom whiz. The defender of the innocent. So here I am doing corporate work, and if I ever see the inside of a courtroom, that means I've done something wrong."

"I guess it's hard to make a living with a criminal practice."

"You can do okay," he said, "but you spend your life with the scum of the earth, and you do everything you can to keep them from getting what they damn well deserve. Of course I didn't know any of that when I was seventeen and starry-eyed over *To Kill a Mockingbird*."

"You were my first boyfriend."

"You were my first real girlfriend."

She thought, Oh? And how many unreal ones were there? And what made her real by comparison? Because she'd slept with him?

Had he been a virgin the first time they had sex? She hadn't given the matter much thought at the time, and had been too intent upon her own role in the proceedings to be aware of his experience or lack thereof. It hadn't really mattered then, and she couldn't see that it mattered now.

And, she'd just told him, he'd been her first boyfriend. No need to qualify that; he'd truly been her first boyfriend, real or otherwise.

But she hadn't been a virgin. She'd crossed that barrier two years earlier, a month or so after her thirteenth birthday, and had had sex in one form or another perhaps a hundred times before she hooked up with Doug.

Not with a boyfriend, however. I mean, your father couldn't be your boyfriend, could he?

Lucas lived alone in a large L-shaped studio apartment on the top floor of a new building. "I'm the first tenant the place has ever had," he told her. "I've never lived in something brand-spanking-new before. It's like I've taken the apartment's virginity."

"Now you can take mine."

"Not quite. But this is better. Remember, I told you my lucky number."

"Six."

"There you go."

And just when, she wondered, had six become his lucky number? When she'd acknowledged five partners? Probably, but never mind. It was a good-enough line, and one he was no doubt feeling proud of right about now, because it had worked, hadn't it?

As if he'd had any chance of failing . . .

He made drinks, and they kissed, and she was pleased but not surprised to note that the requisite chemistry was there. And, keeping it company, there was that delicious surge of anticipatory excitement that was always present on such occasions. It was at once sexual and nonsexual, and she felt it even when the chemistry was not present, even when the sexual act was destined to be perfunctory at best, and at worst distasteful. Even then she'd feel that rush, that urgent excitement, but it was greatly increased when she knew the sex was going to be good.

He excused himself and went to the bathroom, and she opened her purse and found the little unlabeled vial she kept in the change compartment. She looked at it and at the drink he'd left on the table, but in the end she left the vial in her purse, left his drink untouched.

As it turned out, it wouldn't have mattered. When he emerged from the bathroom he reached not for his drink but for her instead, and it was as good as she'd known it would be, inventive and eager and passionate, and finally they fell away from each other, spent and sated.

"Wow," he said.

"That's the right word for it."

"You think? It's the best I can come up with, and yet it somehow seems inadequate. You're—"

"What?"

"Amazing. I have to say this, I can't help it. It's almost impossible to believe you've had so little experience."

"Because I'm clearly jaded?"

"No, just because you're so good at it. And in a way that's the complete opposite of jaded. I swear to God this is the last time I'll ask you, but were you telling the truth? Have you really only been with five men?"

She nodded.

"Well," he said, "now it's six, isn't it?"

"Your lucky number, right?"

"Luckier than ever," he said.

"Lucky for me, too."

She was glad she hadn't put anything in his drink, because after a brief rest they made love again, and that wouldn't have happened otherwise.

"Still six," he told her afterwards, "unless you figure I ought to get extra credit."

She said something, her voice soft and soothing, and he said something, and that went on until he stopped responding. She lay beside him, in that familiar but ever-new combination of afterglow and anticipation, and then finally she slipped out of bed, and a little while later she let herself out of his apartment.

All by herself in the descending elevator, she said out loud, "Five."

A second round of Rob Roys arrived before their entrées. Then the waiter brought her fish and his steak, along with a glass of red wine for him and white for her. She'd had only half of her second Rob Roy, and she barely touched her wine.

"So you're in New York," he said. "You went there straight from college?"

She brought him up to date, keeping the responses vague for fear of contradicting herself. The story she told was all fabrication; she'd never even been to college, and her job résumé was a spotty mélange of waitressing and office temp work. She didn't have a career, and she worked only when she had to.

If she needed money—and she didn't need much, she didn't live high—well, there were other ways to get it beside work.

But today she was Connie Corporate, with a job history to match her clothes, and yes, she'd gone to Penn State and then tacked on a Wharton MBA, and ever since she'd been in New York, and she couldn't really talk about what had brought her to Toledo, or even on whose behalf she was traveling, because it was all hush–hush for the time being, and she was sworn to secrecy.

"Not that there's a really big deal to be secretive about," she said, "but, you know, I try to do what they tell me."

"Like a good little soldier."

"Exactly," she said, and beamed across the table at him.

"You're my little soldier," her father had told her. "A trooper, a little warrior."

In the accounts she sometimes found herself reading, the father (or the stepfather, or the uncle, or the mother's boyfriend, or even the next-door neighbor) was a drunk and a brute, a bloody-minded savage, forcing himself upon the child who was his helpless and unwilling partner. She would get angry, reading those case histories. She would hate the male responsible for the incest, would sympathize with the young female victim, and her blood would surge in her veins with the desire to even the score, to exact a cruel but just vengeance. Her mind supplied scenarios—castration, mutilation, disembowelment—all of them brutal and heartless, all richly deserved.

But her own experience was quite unlike what she read.

Some of her earliest memories were of sitting on her father's lap, his hands touching her, patting her, petting her. Sometimes he was with her at bath time, making sure she soaped and rinsed herself thoroughly. Sometimes he tucked her in at night, and sat by the side of the bed stroking her hair until she fell asleep.

Was his touch ever inappropriate? Looking back, she thought that it probably was, but she'd never been aware of it at the time. She knew that she loved her daddy and he loved her, and that there was a bond between them that excluded her mother. But it never consciously occurred to her that there was anything wrong about it.

Then, when she was thirteen, when her body had begun to change, there was a night when he came to her bed and slipped beneath the covers. And he held her and touched her and kissed her.

The holding and touching and kissing were different that night, and she recognized it as such immediately, and somehow knew that it would be a secret, that she could never tell anybody. And yet no enormous barriers were crossed that night. He was very gentle with her, always gentle, and his seduction of her was infinitely gradual. She had since read how the Plains Indians took wild horses and domesticated them, not by breaking their spirit but by slowly, slowly, winning them over, and the description resonated with her immediately, because that was precisely how her father had turned her from a child who sat so innocently on his lap into an eager and spirited sexual partner.

He never broke her spirit. What he did was awaken it.

He came to her every night for months, and by the time he took her virginity she had long since lost her innocence, because he had schooled her quite thoroughly in the sexual arts. There was no pain on the night he led her across the last divide. She had been well prepared, and was entirely ready.

Away from her bed, they were the same as they'd always been.

"Nothing can show," he'd explained. "No one would understand the way you and I love each other. So we must not let them know. If your mother knew—"

He hadn't needed to finish that sentence.

"Someday," he'd told her, "you and I will get in the car, and we'll drive to some city where no one knows us. We'll both be older then, and the difference in our ages won't be that remarkable, especially when we've tacked on a few years to you and shaved them off of me. And we'll live together, and we'll get married, and no one will be the wiser."

She tried to imagine that. Sometimes it seemed like something that could actually happen, something that would indeed come about in the course of time. And other times it seemed like a story an adult might tell a child, right up there with Santa Claus and the Tooth Fairy.

"But for now," he'd said more than once, "for now we have to be warriors. You're my little soldier, aren't you? Aren't you?"

"I get to New York now and then," Doug Pratter said.

"I suppose you and your wife fly in," she said. "Stay at a nice hotel, see a couple of shows."

"She doesn't like to fly."

"Well, who does? What they make you go through these days, all in the name of security. And it just keeps getting worse, doesn't it? First they started giving you plastic utensils with your in-flight meal, because there's nothing as dangerous as a terrorist with a metal fork. Then they stopped giving you a meal altogether, so you couldn't complain about the plastic utensils."

"It's pretty bad, isn't it? But it's a short flight. I don't mind it that much. I just open up a book, and the next thing I know I'm in New York."

"By yourself."

"On business," he said. "Not that frequently, but every once in a while. Actually, I could get there more often, if I had a reason to go."

"Oh?"

"But lately I've been turning down chances," he said, his eyes avoiding hers now. "Because, see, when my business is done for the day I don't know what to do with myself. It would be different if I knew anybody there, but I don't."

"You know me," she said.

"That's right," he agreed, his eyes finding hers again. "That's right. I do, don't I?"

Over the years, she'd read a lot about incest. She didn't think her interest was compulsive, or morbidly obsessive, and in fact it seemed to her as if it would be more pathological if she were not interested in reading about it.

One case imprinted itself strongly upon her. A man had three daughters, and he had sexual relations with two of them. He was not the artful Daughter Whisperer that her own father had been, but a good deal closer to the Drunken Brute end of the spectrum. A widower, he told the two older daughters that it was their duty to take their mother's place. They felt it was wrong, but they also felt it was something they had to do, and so they did it.

And, predictably enough, they were both psychologically scarred by the experience. Almost every incest victim seemed to be, one way or the other.

But it was their younger sister who wound up being the most damaged of the three. Because Daddy never touched her, she figured there was something wrong with her. Was she ugly? Was she insufficiently feminine? Was there something disgusting about her?

Jeepers, what was the matter with her, anyway? Why didn't he want her?

After the dishes were cleared, Doug suggested a brandy. "I don't think so," she said. "I don't usually drink this much early in the day."

"Actually, neither do I. I guess there's something about the occasion that feels like a celebration."

"I know what you mean."

"Some coffee? Because I'm in no hurry for this to end."

She agreed that coffee sounded like a good idea. And it was pretty good coffee, and a fitting conclusion to a pretty good meal. Better than a person might expect to find on the outskirts of Toledo.

How did he know the place? Did he come here with his wife? She somehow doubted it. Had he brought other women here? She doubted that as well. Maybe it was something he'd picked up at the office water cooler. "*So I took her to this Eye-tie place on Detroit Avenue, and then we just popped into the Comfort Inn down the block, and I mean to tell you that girl was good to go.*"

Something like that.

"I don't want to go back to the office," he was saying. "All these years, and then you walk back into my life, and I'm not ready for you to walk out of it again."

You were the one who walked, she thought. Clear to Bowling Green.

But what she said was, "We could go to my hotel room, but a downtown hotel right in the middle of the city—"

"Actually," he said, "there's a nice place right across the street."

"Oh?"

"A Holiday Inn, actually."

"Do you think they'd have a room at this hour?"

He managed to look embarrassed and pleased with himself, all at the same time. "As a matter of fact," he said, "I have a reservation."

She was four months shy of her eighteenth birthday when everything changed.

What she came to realize, although she hadn't been consciously aware of it at the time, was that things had already been changing for some time. Her father came a little less frequently to her bed, sometimes telling her he was tired from a hard day's work, sometimes explaining that he had to stay up late with work he'd brought home, sometimes not bothering with an explanation of any sort.

Then one afternoon he invited her to go for a ride. Sometimes rides in the family car would end at a motel, and she thought that was what he planned on this occasion. In anticipation, no sooner had he backed the car out of the driveway than she'd dropped her hand into his lap, stroking him, awaiting his response.

He pushed her hand away.

She wondered why, but didn't say anything, and he didn't say anything either, not for ten minutes of sub-urban streets. Then abruptly he pulled into a strip mall, parked opposite a shuttered bowling alley, and said, "You're my little soldier, aren't you?"

She nodded.

"And that's what you'll always be. But we have to stop. You're a grown woman, you have to be able to lead your own life, I can't go on like this. . . ."

She scarcely listened. The words washed over her like a stream, a babbling stream, and what came through to her was not so much the words he spoke but what seemed to underlie those words: *I don't want you anymore.*

After he'd stopped talking, and after she'd waited long enough to know he wasn't going to say anything else, and because she knew he was awaiting her re-sponse, she said, "Okay."

"I love you, you know."

"I know."

"You've never said anything to anyone, have you?"

"No."

"Of course you haven't. You're a warrior, and I've always known I could count on you."

On the way back, he asked her if she'd like to stop for ice cream. She just shook her head, and he drove the rest of the way home.

She got out of the car and went up to her room. She sprawled on her bed, turning the pages of a book without registering their contents. After a few minutes she stopped trying to read and sat up, her eyes focused on a spot on one wall where the wallpaper was misaligned.

She found herself thinking of Doug, her first real boyfriend. She'd never told her father about Doug; of course he knew that they were spending time together, but she'd kept their intimacy a secret. And of course she'd never said a word about what she and her father had been doing, not to Doug or to anybody else.

The two relationships were worlds apart in her mind. But now they had something in common, because they had both ended. Doug's family had moved to Ohio, and their exchange of letters had trickled out. And her father didn't want to have sex with her anymore.

Something really bad was going to happen. She just knew it.

A few days later, she went to her friend Rosemary's house after school. Rosemary, who lived just a few blocks away on Covington, had three brothers and two sisters, and anybody who was still there at dinnertime was always invited to stay.

She accepted gratefully. She could have gone home, but she just didn't want to, and she still didn't want to a few hours later. "I wish I could just stay here overnight," she told Rosemary. "My parents are acting weird."

"Hang on, I'll ask my mom."

She had to call home and get permission. "No one's answering," she said. "Maybe they went out. If you want, I'll go home."

"You'll stay right here," Rosemary's mother said. "You'll call right before bedtime, and if there's still no answer, well, if they're not home, they won't miss you, will they?"

Rosemary had twin beds, and fell asleep instantly in her own. Kit, a few feet away, had this thought that Rosemary's father would let himself into the room, and into her bed, but of course this didn't happen, and the next thing she knew she was asleep.

In the morning she went home, and the first thing she did was call Rosemary's house, hysterical. Rosemary's mother calmed her down, and then she was able to call 911 to report the deaths of her parents. Rosemary's mother came over to be with her, and shortly after that the police came, and it became pretty clear what had happened. Her father had killed her mother and then turned the gun on himself.

"You sensed that something was wrong," Rosemary's mother said. "That's why it was so easy to get you to stay for dinner, and why you wanted to sleep over."

"They were fighting," she said, "and there was

something different about it. Not just a normal argument. God, it's my fault, isn't it? I should have been able to do something. The least I could have done was to say something."

Everybody told her that was nonsense.

After she'd left Lucas's brand-new high-floor apartment, she returned to her own older less-imposing sublet, where she brewed a pot of coffee and sat up at the kitchen table with a pad and paper. She wrote down the numbers one through five in descending order, and after each she wrote a name, or as much of the name as she knew. Sometimes she added an identifying phrase or two. The list began with 5, and the first entry read as follows:

Said his name was Sid. Pasty complexion, gap between top incisors. Met in Philadelphia at bar on Race Street (?), went to his hotel, don't remember name of it. Gone when I woke up.

Hmmm. Sid might be hard to find. How would she even know where to start looking for him?

At the bottom of the list, her entry was simpler and more specific. *Douglas Pratter. Last known address Bowling Green. Lawyer? Google him?*

She booted up her laptop.

Their room in the Detroit Avenue Holiday Inn was on the third floor in the rear. With the drapes drawn and the door locked, with their clothes hastily discarded and the bedclothes as hastily tossed aside, it seemed to her for at least a few minutes that she was fifteen years old again, and in bed with her first boyfriend. She tasted a familiar sweetness in his kisses, a familiar raw urgency in his ardor.

But the illusion didn't last. And then it was just lovemaking, at which each of them had a commendable proficiency. He went down on her this time, which was something he'd never done when they were teenage sweethearts, and the first thought that came to her was that he had turned into her father, because her father had done that all the time.

Afterwards, after a fairly long shared silence, he said, "I can't tell you how many times I've wondered."

"What it would be like to be together again?"

"Well, sure, but more than that. What life would have been like if I'd never moved away in the first place. What would have become of the two of us, if we'd had the chance to let things find their way."

"Probably the same as most high school lovers. We'd have stayed together for a while, and then we'd have broken up and gone separate ways."

"Maybe."

"Or I'd have gotten pregnant, and you'd have married me, and we'd be divorced by now."

"Maybe."

"Or we'd still be together, and bored to death with each other, and you'd be in a motel fucking somebody new."

"God, how'd you get so cynical?"

"You're right, I got off on the wrong foot there.

How about this? If your father hadn't moved you all to Bowling Green, you and I would have stayed together, and our feeling for each other would have grown from teenage hormonal infatuation to the profound mature love it was always destined to be. You'd have gone off to college, and as soon as I finished high school I'd have enrolled there myself, and when you finished law school I'd have my undergraduate degree, and I'd be your secretary and office manager when you set up your own law practice. By then we'd have gotten married, and by now we'd have one child with a second on the way, and we would remain unwavering in our love for one another, and as passionate as ever." She gazed wide-eyed at him. "Better?"

His expression was hard to read, and he appeared to be on the point of saying something, but she turned toward him and ran a hand over his flank, and the prospect of a further adventure in adultery trumped whatever he might have wanted to say. Whatever it was, she thought, it would keep.

"I'd better get going," he said, and rose from the bed, and rummaged through the clothes he'd tossed on the chair.

She said, "Doug? Don't you think you might want to take a shower first?"

"Oh, Jesus. Yeah, I guess I better, huh?"

He'd known where to take her to lunch, knew to make a room reservation ahead of time, but he evidently didn't know enough to shower away her spoor before returning to home and hearth. So perhaps this sort of adventure was not the usual thing for him. Oh, she was fairly certain he tried to get lucky on business trips—those oh-so-lonely New York visits he'd mentioned, for instance—but you didn't have to shower after that sort of interlude, because you were going back to your own hotel room, not to your un-suspecting wife.

She started to get dressed. There was no one wait-ing for her, and her own shower could wait until she was back at her own motel. But she changed her mind about dressing, and was still naked when he emerged from the shower, a towel wrapped around his middle.

"Here," she said, handing him a glass of water. "Drink this."

"What is it?"

"Water."

"I'm not thirsty."

"Just drink it, will you?"

He shrugged, drank it. He went and picked up his undershorts, and kept losing his balance when he tried stepping into them. She took his arm and led him over to the bed, and he sat down and told her he didn't feel so good. She took the undershorts away from him and got him to lie down on the bed, and she watched him struggling to keep a grip on consciousness.

She put a pillow over his face, and she sat on it. She felt him trying to move beneath her, and she watched his hands make feeble clawing motions at the bed-sheet, and observed the muscles working in his lower legs. Then he was still, and she stayed where she was for a few minutes, and an involuntary tremor, a very subtle one, went through her hindquarters.

And what was that, pray tell? Could have been her coming, could have been him going. Hard to tell, and did it really matter?

When she got up, well, duh, he was dead. No surprise there. She put her clothes on, cleaned up all traces of her presence, and transferred all the cash from his wallet to her purse. A few hundred dollars in tens and twenties, plus an emergency hundred-dollar bill tucked away behind his driver's license. She might have missed it, but she'd learned years ago that you had to give a man's wallet a thorough search.

Not that the money was ever the point. But they couldn't take it with them and it had to go somewhere—so it might as well go to her. Right?

How it happened: That final morning, shortly after she left for school, her father and mother had argued, and her father had gone for the handgun he kept in a locked desk drawer and shot her mother dead. He left the house and went to his office, saying nothing to anyone, although a coworker did say that he'd seemed troubled. And sometime during the afternoon he returned home, where his wife's body remained undiscovered. The gun was still there (unless he'd been carrying it around with him during the intervening hours) and he put the barrel in his mouth and blew his brains out.

Except that wasn't really how it happened; it was

how the police figured it out. What did in fact happen, of course, is that she shot her mother before she left for school, and called her father on his cell as soon as she got home from school, summoning him on account of an unspecified emergency. He came right home, and by then she would have liked to change her mind, but how could she with her mother dead in the next room? So she shot him and arranged the evidence appropriately, and then she went over to Rosemary's.

Di dah di dah di dah.

You could see Doug's car from the motel room window. He'd parked in the back and they'd come up the back stairs, never going anywhere near the front desk. So no one had seen her, and no one saw her now as she went to his car, unlocked it with his key, and drove it downtown.

She'd have preferred to leave it there, but her own rental was parked near the Crowne Plaza, so she had to get downtown to reclaim it. You couldn't stand on the corner and hail a cab, not in Toledo, and she didn't want to call one. So she drove to within a few blocks of the lot where she'd stowed her Honda, parked his Volvo at an expired meter, and used the hankie with which he'd cleaned his glasses to wipe away any fingerprints she might have left behind.

She redeemed her car and headed for her own motel. Halfway there, she realized she had no real need to go there. She'd packed that morning and left no traces of herself in her room. She hadn't checked out, electing to keep her options open, so she could go there now with no problem, but for what? Just to take a shower?

She sniffed herself. She could use a shower, no question, but she wasn't so rank that people would draw away from her. And she kind of liked the faint trace of his smell coming off her flesh.

And the sooner she got to the airport, the sooner she'd be out of Toledo.

She managed to catch a 4:18 flight that was scheduled to stop in Cincinnati on its way to Denver. She'd stay in Denver for a while, until she decided where she wanted to go next.

She hadn't had a reservation, or even a set destination, and she took the flight because it was there to be taken. The leg from Toledo to Cincinnati was more than half-empty, and she had a row of seats to herself, but she was stuck in a middle seat from Cincinnati to Denver, wedged between a fat lady who looked to be scared stiff of something, possibly the flight itself, and a man who tapped away at his laptop and invaded her space with his elbows.

Not the most pleasant travel experience she'd ever had, but nothing she couldn't live through. She closed her eyes, let her thoughts turn inward.

After her parents were buried and the estate settled, after she'd finished the high school year and collected her diploma, after a Realtor had listed her house and, after commission and closing costs, netted her a few thousand over and above the outstanding first and second mortgages, she'd stuffed what she could into one of her father's suitcases and boarded a bus.

She'd never gone back. And, until her brief but gratifying reunion with Douglas Pratter, Esq., she'd never been Katherine Tolliver again.

On the tram to Baggage Claim, a businessman from Wichita told her how much simpler it had been getting in and out of Denver before they built Denver International Airport. "Not that Stapleton was all that wonderful," he said, "but it was a quick, cheap cab ride from the Brown Palace. It wasn't stuck out in the middle of a few thousand square miles of prairie."

It was funny he should mention the Brown, she said, because that's where she was staying. So of course he suggested she share his cab, and when they reached the hotel and she offered to pay half, well, he wouldn't hear of it. "My company pays," he said, "and if you really want to thank me, why don't you let the old firm buy you dinner?"

Tempting, but she begged off, said she'd eaten a big lunch, said all she wanted to do was get to sleep. "If you change your mind," he said, "just ring my room. If I'm not there, you'll find me in the bar."

She didn't have a reservation, but they had a room for her, and she sank into an armchair with a glass of water from the tap. The Brown Palace had its own artesian well, and took great pride in its water, so how could she turn it down?

"Just drink it," she'd told Doug, and he'd done what she told him. It was funny, people usually did.

"Five," she'd told Lucas, who'd been so eager to be number six. But he'd managed it for only a matter of minutes, because the list was composed of men who could sit around that mythical table and tell each other how they'd had her, and you had to be alive to do that. So Lucas had dropped off the list when she'd chosen a knife from his kitchen and slipped it right between his ribs and into his heart. He fell off her list without even opening his eyes.

After her parents died, she didn't sleep with anyone until she'd graduated and left home for good. Then she got a waitress job, and the manager took her out drinking after work one night, got her drunk, and performed something that might have been date rape; she didn't remember it that clearly, so it was hard to say.

When she saw him at work the next night he gave her a wink and a pat on the behind, and something came into her mind, and that night she got him to take her for a ride and park on the golf course, where she took him by surprise and beat his brains out with a tire iron.

There, she'd thought, Now it was as if the rape— if that's what it was, and did it really matter what it was? Whatever it was, it was as if it had never happened.

A week or so later, in another city, she quite deliberately picked up a man in a bar, went home with him, had sex with him, killed him, robbed him, and left him there. And that set the pattern.

Four times the pattern had been broken, and those four men had joined Doug Pratter on her list. Two of them, Sid from Philadelphia and Peter from Wall Street, had escaped because she drank too much. Sid was gone when she woke up. Peter was there, and in the mood for morning sex, after which she'd laced his bottle of vodka with the little crystals she'd meant to put in his drink the night before. She'd gone away from there wondering who'd drink the vodka. Peter? The next girl he managed to drag home? Both of them?

She thought she'd read about it in the papers, sooner or later, but if there'd been a story it escaped her attention, so she didn't really know whether Peter deserved a place on her list.

It wouldn't be hard to find out, and if he was still on the list, well, she could deal with it. It would be a lot harder to find Sid, because all she knew about him was his first name, and that might well have been improvised for the occasion. And she'd met him in Philadelphia, but he was already registered at a hotel, so that meant he was probably from someplace other than Philadelphia, and that meant the only place she knew to look was the one place where she could be fairly certain he didn't live.

She knew the first and last names of the two other men on her list. Graham Weider was a Chicagoan she'd met in New York; he'd taken her to lunch and to bed, then jumped up and hurried her out of there, claiming an urgent appointment and arranging to meet her later. But he'd never turned up, and the desk at his hotel told her he'd checked out.

So he was lucky, and Alan Reckson was lucky in another way. He was an infantry corporal on leave before they shipped him off to Iraq, and if she'd realized that she wouldn't have picked him up in the first place, and she wasn't sure what kept her from doing to him as she did to the other men who entered her life. Pity? Patriotism? Both seemed unlikely, and when she thought about it later she decided it was simply because he was a soldier. That gave them something in common, because weren't they both warriors? Wasn't she her father's little soldier?

Maybe he'd been killed over there. She supposed she could find out. And then she could decide what she wanted to do about it.

Graham Weider, though, couldn't claim combatant status, unless you considered him a corporate warrior. And while his name might not be unique, neither was it by any means common. And it was almost certainly his real name, too, because they'd known it at the front desk. Graham Weider, from Chicago. It would be easy enough to find him, when she got around to it.

Of them all, Sid would be the real challenge. She sat there going over what little she knew about him and how she might go about playing detective. Then she treated herself to another half glass of Brown Palace water and flavored it with a miniature of Johnnie Walker from the minibar. She sat down with the drink and shook her head, amused by her own behavior. She was dawdling, postponing her shower, as if she couldn't bear to wash away the traces of Doug's lovemaking.

But she was tired, and she certainly didn't want to wake up the next morning with his smell still on her. She undressed and stood for a long time in the shower, and when she got out of it, she stood for a moment alongside the tub and watched the water go down the drain.

Four, she thought. Why, before you knew it, she'd be a virgin all over again.

Carrie Vaughn

Here's a powerful look at a part of World War II history that's still almost unknown by most people even here in the twenty-first century: the vital role played by the pilots of the Women Airforce Service Pilots or WASP. Who couldn't fight in combat, but who could—and did—die.

Bestseller Carrie Vaughn is the author of a wildly popular series of novels detailing the adventures of Kitty Norville, a radio personality who also happens to be a werewolf, and who runs a late-night call-in radio advice show for supernatural creatures. The Kitty books include *Kitty and The Midnight Hour, Kitty Goes to Washington, Kitty Takes a Holiday,* and *Kitty and the Silver Bullet.* Vaughn's short work has appeared in *Jim Baen's Universe, Asimov's Science Fiction, Inside Straight, Realms of Fantasy, Paradox, Strange Horizons, Weird Tales, All-Star Zeppelin Adventure Stories,* and elsewhere. *Kitty and the Dead Man's Hand* and *Kitty Raises Hell* are the newest Kitty novels, published in 2009. Vaughn lives in Colorado.

The Girls from Avenger

JUNE 1943

The sun was setting over Avenger Field when Em and a dozen others threw Mary into the so-called Wishing Well, the wide round fountain in front of the trainee barracks. A couple of the girls grabbed her arms; a couple more grabbed her feet and hauled her off the ground. Mary screamed in surprise, and Em laughed— she should have known this was coming, it happened to everyone after they soloed. But she remembered from her own dunking the week before, it was hard not to scream out of sheer high spirits.

Em halted the mob of cheering women just long enough to pull off Mary's leather flight jacket—then she was right there at Mary's shoulders, lifting her over the stone lip of the pool of water. Mary screamed again—half screamed, half laughed, rather—and splashed in, sending a wave over the edge. On her knees now, her sodden jumpsuit hanging off her like a sack, she splashed them all back. Em scrambled out of the way.

Applause and laughter died down, and Mary started climbing over the edge.

"Don't forget to grab your coins," Em told her.

"Oh!" She dived back under the water, reached around for a moment, then showed Em her prize—a couple of pennies in her open palm. Mary was young, twenty-two, and her wide, clear eyes showed it. Her brown hair was dripping over her face and she looked bedraggled, grinning. "I'm the luckiest girl in the world!"

Whenever one of the trainees at the Women's Flight Training Detachment at Avenger Field had a test or a check-out flight, she tossed a coin into the fountain for good luck. When she soloed for the first time, she could take two out, for luck. Em's coins were still in her pocket.

Em reached out, and Mary grabbed her hand. "Come on, get out of there. I think Suze has a fifth of whiskey with your name on it hidden under her mattress."

Mary whooped and scrambled out. She shook out her jumpsuit; sheets of water came off it, and she laughed all over again.

Arm in arm, they trooped to the barracks, where someone had a radio playing and a party had already started.

DECEMBER 1943

In an outfit like the WASP, everyone knew everyone and news traveled fast.

Em heard about it as soon as she walked into the

barracks at New Castle. Didn't have time to even put her bag down or slide her jacket off before three of the others ran in from the hall, surrounded her, and started talking. Janey gripped her arm tight like she was drowning, and Em let her bag drop to the floor.

"Did you hear?" Janey said. Her eyes were red from crying, Tess looked like she was about to start, and Patty's face was white. Em's stomach turned, because she already knew what they were going to say.

"Hear what?" she asked. Delaying the inevitable, like if she could draw this moment out long enough, the news wouldn't be true.

"A crash, out at Romulus," Patty said.

Em asked what was always the first question: "Who?"

"Mary Keene."

The world flipped, her heart jumped, and all the blood left her head. No, there was a mistake, not Mary. Rumors flew faster than anything. She realized Patty didn't look so worried because of the crash; she was worried about Em.

"What happened?" Always the second question.

"I don't know, just that there was a crash."

"Mary, is she—?"

Janey's tears fell and her voice was tight. She squeezed Em harder. "Oh, Em! I'm so sorry. I know you were friends—I'm so sorry."

If Em didn't get out of here now, she'd have to hug them all and start crying with them. She'd have to think about how to act and what to say and what to do next. She'd have to listen to the rumors and try to sort out what had really happened.

She pushed by them, got past their circle, ignored it when Patty touched her arm, trying to hold her back. Left her bag behind, thought that she ought to drag it with her because it had dirty clothing in it. Maybe somebody called to her, but she just wanted to be alone.

She found her room, sat on her cot, and stared at the empty cot against the other wall. She bunked with Mary, right here in this room, just as they had at Avenger. Doubled over, face to her lap, she hugged herself and wondered what to do next.

This didn't happen often enough to think it could happen to you, or even someone you knew. A year of women flying Army planes, and it had happened less than a dozen times. There were few enough of them all together that Em had known some of them, even if they hadn't been friends. Seen them at training or waved on the way to one job or another.

It had happened often enough that they had a system.

Em knocked on the last door of the barracks and collected money from Ruth and Liz. She didn't have to explain what it was for when she held the cup out. It had been like that with everyone, the whole dozen of them on base at the moment. Em would take this hundred and twenty dollars, combine it with the hundred or so sent in from the women at Sweetwater and

Houston, and she'd use it to take Mary back to Dayton. None of them were officially Army, so Uncle Sam didn't pay for funerals. It seemed like a little thing to complain about, especially when so many of the boys overseas were dying. But Mary had done her part, too. Didn't that count for something?

"Have you found out what happened yet?" Liz asked. Everyone had asked that, too.

Em shook her head. "Not a thing. I called Nancy, but they're not telling her anything either."

"You think it was bad?" Liz said. "You think that's why they're hushing it up?"

"They're hushing it up because they don't like to think about women dying in airplanes," she said. Earlier in the year, she'd been told point blank by a couple of male pilots that the only women who belonged on planes were the ones painted on the noses. That was supposed to be clever. She was supposed to laugh and flirt. She'd just walked away.

Running footsteps sounded on the wood floor and they looked up to see Janey racing in. The panic in her eyes made Em think that maybe it had happened again, that someone else had gone and crashed and that they'd have to pass the cup around again, so soon.

Janey stopped herself by grabbing Em's arm and said, "There's a bird in from Romulus, a couple of guys in a B-26. You think maybe they know what happened?"

They'd have a better idea than anyone. They might even have seen something. "Anyone talk to them yet?" Em said. Janey shook her head.

A line on the rumor mill. Em gave her colleagues a grim smile and headed out.

She couldn't walk by the flight line without stopping and looking, seeing what was parked and what was roaring overhead. The place was swarming, and it always made her heart race. It was ripe with potential—something *big* was happening here. *We're fighting a war here, we really are.* She took a deep breath of air thick with the smell of fuel and tarmac. Dozens of planes lined up, all shapes and sizes, a dozen more were taking off and landing. Hangar doors stood open revealing even more, and a hundred people moved between them all, working to keep the sound of engines loud and sweet.

This time, she wasn't the only one stopping to look, because a new sound was rocketing overhead, a subtly different rumble than the ones she normally heard out here. Sure enough, she heard the engine, followed the sound, and looked up to see a bulldog of a fighter buzz the field, faster than sin. She shaded her eyes against a bright winter sun and saw the P-51 Mustang—so much more graceful and agile than anything else in the sky. The nose tapered to a sleek point, streamlined and fast, like a rocket. Not like the clunky, snub-nosed trainers. Granted, clunky trainers served a purpose—it was easier for a pilot in training to correct a mistake at a hundred miles an hour than it was at three hundred. But Em had to wonder what it felt like to really *fly*. Some way, somehow, she was going to get up in one of those birds someday. She was going to find out what it was like to have 1,500 horsepower at her command.

If she were male, her training wouldn't stop with the little single-engine trainers the WASP ferried back and forth from training base to training base, where they were flown by the men who would move on to pursuits and bombers, and from there to combat. If she were male, she'd be flying bigger, faster, meaner planes already. Then she'd go overseas to fly them for real.

As Janey had said, a B-26 Marauder—a fast, compact two-engine bomber—crouched out on the tarmac, a couple of mechanics putting fuel into her. She was probably stopped for a refuel on her way to somewhere else. That meant Em probably had only one chance to talk to the pilots. She continued on to the ops center. The door to the briefing room was closed, but she heard voices inside, muffled. Against her better judgment, she put her ear to the door and listened, but the talk was all routine. The bomber was on its way to Newark for transport overseas, and the pilot was a combat instructor, just off the front.

Em sat in a chair across the hall and waited. Half an hour later, the door opened. The two guys who emerged were typical flyboys, leather jackets, sunglasses tucked in the pockets, khaki uniforms, short cropped hair, and Hollywood faces. Lieutenant bars on the shoulders.

When Em stood at attention, smoothing her trousers and trying not to worry if her collar was straight, the men looked startled. She didn't give them time to try to figure out what to do with her. "I'm sorry to bother you. My name's Emily Anderson, and I'm with the WASP squadron here. I got word that you just flew in from Romulus this morning. I was wondering if I could ask you something."

The taller of the two edged toward the door. "I have to go check on . . . on something. Sorry." His apology was quick and not very sincere.

The remaining pilot looked even more stricken and seemed ready to follow his buddy.

"Please, just a quick question," she said, hating to sound like she was begging. She ought to be charming him.

His wary look deepened, a defensive, thin-lipped frown that made her despair of his taking her seriously. He hesitated, seeming to debate with himself before relenting. "What can I help you with, Miss Anderson?"

She took a deep breath. "I'm trying to find out about a crash that happened near Romulus Field three days ago. A WASP was the pilot. Mary Keene. Sir, she was a friend of mine, and we—the other WASP and I—we just want to know what happened. No one will tell us anything."

He could have denied knowing anything, shaken his head, and walked out, and she wouldn't have been able to do anything, and she wouldn't have been more worried than she already was. But he hesitated. His hands fidgeted with the edge of his jacket, and he glanced at the door, nervous. He knew. Not just that, it was something he didn't want to talk about, something awful.

She pressed. "You know what it's like when something like this happens and they won't tell you anything."

He shook his head and wouldn't meet her gaze. "I shouldn't tell you this."

"Why not? Because it's classified? Or because I'm female and you think I can't handle it?"

The lieutenant pursed his lips. He'd been in combat, might even have faced down enemy fighters, but he didn't seem to want to stand up to her.

"It was a collision," he said finally.

Em had worked out a dozen scenarios, everything from weather to mechanical failure. She was even braced to hear that Mary had made a mistake. A million things could go wrong in the air. But a collision?

"That doesn't make sense, Mary had almost seven hundred hours in the air, she was too experienced for that."

He got that patronizing look a lot of male pilots had when dealing with WASP, like she couldn't possibly know what she was talking about. "I told you I shouldn't have said anything."

"A collision with whom? Did the other pilot make it? What were they doing that they ran into each other? Did you see it?"

"I don't know the details, I'm sorry."

"The Army won't even tell me what she was flying when she went down," she said.

He stepped closer, conspiratorially, as if afraid that

someone was listening in. Like this really was classified.

"Look, Miss Anderson, you seem like a nice girl.
Why are you doing this? Why are any of you risking
your lives like this? Why not stay home, stay safe—?"

"And plant a Victory Garden like a good girl? Sit by
the radio and wait for someone to tell me it's going to
be all right, and that my husband'll come home safe? I
couldn't do that, Lieutenant. I had to do something."

The arguments against women flyers tended to stall
out at this point, into vague statements about what was
ladylike, what well-bred girls ought to be doing, how
women weren't strong enough to handle the big planes
even though they'd proved themselves over and over
again. A year of women flying should have shut the
naysayers up by now. It hadn't.

The lieutenant didn't say anything.

She said, "Is there someone else I can talk to?"

"Look, I don't know, I'm working off rumors like
everyone else. I can't help you. I'm sorry." He fled,
backing to the door and abandoning Em to the empty
corridor.

The WASP all liked Colonel Roper, who commanded
the Second Ferry Group at New Castle. At some of the
other bases, commanders had given WASP the cold
shoulder, but here, he'd treated them with respect and
made it policy that the rest of the group do likewise.
He didn't constantly ask them if they could do the
job—he just gave them the job.

She went to him with the lieutenant's story.

His office door was open and he saw her coming. As he was glancing up, a frown drew lines around his mouth. He was young for a colonel, maybe a little rounder than most guys in the Army, but high-spirited. His uniform jacket was slung over the back of his chair.

"I'm sorry, Anderson, I don't have any news for you," he told her before she'd said a word.

She ducked her gaze and blushed. She'd been in here every day looking for news about Mary's death.

"Sorry, sir," she said, standing at the best attention she knew, back straight and hands at her sides. "But I just talked to the pilots of that B-26 that came in from Romulus. Sir, they told me Mary crashed in a collision. They wouldn't tell me anything else."

Roper's lips thinned, his brow creased. "A collision—Mary wouldn't get herself in that kind of mess."

"I know. Sir, something's not right. If there's anything you can do, anything you can find out—"

He scratched out a note on a pad of paper. "The crash report ought to be filed by now. I'll get a copy sent over."

That meant a few more days of waiting, but it was progress. They'd get the report, and that would be that. But she still wanted to *talk* to someone. Someone who'd seen it, someone who knew her. If there was a collision, another pilot was involved. If she could just find out who.

"Thank you, sir," she said.

"You're welcome. Anderson—try to get some sleep. You look beat."

She hadn't even been thinking about being tired. She'd been running on fumes. "Yes, sir."

Mary Keene came from the kind of family that did everything just so, with all the right etiquette. A car from the funeral home was waiting at the train station, along with Mary's father. Em recognized him from the family picture Mary kept in their room.

Em, dressed in her blue uniform—skirt straight, collar pressed, lapels smooth, insignia pins and wings polished—jumped to the platform before the train slowed to a complete stop and made her way to the luggage car. She waited again. It should have been raining; instead, a crisp winter sun shone in a blue sky. Perfect flying weather. She was thankful for the wool uniform, because a cold wind blew in over a flat countryside.

Men from the funeral home retrieved the casket while Mr. Keene thanked her for coming, shaking her hand with both of his and frowning hard so he wouldn't cry.

"I thought I'd be meeting one of my boys here like this. Not Mary."

Em bowed her head. No one ever knew quite what to say about a woman coming home from war in a casket. If one of Mr. Keene's sons had been killed, the family would put a gold star in the window to replace the blue one showing loved ones serving in combat. They'd be able to celebrate their war hero. Mary wouldn't get any of that, not even a flag on her casket.

Mr. Keene left in his own car. Em would go with Mary to the funeral home, then call a cab and find a hotel to stay at until the funeral tomorrow. One of the men from the mortuary took Em aside before they left.

"I'm given to understand Miss Keene passed on in an airplane crash."

"That's right."

He was nervous, not looking at her, clasping his hands. Em thought these guys knew how to deal with anything.

"I'm afraid I have to ask—I wasn't given any information," he said. "The family has traditionally held open-casket services—will this be possible?"

Or had she burned, had she been smashed beyond recognition, was there anything left? . . . Em's lips tightened. Stay numb, stay focused, just like navigating a fogbank.

"No, I don't think it will," she said.

The man lowered his gaze, bowing a little, and returned to his car.

Em logged thirty hours the next week in trainers, two AT-6s and a BT-13, flying from one end of the country to the other. One morning, she'd woken up in the barracks and had to look outside the window to remember where she was. She kept an eye on other logs and flight plans coming in and out of each base, and kept looking for people who'd been at Romulus last week. Everyone knew about the crash, but other than the fact that a WASP had been killed, nobody treated it like anything unusual. This was wartime, after all.

Arriving back at New Castle on the train after ferrying another round of BT-13s to Houston, she dropped her bag off at the barracks and went to see Colonel Roper. She still had her jumpsuit and flight jacket on, and she really needed a shower. And a meal. And sleep. But maybe this time he had news.

"Sir?" she said at his doorway.

He looked hard at her, didn't say a word. Self-consciously, she pushed her hair back behind her ears. Maybe she should have washed up first. She tried again. "Sir?"

"You're right, Anderson," he said finally. "Something's not right. The crash report's been classified."

She stared. "But that doesn't make any sense."

"I have something for you."

He handed her a folded paper that looked suspiciously like orders. She'd been in the air for three days. She hadn't been back in her own room for a week. She didn't want another mission; she didn't want orders. But you never said no; you never complained.

Her despair must have shown, because Roper gave a thin smile. "I saved this one just for you. I have an AT-11 needs to go to Romulus and I thought you're just the pilot to do it."

Exhaustion vanished. She could fly a month straight if she had to.

He continued, "In fact, you look a little tired. Why don't you spend a few days out there while you're at it? Take a break, meet the locals."

Do some digging, in other words.

"Thank you, sir," she said, a little breathlessly.

"Bring me back some facts, Anderson."

Last June, right after graduation and before transferring to New Castle, Em and Mary flew together on a cross-country training hop from Sweetwater to Dallas. It was the kind of easy trip where Em could sit back and actually enjoy flying. The kind of trip that reminded her why she was even doing this. She could lean back against the narrow seat, look up and all around through the narrow, boxy canopy at nothing but blue sky. Free as air.

"Hey Em, take the stick for a minute," Mary said, shouting over the rumble of the engine, when they'd almost reached Love Field at Dallas.

From the back seat of their BT-13 Valiant, craning her neck to peer over Mary's shoulder, Em saw her drop the stick and start digging in one of the pockets of her jacket. Em hadn't yet taken over on the dual controls. The Valiant was a trainer and could be flown from either the front or back seat, and every trainee sitting in front had had the controls yanked away from them by the instructor in back at least once. The plane was flying trim so Em didn't panic too much; she had a little time to put a steadying hand on the stick.

"What are you doing up there?" Em asked. Mary turned just enough so Em could see her putting on lipstick, studying her work in a compact mirror. She'd had enough practice putting on lipstick in airplanes that the teeth-rattling vibrations of the engine didn't affect her at all. Em laughed. "No one up here cares about your lipstick."

Mary looked a little ridiculous, leather cap mashing down her hair, goggles up on her forehead, painting her lips. So this was why she wanted to fly with the canopy closed on such a warm, beautiful day, making the cockpit hot and stuffy. She didn't want to be all ruffled when they landed.

"I have to be ready. There might be some handsome young officer just waiting for me to catch his eye. Oh, I hope we get there in time for dinner. This bucket's so slow. You think they'll ever give us anything faster to fly?"

"A real plane, you mean?" Em said. It was an old joke.

"I wouldn't say *that*. This bird's real enough. If you don't mind going *slow*."

Em looked out the canopy stuck up top in the middle of the fuselage. "We have to get there and land before you can catch your handsome young officer's eye. Do you know where we are?" They were flying low-level and cross-country; Em searched for landmarks, which was quite a trick in the middle of Texas.

"Don't fret, we're right on course. Bank left—there's the main road, see?"

Em nudged the stick and the plane tipped, giving her a wide view past the wing and its Army star to the earth below, and the long straight line of paved road leading to Dallas. Mary seemed to have an instinct for these sorts of things.

"You really do have this all planned out," Em said. "You'll be heading straight from the flight line to the Officer's Club, won't you?"

Mary had a pout in her voice. "I might stop to brush my hair first." Em laughed, and Mary looked over her shoulder. "Don't give me a hard time just because I'm not already married off to a wonderful man like you are."

Em sighed. She hadn't seen her husband in almost a year. The last letter she'd had from him was postmarked Honolulu, three weeks ago. He hadn't said where he was sailing to—couldn't, really. All she knew was that he was somewhere in the middle of a big wide ocean, flying Navy dive-bombers off a carrier. Sometimes she wished she weren't a pilot, because she knew exactly what could go wrong for Michael. Then again, maybe he was flying right now—it was midmorning in the Pacific—cruising along for practice on a beautiful day and thinking of her, the way she was thinking of him.

"Em?" Mary said, still craned over to look at Em the best she could over the back of her seat.

"Sorry. You just got me thinking about Michael."

Em could just see Mary's wide red smile, her excitable eyes. "You really miss him, don't you?"

"Of course I do."

Mary sighed. "That's so romantic."

Em almost laughed again. "Would you listen to you? There's nothing romantic about waking up every day wondering if he's alive or dead." She was only twenty-four, too young to be a widow, surely. She had to stop this or she'd start crying and have to let Mary land the plane. Shaking her head, she looked away, back to the blue sky outside the canopy, scattered clouds passing by.

"It's just that being in love like that? I've never been in love like that. Except maybe with Clark Gable." She grinned.

Em gratefully kept the joke going. "Don't think for a minute Clark Gable's going to be on the ground when we get there."

"You never know. These are strange times. He enlisted, did you know that? I read about it. Him and Jimmy Stewart both—and Jimmy Stewart's a pilot!"

"And maybe they'll both be at Dallas, just for you."

"Hope springs eternal," Mary said smugly. "I've got my lucky pennies, you know."

"All right, but if they're there, you *have* to ask them to dance."

"It's a deal," Mary said brightly, knowing she'd never have to make good on it. Because Clark Gable and Jimmy Stewart were *not* at Dallas. But if something like that was going to happen to anyone, it would happen to Mary.

A few minutes later, Em leaned forward to listen. Sure enough, Mary was singing. "Don't sit under the apple tree, with anyone else but me, anyone else but me . . ."

Em joined in, and they sang until they were circling over the field to land.

———

After shutting down the engine, she sat in her cockpit and took a look down the flight line at Romulus, in freezing Michigan. The sight never failed to amaze her—a hundred silver birds perched on the tarmac, all that power, ready and waiting. The buzzing of engines was constant; she could feel the noise in her bones.

This was the last runway Mary took off from.

Sighing, she filled out the plane's 1-A, collected her bag and her logbook, and hoisted herself out of the cockpit and onto the tarmac. Asked the first guy she saw, a mechanic, where the WASP barracks were. The wary look on his face told her all she needed to know about what the men on this base thought of WASP. She'd heard the rumors—they traded stories about which bases welcomed them and which wanted nothing to do with women pilots. She wasn't sure she believed the stories about someone putting sugar in the fuel tank of a WASP's plane at Camp Davis, causing it to crash—mostly because she didn't think anyone would do that to a plane. But those were the sorts of stories people told.

She made her way to the barracks. After a shower, she'd be able to face the day a little easier.

After the shower, Em, dressed in shirt and trousers, was still drying her hair when a group of women came into the barracks—three of them, laughing and wind-blown, peeling off flight jackets and scrubbing fingers through mussed hair. They quieted when they saw her, and she set her towel aside.

"Hi."

One of them, a slim blonde with mischief in her eyes, the kind of woman the brass liked to use in press photos, stepped forward, hand outstretched.

"Hi. You must be the new kid they were talking about back in ops. I'm Lillian Greshing."

"Em Anderson," she said, shaking her hand. "I'm just passing through. I hope you don't mind, I used one of the towels on the shelf. There weren't any names or labels—"

"Of course not, that's what they're there for. Hey—we were going to grab supper in town after we get cleaned up. Want to come along? You can catch us up on all the gossip."

Em's smile went from polite to warm, as she felt herself among friends again. "That sounds perfect."

The four women found a table in the corner of a little bar just off base. The Runway wasn't fancy; it had a Christmas tree decorated with spots of tinsel and glass bulbs in a corner, a pretty good bar, and a jukebox playing swing. The dinner special was roast chicken, mashed potatoes, and a bottle of beer to wash it down.

"What're they transferring WASP to Camp Davis for?" Betsy, a tall woman with a narrow face and a nervous smile, asked when Em passed on the rumor.

"Don't know," Em said. "Nobody'll say. But Davis is a gunnery school." More speculative murmurs ran around the table.

"Target towing. Wanna bet?" Lillian said.

"I'll stick to the job I have, thank you very much," Betsy said, shivering.

Em felt her smile grow thin and sly. "Not me. Nursing along slowpoke trainers? We can do better than that."

"You *want* to fly planes while some cross-eyed greenhorn shoots at you?"

"Nope," Em said. "I want to transition to pursuits."

"It'll never happen," Lillian said, shaking her head, like she needed the emphasis. "The old cronies like Burnett will never let it happen."

"Burnett?"

"Colonel. Runs this lovely little operation." She gestured in the direction of the airfield. Smoke trailed behind her hand to join the rest of the haze in the air.

"What's he like?" Em asked.

That no one answered with anything more than sidelong glances and rolled eyes told her enough. Romulus was a cold-shoulder base.

Em pressed on. "We'll get there. Nancy Love has five girls in transition out at Palm Springs already. The factories are all working overtime building bombers and fighters, and ATC doesn't have enough pilots to ferry them to port. They're going to have to let us fly 'em, whether they like it or not."

Betsy was still shaking her head. "Those birds are too dangerous."

Mary got killed in a trainer, Em wanted to say. "We can do it. We're capable of it."

Lillian said with a sarcastic lilt, "Burnett would say

we're not strong enough. That we wouldn't be able to even get something like a Mustang off the ground."

"He's full of it," Em said. "I can't *wait* to get my hands on one of those."

Betsy, smiling vaguely, looked into her beer. "I don't know how I'd explain flying fighters to my husband. He's barely all right with my flying at all."

"So don't tell him," Lillian said. Shocked giggles met the proclamation.

Round-eyed Molly, blond hair in a ponytail, leaned in. "Don't listen to her, she's got three boyfriends at three different fields. She doesn't understand about husbands." More giggling.

Em smiled. "Betsy, is he overseas?"

"England," she said. "He's a doctor." Her pride was plain.

"You've got a ring there, Em," Molly said to the band on Em's finger. "You married or is that to keep the flyboys off you?"

"He's Navy," Em said. "He's on a carrier in the Pacific."

After a sympathetic hesitation, Lillian continued. "What does he think about you flying?"

Em donned a grin. "I met him when we were both taking flying lessons before the war. He can't argue about me flying. Besides, I have to do something to keep my mind off things."

Lillian raised her bottle. "Here's to the end of the war."

They raised their glasses and the toasts were heartfelt.

The quiet moment gave Em her opening—time to start in on the difficult gossip, what she'd come here to learn. "What do you all know about Mary Keene's crash last week?"

No one would look at her. Betsy bit a trembling lip and teared up, and Molly fidgeted with her glass. Lillian's jaw went taut with a scowl. She ground her cigarette into the ashtray with enough force to destroy what was left of it.

"It happened fifty miles out," Lillian said, her voice quiet. "Nobody saw anything, we just heard it when the fire truck left. All we know is a group of seven planes went out—BT-13s, all of 'em—and an hour later six came back and nobody would tell us a thing. Just that Mary'd been killed. You knew her, I take it?"

"We were in the same class at Avenger," Em said. "We were friends."

"I'm sorry," Lillian said. "She was only here a couple of days but we all liked her a lot."

Molly handed Betsy a handkerchief; she dabbed her eyes with it.

"I was told the accident report was classified, and that doesn't make any sense. Some guys who were here last week told me there was a collision."

Lillian leaned close and spoke softly, like this was some kind of conspiracy. "That's what we heard, and one of the planes came back with a wheel all busted up, but Burnett clamped down on talk so fast, our heads spun. Filed away all the paperwork and wouldn't answer any questions. We don't even know who else was flying that day."

"He can't do that," Em said. "Couldn't you go after him? Just keep pushing—"

"It's Burnett," Lillian said. "Guy's a brick wall."

"Then go over his head."

"And get grounded? Get kicked out? That's what he's threatened us with, for going over his head," Lillian said, and Em couldn't argue. But technically, she wasn't part of his squadron, and he couldn't do anything to her. She could ask her questions.

Another group from the field came in then, flyboys by their leather jackets with silver wings pinned to the chest. Ferry Division, by the insignia. Not so different from the girls, who were wearing trousers and blouses, their jackets hanging off their chairs—a group gathered around a table, calling for beers and talking about the gossip, flying, and the war.

Pretty soon after their arrival, a couple of them went over to the jukebox and put in a few coins. A dance tune came up, something just fast enough to make you want to get out of your seat—Glenn Miller, "Little Brown Jug." Lillian rolled her eyes and Molly hid a smile with her hand; they all knew what was coming next.

Sure enough, the guys sauntered over to their table. Em made sure the hand with her wedding band was out and visible. Not that that stopped some men. Just a dance, they'd say. But she didn't want to, because it would make her think about Michael.

Lillian leaned back in her chair, chin up and shoulders squared, and met their gazes straight on. The others looked on like they were watching a show.

They weren't bad looking, early thirties maybe. Slightly rumpled uniforms and nice smiles. "Would any of you ladies like a dance?"

The women glanced at each other—would any of them say yes?

Lillian, brow raised, blond curls falling over her ears so artfully she might have pinned them there, said, "What makes you boys think you could keep up with any of us?"

The guys glanced at each other, then smiled back at Lillian. Gauntlet accepted. "We'd sure like to give it a try."

Nobody was making a move to stand, and Lillian again took the lead—breaking the boys' hearts for fun. "Sorry to disappoint you, but the girls and I spent all day putting repaired AT-6s through their paces and we're beat. We were looking forward to a nice, quiet evening."

The guy standing at the first one's shoulder huffed a little. "Lady pilots," he might have muttered.

The first guy seemed a little daunted. "Well, maybe you'll let us pull over a couple of chairs and buy you a round?"

Magic words, right there. Lillian sat up and made a space at the table. "That'll be all right."

Another round of beers arrived a moment later.

The men were nice enough, Ferry Division boys flying pursuits and bombers from the factories. Em asked questions—how many, what kind, where were they going, what was it like?—and ate up the answers. They seemed happy enough to humor her, even if they did come off on the condescending side—isn't that cute, a girl who wants to fly fast planes.

The attitude was easy enough to ignore. Every WASP had a story about being chatted up by some flyboy at a bar, him bragging about piloting hotshot planes and ending with the "I ship out to Europe tomorrow, honey," line; then seeing the look of shock on the guy's face the next day when he spotted her on the flight line climbing into her own cockpit. That was funny every damn time.

Lillian leaned over to Jim, the guy who'd talked to them first, and said, "Do your friends want to come on over and join us? We could make a real party of it."

A couple of the guys already had, but a few remained at the other table, talking quietly and nursing beers. They didn't pay much attention to the other group, except for one guy, with a round face and slicked-back hair, who kept his jacket on even though the room had grown warm.

Grinning, Jim leaned forward and lowered his voice. "I think you all make some of the boys nervous."

Em smiled and ducked her gaze while the other women giggled.

Lillian almost purred. "We're not flying now, I don't see why they should be nervous. We're not going to crash into them." Em looked away at that. It was just a joke, she told herself.

Jim tilted his head to the sullen-looking pilot. "Frank there almost walked back out again when he saw you girls sitting here."

"What, afraid of little old us?" Lillian said, and the

others laughed. The sullen-looking pilot at the other table, Frank, seemed to sink into his jacket a little further.

Jim shrugged. "His loss, right?"

Em agreed. Anyone had an issue with women pilots, it was their problem, not hers.

Em had to go at the mystery backwards. The accident report wasn't available, so she dug through the flight logs to see who else was flying that day. Who else was in the air with Mary.

She made her way to ops, a big square prefab office building off the airstrip, around lunchtime the next day, when she was less likely to run into people. The move paid off—only a secretary, a woman in civilian clothes, was on duty. Em carried her logbook in hand, making her look more official than not, and made up some excuse about being new to the base and needing to log her next flight and where should she go? The secretary directed her to an adjoining room. There, Em found the setup familiar: maps pinned to the wall, chalkboards with instructions written on them, charts showing planes and schedules, and a wall of filing cabinets.

Every pilot taking off from the field was supposed to file a flight plan, which were kept in ops. Mary's plan—and the plans of anyone else who was flying that day and might have collided with her—should be here. She rubbed her lucky pennies together and got to work.

The luck held: the files were marked by day and in order. Flipping through, Em found the pressboard folder containing the forms from that day. Taking the folder to an empty desk by the wall, she began studying, reconstructing in her mind what the flight line had looked like that day.

Mary had been part of a group ferrying seven BT-13 Valiants from Romulus to Dallas. She wasn't originally part of the group; she'd been at Romulus overnight after ferrying a different BT-13. But they had an extra plane, and like just about any WASP, she would fly anything she was checked out on, anything a commander asked her to fly. Those were the bare facts. That was the starting point. Less than an hour after takeoff, Mary had crashed. A collision—which meant it must have been one of the other planes in the group.

WASP weren't authorized for close-formation flying. When they did fly in groups, they flew loose, with enough distance between to prevent accidents—at least five hundred feet. Mary was the only WASP in the group, but the men should have followed the same procedure and maintained a safe distance. Just saying "collision" didn't tell the story, because only one plane hit the ground, and only one pilot died.

The accident had eyewitnesses: the other six pilots in the group, who were flying with Mary when she crashed. She started jotting down names and the ID numbers of the planes they'd been flying.

"What do you think you're doing?"

Startled, Em flinched and looked up to find a lanky

man just past forty or so, his uniform starched and perfect, standing in the doorway, hands clenched, glaring. Silver eagles on his shoulders—this must be Colonel Burnett. Reflexively, she crumpled her page of notes and stuffed it in her pocket. The move was too obvious to hide. Gathering her thoughts, she stood with as much attention as she could muster—part of her mind was still on those six pilots.

She'd spent enough time in the Army Air Force to know how men like Burnett operated: they intimidated, they browbeat. They had their opinions and didn't want to hear arguments. She just had to keep from letting herself get cowed.

"Filing a flight plan, sir." She kept the lie short and simple, so he wouldn't have anything to hold against her.

"I don't think so," he said, looking at the pages spread out on the desk.

They were in a standoff. She hadn't finished, and wanted to get those last couple of names. Burnett didn't look like he was going to leave.

"It's true," she bluffed. "BT-13 to Dallas." Mary's last flight plan; that might have been pushing it.

"You going to show me what's in your pocket there?"

"Grocery list," she said, deadpan.

He stepped closer, and Em had to work not to flinch away from the man.

"Those are papers from last week," he said, pointing at the plans she'd been looking at.

"Yes, sir."

His face reddened, and she thought he might start screaming at her, drill-sergeant style. "Who authorized you to look at these?"

Somebody had to speak up. Somebody had to find the truth. That allowed her to face him, chin up. "Sir, I believe the investigation into that crash ended prematurely, that all the information hasn't been brought to light."

"That report was filed. There's nothing left to say. You need to get out of here, missy."

Now he was just making her angry. He probably expected her to wilt—he probably yelled at all the women because he expected them to wilt. She stepped forward, feeling her own flush starting, her own temper rising. "Why was the report buried? I just want to know what really happened."

"I don't have to explain anything to you. You're a civilian. You're just a civilian."

"What is there to explain, sir?"

"Unless you march out of here right now, I'll have you arrested for spying. Don't think the Army won't shoot a woman for treason!"

Em expected a lot of threats—being grounded, getting kicked out of the WASP, just like Lillian said. But being shot for treason? What the hell was Burnett trying to hide?

Em was speechless, and didn't have any fight left in her after that. She marched out with her logbook, just as Burnett told her to, head bowed, unable to look at him. Even though she really wanted to spit at him. In the corner of her gaze, she thought she saw him smile, like he thought he'd won some kind of victory over her. Bullying a woman, and he thought that made him tough. By the time she left the building, her eyes were watering. Angrily, she wiped the tears away.

Well away from the building, she stopped to catch her breath. Crossed her arms, waited for her blood to cool. Looked up into the sky, turning her face to the clouds. The day was overcast, the ceiling low, a biting wind smelling of snow. Terrible weather for flying. But she'd go up in a heartbeat, in whatever piece-of-junk trainer was available, just to get away from here.

One of the lessons you learned early on: Make friends with the ground crew. When some of the trainers they flew had seen better days and took a lot of attention to keep running, sweet-talking a mechanic about what was wrong went further than complaining. Even if the wreckage from Mary's plane was still around—it would have already been picked over for aluminum and parts—Em wouldn't have been able to tell what had happened without seeing the crash site. She needed to talk to the recovery team.

Lillian told her that a Sergeant Bill Jacobs's crew had been the one to recover Mary's Valiant. He'd know a lot that hadn't made it into the records, maybe even be able to tell her what happened. If she could sweet-talk him. She touched up her lipstick, repinned her hair, and tapped her lucky pennies.

On the walk to the hangar, she tried to pound out her bad mood, to work out her anger and put herself in a sweet-talking frame of mind. *Hey there, mind telling me about a little ol' plane crash that happened last week?* She wasn't so good at sweet-talking, not like Lillian was. Not like Mary had been.

The main door of the hangar was wide open to let in the afternoon light. In the doorway, she waited a moment to let her eyes adjust to the shadows. A B-24 was parked inside, two of its four engines open and half-dismantled. The couple of guys working on each one called a word to the other now and then, asking for a part or advice. A radio played Duke Ellington.

The hangar had a strangely homey feel to it, with its atmosphere of grease and hard work, the cheerful music playing and the friendly banter between the mechanics. This might have been any airport repair shop, if it weren't for the fact they were working on a military bomber.

Em looked around for someone who might be in charge, someone who might be Jacobs. In the back corner, she saw the door to an office and headed there. Inside, she found what she was probably looking for: a wide desk stacked with papers and clipboards. Requisitions, repair records, inventories, and the like, she'd bet. Maybe a repair order for a BT-13 wounded in a collision last week?

She was about to start hunting when a man said, "Can I help you, miss?"

A man in Army coveralls and a cap stood at the doorway. Scraping together all the charm she could manage, she straightened and smiled. She must have made quite a silhouette in her trousers and jacket because he looked a bit stricken. He glanced at the insignia on her collar, the patches on her jacket, and knew what, if not who, she was.

"Sergeant Jacobs?" she said, smiling.

"Yes, ma'am."

Her smile widened. "Hi, I'm Emily Anderson, in from New Castle." She gestured vaguely over her shoulder. "They told me you might be able to help me out."

He relaxed, maybe thinking she was only going to ask for a little grease on a squeaky canopy.

She said, "The crash last week. The one the WASP died in. Can you tell me what happened?" Her smile had stiffened; her politeness was a mask.

Jacobs sidled past her in an effort to put himself between her and the desk—the vital paperwork. He began sorting through the mess on the desk, but his movements were random. "I don't know anything about that."

"You recovered the plane. You saw the crash site."

"It was a mess. I can't tell you what happened."

"What about the other plane? How badly was it damaged?"

He looked at her. "How do you know there was another plane?"

"I heard there was a collision. Who was flying that other plane? Can you at least tell me that much?"

"I can't help you, I'm sorry." He shook his head, like he was shaking off an annoying fly.

"Sergeant Jacobs, Mary Keene was my friend."

When he looked at her, his gaze was tired, pitying. "Ma'am, please. Let it go. Digging this up isn't going to fix anything."

"I need to know what really happened."

"The plane crashed, okay? It just crashed. Happens all the time, I hate to say it, but it's so."

Em shook her head. "Mary was a good pilot. *Something* had to have happened."

Jacobs looked away. "She switched off the engine."

"What?"

"She'd lost part of a wing—there was no way she could pull out of it. But before she hit the ground, she had time to turn off the engine so it wouldn't catch fire. So the plane wouldn't burn. She knew what was going to happen and she switched it off."

Mary, sitting in her cockpit, out of control after whatever had hit her, calmly reaching over to turn off the ignition, knowing the whole time she maybe wasn't going to make it—

"Is that supposed to make me feel better?" Em said.

"No. I'm sorry, ma'am. It's just you're right. She was a good pilot."

"Then why won't you—?"

A panicked shouting from the hangar caught their attention—"Whoa whoa, hold that thing, it's gonna drop"—followed by the ominous sound of metal crashing to concrete. Jacobs dashed out of the office to check on his crew.

Em wasn't proud; she went through the stack of papers while he was occupied.

The fact that Mary had crashed and died was becoming less significant to Em than the way everyone was acting about it. Twitchy. Defensive. Like a pilot towing targets for gunnery training, wondering if the wet-behind-the-ears gunners were going to hit you instead. These guys, everyone who knew what had happened, didn't want to talk about it, didn't want her to ask about it, and were doing their damnedest to cover this up. What were all these people hiding? Or, what were they protecting?

It wasn't a hard answer, when she put it like that: the other pilot. They were protecting the pilot who survived the collision.

She dug through repair orders. Mary's plane had crashed—but the other plane hadn't. It still would have been damaged, and there'd be paperwork for that. She looked at the dates, searching for *that* date. Found it, found the work order for a damaged BT-13. Quickly, she retrieved the list of names she'd taken from the flight plans. She'd copied only half of them before Burnett interrupted her. She had a fifty-fifty chance of matching the name on the work order. Heads or tails?

And there it was. When she compared ID numbers with the ones on the work order, she found the match she was looking for: Frank Milliken. The other pilot's name was Frank Milliken.

She marched out of the office and into hangar. Jacobs was near the B-24 wing, yelling at the guys who had apparently unbolted and dropped a propeller. He might have followed her with a suspicious gaze as she left, but he couldn't do anything about it now, could he?

She kept her eyes straight ahead and didn't give him a chance to stop her.

"You know Frank Milliken?" she asked Lillian when she got back to the barracks.

"By name. He's one of the Third Ferry Group guys—he was part of Jim's bunch of clowns last night," she said.

Em tried to remember the names she'd heard, to match them up with the faces, the guys who talked to them. "I don't remember a Frank," she said.

"He's the sulky guy who stayed at the table."

Ah . . . "You know anything about him?"

"Not really. They kind of run together when they're all flirting with you at once." She grinned. "What about him?"

"I think he was in the plane that collided with Mary's last week."

"What?" she said with a wince and tilted head, like she hadn't heard right.

"I've got a flight plan and a plane ID number on a repair order that says it was him."

Clench-jawed anger and an anxious gaze vied with each other and ended up making Lillian look young and confused. "What do we do?"

"I just want to find out what happened," Em said. She just wanted to sit down with the guy, make him walk her through it, explain who had flown too close to whom, whether it was accident, weather, a gust of wind, pilot error—anything. She just wanted to know.

"You sure?" Lillian said. "This is being hushed up for a reason. It can't be anything good. Not that *anything* is going to make this better, but—well, you know what I mean. Em, what if—what if it was Mary's fault? Are you ready to hear that? Are you ready to hear that this was a stupid accident and Burnett's covering it up to make his own record a little less dusty?"

Em understood what Lillian was saying—it didn't matter how many stories you made up for yourself; the truth could always be worse. If something—God forbid—ever happened to Michael, would she really want to know what killed him? Did she really want to picture that?

Shouldn't she just let Mary go?

Em's smile felt thin and pained. "We have to look out for each other, Lillian. No one else is doing it for us, and no one else is going to tell our stories for us. I have to know."

Lillian straightened, and the woman's attitude won out over her confusion. "Right, then. Let's go find ourselves a party."

Em and Lillian parked at the same table at the Runway, but didn't order dinner tonight. Em's stomach was churning; she couldn't think of eating. She and Lillian drank sodas and waited.

"What if they don't come?" Em said.

"They'll be here," Lillian said. "They're here every night they're on base. Don't worry."

As they waited, a few of the other girls came in and joined them, and they all had a somber look, frowning, quiet. Em didn't know how, but the rumor must have traveled.

"Is it true?" Betsy asked, sliding in across from Em. "You found out what happened to Mary?"

"That's what we need to see," she said, watching the front door, waiting.

The men knew something was up as soon as they came in and found the women watching them. The mood was tense, uncomfortable. None of them were smiling. And there he was, with his slicked-back hair, hunched up in his jacket like he was trying to hide. He hesitated inside the doorway along with the rest of the guys—if he turned around to leave this time, Em didn't think Jim or the others would try to stop him.

Em stood and approached them. "Frank Milliken?"

He glanced up, startled, though he had to have seen her coming. The other guys stepped away and left him alone in a space.

"Yeah?" he said warily.

Taking a breath, she closed her eyes a moment to steel herself. Didn't matter how much she'd practiced this speech in her mind, it wasn't going to come out right. She didn't know what to say.

"Last week, you were flying with a group of BT-13s. There was a collision. A WASP named Mary Keene crashed. I'm trying to find out what happened. Can you tell me?"

He was looking around, glancing side to side as if searching for an escape route. He wasn't saying anything, so Em kept on. "Your plane was damaged—I saw the work order. So I'm thinking your plane was involved and you know exactly what happened. Please, I just want to know how a good pilot like Mary crashed."

He was shaking his head. "No. I don't have to talk to you. I don't have to tell you anything."

"What's wrong?" Em pleaded. "What's everyone trying to hide?"

"Let it go. Why can't you just let it go?" he said, refusing to look at her, shaking his head like he could ward her away. Lillian was at Em's shoulder now, and a couple of the other WASP had joined them, standing in a group, staring down Milliken.

If Em had been male, she could have gotten away with grabbing his collar and shoving him to the wall, roughing him up a little to get him to talk. She was on the verge of doing it anyway; then wouldn't he be surprised?

"It was your fault, wasn't it?" She had the sudden epiphany. It was why he couldn't look at her, why he didn't even want to be here with WASP sitting at the next table. "What happened? Did you just lose control? Was something wrong with your plane?"

"It was an accident," he said softly.

"But what happened?" Em said, getting tired of

asking, not knowing what else to do. He had six women staring him down now, and a handful of men looking back and forth between them and him. Probably wondering who was going to start crying first.

"Why don't you just tell her, Milliken," Jim said, frowning.

"Please, no one will tell me—"

"It was an accident!" His face was flush; he ran a shaking hand over his hair. "It was just a game, you know? I only buzzed her a couple of times. I thought it'd be funny—it was supposed to be funny. You know, get close, scare her a little. But—it was an accident."

He probably repeated it to himself so often, he believed it. But when he spoke it out loud, he couldn't gloss the crime of it: he'd broken regs, buzzed Mary in the air, got closer than the regulation five hundred feet, thought he could handle the stunt—and he couldn't. He'd hit her instead, crunched her wing. She'd lost control, plowed into the earth. Em could suddenly picture it so clearly. The lurch as the other plane hit Mary, the dive as she went out of control. She'd have looked out the canopy to see the gash in her wing, looked the other way to see the ground coming up fast. She'd have hauled on the stick, trying to land nose up, knowing it wasn't going to work because she was going too fast, so she turned off the engine, just in case, and hadn't she always wanted to go faster—

You tried to be respectful, to be a good girl. You bought war bonds and listened to the latest news on the radio. You prayed for the boys overseas, and most of all you didn't rock the boat, because there were so many other things to worry about, from getting a gallon of rationed gas for your car to whether your husband was going to come home in one piece.

They were a bunch of Americans doing their part. She tried to let it go. Let the anger drain away. Didn't work. The war had receded in Em's mind to a small noise in the background. She had this one battle to face.

With Burnett in charge, nothing would happen to Milliken. The colonel had hushed it up good and tight because he didn't want a more involved investigation, he didn't want the lack of discipline among his male flyers to come out. Milliken wouldn't be court-martialed and grounded, because trained pilots were too valuable. Em couldn't do anything more than stand here and stare him down. How could she make that be enough?

"Mary Keene was my friend," she said softly.

Milliken said, his voice a breath, "It was an accident. I didn't mean to hit her. I'm sorry. I'm sorry, all right?"

Silence cut like a blade. None of the guys would look at her.

Em turned and walked out, flanked by the other WASP.

Outside, the sun had set, but she could still hear airplane engines soaring over the airfield, taking off and landing, changing pitch as they roared overhead. The air smelled of fuel, and the field was lit up like stars fallen to earth. The sun would shine again tomorrow no matter what happened, and nothing had changed. She couldn't tell if she'd won. She slumped against the wall, slid to the ground, put her face to her knees and her arms over her head, and cried. The others gathered around her, rested hands on her shoulders, her arms. Didn't say a word, didn't make a big production. Just waited until she'd cried herself out. Then Lillian and Betsy hooked their arms in hers and pulled her back to the barracks, where one of the girls had stashed a bottle of whiskey.

The last time Em saw Mary was four days before she died.

Em reached the barracks after coming off the flight line to see Mary sitting on the front steps with her legs stretched out in front of her, smoking a cigarette and staring into space. Em approached slowly and sat beside her. "What's gotten into you?"

Mary donned a slow, sly smile. "It didn't happen the way I thought it would, the way I planned it."

"What didn't?"

She tipped her head back so her honey brown curls fell behind her and her tanned face looked into the sky. "I was supposed to step out of my airplane, chin up and beautiful, shaking my hair out after I took off my cap, and my handsome young officer would be standing there, stunned out of his wits. That didn't happen."

Em was grinning. This ought to be good. "So what did happen?"

"I'd just climbed out of my Valiant and I wanted to check the landing gear because it was feeling kind of wobbly when I landed. So there I was, bent over when I heard some guy say, 'Hey, buddy, can you tell me where to find ops?' I just about shot out of my boots. I stood up and looked at him, and his eyes popped. And I swear to you he looked like Clark Gable. Not *just* like, but close. And I blushed red because the first thing he saw of me was my . . . my fanny stuck up in the air! We must have stood there staring at each other in shock for five minutes. Then we laughed."

Now Em was laughing, and Mary joined in, until they were leaning together, shoulder to shoulder.

"So, what," Em said. "It's true love?"

"I don't know. He's nice. He's a captain in from Long Beach. He's taking me out for drinks later."

"You are going to have the best stories when this is all over," Em said.

Mary turned quiet, thoughtful. "Can I tell you a secret? Part of me doesn't want the war to end. I don't want *this* to end. I just want to keep flying and carrying on like this forever. They won't let us keep flying when the boys come home. Then I'll have to go back home, put on white gloves and a string of pearls and start acting respectable." She shook her head. "I don't really mean that, about the war. It's got to end sometime, right?"

"I hope so," Em said softly. Pearl Harbor had been almost exactly two years ago, and it was hard to see an end to it all.

"Sometimes I wish my crazy barnstormer uncle hadn't ever taken me flying, then I wouldn't feel like this. Oh, my dad was so mad, you should have seen it. But once I'd flown I wasn't ever going to go back. I'm not ever going to quit, Em."

"I know." They sat on the stoop, watching and listening to planes come in over the field, until Mary went to get cleaned up for her date.

Em sat across from Colonel Roper's desk and waited while he read her carefully typed report. He read it twice, straightened the pages, and set it aside. He folded his hands together and studied her.

"How are you doing?"

She paused a moment, thinking about it rather than giving the pat "just fine" response. Because it wasn't true, and he wouldn't believe her.

"Is it worth it, sir?" He tilted his head, questioning, and she tried to explain. "Are we really doing anything for the war? Are we going to look back and think she died for nothing?"

His gaze dropped to the desk while he gathered words. She waited for the expected platitudes, the gushing reassurances. They didn't come.

"You want me to tell you Mary's death meant something, that what she was doing was essential for the war, that her dying is going to help us win. I can't do that." He shook his head. Em almost wished he would sugarcoat it. She didn't want to hear this. But she was also relieved that he was telling the truth. Maybe the bad-attitude flyboys were right, and the WASP were just a gimmick.

He continued. "You don't build a war machine so that taking out one cog makes the whole thing fall apart. Maybe we'll look back on this and decide we could have done it all without you. But, Emily—it would be a hell of a lot harder. We wouldn't have the pilots we need, and we wouldn't have the planes where we need them. And there's a hell of a lot of war left to fight."

She didn't want to think about it. You could take all the numbers, all the people who'd died over the last few years and everything they'd died for, and the numbers on paper might add up, but you start putting names and stories to the list and it would never add up, never be worth it. She just wanted it to be over; she wanted Michael home.

Roper sorted through a stack of papers on the corner of his desk and found a page he was looking for. He made a show of studying it for a long moment, giving her time to draw her attention from the wall where she'd been staring blankly. Finally, she met his gaze across the desk.

"I have transfer orders here for you. If you want them."

She shook her head, confused, wondering what she'd done wrong. Wondering if Burnett was having his revenge on her anyway, after all that had happened.

"Sir," she said, confused. "But . . . where? Why?"

"Palm Springs," he said, and her eyes grew wide, a spark in her heart lit, knowing what was at Palm Springs. "Pursuit School. If you're interested."

MARCH 1944

Em settled in her seat and reached up to close the canopy overhead. This was a one-seater, compact, nestled into a narrow, streamlined fuselage. The old trainers were roomy by comparison. She felt cocooned in the seat, all her controls and instruments at hand.

She started the engine; it roared. She could barely hear herself call the tower. "This is P-51 21054 requesting clearance for takeoff."

Her hands on the stick could feel this thing's power running into her bones. She wasn't going to have to push this plane off the ground. All she'd have to do was give it its head and let it go.

A voice buzzed in her ear. "P-51 21054, this is Tower, you are cleared for takeoff."

This was a crouched tiger preparing to leap. A rocket ready to explode. The nose was higher than the tail; she couldn't even see straight ahead—just straight up, past sleek silver into blue sky.

She eased the throttle forward, and the plane started moving. Then it *really* started moving. The tail lifted—she could see ahead of her now, to the end of the runway. Her speed increased, and she watched the dials in front of her. At a hundred miles per hour, she pulled back on the stick, *lifted*, and left earth behind.

Climbed *fast*, into clear blue sky, like a bullet, like a hawk. She glanced over her shoulder; the airstrip was already tiny. Nothing but open sky ahead, and all the speed she could push out of this thing.

This was heaven.

"Luckiest girl in the world," she murmured, thinking that Mary would have loved this.

James Rollins

A blood-soaked arena and gladiators circling each other for the kill . . . a scene familiar from many books and movies, except that this isn't Ancient Rome, and the battle-scarred warriors aren't quite what you'd expect either. In fact, many things are different. The blood is the same, though. And the death. And the courage.

An amateur spelunker, a veterinarian, and a PADI-certified scuba enthusiast, James Rollins is a *New York Times* bestselling author of contemporary thrillers (many with strong fantastic elements) such as *Subterranean, Excavation, Ice Hunt, Deep Fathom,* and *Amazonia,* as well as a series of novels detailing the often world-saving adventures of the SIGMA Force, including *Sandstorm, Map of Bones, Black Order,* and *The Judas Strain.* His most recent books are a novelization of *Indiana Jones and the Kingdom of the Crystal Skull* and the novel *The Last Oracle.* He lives with his family in Sacramento, California, where he runs a veterinary practice.

The Pit

The large dog hung from the bottom of the tire swing by his teeth. His back paws swung three feet off the ground. Overhead, the sun remained a red blister in an achingly blue sky. After so long, the muscles of the dog's jaw had cramped to a tight knot. His tongue had turned to a salt-dried piece of leather, lolling out one side. Still, at the back of his throat, he tasted black oil and blood.

But he did not let go.

He knew better.

Two voices spoke behind him. The dog recognized the gravel of the yard trainer. But the second was someone new, squeaky and prone to sniffing between every other word.

"How long he be hangin' there?" the stranger asked.

"Forty-two minutes."

"No shit! That's one badass motherfucker. But he's not pure pit, is he?"

"Pit and boxer."

"True nuff? You know, I got a Staffordshire bitch be ready for him next month. And let me tell you, she puts the mean back in bitch. Cut you in on the pups."

"Stud fee's a thousand."

"Dollars? You cracked or what?"

"Fuck you. Last show, he brought down twelve motherfuckin' Gs."

"Twelve? You're shittin' me. For a dogfight?"

The trainer snorted. "And that's after paying the house. He beat that champion out of Central. Should seen that Crip monster. All muscle and scars. Had twenty-two pounds on Brutus here. Pit ref almost shut down the fight at the weigh-in. Called my dog ring bait! But the bastard showed 'em. And those odds paid off like a crazy motherfucker."

Laughter. Raw. No warmth behind it.

The dog watched out of the corner of his eye. The trainer stood to the left, dressed in baggy jeans and a white T-shirt, showing arms decorated with ink, his head shaved to the scalp. The newcomer wore leather and carried a helmet under one arm. His eyes darted around.

"Let's get out of the goddamn sun," the stranger finally said. "Talk numbers. I got a kilo coming in at the end of the week."

As they stepped away, something struck the dog's flank. Hard. But he still didn't let go. Not yet.

"Release!"

With the command, the dog finally unclamped his jaws and dropped to the practice yard. His hind legs were numb, heavy with blood. But he turned to face the two men. Shoulders up, he squinted against the sun. The yard trainer stood with his wooden bat. The newcomer had his fists shoved into the pockets of his jacket and took a step back. The dog smelled the stranger's fear, a bitter dampness, like weeds soaked in old urine.

The trainer showed no such fear. He held his bat with one hand and scowled his dissatisfaction. He reached down and unhooked the plate of iron that hung from the dog collar. The plate dropped to the hard-packed dirt.

"Twenty-pound weight," the trainer told the stranger. "I'll get him up to *thirty* before next week. Helps thicken the neck up."

"Any thicker, and he won't be able to turn his head."

"Don't want him to *turn* his head. That'll cost me a mark in the ring." The bat pointed toward the line of cages. A boot kicked toward the dog's side. "Get your ass back into the kennel, Brutus."

The dog curled a lip, but he swung away, thirsty and exhausted. The fenced runs lined the rear of the yard. The floors were unwashed cement. From the neighboring cages, heads lifted toward him as he approached, then lowered sullenly. At the entrance, he lifted his leg and marked his spot. He fought not to tremble on his numb back leg. He couldn't show weakness.

He'd learned that on the first day.

"Git in there already!"

He was booted from behind as he entered the cage. The only shade came from a scrap of tin nailed over the back half of the run. The fence door clanged shut behind him.

He lumbered across the filthy space to his water dish, lowered his head, and drank.

Voices drifted away as the two headed toward the house. One question hung in the air. "How'd that monster get the name Brutus?"

The dog ignored them. That memory was a shard of yellowed bone buried deep. Over the past two winters, he'd tried to grind it away. But it had remained lodged, a truth that couldn't be forgotten.

He hadn't always been named Brutus.

"C'mere, Benny! That's a good boy!"

It was one of those days that flowed like warm milk, so sweet, so comforting, filling every hollow place with joy. The black pup bounded across the green and endless lawn. Even from across the yard, he smelled the piece of hot dog in the hand hidden behind the skinny boy's back. Behind him, a brick house climbed above a porch encased in vines and purple flowers. Bees buzzed, and frogs croaked a chorus with the approach of twilight.

"Sit! Benny, sit!"

The pup slid to a stop on the dewy grass and dropped to his haunches. He quivered all over. He wanted the hot dog. He wanted to lick the salt off those fingers. He wanted a scratch behind the ear. He wanted this day to never end.

"There's a good boy."

The hand came around, and fingers opened. The pup stuffed his cold nose into the palm, snapped up the piece of meat, then shoved closer. He waggled his whole hindquarters and wormed tighter to the boy.

Limbs tangled, and they both fell to the grass.

Laughter rang out like sunshine.

"Watch out! Here comes Junebug!" the boy's mother called from the porch. She rocked in a swing as she watched the boy and pup wrestle. Her voice was kind, her touch soft, her manner calm.

Much like the pup's own mother.

Benny remembered how his mother used to groom his forehead, nuzzle his ear, how she kept them all safe, all ten of them, tangled in a pile of paws, tails, and mewling complaints. Though even that memory was fading. He could hardly picture her face any longer, only the warmth of her brown eyes as she'd gazed down at them as they fed, fighting for a teat. And he'd had to fight, being the smallest of his brothers and sisters. But he'd never had to fight alone.

"Juneeeee!" the boy squealed.

A new weight leaped into the fray on the lawn. It was Benny's sister, Junebug. She yipped and barked and tugged on anything loose: shirtsleeve, pant leg, wagging tail. The last was her specialty. She'd pulled many of her fellow brothers and sisters off a teat by their tails, so Benny could have his turn.

Now those same sharp teeth clamped onto the tip of Benny's tail and tugged hard. He squealed and leaped straight up—not so much in pain, but in good-hearted play. The three of them rolled and rolled across the yard, until the boy collapsed on his back in surrender, leaving the brother and sister free to lick his face from either side.

"That's enough, Jason!" their new mother called from the porch.

"Oh, Mom . . ." The boy pushed up on one elbow, flanked by the two pups.

The pair stared across the boy's chest, tails wagging, tongues hanging, panting. His sister's eyes shone at him in that frozen moment of time, full of laughter, mischief, and delight. It was like looking at himself.

It was why they'd been picked together.

"Two peas in a pod, those two," the old man had said as he knelt over the litter and lifted brother and sister toward the visitors. "Boy's right ear is a blaze of white. Girl's left ear is the same. Mirror images. Make quite a pair, don't you think? Hate to separate them."

And in the end, he didn't have to. Brother and sister were taken to their new home together.

"Can't I play a little longer?" the boy called to the porch.

"No argument, young man. Your father will be home in a bit. So get cleaned up for dinner."

The boy stood up. Benny read the excitement in his sister's eyes. It matched his own. They'd not understood anything except for the mother's last word.

Dinner.

Bolting from the boy's side, the pair of pups raced toward the porch. Though smaller, Benny made up for his size with blazing speed. He shot across the yard toward the promise of a full dinner bowl and maybe a biscuit to chew afterwards. Oh, if only—

—then a familiar tug on his tail. The surprise attack from behind tripped his feet. He sprawled nose-first into the grass and slid with his limbs splayed out.

His sister bounded past him and up the steps.

Benny scrabbled his legs under him and followed. Though outsmarted as usual by his bigger sister, it didn't matter. His tail wagged and wagged.

He hoped these days would never end.

"Shouldn't we pull his ass out of there?"

"Not yet!"

Brutus paddled in the middle of the pool. His back legs churned the water, toes splayed out. His front legs fought to keep his snout above the water. His collar, a weighted steel chain, sought to drag him to the cement bottom. Braided cords of rope trapped him in the middle of the concrete swimming pool. His heart thundered in his throat. Each breath heaved with desperate sprays of water.

"Yo, man! You gonna drown 'im!"

"A little water won't kill him. He got a fight in two days. A big-ass show. I got a lot riding on it."

Paddling and wheeling his legs, water burned his eyes. His vision darkened at the edges. Still he saw the pit trainer off to the side, in trunks, no shirt. On his bare chest was inked two dogs snarling at each other. Two other men held the chains, keeping him from reaching the edge of the pool.

Bone-tired and cold, his back end began to slip deeper. He fought, but his head bobbed under. He took a gulp into his lungs. Choking, he kicked and got his nose above water again. He gagged his lungs clear. A bit of bile followed, oiling the water around his lips. Foam frothed from his nostrils.

"He done in, man. Pull 'im out."

"Let's see what he's got," the trainer said. "Bitch been in there longer than he ever done."

For another stretch of painful eternity, Brutus fought the pull of the chain and the waterlogged weight of his own body. His head sank with every fourth paddle. He breathed in as much stinging water as he did air. He had gone deaf to anything but his own hammering heart. His vision had shrunk to a blinding pinpoint. Then finally, he could no longer fight to the surface. More water flowed into his lungs. He sank—into the depths and into darkness.

But there was no peace.

The dark still terrified him.

The summer storm rattled the shutters and boomed with great claps that sounded like the end of all things. Spats of rain struck the windows, and flashes of lightning split the night sky.

Benny hid under the bed with his sister. He shivered against her side. She crouched, ears up, nose out. Each rumble was echoed in her chest as she growled back at the threatening noise. Benny leaked some of his terror, soaking the carpet under him. He was not so brave as his big sister.

. . . *boom, boom,* BOOM . . .

Brightness shattered across the room, casting away all shadows.

Benny whined and his sister barked.

A face appeared from atop the bed and leaned down to stare at them. The boy, his head upside down, lifted a finger to his lips. "Shh, Junie, you'll wake Dad."

But his sister would have none of that. She barked and barked, trying to scare off what lurked in the storm. The boy rolled off his bed and sprawled on the floor. Arms reached and scooped them both toward him. Benny went willingly.

"Eww . . . you're all wet."

Junie squirmed loose then ran around the room, barking, tail straight back, ears pricked high.

"Sheesh," the boy said, trying to catch her while cradling Benny.

A door banged open out in the hall. Footsteps echoed. The bedroom door swung open. Large bare legs like tree trunks entered. "Jason, son, I got to get up early."

"Sorry, Dad. The storm's got them spooked."

A long heavy sighed followed. The large man caught Junie and swung her up in his arms. She slathered his face with her tongue, tail beating against his arms. Still, she growled all the time as the sky rumbled back at them.

"They're going to have to get used to these storms," the man said. "These thunder-bumpers will be with us all summer."

"I'll take them downstairs. We can sleep on the

sofa on the back porch. If they're with me . . . maybe that'll help 'em get used to it."

Junie was passed to the boy.

"All right, son. But bring an extra blanket."

"Thanks, Dad."

A large hand clapped on the boy's shoulder. "You're taking good care of them. I'm proud of you. They're really getting huge."

The boy struggled with the two squirming pups and laughed. "I know!"

A few moments later, all three of them were buried in a nest of blankets atop a musty sofa. Benny smelled mice spoor and bird droppings, brought alive by the wind and dampness. Still, with all of them together, it was the best bed he'd ever slept in. Even the storm had quieted, though a heavy rain continued to pelt from the dark moonless skies. It beat against the shingled roof of the porch.

Just as Benny finally calmed enough to let his eyelids droop closed, his sister sprang to her feet, growling again, hackles up. She slithered out from under the blankets without disturbing the boy. Benny had no choice but to follow.

What is it? . . .

Benny's ears were now up and swiveling. From the top step of the porch, he stared out into the storm-swept yard. Tree limbs waved. Rain chased across the lawn in rippling sheets.

Then Benny heard it, too.

A rattle of the side gate. A few furtive whispers.

Someone was out there!

His sister shot from the porch. Without thinking, Benny ran after her. They raced toward the gate.

Whispers turned into words. "Quiet, asshole. Let me see if the dogs are back there!"

Benny saw the gate swing open. Two shadowy shapes stepped forward. Benny slowed—then caught the smell of meat, bloody and raw.

"What'd I tell ya?"

A tiny light bloomed in the darkness, spearing his sister. Junie slowed enough for Benny to catch up to her. One of the strangers dropped to a knee and held out an open palm. The rich, meaty smell swelled.

"You want it, don't cha? C'mon, you little bitches."

Junie snuck closer, more on her belly, tail twitching in tentative welcome. Benny sniffed and sniffed, nose up. The tantalizing odor drew him along behind his sister.

Once near the gate, the two dark shapes leaped on them. Something heavy dropped over Benny and wrapped tightly around him. He tried to cry out, but fingers clamped over his muzzle and trapped his scream to a muffled whine. He heard the same from his sister.

He was hauled up and carried away.

"Nothing like a stormy night to pick up bait. No one ever suspects. Always blame the thunder. Thinks it scared the little shits into running off."

"How much we gonna make?"

"Fifty a head easy."

"Nice."

Thunder clapped again, marking the end of Benny's old life.

Brutus entered the ring. The dog kept his head lowered, shoulders high, ears pulled flat against his skull. His hackles already bristled. It still hurt to breathe deeply, but the dog hid the pain. Buried in his lungs, a dull fire burned from the pool water, flaring with each breath. Cautiously, he took in all the scents around him.

The sand of the ring was still being raked clean of the blood from the prior fight. Still, the fresh spoor filled the old warehouse, along with the taint of grease and oil, the chalk of cement, and the bite of urine, sweat, and feces from both dog and man.

The fights had been going on from sunset until well into the night.

But no one had left.

Not until this match was over.

The dog had heard his name called over and over: "Brutus . . . man, look at the *cojones* on that *monstruo* . . . he a little-ass bastard, but I saw Brutus take on a dog twice his size . . . tore his throat clean open . . ."

As Brutus had waited in his pen, people trailed past, many dragging children, to stare at him. Fingers pointed, flashes snapped, blinding him, earning low growls. Finally, the handler had chased them all off with his bat.

"Move on! This ain't no free show. If you like him so goddamned much, go place a fucking bet!"

Now as Brutus passed through the gate in the ring's three-foot-tall wooden fence, shouts and whistles greeted him from the stands, along with raucous laughter and angry outbursts. The noise set Brutus's heart pounding. His claws dug into the sand, his muscles tensed.

They were the first to enter the ring.

Beyond the crowd spread a sea of cages and fenced-in pens. Large shadowy shapes stirred and paced.

There was little barking.

The dogs knew to save their strength for the ring.

"You'd better not lose," the pit handler mumbled, and tugged on the chain hooked to the dog's studded collar. Bright lights shone down into the pit. It reflected off the handler's shaved head, revealing the ink on his arms, black and red, like bloody bruises.

The pair kept to the ring's edge and waited. The trainer slapped the dog's flank, then wiped his wet hand on his jeans. Brutus's coat was still damp. Prior to the fight, each dog had been washed by their opponent's handler, to make sure there was no slippery grease or poison oils worked into the coat to give a dog an advantage.

As they waited for their opponent to enter the ring, Brutus smelled the sheen of excitement off the handler. A sneer remained frozen on the man's face, showing a hint of teeth.

Beyond the fence, another man approached the edge of the ring. Brutus recognized him by the way he sniffed between his words and the bitter trace of fear that accompanied him. If the man had been another dog, he would've had his tail tucked to his belly and a whine flowing from his throat.

"I placed a buttload on this bastard," the man said as he stepped to the fence and eyed Brutus.

"So?" his handler answered.

"I just saw Gonzales's dog. Christ, man, are you nuts? That monster's half bull mastiff."

The handler shrugged. "Yeah, but he got only one good eye. Brutus'll take him down. Or at least, he'd better." Again the chain jerked.

The man shifted behind the fence and leaned closer. "Is there some sort of fix going on here?"

"Fuck you. I don't need a fix."

"But I heard you once owned that other dog. That one-eyed bastard."

The handler scowled. "Yeah, I did. Sold him to Gonzales a couple years ago. Didn't think the dog would live. After he lost his fuckin' eye and all. Bitch got all infected. Sold him to that Spic for a couple bottles of Special K. Stupidest deal I ever made. Dog gone and made that beaner a shitload of money. He's been rubbin' it in my face ever since. But today's payback."

The chain yanked and lifted Brutus off his toes.

"You'd better not lose this show. Or we might just have ourselves another barbecue back at the crib."

The dog heard the threat behind the words. Though he didn't fully understand, he sensed the meaning. *Don't lose.* Over the past two winters, he'd seen defeated dogs shot in the head, strangled to death with their own chains, or allowed to be torn to pieces in the ring. Last summer, a bull terrier had bit Brutus's handler in the calf. The dog had been blood-addled after losing a match and had lashed out. Later, back at the yard, the bull terrier had tried mewling for forgiveness, but the handler had soaked the dog down and set him on fire. The flaming terrier had run circles around the yard, howling, banging blindly into runs and fences. The men in the yard had laughed and laughed, falling down on their sides.

The dogs in their kennels had watched silently.

They all knew the truth of their lives.

Never lose.

Finally, a tall skinny man stepped to the center of the ring. He lifted an arm high. "Dogs to your scratch lines!"

The far gate of the ring opened, and a massive shape bulled into the ring, half-dragging his small, beefy handler, a man who wore a big grin and a cowboy hat. But Brutus's attention fixed to the dog. The mastiff was a wall of muscle. His ears had been cropped to nubs. He had no tail. His paws mashed deep into the sand as he fought toward the scratch line.

As the beast pulled forward, he kept his head cocked to the side, allowing his one eye to scan the ring. The other eye was a scarred knot.

The man in the center of the ring pointed to the two lines raked into the sand. "To the scratch! It's the final show of the night, folks! What you've been waiting for! Two champions brought together again! Brutus against Caesar!"

Laughter and cheers rose from the crowd. Feet pounded on the stands' boards.

But all Brutus heard was that one name.

Caesar.

He suddenly trembled all over. The shock rocked through him as if his very bones rattled. He fought to hold steady and stared across at his opponent—and remembered.

"Caesar! C'mon, you bastard, you hungry or not?"

Under the midmorning sun, Benny hung from a stranger's hand. Fingers scruffed the pup's neck and dangled him in the center of a strange yard. Benny cried and piddled a stream to the dirt below. He saw other dogs behind fences. Smelled more elsewhere. His sister was clutched in the arms of one of the men who'd nabbed them out of their yard. His sister barked out sharply.

"Shut that bitch up. She's distracting him."

"I don't want to see this," the man said, but he pinched his sister's muzzle shut.

"Oh, grow some damn balls. Whatcha think I paid you a hundred bucks for? Dog's gotta eat, don't he?" The man dug his fingers tighter into Benny's scruff and shook him hard. "And bait is bait."

Another man called from the shadows across the yard. "Hey, Juice! How much weight you want on the sled this time?"

"Go for fifteen bricks."

"Fifteen?"

"I need Caesar muscled up good for the fight next week."

Benny heard the knock and scrape of something heavy.

"Here he comes!" the shadow man called over. "He must be hungry!"

Out of the darkness, a monster appeared. Benny had never seen a dog so large. The giant heaved against a harness strapped across his chest. Ropes of drool trailed from the corner of his lips. Claws dug into the dark dirt as he hauled forward. Behind him, attached to the harness, was a sled on steel runners. It was piled high with blocks of cement.

The man holding Benny laughed deep in his throat. "He be damned hungry! Haven't fed him in two days!"

Benny dribbled out more of his fear. The monster's gaze was latched on to him. Benny read the red, raw hunger in those eyes. The drool flowed thicker.

"Hurry it up, Caesar! If you want your breakfast!"

The man took a step back with Benny.

The large brute pulled harder, shouldering into the harness, his long tongue hanging, frothing with foam. He panted and growled. The sled dragged across the dirt with the grating sound of gnawed bone.

Benny's heart hammered in his small chest. He tried to squirm away, but he couldn't escape the man's iron grip . . . or the unwavering gaze of the monster. It was coming for him. He wailed and cried.

Time stretched to a long sharp line of terror.

Steadily the beast came at him.

Finally, the man burst out a satisfied snort. "Good enough! Unhook him!"

Another man ran out of the shadows and yanked on a leather lead. The harness dropped from the monster's shoulders, and the huge dog bounded across the yard, throwing slather with each step.

The man swung his arm back, then tossed Benny forward. The pup flew high into the air, spinning tail over ear. He was too terrified to scream. As he spun, he caught glimpses below of the monster pounding after him—but he also spotted his sister. The man who held Junie had started to turn away, not wanting to watch. He must have loosened his grip enough to let Junie slip her nose free. She bit hard into his thumb.

Then Benny hit the ground and rolled across the yard. The impact knocked the air from his chest. He lay stunned as the larger dog barreled toward him. Terrified, Benny used the only advantage he had—his speed.

He rolled to his feet and darted to the left. The big dog couldn't turn fast enough and skidded past where he'd landed. Benny fled across the yard, tucking his back legs under his front in his desperation to go faster. He heard the huffing of the monster at his tail.

If he could just get under the low sled, hide there . . .

But he didn't know the yard. One paw hit a broken tile in the scrubby weeds, and he lost his footing. He hit his shoulder and rolled. He came to rest on his side as the huge dog lunged at him.

Benny winced. Desperate, he exposed his belly and

piddled on himself, showing his submission. But it didn't matter. Lips rippled back from yellow teeth.

Then the monster suddenly jerked to a stop in mid-lunge, accompanied by a surprised yelp. The brute spun around. Benny saw something attached to his tail.

It was Junie. Dropped by her captor, she had come at the monster with her usual sneak attack. The monster spun several more times as Junie remained clamped to his tail. This was no playful nip. She must've dug in deep with her sharp teeth. In attempting to throw her off, the large dog only succeeded in stripping more fur and skin from his tail as Junie was tossed about.

Blood sprayed across the dirt.

But finally even Junie couldn't resist the brute's raw strength. She went flying, her muzzle bloody. The monster followed and landed hard on her. Blocked by his bulk, Benny couldn't see—but he heard.

A sharp cry from Junie, followed by the crunch of bone.

No!

Benny leaped to his feet and ran at the monster. There was no plan—only a red, dark anger. He speared straight at the monster. He caught a glimpse of a torn leg, bone showing. The monster gripped his sister and shook her. She flopped limply. Crimson sprayed, then poured from his lips, mixed with drool.

With the sight, Benny plummeted into a dark place, a pit from which he knew he'd never escape. He leaped headlong at the monster and landed on the brute's face. He clawed and bit and gouged, anything to get him to let his sister go.

But he was so much smaller.

A toss of the blocky head, and Benny went flying away—forever lost in blood, fury, and despair.

As Brutus stared at Caesar, it all came back. The past and present overlapped and muddled into a crimson blur. He stood at the scratch line in the ring without remembering walking to it. He could not say who stood at the line.

Brutus or Benny.

After the mutilation of his sister, Benny had been spared a brutal death. The yard trainer had been impressed by his fire. *"A real Brutus, this one. Taking on Caesar all alone! Fast, too. See him juke and run. Maybe he's too good for just bait."*

Caesar had not fared so well after their brief fight. During the attack, a back claw had split the large dog's eyelid and sliced across his left eye, blinding that side. Even the tail wound from Junie's bite had festered. The yard trainer had tried cutting off his tail with an ax and burning the stub with a flaming piece of wood. But the eye and tail got worse. For a week, the reek of pus and dying flesh flowed from his kennel. Flies swarmed in black gusts. Finally, a stranger in a cowboy hat arrived with a wheelbarrow, shook hands with the handler, and hauled Caesar away, muzzled, feverish, and moaning.

Everyone thought he'd died.

They'd been wrong.

Both dogs toed the scratch line in the sand. Caesar did not recognize his opponent. No acknowledgment shone out of that one eye, only bloodlust and blind fury. The monster lunged at the end of his chain, digging deep into the sand.

Brutus bunched his back legs under him. Old fury fired through his blood. His muzzle snarled into a long growl, one rising from his very bones.

The tall skinny man lifted both arms. "Dogs ready!" He brought his arms down while stepping back. "Go!"

With a snap, they were loosed from their chains. Both dogs leaped upon one another. Bodies slammed together amid savage growls and flying spittle.

Brutus went first for Caesar's blind side. He bit into the nub of ear, seeking a hold. Cartilage ripped. Blood flowed over his tongue. The grip was too small to hold for long.

In turn, Caesar struck hard, using his heavier bulk to roll Brutus. Fangs sank into his shoulder. Brutus lost his hold and found himself pinned under that weight. Caesar bodily lifted him and slammed him into the sand.

But Brutus was still fast. He squirmed and twisted until he was belly to belly with the monster. He jackrabbit punched up with his back legs and broke Caesar's hold on his shoulder. Loosed, Brutus went for the throat above him. But Caesar snapped down at him at the same time. They ended muzzle to muzzle, tearing at each other. Brutus on bottom, Caesar on top.

Blood spat and flew.

He kicked again and raked claws across the tender belly of his opponent, gouging deep—then lunged up and latched on to Caesar's jowl. Using the hold, he kicked and hauled his way out from under the bulk. He kept to the beast's left, his blind side.

Momentarily losing sight of Brutus, Caesar jagged the wrong direction. He left his flank open. Brutus lashed out for a hind leg. He bit deep into the thick meat at the back of the thigh and chomped with all the muscles in his jaws. He yanked hard and shook his head.

In that moment of raw fury, Brutus flashed to a small limp form, clamped in bloody jaws, shaken and broken. A blackness fell over his vision. He used his entire body—muscle, bone, and blood—to rip and slash. The thick ligament at the back of the leg tore away from the ankle.

Caesar roared, but Brutus kept his grip and hauled up onto his hind legs. He flipped the other onto his back. Only then did he let go and slam on top of the other. He lunged for the exposed throat and bit deep. Fangs sank into tender flesh. He shook and ripped, snarled and dug.

From beyond the blackness, a whistle blew. It was the signal to break hold and return to their corners. Handlers ran up.

"Release!" his trainer yelled and grabbed the back of his collar.

Brutus heard the cheering, recognized the command. But it was all far away. He was deep in the pit.

Hot blood filled his mouth, flowed it into his lungs,

soaked into the sand. Caesar writhed under him. Fierce growling turned into mewling. But Brutus was deaf to it. Blood flowed into all the empty places inside him, trying to fill it up, but failing.

Something struck his shoulders. Again and again. The handler's wooden bat. But Brutus kept his grip locked on the other dog's throat. He couldn't let go, trapped forever in the pit.

Wood splintered across his back.

Then a new noise cut through the roaring in his ears. More whistles, sharper and urgent, accompanied by the strident blare of sirens. Flashing lights dazzled through the darkness. Shouts followed, along with commands amplified to a piercing urgency.

"This is the police! Everyone on your knees! Hands on heads!"

Brutus finally lifted his torn muzzle from the throat of the other dog. Caesar lay unmoving on the sand, soaked in a pool of blood. Brutus lifted his eyes to the chaos around him. People fled the stands. Dogs barked and howled. Dark figures in helmets and carrying clear shields closed a circle around the area, forming a larger ring around the sand pit. Through the open doors of the warehouse, cars blazed in the night.

Wary, Brutus stood over the body of the dead dog.

He felt no joy at the killing. Only a dead numbness.

His trainer stood a step away. A string of anger flowed from the man's lips. He threw the broken stub of his bat into the sand. An arm pointed at Brutus.

"When I say release, you *release*, you dumb sack of shit!"

Brutus stared dully at the arm pointed at him, then to the face. From the man's expression, Brutus knew what the handler saw. It shone out of the dog's entire being. Brutus was trapped in a pit deeper than anything covered in sand, a pit from which he could never escape, a hellish place of pain and hot blood.

The man's eyes widened, and he took a step back. The beast stalked after him, no longer dog, only a creature of rage and fury.

Without warning—no growl, no snarl—Brutus lunged at the trainer. He latched on to the man's arm. The same arm that dangled pups as bait, an arm attached to the real monster of the sandy ring, a man who called horrors out of the shadows and set dogs on fire.

Teeth clamped over the pale wrist. Jaws crushed down. Bones ground and crackled under the pressure.

The man screamed.

From the narrow corner of one eye, Brutus watched a helmeted figure rush at them, an arm held up, pointing a black pistol.

A flash from the muzzle.

Then a sizzle of blinding pain.

And at last, darkness again.

Brutus lay on the cold concrete floor of the kennel. He rested his head on his paws and stared out the fenced gate. A wire-framed ceiling lamp shone off the whitewashed cement walls and lines of kennels.

He listened with a deaf ear to the shuffle of other dogs, to the occasional bark or howl.

Behind him, a small door led to an outside fenced-in pen. Brutus seldom went out there. He preferred the shadows. His torn muzzle had been knitted together with staples, but it still hurt to drink. He didn't eat. He had been here for five days, noting the rise and fall of sunlight through the doorway.

People came by occasionally to stare at him. To scribble on a wooden chart hanging on his door. Men in white jackets injected him twice a day, using a noose attached to a long steel pole to hold him pinned to the wall. He growled and snapped. More out of irritation than true anger. He just wanted to be left alone.

He had woken here after that night in the pit.

And a part of him still remained back there.

Why am I still breathing?

Brutus knew guns. He recognized their menacing shapes and sizes, the tang of their oils, the bitter reek of their smoke. He'd seen scores of dogs shot, some quickly, some for sport. But the pistol that had fired back at the ring had struck with a sizzle that twisted his muscles and arched his back.

He lived.

That, more than anything, kept him angry and sick of spirit.

A shuffle of rubber shoes drew his attention. He didn't lift his head, only twitched his eyes. It was too early for the pole and needles.

"He's over here," a voice said. "Animal Control just got the judge's order to euthanasize all the dogs this morning. This one's on the list, too. Heard they had to Taser him off his own trainer. So I wouldn't hold out much hope."

Brutus watched three people step before his kennel. One wore a gray coverall zippered up the front. He smelled of disinfectant and tobacco.

"Here he is. It was lucky we scanned him and found that old HomeAgain microchip. We were able to pull up your address and telephone. So you say someone stole him from your backyard?"

"Two years ago," a taller man said, dressed in black shoes and a suit.

Brutus pulled back one ear. The voice was vaguely familiar.

"They took both him and his littermate," the man continued. "We thought they'd run off during a thunderstorm."

Brutus lifted his head. A boy pushed between the two taller men and stepped toward the gate. Brutus met his eyes. The boy was older, taller, more gangly of limb, but his scent was as familiar as an old sock. As the boy stared into the dark kennel, the initial glaze of hope in his small face crumbled away into horror.

The boy's voice was an appalled squeak. "Benny?"

Shocked and disbelieving, Brutus slunk back on his belly. He let out a low warning growl as he shied away. He didn't want to remember . . . and especially didn't want this. It was too cruel.

The boy glanced over his shoulder to the taller man. "It is Benny, isn't it, Dad?"

"I think so." An arm pointed. "He's got that white

blaze over his right ear." The voice grew slick with dread. "But what did they do to him?"

The man in the coveralls shook his head. "Brutalized him. Turned him into a monster."

"Is there any hope for rehabilitation?"

He shook his head and tapped the chart. "We had all the dogs examined by a behaviorist. She signed off that he's unsalvageable."

"But, Dad, it's *Benny*...."

Brutus curled into the back of the run, as deep into the shadows as he could get. The name was like the lash of a whip.

The man pulled a pen from his coverall pocket. "Since you're still legally his owners and had no part in the dogfighting ring, we can't put him down until you sign off on it."

"Dad..."

"Jason, we had Benny for two *months*. They've had him for two *years*."

"But it's still Benny. I know it. Can't we try?"

The coverall man crossed his arms and lowered his voice with warning. "He's unpredictable and damn powerful. A bad combination. He even mauled his trainer. They had to amputate the man's hand."

"Jason..."

"I know. I'll be careful, Dad. I promise. But he deserves a chance, doesn't he?"

His father sighed. "I don't know."

The boy knelt down and matched Brutus's gaze. The dog wanted to turn away, but he couldn't. He locked eyes and slipped into a past he'd thought long buried away, of fingers clutching hot dogs, chases across green lawns, and endless sunny days. He pushed it all way. It was too painful, too prickled with guilt. He didn't deserve even the memory. It had no place in the pit.

A low rumble shook through his chest.

Still, the boy clutched the fence and faced the monster inside. He spoke with the effortless authority of innocence and youth.

"It's *still* Benny. Somewhere in there."

Brutus turned away and closed his eyes with an equally firm conviction.

The boy was wrong.

Brutus slept on the back porch. Three months had passed and his sutures and staples were gone. The medicines in his food had faded away. Over the months, he and the family had come to an uneasy truce, a cold stalemate.

Each night, they tried to coax him into the house, especially as the leaves were turning brown and drifting up into piles beneath the hardwoods and the lawn turned frosty in the early morning. But Brutus kept to his porch, even avoiding the old sofa covered in a ragged thick comforter. He kept his distance from all things. He still flinched from a touch and growled when he ate, unable to stop himself.

But they no longer used the muzzle.

Perhaps they sensed the defeat that had turned his

heart to stone. So he spent his days staring across the yard, only stirring occasionally, pricking up an ear if a stray squirrel should dare bound along the fencerow, its tail fluffed and fearless.

The back door opened, and the boy stepped out onto the porch. Brutus gained his feet and backed away.

"Benny, are you sure you don't want to come inside? I made a bed for you in the kitchen." He pointed toward the open door. "It's warm. And look, I have a treat for you."

The boy held out a hand, but Brutus already smelled the bacon, still smoking with crisply burned fat. He turned away. Back at the training yard, the others had tried to use bait on him, too. But after his sister, Brutus had always refused, no matter how hungry.

The dog crossed to the top step of the porch and lay down.

The boy came and sat with him, keeping his distance.

Brutus let him.

They sat for a long time. The bacon still in his fingers. The boy finally nibbled it away himself. "Okay, Benny, I have some homework."

The boy began to get up, paused, then carefully reached out to touch him on the head. Brutus didn't growl, but his fur bristled. Noting the warning, the boy sagged, pulled back his hand, and stood up.

"Okay. See ya in the morning, Benny boy."

He didn't watch the boy leave, but he listened for the

door to clap shut. Satisfied that he was alone, he settled his head to his paws. He stared out into the yard.

The moon was already up, full-faced and bright. Lights twinkled. Distantly, he listened as the household settled in for the night. A television whispered from the front room. He heard the boy call down from the upstairs. His mother answered.

Then suddenly Brutus was on his feet, standing stiff, unsure what had drawn him up. He kept dead still. Only his ears swiveled.

A knock sounded on the front door.

In the night.

"I'll get it," the mother called out.

Brutus twisted, bolted for the old sofa on the porch, and climbed half into it, enough to see through the picture window. The view offered a straight shot down the central dark hallway to the lighted front room.

Brutus watched the woman step to the door and pull it open.

Before she'd gotten it more than a foot wide, the door slammed open. It struck her and knocked her down. Two men charged inside, wearing dark clothes and masks pulled over their heads. Another kept watch by the open door. The first man backed into the hallway and kept a large pistol pointed toward the woman on the floor. The other intruder sidled to the left and aimed a gun toward someone in the dining room.

"DON'T MOVE!" the second gunman shouted.

Brutus tensed. He knew that voice, graveled and merciless. In an instant, his heart hammered in his chest, and his fur flushed up all over his body, quivering with fury.

"Mom? Dad?" The boy called from the top of the stairs.

"Jason!" the father answered from the dining room. "Stay up there!"

The leader stepped farther into the room. He shoved his gun out, holding it crooked. "Old man, sit your ass down!"

"What do you want?"

The gun poked again. "Yo! Where's my dog?"

"Your dog?" the mother asked on the floor, her voice trembling with fear.

"Brutus!" the man hollered. He lifted his other arm and bared the stump of a wrist. "I owe that bitch some payback . . . and that includes anyone taking care of his ass! In fact, we're going to have ourselves an old-fashioned barbecue." He turned to the man in the doorway. "What are you waiting for? Go get the gasoline?"

The man vanished into the night.

Brutus dropped back to the porch and retreated to the railing. He bunched his back legs.

"Yo! Where you keeping my damn dog? I know you got him!"

Brutus sprang forward, shoving out with all the strength in his body. He hit the sofa and vaulted over it. Glass shattered as he struck the window with the crown of his skull. He flew headlong into the room and landed in the kitchen. His front paws struck the floor before the first piece of glass. He bounded away as shards crashed and skittered across the checker-board linoleum.

Down the hall, the first gunman began to turn, drawn by the noise. But he was too late. Brutus flew down the hall and dived low. He snatched the gunman by the ankle and ripped the tendon, flipping the man as he ran under him. The man's head hit the corner of a walnut hall table, and he went down hard.

Brutus spotted a man out on the front porch, frozen in midstep, hauling two large red jugs. The man saw Brutus barreling toward him. His eyes got huge. He dropped the jugs, spun around, and fled away.

A pistol fired, deafening in the closed space. Brutus felt a kick in his front leg. It shattered under him, but he was already in midleap toward the one-handed gunman, his old trainer and handler. Brutus hit him like a sack of cement. He head-butted the man in the chest. Weight and momentum knocked the legs out from under the man. They fell backwards together.

The pistol blasted a second time.

Something burned past Brutus's ear, and plaster rained down from the ceiling.

Then they both hit the hardwood floor. The man landed flat on his back, Brutus on top. The gun flew from his fingers and skittered under the dining room chair.

His trainer tried to kick Brutus away, but he'd taught the dog too well. Brutus dodged the knee. With a roar, he lunged for the man's throat. The man grabbed one-handed for an ear, but Brutus had lost most of the flap in an old fight. The ear slipped from the man's grip, and Brutus snapped for the tender neck. Fangs sank for the sure kill.

Then a shout barked behind him. "Benny! No!"

From out the corner of an eye, he saw the father crouched by the dining room table. He had recovered the pistol and pointed it at Brutus.

"Benny! Down! Let him go!"

From the darkness of the pit, Brutus growled back at the father. Blood flowed as Brutus clamped harder on his prey. He refused to release. Under him, the trainer screamed and gurgled. One fist punched blindly, but Brutus ground his jaws tighter. Blood flowed more heavily.

"Benny, let him go now!"

Another sharper voice squeaked in fear. It came from the stairs. "No, Dad!"

"Jason, I can't let him kill someone."

"Benny!" the boy screamed. "Please, Benny!"

Brutus ignored them. He wasn't Benny. He knew the pit was where he truly belonged, where he'd always end up. As his vision narrowed and darkness closed over him, he let himself fall deeper into that black, bottomless well, dragging the man with him. Brutus knew he couldn't escape; neither would he let this one go.

It was time to end all this.

But as Brutus sank into the pit, slipping away into the darkness, something stopped him, held him from falling. It made no sense. Though no one was behind him, he felt a distinct tug. On his tail. Holding him steady, then slowly drawing him back from the edge of the pit. Comprehension came slowly, seeping through the despair. He knew that touch. It was familiar as his own heart. Though it had no real strength, it broke him, shattered him into pieces.

He remembered that tug, from long ago, her special ambush.

Done to protect him.

Ever his guardian.

Even now.

And always.

No, Benny . . .

"No, Benny!" the boy echoed.

The dog heard them both, the voices of those who loved him, blurring the line between past and present—not with blood and darkness, but with sunlight and warmth.

With a final shake against the horror, the dog turned his back on the pit. He unclamped his jaws and tumbled off the man's body. He stood on shaking limbs.

To the side, the trainer gagged and choked behind his black mask. The father closed in on him with the gun.

The dog limped away, three-legged, one forelimb dangling.

Footsteps approached from behind. The boy appeared at his side and laid a palm on his shoulder. He left his hand resting there. Not afraid.

The dog trembled, then leaned into him, needing reassurance.

And got it.

"Good boy, Benny. Good boy."

The boy sank to his knees and hugged his arms around the dog.

At long last . . . Benny let him.

David Morrell

A soldier's life often depends on his fellow soldiers, forging a bond that can be closer than that of brothers. But what happens when it's your brothers who are trying to *kill* you? . . .

The creator of Rambo, one of the best-known warriors in contemporary fiction, David Morrell is a bestselling author who has over eighteen million copies of his novels in print, and whose thrillers have been translated into twenty-six languages and turned into record-breaking films as well as top-rated TV miniseries. His famous first novel, *First Blood*, was the origin of the character Rambo. He is also the author of more than twenty-eight other books, including the classic Brotherhood of the Rose spy trilogy, *The Fifth Profession, Assumed Identity, The Covenant of the Flame, Extreme Denial, Desperate Measures, Creepers*, and many others. His short fiction has been collected in *Black Evening* and *Nightscape*, and he's also produced a book of writing advice, *The Successful Novelist*, as well as other nonfiction books. Best known for his thrillers, he has also written horror, fantasy, and historical novels, and has three times won the

Bram Stoker Award. The International Thriller Writers organization honored him with its prestigious Thriller Master Award. His most recent book is *The Shimmer*. He lives in Santa Fe, New Mexico.

My Name Is Legion

*The mission is sacred. You will see it through to the
end at any price.*

—Part of the French Foreign Legion's
Code of Honor

Syria
June 20, 1941

"The colonel found someone to carve a wooden
hand."

Hearing Durado's voice behind him, Kline didn't
turn. He kept his gaze focused between the two boulders that protected him from sniper fire. Propped
against a rocky slope, he stared toward the yellow
buildings in the distance.

"Wooden hand?" The reference didn't puzzle Kline,
but the timing did. "This isn't April."

"I guess the colonel figures we need a reminder,"
Durado said.

"Considering what'll happen tomorrow, he's probably right."

"The ceremony's at fifteen hundred hours."

"Can't go," Kline said. "I'm on duty here till dark."

"There'll be a second ceremony. The sergeant told me to come back later and take your place so you can attend."

Kline nodded his thanks. "Reminds me of when I was a kid and my family went to church. The colonel's become our preacher."

"See anything out there?" Durado asked.

"Nothing that moves—except the heat haze."

"Tomorrow will be different."

Kline heard the scrape of rocks under combat boots as Durado walked away. A torn blanket was over him. His uniform was minimal—tan shorts and a short-sleeved shirt, faded by the desert sun. His headgear was the Legion's famed *kepi blanc*, a white cap with a flat, round top and black visor. It too was badly faded by the sun. A flap at the back covered his neck and ears, but for further protection, Kline relied on the blanket to shield his bare legs and arms and keep the rocks on each side from absorbing so much heat that they burned him.

His bolt-action MAS 36 rifle was next to him, ready to be sighted and fired if a sniper showed himself. Of course, that would reveal Kline's position, attracting enemy bullets, forcing him to find a new vantage point. Given that he'd smoothed the ground and made this emplacement as comfortable as possible, he preferred to hold his fire until tomorrow.

Enemy bullets? Those words had automatically come to mind, but under the circumstances, they troubled him.

Yes, pulling the trigger could wait until tomorrow.

Kline wasn't his real name. Seven years earlier, in 1934, he'd arrived at the Old Fort in the Vincennes area of Paris, where he'd volunteered to join the French Foreign Legion, so-called because the unit was the only way foreigners could enlist in the French army.

"American," a sergeant had sniffed.

Kline had received a meal of coffee, bread, and watery bean soup. In a crowded barracks, he slept on a straw-filled mattress at the top of a three-tiered metal bunk. Two days later, he and twenty other newcomers, mostly Spaniards, Italians, and Greeks, with one Irishman, were transported via train south to Marseilles. They were herded into the foul-smelling lower hold of a ship, where they vomited for two days during a rough voyage across the Mediterranean to Algeria. At last, trucks took them along a dusty, jolting road to the Legion's headquarters at the remote desert town of Sidi Bel Abbès. The heat was overwhelming.

There, Kline's interrogation had started. Although the Legion had a reputation for attracting criminals on the run from the law, in reality it understood the difficulty of making disciplined soldiers out of them and didn't knowingly accept the worst offenders. As a consequence, each candidate was questioned in detail, his background investigated as thoroughly as possible. Many volunteers, while not criminals, had reached a dead end in their lives and wanted a new start, along with the chance to become French citizens.

If the Legion accepted them, they were allowed to choose a new name and received new identities.

Certainly, Kline had reached a dead end. Before arriving in France and volunteering for the Legion, he'd lived in the United States, in Springfield, Illinois, where the Great Depression had taken away his factory job and kept him from supporting his wife and infant daughter. He'd made bad friends and acted as the lookout for a bank robbery in which a guard was killed and the only cash taken was $24.95. During the month he'd spent eluding the police, his daughter had died from whooping cough. His grief-crazed wife had slit her wrists, bleeding to death. The single thing that had kept Kline from doing the same was his determination to punish himself, and that goal had finally prompted him to do the most extreme thing he could imagine. Responding to an article in a newspaper that he happened to find on a street, he ended his anguished wandering by working as a coal shoveler on a ship that took him to Le Havre in France, from where he walked all the way to Paris and enlisted in the Legion.

According to the newspaper article, no way of life could be more arduous, and Kline was pleased to discover that the article understated the facts. Managing to hide his criminal past, he endured a seemingly endless indoctrination of weapons exercises, hand-to-hand combat drills, forced marches, and other tests of endurance that gave him satisfaction because of the pain they caused. In the end, when he received the certificate that formally admitted him to the Legion, he felt that he had indeed made a new start. Never forgiving himself or the world or God for the loss of his family, he felt an unexpected deep kinship with a group that had "Living by Chance" as part of its credo.

The Irishman called himself Rourke. Because he and Kline were the only men who spoke English in their section of volunteers, they became friends during their long months of training. Like everyone else in the Legion, Rourke referred only vaguely to his past, but his skill with rifles and explosives made Kline suspect that he'd belonged to the Irish Republican Army, that he'd killed British soldiers in an effort to make the British leave his country, and that he'd sought refuge in the Legion after the British Army had vowed to use all its resources to hunt him down.

"I don't suppose you're a Roman Catholic," Rourke said one night after they completed a fifty-mile march in punishing heat. His upward-tilted accent sounded melodic, despite his pain as they bandaged the blisters on their feet.

"No, I'm a Baptist," Kline answered, then corrected himself. "At least, that's how I was raised. I don't go to church anymore."

"I didn't see many Baptists in Ireland," Rourke joked. "Do you know your Bible?"

"My father read from it out loud every night."

" 'My name is legion,' " Rourke quoted.

" 'For we are many,' " Kline responded. "The gospel

according to Mark. A possessed man says that to Jesus, trying to explain how many demons are in him. . . . Legion." The word made Kline finally understand where Rourke was taking the conversation. "You're comparing us to devils?"

"After putting us through that march, the sergeant qualifies as one."

Kline couldn't help chuckling.

"For certain, the sergeant wants the *enemy* to think we're devils," Rourke said. "That's what the Mexican soldiers called the legionnaires after the battle at Camerone, isn't it?"

"Yes. 'These are not men. They're demons.' "

"You have a good memory."

"I wish I didn't."

"No more than I." Rourke's normally mischievous eyes looked dull. His freckles were covered with dust. "Anyway, after a march like that, we might as well be devils."

"How do you figure?"

Wiping blood from his feet, Rourke somehow made what he said next sound like another joke. "We understand what it feels like to be in hell."

Rourke was gone now.

Kline's years in the Legion had taught him to banish weak emotions. Nonetheless, the loss of his friend made him grieve. As he stared between the boulders toward the seemingly abandoned sandstone buildings, he thought about the many conversations he and Rourke had shared. In 1940, as Germany increasingly threatened Europe, they'd fought side-by-side in the concrete fortifications of the Maginot Line that France had built along its border with Germany. Their unit endured relentless assaults from machine guns, tanks, and dive-bombers, counterattacking whenever the Germans showed the slightest sign of weakness.

The casualties were massive. Still, Kline, Rourke, and their fellow legionnaires continued fighting. When the officer in charge of a regular French unit insisted that no one had a chance and that surrender to the Germans was the only reasonable choice, the Legion commander had shot him to death. A second French officer tried to retaliate, and this time, it was Kline who did the shooting, defending his commander, whose back was turned. Every legionnaire understood. From their first day of training, absolutes were drilled into them, and one of them was, *Never surrender your arms*.

"What do Baptists believe?" Rourke asked the night after another battle. They were cleaning their rifles.

"God punishes us for our sins," Kline answered.

"What can you do to be saved?"

"Nothing. It all depends on Christ's mercy."

"Mercy?" Rourke's thin face tightened as he considered the word. "Seen much of that?"

"No."

"Me, neither," Rourke said.

"What do *Catholics* believe about being saved?" Kline asked.

"We say we're sorry for our sins and do penance to prove we mean it."

Thinking of his wife and daughter, of how he'd left them alone while he'd helped in the bank robbery, of how his wife had committed suicide after his daughter had died, Kline asked, "But what if your sin's so bad that you can't possibly make up for it?"

"I ask myself that a lot. I was an altar boy. I almost went into the seminary. But maybe I'm in the wrong religion. You say God punishes us for our sins and our only hope is to depend on His mercy? Makes sense to me."

That was when Kline decided that Rourke hadn't joined the Legion to avoid being hunted by the British Army. No, he was in the Legion because, like Kline, he'd done something horribly wrong and was punishing himself.

Kline missed his friend. Staring between the boulders, he sought distraction from his regrets by reaching for his canteen under the blanket that protected him from the sun. He unscrewed it and withdrew his gaze from the ancient sandstone buildings only long enough to drink the metallic-tasting, warm water.

He focused again on the target. Men with rifles were over there, watching this ridge. Of that, he had no doubt. There would be a battle tomorrow. Of that, he had no doubt, either.

Behind him, footsteps approached, dislodging rocks.

Durado's voice said, "The first ceremony's over. I'll take your place."

"Everything's quiet," Kline reported.

"It won't be tomorrow. The captain says we're definitely going in."

Kline pulled the blanket off him, feeling the harsh rays of the sun on his now-exposed arms and legs. Careful to stay low, he made his way along the bottom of the rocky slope. After passing other sentry emplacements, he reached the main part of camp, where half the Thirteenth Demi-Brigade was in formation next to its tents.

The air was blindingly bright as the colonel stepped onto a boulder, facing them. His name was Amilakvari. He was a Russian who'd escaped the Communist revolution when he was eleven and joined the Legion when he was twenty. Now in his mid-thirties, he looked gaunt and sinewy after months of desert combat. Nonetheless, he wore a full-dress uniform.

Despite his Russian background, the colonel addressed the legionnaires in French, their common language, even though privately most still spoke their native language and formed friendships on the basis of it, as Kline had done with Rourke. Solemn, the colonel raised a hand, but the hand didn't belong to him. It had been carved from a block of wood, the palm and the fingers amazingly lifelike.

Neither Kline nor anyone else needed to be told that it was supposed to be a replica of the wooden hand of the Legion's greatest hero, Captain Jean Danjou. All of them knew by heart the events that the colonel was about to describe, and every battle-hardened one of them also knew that, before the ceremony was completed, tears would stream down his face.

Camarón, Mexico. The Legion called it Camerone.

As many times as Kline had heard the story, with each telling it became more powerful. Listening to the colonel recite it, Kline sensed he was there, feeling the cool night air as the patrol set out at 1 A.M. on April 30, 1863.

They were on foot: sixty-two soldiers, three officers, and Captain Danjou, a decorated combat veteran with a gallant-looking goatee and mustache. Few understood why they were in Mexico, something to do with a pact between Napoléon III of France and Emperor Maximilian of Austria, a scheme to invade Mexico while the United States was distracted by its Civil War. But legionnaires were indifferent to politics. All they cared about was completing any mission they were assigned.

The French force had arrived at the port of Veracruz in the Gulf of Mexico, where they immediately discovered an enemy as lethal as the Mexican soldiers and furious civilians who resisted them. The ravages of yellow fever killed a third of them and forced them to move their headquarters sixty miles inland to the elevated town of Córdoba, where they hoped the air would be less contaminated. The shift in location meant that the supply route between Veracruz and Córdoba needed to be kept open, and the responsibility for doing that fell to patrols like the one Captain Danjou commanded.

Kline imagined the long night of walking along the remote, barren road. At dawn, the legionnaires were allowed to stop for breakfast, but as they searched for wood to build cook fires, a sentry pointed to the west.

"Mexican cavalry!"

The dust raised by the approaching horses made it difficult to count the number of riders, but this much was clear—there were hundreds and hundreds of them.

"Form a square!" Danjou ordered.

The men assembled in rows that faced each direction. The first row knelt while the second stood, their rifles aimed over the heads of the men kneeling in front.

The Mexican cavalry charged. As one, the legionnaires in the first row fired, breaking the attack. While they reloaded, the men behind them aimed, ready to fire if ordered.

Knowing that he'd gained only a little time, Danjou studied the open area around him, in search of cover. To the east, a ruined hacienda attracted his attention. He urged his men toward it, but again, the Mexicans charged, and again, the legionnaires fired, their fusillade dispersing the attack.

"Keep moving!" Danjou yelled.

Nearing the ruins, he peered over his shoulder and saw foot soldiers joining the Mexican cavalry. Out of breath, he and his patrol raced into a rubble-littered courtyard.

"Close the gates! Barricade them!"

Danjou assessed where they were. The hacienda

had dilapidated farm buildings arranged in a fifty-yard square. A stone wall enclosed it. In places, the barrier was ten feet high, but at other spots, it had collapsed, forming a chest-high heap of stones.

"Spread out! Take cover!"

A sentry scurried up a ladder to the top of a stable and reported the dust of more horsemen and infantry arriving.

"I see sombreros in every direction!"

"How many?" Danjou yelled.

"At least two thousand."

Danjou quickly calculated the ratio: thirty to one.

"There'll soon be a lot less of them!" he shouted to his men.

He got the laugh that he'd hoped for. But his billowy red pants and dark blue jacket were soaked with sweat from the urgent retreat toward the hacienda. In contrast, his mouth was dry, and he knew that, as the day grew hotter, his men would be desperate for water.

A quick search of the ruins revealed that there wasn't any, however. But that wasn't the case with the Mexicans. A nearby stream provided all the water the enemy could want. Danjou's lips felt drier at the thought of it.

"A rider's coming!" the sentry yelled. "He's got a white flag!"

Danjou climbed the ladder to the top of the stable. The movement was awkward for him. He had only one intact hand. Years earlier, his left one had been blown off by a musket. Undaunted, he'd commissioned a carver to create an ornate wooden replacement. Its lacquer was flesh-colored. Its fingers had hinges that made them flexible. It had a black cuff into which he inserted the stump of his wrist. By moving the stump against leather strips inside the cuff, he had taught himself to make the wooden fingers move.

Keeping that artificial hand out of sight behind his back, lest it be interpreted as a weakness, Danjou peered down at a Mexican officer who rode to him. The many languages of Danjou's legionnaires had forced him to become multilingual.

"You're outnumbered," the Mexican officer said. "You don't have water. You'll soon run out of food. Surrender. You'll be treated fairly."

"No," Danjou said.

"But to stay is to die."

"We won't lay down our arms," Danjou emphasized.

"This is foolishness."

"Try to attack us, and you'll learn how foolish *that* is."

Enraged, the Mexican officer rode away.

Danjou descended the ladder as quickly as he could. Even though he shouted encouragement to his men, he was troubled that the hacienda was situated in low terrain. The elevated ground beyond it allowed enemy riflemen to shoot down past the walls and into the compound.

Mexican snipers opened fire, providing cover for another cavalry charge. The dust the horses raised provided cover for advancing infantry. Bullets walloped through the wood of the buildings and shattered chunks of stone from the walls. But despite the unrelenting barrage, the disciplined volleys from the legionnaires repelled attack after attack.

By 11 A.M., the heat of the sun was crushing. The barrels of their rifles became too hot to touch. Twelve legionnaires were dead.

Danjou urged the remainder to keep fighting. Gesturing with his wooden hand, he rushed from group to group and personally made each man know that he counted on him. As he crossed the courtyard to help defend a wall, he lurched back, struck in the chest by a sniper's bullet.

A legionnaire who ran to help him heard him murmur with his last anguished breath, "Never give up."

Danjou's second-in-command took charge, shouting to the men, making them swear to fight harder in Danjou's honor. "We may die, but we'll never surrender!"

With two thousand Mexicans shooting, the enormous number of bullets hitting the compound—perhaps as many as eight thousand per minute—would have felt overwhelming, like the modern equivalent of being strafed by numerous machine guns. The noise alone would have been agony. Buildings crumbled. Gun smoke filled the air.

The farmhouse caught fire, perhaps ignited by muzzle flashes. Smoke from it further hampered vision and made the legionnaires struggle to breathe. But they kept shooting, repelling more attacks, ignoring more pleas to surrender.

By four in the afternoon, only twelve legionnaires

remained alive. By 6 P.M., the number of men able to fight had been reduced to five. As the Mexicans burst into the compound, the handful of survivors fired their last remaining ammunition, then attacked with fixed bayonets, rushing through the smoke, stabbing and clubbing.

A private was shot nineteen times while he tried to shield his lieutenant. Two others were hit and fell, but one struggled to his feet and joined his last two comrades. They stood back to back, thrusting with their bayonets.

The Mexican officer, who'd spoken to Danjou earlier, had never seen fighting like it.

"Stop!" he ordered his men.

He spun toward the survivors. "For God's sake, this is pointless. Surrender."

"We won't give up our weapons," a wounded legionnaire insisted.

"Your weapons? Are you trying to negotiate with me?" the Mexican asked in amazement.

The bleeding legionnaire wavered, trying not to fall. "We might be your prisoners, but we won't give up our weapons."

The Mexican gaped. "You don't have any ammunition. Your rifles are almost useless anyhow. Keep the damned things."

"And you need to allow us to take care of our wounded."

Astonished by their audacity, the Mexican officer grabbed the sinking legionnaire and said, "To men like you, I can't refuse anything."

Kline stood under the stark Syrian sun, listening to his commander describe the battle at Camerone.

Kline had heard the details many times, but with each telling, they gained more power. In his imagination, he smelled the blood, heard the buzzing of the flies on the corpses, and tasted the bitter smoke from the gunpowder and the burning buildings. The screams of the dying seemed to echo around him. He felt his eyes mist with emotion and took for granted that the men around him felt the same.

All the while, the colonel held up the wooden hand, a replica of Danjou's wooden hand, which had been recovered after the long-ago battle. The original hand was now protected in a glass case at Legion headquarters. Each year on April 30, the anniversary of the battle, the hand was carried around a crowded assembly room, allowing everyone to gaze at the Legion's most precious relic. On that same day, a similar memorial—minus the hand—occurred at every Legion base around the world. It was the most important ritual in the Legion's year.

But no one had ever arranged for a replica of Danjou's hand to be carved. No one had ever gone this far to imitate the ceremony as it took place each year at Legion headquarters. Moreover, this wasn't April 30. Given what was scheduled to happen the next morning, Kline understood that the wrong date reinforced how determined the colonel was to remind him and his fellow legionnaires of their heritage.

Standing on the boulder, holding the wooden hand above his head, the colonel spoke so forcefully that no one could fail to hear.

"Each of the sixty-six legionnaires at that battle carried sixty rounds of ammunition. Every round was used. That means they fired thirty-eight hundred rounds. Despite the heat and thirst and dust and smoke, they killed almost four hundred of the enemy. Think of it—one out of every ten bullets found its mark. Astonishing, given the circumstances. Those legionnaires were offered repeated opportunities to surrender. At any time, they could have abandoned their mission, but they refused to dishonor the legion or themselves.

"Tomorrow, remember those heroes. Tomorrow, *you* will be heroes. No legionnaire has ever encountered what all of you will face in the morning. We never walk away from a mission. We never fail to honor our obligations. What is our motto?"

"The Legion Is Our Country!" Kline and everybody else automatically shouted.

"I can't hear you!"

"The Legion Is Our Country!"

"What is our second motto?"

"Honor and Nobility!"

"Yes! Never forget that! Never forget Camerone! Never disgrace the Legion! Never fail to do your duty!"

Brooding about the bleak choice he would face the next morning, Kline returned along the bottom of the rocky slope. Barely noticing the numerous sentries along the way, he came to where Durado lay under the blanket and peered between the two boulders toward the outskirts of Damascus.

"You're back already? Just when I was getting comfortable," Durado said.

Kline half smiled. The humor reminded him of the jokes that Rourke had used to make.

Heat radiated off the rocks.

"Do you think the colonel's speech made a difference?" Durado squirmed to the bottom of the slope.

"We won't know until tomorrow," Kline answered, taking his place between the boulders. "No legionnaire's ever been forced into this situation before."

"Well, we do what we need to," Durado said, starting to walk away.

"Yes, God punishes us for our sins," Kline murmured.

Durado stopped and turned. "What? I didn't quite hear what you said."

"Just talking to myself."

"I thought you said something about God."

"Did you ever realize that it didn't need to happen?" Kline asked.

"Realize that *what* didn't need to happen?"

"Camerone. The legionnaires were out of water. They had almost no food. Their ammunition was limited. In that heat, after three days without anything to drink, they'd have been unconscious or worse. All the Mexicans needed to do was wait."

"Maybe they were afraid reinforcements would arrive before then," Durado suggested.

"But why would the Mexicans have been afraid?" Kline asked. "There were so many of them that a rescue column wouldn't have had a chance. If they'd set it up right and made it seem that only a couple of hundred Mexicans surrounded the hacienda, they could have lured the reinforcements into an ambush."

"So what's your point?"

"Just what I said—sometimes, battles don't need to happen."

"Like tomorrow's?" Durado asked.

Kline pointed toward the buildings. "Maybe they'll surrender."

"Or maybe they hope *we'll* surrender. Is that going to happen?"

"Of course not." Kline quoted from the Legion's Code of Honor, which all recruits were required to memorize at the start of their training. "'Never surrender your arms.'"

"And *they* won't do it, either," Durado said.

"But in the end, France was forced to leave Mexico. Camerone made no difference," Kline told him.

"Be careful. You'd better not let the colonel hear you talking this way."

"Maybe tomorrow's battle won't make a difference, either."

"Thinking isn't our business." Now it was Durado's turn to quote from the Legion's Code of Honor. "'The mission is sacred. You will see it through to the end, at any price.'"

"'At any price.'" Kline exhaled. "You're absolutely

right. I'm not paid to think. Tomorrow, I'll fight as hard as you."

"God punishes us for our sins? Is that what you said earlier?" Durado asked. "The things I've seen in this war prove He doesn't exist. Otherwise, they never would have been allowed to happen."

"Unless this battle tomorrow is God's way of paying us back."

"For our sins?"

"For the things we'd give anything to forget."

"In that case, God help us." Again, the irony in Durado's voice reminded Kline of Rourke.

Kline lay under the blanket, staring across the rocky hill toward the buildings that seemed to waver in the heat. He knew that soldiers just like him watched from their own hiding places over there. With their weapons beside them, they brooded behind the city's walls, parapets, turrets, and gates, knowing that soon, probably the next morning, the battle would begin.

Kline was struck by how different things had been a year earlier. When the Germans had broken through the concrete battlements of the Maginot Line and invaded France, the only tactic that had made sense was for him and Rourke and the rest of the legionnaires to fight a retreating action, trying to slow the German advance as much as possible.

And we still might have beaten them, Kline thought, if the Germans hadn't realized the mistake they were about to make.

The risk to the invading army had been that a rush to occupy all of France would overextend their supply lines, leaving them vulnerable to devastating hit-and-run attacks by French civilians and the remainder of the French military. Without supplies, the Germans would have been helpless. To prevent that from happening, they'd developed the brilliant strategy of consolidating their forces in the northern and western parts of the country, an area that included Paris. Meanwhile, their massive threatening presence had convinced the rest of France that total occupation was only a matter of time, that it was better to capitulate and negotiate for favorable terms.

So the bastards in the south became collaborators, Kline thought.

The deal was that the southern two-fifths of France would remain free of German soldiers. Meanwhile, France would form a new government based in the community of Vichy in the central part of the country. In theory, this government was neutral to Germany, but in reality, the Vichy regime was so eager to placate the Germans that they were more than happy to hand over Jews or any other "undesirables" that the Germans wanted.

The rest of France might as well have been invaded. The result was the same, Kline thought. *Maybe they could justify collaborating if they'd made an effort to resist. But as it was, they just surrendered and acted like the enemy.*

He painfully remembered the last time he'd seen Rourke. Along with a remnant of their legionnaire unit, they'd been hiding in an abandoned French barn, waiting for nightfall when they could slip out and elude patrols by the Vichy militia.

Their radioman picked up a wireless signal that he quickly reported. "The Thirteenth Demi-Brigade shipped back from fighting in Norway."

All the men hiding in the barn sat up from the straw they lay on. The context didn't need to be explained— the Legion had been fighting on two fronts, and the Thirteenth's objective had been Norway. But like the Legion's unit on the Maginot Line, the Thirteenth had been forced to withdraw.

"They landed at Brest," the radioman continued.

The men nodded, well aware that Brest was the westernmost port in France.

"When they realized France had capitulated and that the Germans were about to occupy the port, they hurried back on the ships and headed toward England."

"So they're going to help the Allies try to retake France?" Kline asked.

"Yes," the radioman said. "But not all of them went to England."

Rourke straightened. "What do you mean?"

"Some decided to go back to headquarters in Algeria."

The legionnaires remained silent for a moment, analyzing the significance of this information. Another reason Germany had resisted invading all of France was that the move would have made enemies of Algeria and Morocco: French territories in North Africa. But by persuading France to form the Vichy government, a supposedly neutral regime that was in effect a puppet government, Germany gained indirect control of those French territories and prevented the legionnaires stationed there from helping England.

"They're going to fight *against* the Brits?" Kline asked in shock.

"It's more like they're hoping Algeria will remain neutral. That way, they'll be able to sit out the rest of the war without fighting *anybody*," the radioman explained.

"Lots of damned luck to them," someone said.

"The message came from England," the radioman continued. "From Brigadier General de Gaulle."

"Who's he?"

"I never heard of him, either," the radioman continued. "But apparently he's in charge of something called the Free French Forces, and that includes the legionnaires who went to England. He wants every French soldier to get there somehow and regroup. The fight's not over."

"Thank God, somebody's got some balls," another legionnaire said. "I guess we know which way we're going tonight. South to the coast. We'll get our hands on a boat and head toward England."

Most of the men readily agreed. They'd been born and raised in Spain, Portugal, Greece, or any number of other countries, but all were now French citizens and felt loyal to the nation they'd been fighting to protect.

Kline couldn't help noticing that some were pensively quiet, however. Evidently, the previous year of fighting made the idea of sitting out the war in Algeria appealing.

Kline also couldn't help noticing that Rourke was one of the men who remained quiet.

At dark, as the group sneaked from the barn, Kline motioned for Rourke to wait.

"I get the feeling you're not going to England with us," he said when the two of them were alone.

In the shadows, Rourke took a moment to answer. "Yes. When we reach the Mediterranean, I'll find a way across to Algeria."

"You've had enough fighting?"

"It's got nothing to do with sitting out the war. Believe me, I'm happy to fight the Germans." Rourke paused. "But I can't go to England."

"I don't understand."

"You and I never talked about our pasts, my friend." Rourke put a hand on his shoulder. "But I think you guessed a lot about mine. If I go back to England, I might end up serving next to the same British soldiers who hunted me in Ireland before I joined the Legion. Don't get me wrong. I didn't join the Legion to escape them."

"I know. You joined to do penance."

"See, we understand each other," Rourke said. "I once told you that Catholics need to tell God they're sorry for their sins and then do whatever's necessary to prove they mean it."

"I remember."

"Well, how can I keep doing penance if some bastard British Tommy recognizes me and shoots me?"

From the darkness outside the barn, a legionnaire whispered, "Kline, we need to get moving."

"I'll be there in a second," he murmured through the rickety door.

He turned to Rourke. "Take care of yourself."

"Don't worry," Rourke said, shaking hands with him. "We'll cross paths again after the war."

But Rourke had been wrong. It wasn't after the war that they would cross paths. Soon after the split in the Legion, some men going to England, others going to Algeria, the Vichy government ordered the legionnaires in Algeria to assist the German army.

By June of 1941, when the Allies fought to liberate Syria from the invaders, Kline's Legion unit was helping the British. Meanwhile, a different Legion unit, the Vichy brigade, was helping the Germans.

In the morning, Kline knew, the unthinkable would occur. Battling for Damascus, legionnaires who had trained together, bivouacked together, gotten drunk together, and fought together, would now fight each other, and unless Rourke had already died in combat, he would be one of those whom Kline would attack.

As the sun began to set, Durado returned one last time, assigned to sentry duty for the night.

The intense heat continued to weigh on them.

"Still quiet over there?" Durado asked.

"No sign of anyone. Maybe they pulled back," Kline hoped.

"I doubt it."

"Me, too. They know *we* won't pull back."

"But surely they realize they're on the wrong side," Durado said.

"Probably they're saying the same thing about us."

"What do you mean?"

"*They're* the ones fighting for France."

"For a government sucking up to the damned Germans," Durado said.

"Even so, it's the only French government there is. Do you remember what Commander Vernerey said when the Allies told him to fight the Germans in Norway?"

"If I heard, I've forgotten."

"Legionnaires fighting in snow instead of sand. He knew how crazy that was. But he didn't argue with his orders. He said, 'What is my aim? To take the port of Narvik. For the Norwegians? The phosphates? The anchovies? I haven't the slightest idea. But I have my mission, and I shall take Narvik.'"

"Yes," Durado said. "We have our mission."

"Something's moving over there," Kline said.

Durado squirmed next to him and peered between the boulders.

At a gate in the Damascus wall, a white flag appeared. Several legionnaires emerged, recognizable because each man's cap was the Legion's traditional white kepi. Unlike the shorts and short-sleeved shirts that Kline's unit wore, the uniform of the opposing legionnaires consisted of full-length sleeves and pants.

In the last of the setting sun, they formed a line against the wall, stood at attention, and formally presented arms to Kline's unit.

Kline strained to distinguish their faces, unable to tell if Rourke was among them. Even so, he had no doubt that, if he got closer, he'd be able to call each of them by his first name.

At once, he gripped the boulder on his right. Using it for leverage, he stood.

"What are you doing?" Durado asked in alarm.

But Kline wasn't the only man who stood. All along the ridge, sentry after sentry rose to his feet.

Soon Durado did, also.

Someone yelled, "Present . . . arms!"

The line of sentries imitated their brethren across the way. Kline's chest felt squeezed as he went through the ritual that ended with him holding his rifle close to him, the butt toward the ground, the barrel toward the sky.

From somewhere in Damascus, a bugle played, echoing across the valley. The song, *"Le Boudin,"* was familiar to every legionnaire, who learned it by heart at the start of his training. It dated back to the nineteenth century, when Belgium had refused to allow its citizens to join the Legion. As the pulsing melody faded to a close, a bugler on the Demi-Brigade's side took it up. Soon voices joined in, filling the valley with the normally comical lyric about blood sausage and how the Legion wouldn't share any with the Belgians because they were shitty marksmen.

"*Le Boudin*" was followed by another favorite from the first day of training, "*La Legion Marche*." Its energy expanded Kline's chest and made him sing so hard that he risked becoming hoarse. Even though his voice was only one of thousands on both sides of the valley, nonetheless he did his best to make Rourke hear him.

> The Legion marches toward the front.
> Singing, we are heirs to our traditions,
> One with the Legion.

The song praised Honor and Loyalty, virtues that gave the Legion strength. But Kline's voice faltered as he realized that absolute loyalty to a mission was what had brought the Legion to this moment.

When the lyrics reached their refrain, a section of it made Kline stop singing entirely.

> We don't only have weapons.
> The devil marches with us.

He couldn't help remembering the conversation he'd had with Rourke when they'd enlisted long ago.

"'My name is Legion,'" Rourke had said.

"'For we are many,'" Kline had responded. "A possessed man says that to Jesus, trying to explain how many demons are in him."

From Damascus and from this ridge, each side now repeated the song's refrain, their voices rising.

The devil marches with us.

As the sun dipped completely behind the horizon, the music sank as well, echoing faintly, descending into silence.

Enveloped by darkness, Kline stood at the bottom of the ridge, staring up at the cold glint of the emerging stars.

He left Durado and made his way to the mess tent. Although he had no appetite, he knew that he would need all his strength in the morning, so he ate the bread and bacon that was served, and drank bitter coffee. Many other men sat around him. None said a word.

Later, in the shadows of his tent, he wondered what Rourke had done that was so horrible it had made him join the Legion as his punishment. Had he set a roadside bomb intended for a British army convoy, only to see it blow apart a school bus full of children? Or had he set fire to a house occupied by an Irish family who supposedly had revealed the IRA's battle plans to the British, only to discover that he'd set the wrong house ablaze, that the family who'd burned to death was innocent? Would those things be terrible enough to make someone like Rourke hate himself? In his nightmares, did he hear the screams of the dying children, just as Kline imagined his wife sobbing over the corpse of their daughter, reaching for a razor blade to slit her wrists while Kline hid from the police because of a bank robbery in which a guard had been killed for $24.95?

Everybody ran in different directions, Kline remembered. *I never got even a dollar.*

Imagining the relentless coughing that had racked and smothered his daughter, he thought, *I should have been with them.*

He remained awake for a long time, staring at the top of the tent.

Explosions shook him from a troubled sleep, so many roaring blasts that he couldn't distinguish them. The ground, the tent, the air—everything trembled. The first shock waves slapped his ears, making them ring. But amid the persistent heavy rumbles, his ears quickly became numb, as if muffled by cotton batting. He grabbed his rifle and charged from the tent, seeing the chaos of a camp being struck by artillery shells. Powerful flashes illuminated the darkness as rocks, tents, and men disintegrated in the blasts.

Murky silhouettes of legionnaires ran desperately toward the cover of boulders, toward pits they'd dug, toward anything that would shield them from flying debris. The camp's own artillery returned fire, howitzers and tanks shuddering as they blasted shells toward Damascus.

Burning blasts erupted from the sandstone buildings over there. They and the muzzle flashes of the cannons turned the darkness into a pulsing twilight that allowed Kline to see his way toward a rock wall behind which he dived before a nearby blast sent shrapnel streaking over it.

The bombardment went on for hours. When it finally ended, the air was thick with dust and smoke. Despite the continued ringing in Kline's ears, he heard officers yelling, "*Allez! Allez!* Get on your feet, you lazy bastards! Attack!"

Kline came to his feet, the dust so thick that he sensed more than saw the men around him doing the same.

He and the others scurried up the ridge. Sometimes they slipped on loose stones, but that was the only thing that held them back. Kline sensed their determination as they reached the top and increased speed, charging past boulders toward the wall.

The dust still hovered, giving them shelter, but soon it thinned, and the moment they emerged from it, visible now, running toward the wall, the legionnaires opposing them opened fire. Kline felt a man beside him lurch back. A man ahead of him dropped.

But Kline kept charging, shooting toward movement on the parapets. At once, a portion of the wall blew apart from a cannon shell. A second explosion widened the opening.

Kline paused only long enough to yank the pin from a grenade and hurl the grenade as far as he could through the gap in the wall. Other legionnaires did the same, diving to the ground the same as Kline did, waiting for the multiple blasts to clear their way.

He scrambled over the rubble and entered a court-yard. Among stone buildings, narrow alleys led in various directions. A bullet struck near him, throwing up chunks of sandstone. He whirled toward a window and fired, not knowing if he hit anyone before he charged on. Then he reached one of the alleys and aimed along it. Joined by other legionnaires, he moved slowly now, prepared to fire at any target.

Shots seemed to ring out everywhere. Explosions rumbled as Kline pressed forward, smelling gunpowder and hearing screams. The buildings were no taller than three stories. Smoke drifted over them, some of it settling into the alley, but he didn't allow it to distract him. The doors and windows ahead were all he cared about.

A man next to him screamed and fell. Kline fired toward the ground-floor window from which the shot had come, and this time, he saw blood fly. A legionnaire near him hurled a grenade through the same window, and the moment after it exploded, they crashed through a doorway, firing.

Two soldiers lay dead on the floor. Their white legionnaire's caps were spattered with blood. Their uniforms had the long sleeves and full-length pants of the opposing side. Kline recognized both of them. Rinaldo and Stavros. He'd trained with them, marched with them, shared tents with them, and sung with them at breakfast in the mess hall at Sidi-bel-Abbes.

Stairs led upward. From above, Kline heard shots. Aiming, he and the other legionnaire checked a neighboring room, then approached the steps. As they climbed, a quick glance toward his companion showed Kline that he was again paired with Durado. The Spaniard's normally tan complexion was now sallow.

Neither spoke as they stalked higher.

Above, the shots persisted, presumably directed toward the alley they'd left or else toward the alley on the opposite side of the building. Perhaps the numerous explosions in the area had prevented the shooter from realizing that this building had been hit by a grenade. Or perhaps the shooter wasn't alone. Perhaps he continued firing while another soldier watched the stairs, hoping to draw Kline and Durado into a trap.

Sweat trickled down Kline's face. Nearing the top, he armed another grenade and threw it into a room. Immediately, he and Durado ducked down the stairs, protecting themselves from the force of the blast. They straightened and charged the rest of the way up, shooting as they entered the room.

No one was there. A neighboring room was deserted, also. At the last moment, the shooter must have hurried the rest of the way up the stairs, taking refuge on the third and final floor.

Kline and Durado took turns replacing the magazines on their rifles. Again they crept up, and this time, it was Durado who threw the grenade. An instant after the explosion, they ran to the top, but amid the smoke of the explosion, they still didn't find anyone.

In the far corner, a ladder led to an open hatch in the roof.

Durado's voice was stark. "I'm not going up there."

Kline understood. Their quarry was probably lying on the roof, aiming toward the hatch, ready to blow off the head of anyone who showed himself through the small opening. There was no way to know which way to throw a grenade to try to clear the roof.

"Maybe he ran across to another building," Kline said.

"And maybe not. I won't climb up there to find out."

"Right. To hell with him," Kline said. He peered through an open window and saw a sniper in a window across from him. The sniper wore a white legionnaire's cap. His sleeves were long. As the man aimed down toward an alley, Kline shot him before he had the chance to pull the trigger.

Durado pointed. "Snipers all along the roofs!"

Kline worked the bolt on his rifle and fired through the window. Worked the bolt and fired. The movement became automatic. Hearing Durado do the same through an opposite window, he loaded a fresh magazine and continued shooting in a frenzy. His uniform was drenched with sweat. Struck by his bullets, white-capped men with long-sleeved shirts slumped on the roofs or else toppled into the alleys.

An explosion shoved Kline forward, almost propelling him through the window. He managed to twist sideways and slam against the window's frame before he would have gone through. His back stung, and his shirt felt more soaked, but this time, he knew it was from blood.

Trying to recover from the shock wave, he spun toward the room and realized that the explosion had come from the far corner. The ladder was in pieces. The man on the roof had dropped a grenade through the hatch.

"Durado!"

There wasn't any point in running to try to help him. Durado had been shooting through a window near the ladder. The grenade had exploded next to him, tearing him open. His blood was everywhere. His gaping intestines lay around him. Already, the flies settled on him.

Kline aimed toward the ceiling's open hatch. Abruptly, numerous bullets sprayed through the window next to him. The snipers across from him had realized the direction from which his shots had come. If the wall hadn't been made of thick sandstone, their bullets would have come through and killed him. Even so, the wall would eventually disintegrate from the unrelenting barrage. He couldn't stay in the room much longer.

When another grenade dropped through the hatch, Kline dived toward the stairs. The impact made him wince as he rolled down, feeling the edges of the steps against his bleeding back. The explosion roared behind him. He groaned when he hit the bottom, but he kept rolling.

He deliberately made loud noises, striking his boots hard as he clattered down the final section of the stairs. At the bottom, he fired once, hoping to give the impression that he shot at someone before he left the building. Then he silently crept up to the middle floor and hid in the adjacent room.

The most difficult part about standing still and waiting was trying to control the sound of his breathing. His chest heaved. He was sure that the strident sound of air going through his nostrils would give him away. He worked desperately to breathe less fast, but that only increased the urgency in his lungs. His heart seemed about to explode.

A minute passed.

Two.

Blood trickled down Kline's injured back. Outside, the explosions and shots continued.

I'm wasting my time, Kline thought. *I ought to be outside, helping.*

The moment he started to leave, he heard a shot from the floor above him, and smiled. The man on the roof had finally decided that the building was clear. He'd jumped down to continue shooting from the cover of a window.

Kline emerged from the room. Hearing another shot above him, he eased up the stairs. He paused, waiting for another shot and the sound of the rifle's bolt being pulled back. Those noises concealed his own sounds as he came to the top of the stairs and fired, hitting the man in the back.

The legionnaire, who wore long pants, slumped forward, his head on the windowsill. Kline recognized the back of his brawny neck. His name was Arick. He was a German, who'd been part of Kline's group of volunteers back in 1934. Outside, other Germans fought each other, some for the Vichy Legion, some for the Free French Legion. But where a legionnaire had been born and raised made no difference.

The Legion Is Our Only Country, Kline thought. *God help us.*

He turned to race down the stairs and reenter the battle. He reached the second floor. He hurried to the first at the same moment a man left the chaos outside, rushing into the demolished room. He wore the Legion's white kepi. Long pants.

He gaped at Kline.

Kline gaped, as well.

The man was even thinner than when Kline had last seen him, his freckles almost hidden by the dust of battle.

"Rourke."

The name barely escaped Kline's mouth before he shot Rourke in the chest. The pressure of his finger on the trigger was automatic, the result of countless drills in which self-preservation preceded thought.

Rourke staggered back, hit a wall, and slid down, leaving a streak of blood. He squinted at Kline, as if trying to focus his dimming eyes.

He trembled and lay still.

"Rourke," Kline said again.

He went to the open doorway, fired at an opposing legionnaire, and hurried into the tumult of the alley, hoping to die.

———

The battle persisted into the next day. By sunset, the Vichy Legion had been routed. Damascus had fallen to the Allies.

Exhausted, his back crusted with scabs, Kline lay with other legionnaires in the rubble of a building. It was difficult to find a comfortable position among the debris. They licked the last drops of water from the brims of their canteens. They chewed the last of the stale biscuits in their rations.

As the sun set and the cold stars appeared, Kline peered up at the vastness. He was puzzled by the casualty figures that had been reported to his group of men. On his side, only 21 legionnaires had been killed and 47 wounded. But of the opposing legionnaires, 128 had been killed while 728 had been wounded.

The contrast was so great that Kline had difficulty making sense of it.

They had plenty of time to secure their defenses within the city, he thought. *They had buildings to shield them from our bullets while we attacked across open ground. We were easy targets. They should have been able to stop us from reaching the walls.*

An unnerving thought squirmed through his mind. *Did they hold back? Did they shoot to miss? Did they hope to appear to fight when all they wanted was for the battle to end as soon as their pride would allow?*

Kline recalled speaking with Durado about whether the men in the Vichy Legion knew they were on the wrong side, the aggressor's side, the invader's side.

The snipers whom Kline had seen in windows and

on rooftops—had they been merely firing but not aiming? Had they been looking for an honorable way to *lose* the fight?

Kline remembered turning in surprise as Rourke had hurried through the doorway into the wreckage of the room. Kline had shot him reflexively. Searching his memory, Kline sought to focus on Rourke's rifle. Had Rourke been raising it, about to shoot? Or had Rourke been about to lower it and greet his friend?

There was no way to tell. Everything had happened too quickly.

I did what I was trained to do, Kline thought. *The next instant, Rourke might have shot me.*

But then again, he might not *have.*

Would our friendship have meant more to him than his duty as a legionnaire? Kline wondered. *Or would Rourke's training have made him pull the trigger?*

Peering up toward the sky, Kline noticed that there were even more stars. Their glint was colder—bitterly so—as a new, more unnerving thought took possession of him. He remembered the many times that he and Rourke had talked about salvation.

"What do Baptists believe?" Rourke had asked.

"God punishes us for our sins," Kline had answered.

Kline now suspected that manipulating him into killing his friend was another way for God to punish him.

"What do *Catholics* believe about being saved?" Kline had asked.

The former altar boy had replied, "We tell God

we're sorry for our sins and do penance to prove we mean it."

Penance.

Thinking of his dead wife and daughter, thinking of the dead bank guard, thinking of Rourke, he murmured, his voice breaking, "I'm sorry."

Diana Gabaldon

International bestseller Diana Gabaldon is the winner of a Quill Award (for science fiction/fantasy/horror), a RITA Award (for best book of the year, genre unspecified), given by the Romance Writers of America, and the Corine International Prize for Fiction—all for the same series of books. Her hugely popular Outlander series includes *Outlander, Dragonfly in Amber, Voyager, Drums of Autumn, The Fiery Cross, A Breath of Snow and Ashes,* and *An Echo in the Bone.* The bestselling Lord John stories are a subset of the main Outlander series, historical mysteries featuring Lord John Grey, an important minor character from the main novels. Lord John's adventures include *Lord John and the Private Matter, Lord John and the Brotherhood of the Blade,* and *Lord John and the Hand of Devils* (a collection of shorter pieces that includes "Lord John and the Hell-fire Club," "Lord John and the Succubus," and "Lord John and the Haunted Soldier"). A graphic novel, *The Exile* (based on *Outlander,* with artwork by Hoang Nguyen), is due to be released in September 2010. She has also written *The Outlandish Companion,* a nonfiction reference/guide/addendum that covers the first four volumes of the series (the second volume of the *Companion* is due out in a year or so), and is working on a contemporary mystery (working title: *Red Ant's Head*).

Here she takes her swashbuckling military adventurer, Lord John Grey, on a journey to the New World, where at the Siege of Quebec, he faces dangers much more subtle than the usual shot, shell, and steel.

The Custom of the Army

All things considered, it was probably the fault of the electric eel. John Grey could—and for a time, did—blame the Honorable Caroline Woodford as well. And the surgeon. And certainly that blasted poet. Still . . . no, it was the eel's fault.

The party had been at Lucinda Joffrey's house. Sir Richard was absent; a diplomat of his stature could not have countenanced something so frivolous. Electric eel parties were a mania in London just now, but owing to the scarcity of the creatures, a private party was a rare occasion. Most such parties were held at public theaters, with the fortunate few selected for encounter with the eel summoned onstage, there to be shocked and sent reeling like nine-pins for the entertainment of the audience.

"The record is forty-two at once!" Caroline had told him, her eyes wide and shining as she looked up from the creature in its tank.

"Really?" It was one of the most peculiar things he'd seen, though not very striking. Nearly three feet long, it had a heavy squarish body with a blunt head that looked to have been inexpertly molded out of sculptor's clay, and tiny eyes like dull glass beads. It had little in common with the lashing, lithesome eels of the fish-market—and certainly did not seem capable of felling forty-two people at once.

The thing had no grace at all, save for a small thin ruffle of a fin that ran the length of its lower body, undulating as a gauze curtain does in the wind. Lord John expressed this observation to the Honorable Caroline, and was accused in consequence of being poetic.

"Poetic?" said an amused voice behind him. "Is there no end to our gallant major's talents?"

Lord John turned, with an inward grimace and an outward smile, and bowed to Edwin Nicholls.

"I should not think of trespassing upon your province, Mr. Nicholls," he said politely. Nicholls wrote execrable verse, mostly upon the subject of love, and was much admired by young women of a certain turn of mind. The Honorable Caroline wasn't one of them; she'd written a very clever parody of his style, though Grey thought Nicholls had not heard about it. He hoped not.

"Oh, don't you?" Nicholls raised one honey-colored brow at him and glanced briefly but meaningfully at Miss Woodford. His tone was jocular, but his look was not, and Grey wondered just how much Mr. Nicholls had had to drink. Nicholls was flushed of cheek and glittering of eye, but that might be only the heat of the room, which was considerable, and the excitement of the party.

"Do you think of composing an ode to our friend?"

Grey asked, ignoring Nicholls's allusion and gesturing toward the large tank that contained the eel.

Nicholls laughed, too loudly—yes, quite a bit the worse for drink—and waved a dismissive hand.

"No, no, Major. How could I think of expending my energies upon such a gross and insignificant creature, when there are angels of delight such as this to inspire me?" He leered—Grey did not wish to impugn the fellow, but he undeniably leered—at Miss Woodford, who smiled—with compressed lips—and tapped him rebukingly with her fan.

Where was Caroline's uncle? Grey wondered. Simon Woodford shared his niece's interest in natural history, and would certainly have escorted her. . . . Oh, there. Simon Woodford was deep in discussion with Mr. Hunter, the famous surgeon—what had possessed Lucinda to invite *him*? Then he caught sight of Lucinda, viewing Mr. Hunter over her fan with narrowed eyes, and realized that she *hadn't* invited him.

John Hunter was a famous surgeon—and an infamous anatomist. Rumor had it that he would stop at nothing to bag a particularly desirable body—whether human or not. He did move in society, but not in the Joffreys' circles.

Lucinda Joffrey had the most expressive eyes. Her one claim to beauty, they were almond-shaped, amber in color, and capable of sending remarkably minatory messages across a crowded room.

Come here! they said. Grey smiled and lifted his glass in salute to her, but made no move to obey. The eyes narrowed further, gleaming dangerously, then cut abruptly toward the surgeon, who was edging toward the tank, his face alight with curiosity and acquisitiveness.

The eyes whipped back to Grey.

Get rid of him! they said.

Grey glanced at Miss Woodford. Mr. Nicholls had seized her hand in his and appeared to be declaiming something; she looked as though she wanted it back. Grey looked back at Lucinda and shrugged, with a small gesture toward Mr. Nicholls's ochre-velvet back, expressing regret that social responsibility prevented his carrying out her order.

"Not only the face of an angel," Nicholls was saying, squeezing Caroline's fingers so hard that she squeaked, "but the skin as well." He stroked her hand, the leer intensifying. "What do angels smell like in the morning, I wonder?"

Grey measured him up thoughtfully. One more remark of that sort, and he might be obliged to invite Mr. Nicholls to step outside. Nicholls was tall and heavily built, outweighed Grey by a couple of stone, and had a reputation for bellicosity. *Best try to break his nose first*, Grey thought, shifting his weight, *then run him headfirst into a hedge. He won't come back in if I make a mess of him.*

"What are you looking at?" Nicholls inquired unpleasantly, catching Grey's gaze upon him.

Grey was saved from reply by a loud clapping of hands—the eel's proprietor calling the party to order. Miss Woodford took advantage of the distraction to snatch her hand away, cheeks flaming with mortification. Grey moved at once to her side, and put a hand beneath her elbow, fixing Nicholls with an icy stare.

"Come with me, Miss Woodford," he said. "Let us find a good place from which to watch the proceedings."

"Watch?" said a voice beside him. "Why, surely you don't mean to *watch*, do you, sir? Are you not curious to try the phenomenon yourself?"

It was Hunter himself, bushy hair tied carelessly back, though decently dressed in a damson-red suit, and grinning up at Grey; the surgeon was broad-shouldered and muscular, but quite short—barely five foot two, to Grey's five-six. Evidently he had noted Grey's wordless exchange with Lucinda.

"Oh, I think—," Grey began, but Hunter had his arm and was tugging him toward the crowd gathering round the tank. Caroline, with an alarmed glance at the glowering Nicholls, hastily followed him.

"I shall be most interested to hear your account of the sensation," Hunter was saying chattily. "Some people report a remarkable euphoria, a momentary disorientation . . . shortness of breath, or dizziness— sometimes pain in the chest. You have not a weak heart, I hope, Major? Or you, Miss Woodford?"

"Me?" Caroline looked surprised.

Hunter bowed to her.

"I should be particularly interested to see your own response, ma'am," he said respectfully. "So few women have the courage to undertake such an adventure."

"She doesn't want to," Grey said hurriedly.

"Well, perhaps I *do*," she said, and gave him a little frown before glancing at the tank and the long gray form inside it. She gave a little shiver—but Grey recognized it, from long acquaintance with the lady, as a shiver of anticipation, rather than of revulsion.

Mr. Hunter recognized it, too. He grinned more broadly and bowed again, extending his arm to Miss Woodford.

"Allow me to secure you a place, ma'am."

Grey and Nicholls both moved purposefully to prevent him, collided, and were left scowling at each other as Mr. Hunter escorted Caroline to the tank and introduced her to the eel's owner, a dark-looking little creature named Horace Suddfield.

Grey nudged Nicholls aside and plunged into the crowd, elbowing his way ruthlessly to the front.

Hunter spotted him and beamed.

"Have you any metal remaining in your chest, Major?"

"Have I—what?"

"Metal," Hunter repeated. "Arthur Longstreet described to me the operation in which he removed thirty-seven pieces of metal from your chest—most impressive. If any bits remain, though, I must advise you against trying the eel. Metal conducts electricity, you see, and the chance of burns—"

Nicholls had made his way through the throng as well, and gave an unpleasant laugh, hearing this.

"A good excuse, Major," he said, a noticeable jeer in his voice.

He was very drunk indeed, Grey thought. Still—

"No, I haven't," he said abruptly.

"Excellent," Suddfield said politely. "A soldier, I understand you are, sir? A bold gentleman, I perceive—who better to take first place?"

And before Grey could protest, he found himself next to the tank, Caroline Woodford's hand clutching his, her other held by Nicholls, who was glaring malevolently.

"Are we all arranged, ladies and gentlemen?" Suddfield cried. "How many, Dobbs?"

"Forty-five!" came a call from his assistant from the next room, through which the line of participants snaked, joined hand to hand and twitching with excitement, the rest of the party standing well back, agog.

"All touching, all touching?" Suddfield cried. "Take a firm grip of your friends, please, a very firm grip!" He turned to Grey, his small face alight. "Go ahead, sir! Grip it tightly, please—just there, just there before the tail!"

Disregarding his better judgement and the consequences to his lace cuff, Grey set his jaw and plunged his hand into the water.

In the split second when he grasped the slimy thing, he expected something like the snap one got from touching a Leiden jar and making it spark. Then he was flung violently backwards, every muscle in his body contorted, and he found himself on the floor, thrashing like a landed fish, gasping in a vain attempt to recall how to breathe.

The surgeon, Mr. Hunter, squatted next to him, observing him with bright-eyed interest.

"How do you feel?" he inquired. "Dizzy, at all?"

Grey shook his head, mouth opening and closing like a goldfish's, and with some effort, thumped his chest.

Thus invited, Mr. Hunter leaned down at once, unbuttoned Grey's waistcoat and pressed an ear to his shirtfront. Whatever he heard—or didn't—seemed to alarm him, for he jerked up, clenched both fists together and brought them down on Grey's chest with a thud that reverberated to his backbone.

This blow had the salutary effect of forcing breath out of his lungs; they filled again by reflex, and suddenly, he remembered how to breathe. His heart also seemed to have been recalled to a sense of its duty, and began beating again. He sat up, fending off another blow from Mr. Hunter, and sat blinking at the carnage round him.

The floor was filled with bodies. Some still writhing, some lying still, limbs outflung in abandonment, some already recovered and being helped to their feet by friends. Excited exclamations filled the air, and Suddfield stood by his eel, beaming with pride and accepting congratulations. The eel itself seemed annoyed; it was swimming round in circles, angrily switching its heavy body.

Edwin Nicholls was on hands and knees, Grey saw, rising slowly to his feet. He reached down to grasp Caroline Woodford's arms and help her to rise. This she did, but so awkwardly that she lost her balance and fell face-first into Mr. Nicholls. He in turn lost his own balance and sat down hard, the Honorable Caroline atop him. Whether from shock, excitement, drink, or simple boorishness, he seized the moment—and Caroline—and planted a hearty kiss upon her astonished lips.

Matters thereafter were somewhat confused. He had a vague impression that he *had* broken Nicholls's nose—and there was a set of burst and swollen knuckles on his right hand to give weight to the supposition. There was a lot of noise, though, and he had the disconcerting feeling of not being altogether firmly confined within his own body. Parts of him seemed to be constantly drifting off, escaping the outlines of his flesh.

What *was* still inside was distinctly jangled. His hearing—still somewhat impaired from the cannon explosion a few months before—had given up entirely under the strain of electric shock. That is, he could still hear, but what he heard made no sense. Random words reached him through a fog of buzzing and ringing, but he could not connect them sensibly to the moving mouths around him. He wasn't at all sure that his own voice was saying what he meant it to, for that matter.

He was surrounded by voices, faces—a sea of feverish sound and movement. People touched him, pulled him, pushed him. He flung out an arm, trying as much to discover where it was as to strike anyone, but felt the impact of flesh. More noise. Here and there a face he recognized: Lucinda, shocked and furious; Caroline, distraught, her red hair disheveled and coming down, all its powder lost.

The net result of everything was that he was not positive whether he had called Nicholls out, or the reverse. Surely Nicholls must have challenged him? He had a vivid recollection of Nicholls, gore-soaked handkerchief held to his nose and a homicidal light in his narrowed eyes. But then he'd found himself outside, in his shirtsleeves, standing in the little park that fronted the Joffreys' house, with a pistol in his hand. He wouldn't have chosen to fight with a strange pistol, would he?

Maybe Nicholls had insulted him, and he had called Nicholls out without quite realizing it?

It had rained earlier, was chilly now; wind was whipping his shirt round his body. His sense of smell was remarkably acute; it seemed to be the only thing working properly. He smelled smoke from the chimneys, the damp green of the plants, and his own sweat, oddly metallic. And something faintly foul—something redolent of mud and slime. By reflex, he rubbed the hand that had touched the eel against his breeches.

Someone was saying something to him. With difficulty, he fixed his attention on Dr. Hunter, standing by his side, still with that look of penetrating interest. *Well, of course. They'd need a surgeon*, he thought dimly. *Have to have a surgeon at a duel.*

"Yes," he said, seeing Hunter's eyebrows raised in inquiry of some sort. Then, seized by a belated fear that he had just promised his body to the surgeon were he killed, seized Hunter's coat with his free hand.

"You . . . don't . . . touch me," he said. "No . . .

knives. Ghoul," he added for good measure, finally locating the word.

Hunter nodded, seeming unoffended.

The sky was overcast, the only light that shed by the distant torches at the house's entrance. Nicholls was a whitish blur, coming closer.

Suddenly someone grabbed Grey, turned him forcibly about, and he found himself back to back with Nicholls, the bigger man's heat startling, so near.

Shit, he thought suddenly. *Is he any kind of a shot?*

Someone spoke and he began to walk—he thought he was walking—until an outthrust arm stopped him, and he turned in answer to someone pointing urgently behind him.

Oh, hell, he thought wearily, seeing Nicholls's arm come down. *I don't care.*

He blinked at the muzzle-flash—the report was lost in the shocked gasp from the crowd—and stood for a moment, wondering whether he'd been hit. Nothing seemed amiss, though, and someone nearby was urging him to fire.

Frigging poet, he thought. *I'll delope and have done. I want to go home.* He raised his arm, aiming straight up into the air, but his arm lost contact with his brain for an instant, and his wrist sagged. He jerked, correcting it, and his hand tensed on the trigger. He had barely time to jerk the barrel aside, firing wildly.

To his surprise, Nicholls staggered a bit, then sat down on the grass. He sat propped on one hand, the other clutched dramatically to his shoulder, head thrown back.

It was raining quite hard by now. Grey blinked water off his lashes and shook his head. The air tasted sharp, like cut metal, and for an instant, he had the impression that it smelled . . . purple.

"That can't be right," he said aloud, and found that his ability to speak seemed to have come back. He turned to speak to Hunter, but the surgeon had, of course, darted across to Nicholls, was peering down the neck of the poet's shirt. There was blood on it, Grey saw, but Nicholls was refusing to lie down, gesturing vigorously with his free hand. Blood was running down his face from his nose; perhaps that was it.

"Come away, sir," said a quiet voice at his side. "It'll be bad for Lady Joffrey, else."

"What?" He looked, surprised, to find Richard Tarleton, who had been his ensign in Germany, now in the uniform of a lieutenant in the Lancers. "Oh. Yes, it will." Dueling was illegal in London; for the police to arrest Lucinda's guests before her house would be a scandal—not something that would please her husband, Sir Richard, at all.

The crowd had already melted away, as though the rain had rendered them soluble. The torches by the door had been extinguished. Nicholls was being helped off by Hunter and someone else, lurching away through the increasing rain. Grey shivered. God knew where his coat or cloak was.

"Let's go, then," he said.

Grey opened his eyes.

"Did you say something, Tom?"

Tom Byrd, his valet, had produced a cough like a chimney sweep's, at a distance of approximately one foot from Grey's ear. Seeing that he had obtained his employer's attention, he presented the chamber pot at port arms.

"His Grace is downstairs, me lord. With Her Ladyship."

Grey blinked at the window behind Tom, where the open drapes showed a dim square of rainy light.

"Her Ladyship? What, the duchess?" What could have happened? It couldn't be past nine o'clock. His sister-in-law never paid calls before afternoon, and he had never known her to go anywhere with his brother during the day.

"No, me lord. The little 'un."

"The little—oh. My goddaughter?" He sat up, feeling well but strange, and took the utensil from Tom.

"Yes, me lord. His Grace said as he wants to speak to you about 'the events of last night.'" Tom had crossed to the window and was looking censoriously at the remnants of Grey's shirt and breeches, these stained with grass, mud, blood, and powder, and flung carelessly over the back of the chair. He turned a reproachful eye on Grey, who closed his own, trying to recall exactly what the events of last night had been.

He felt somewhat odd. Not drunk, he hadn't been

drunk; he had no headache, no uneasiness of digestion. . . .

"Last night," he repeated, uncertain. Last night had been confused, but he did remember it. The eel party. Lucinda Joffrey, Caroline . . . why on earth ought Hal to be concerned with . . . what, the duel? Why should his brother care about such a silly affair—and even if he did, why appear at Grey's door at the crack of dawn with his six-month-old daughter?

It was more the time of day than the child's presence that was unusual; his brother often did take his daughter out, with the feeble excuse that the child needed air. His wife accused him of wanting to show the baby off—she was beautiful—but Grey thought the cause somewhat more straightforward. His ferocious, autocratic, dictatorial brother, Colonel of his own regiment, terror of both his own troops and his enemies—had fallen in love with his daughter. The regiment would leave for its new posting within a month's time. Hal simply couldn't bear to have her out of his sight.

Thus, he found the Duke of Pardloe seated in the morning room, Lady Dorothea Jacqueline Benedicta Grey cradled in his arm, gnawing on a rusk her father held for her. Her wet silk bonnet, her tiny rabbit-fur bunting, and several letters, some already opened, lay upon the table at the Duke's elbow.

Hal glanced up at him.

"I've ordered your breakfast. Say hallo to Uncle John, Dottie." He turned the baby gently round. She didn't remove her attention from the rusk, but made a small chirping noise.

"Hallo, sweetheart." John leaned over and kissed the top of her head, covered with a soft blond down and slightly damp. "Having a nice outing with Daddy in the pouring rain?"

"We brought you something." Hal picked up the opened letter and, raising an eyebrow at his brother, handed it to him.

Grey raised an eyebrow back and began to read.

"What!" He looked up from the sheet, mouth open.

"Yes, that's what I said," Hal agreed cordially, "when it was delivered to my door, just before dawn." He reached for the sealed letter, carefully balancing the baby. "Here, this one's yours. It came just after dawn."

Grey dropped the first letter as though it were on fire, and seized the second, ripping it open.

"Oh, John," it read without preamble, *"forgive me, I couldn't stop him, I really couldn't, I'm so sorry. I told him, but he wouldn't listen. I'd run away, but I don't know where to go. Please, please do something!"* It wasn't signed, but didn't need to be. He'd recognized the Honorable Caroline Woodford's writing, scribbled and frantic as it was. The paper was blotched and puckered—with tearstains?

He shook his head violently, as though to clear it, then picked up the first letter again. It was just as he'd read it the first time—a formal demand from Alfred, Lord Enderby, to His Grace the Duke of Pardloe, for satisfaction regarding the injury to the honor of his sister, the Honorable Caroline Woodford, by the agency of His Grace's brother, Lord John Grey.

Grey glanced from one document to the other, several times, then looked at his brother.

"What the devil?"

"I gather you had an eventful evening," Hal said, grunting slightly as he bent to retrieve the rusk Dottie had dropped on the carpet. "No, darling, you don't want that anymore."

Dottie disagreed violently with this assertion, and was distracted only by Uncle John picking her up and blowing in her ear.

"Eventful," he repeated. "Yes, it was, rather. But I didn't do anything to Caroline Woodford save hold her hand whilst being shocked by an electric eel, I swear it. Gleeglgleeglgleegl-pppppssssshhhhh," he added to Dottie, who shrieked and giggled in response. He glanced up to find Hal staring at him.

"Lucinda Joffrey's party," he amplified. "Surely you and Minnie were invited?"

Hal grunted. "Oh. Yes, we were, but I had a prior engagement. Minnie didn't mention the eel. What's this I hear about you fighting a duel over the girl, though?"

"What? It wasn't—" He stopped, trying to think. "Well, perhaps it was, come to think. Nicholls—you know, that swine who wrote the ode to Minnie's feet?—he kissed Miss Woodford, and she didn't want him to, so I punched him. Who told you about the duel?"

"Richard Tarleton. He came into White's card-room late last night, and said he'd just seen you home."

"Well, then, you likely know as much about it as

I do. Oh, you want Daddy back now, do you?" He handed Dottie back to his brother and brushed at a damp patch of saliva on the shoulder of his coat.

"I suppose that's what Enderby's getting at." Hal nodded at the Earl's letter. "That you made the poor girl publicly conspicuous and compromised her virtue by fighting a scandalous duel over her. I suppose he's got a point."

Dottie was now gumming her father's knuckle, making little growling noises. Hal dug in his pocket and came out with a silver teething ring, which he offered her in lieu of his finger, meanwhile giving Grey a sidelong look.

"You don't want to marry Caroline Woodford, do you? That's what Enderby's demand amounts to."

"God, no." Caroline was a good friend—bright, pretty, and given to mad escapades, but marriage? Him?

Hal nodded.

"Lovely girl, but you'd end in Newgate or Bedlam within a month."

"Or dead," Grey said, gingerly picking at the bandage Tom had insisted on wrapping round his knuckles. "How's Nicholls this morning, do you know?"

"Ah." Hal rocked back a little, drawing a deep breath. "Well . . . dead, actually. I had rather a nasty letter from his father, accusing you of murder. That one came over breakfast; didn't think to bring it. Did you mean to kill him?"

Grey sat down quite suddenly, all the blood having left his head.

"No," he whispered. His lips felt stiff and his hands had gone numb. "Oh, Jesus. No."

Hal swiftly pulled his snuffbox from his pocket, one-handed, dumped out the vial of smelling-salts he kept in it and handed it to his brother. Grey was grateful; he hadn't been going to faint, but the assault of ammoniac fumes gave him an excuse for watering eyes and congested breathing.

"Jesus," he repeated, and sneezed explosively several times in a row. "I didn't aim to kill—I swear it, Hal. I deloped. Or tried to," he added honestly.

Lord Enderby's letter suddenly made more sense, as did Hal's presence. What had been a silly affair that should have disappeared with the morning dew had become—or would, directly the gossip had time to spread—not merely a scandal, but quite possibly something worse. It was not unthinkable that he *might* be arrested for murder. Quite without warning, the figured carpet yawned at his feet, an abyss into which his life might vanish.

Hal nodded, and gave him his own handkerchief.

"I know," he said quietly. "Things . . . happen sometimes. That you don't intend—that you'd give your life to have back."

Grey wiped his face, glancing at his brother under cover of the gesture. Hal looked suddenly older than his years, his face drawn by more than worry over Grey.

"Nathaniel Twelvetrees, you mean?" Normally, he wouldn't have mentioned that matter, but both men's guards were down.

Hal gave him a sharp look, then looked away.

"No, not Twelvetrees. I hadn't any choice about that. And I did mean to kill him. I meant . . . what led to that duel." He grimaced. "Marry in haste, repent at leisure." He looked at the note on the table and shook his head. His hand passed gently over Dottie's head. "I won't have you repeat my mistakes, John," he said quietly.

Grey nodded, wordless. Hal's first wife had been seduced by Nathaniel Twelvetrees. Hal's mistakes notwithstanding, Grey had never intended marriage with anyone, and didn't now.

Hal frowned, tapping the folded letter on the table in thought. He darted a glance at John and sighed, then set the letter down, reached into his coat and withdrew two further documents, one clearly official, from its seal.

"Your new commission," he said, handing it over. "For Krefeld," he said, raising an eyebrow at his brother's look of blank incomprehension. "You were brevetted lieutenant-colonel. You didn't remember?"

"I—well . . . not exactly." He had a vague feeling that someone—probably Hal—had told him about it, soon after Krefeld, but he'd been badly wounded then, and in no frame of mind to think about the army, let alone to care about battlefield promotion. Later—

"Wasn't there some confusion over it?" Grey took the commission and opened it, frowning. "I thought they'd changed their minds."

"Oh, you do remember, then," Hal said, eyebrow still cocked. "General Wiedman gave it you after the battle. The confirmation was held up, though, because of the inquiry into the cannon explosion, and then the . . . ah . . . kerfuffle over Adams."

"Oh." Grey was still shaken by the news of Nicholls's death, but mention of Adams started his brain functioning again. "Adams. Oh. You mean Twelvetrees held up the commission?" Colonel Reginald Twelvetrees, of the Royal Artillery—brother to Nathaniel, and cousin to Bernard Adams, the traitor awaiting trial in the Tower, as a result of Grey's efforts the preceding autumn.

"Yes. Bastard," Hal added dispassionately. "I'll have him for breakfast, one of these days."

"Not on my account, I hope," Grey said dryly.

"Oh, no," Hal assured him, jiggling his daughter gently to prevent her fussing. "It will be a purely personal pleasure."

Grey smiled at that, despite his disquiet, and put down the commission. "Right," he said, with a glance at the fourth document, which still lay folded on the table. It was an official-looking letter, and had been opened; the seal was broken. "A proposal of marriage, a denunciation for murder, and a new commission—what the devil's that one? A bill from my tailor?"

"Ah, that. I didn't mean to show it to you," Hal said, leaning carefully to hand it over without dropping Dottie. "But under the circumstances . . ."

He waited, noncommittal, as Grey opened the letter and read it. It was a request—or an order, depending how you looked at it—for the attendance of Major Lord John Grey at the court-martial of one

Captain Charles Carruthers, to serve as witness of character for the same. In . . .

"In Canada?" John's exclamation startled Dottie, who crumpled up her face and threatened to cry.

"Hush, sweetheart." Hal jiggled faster, hastily patting her back. "It's all right; only Uncle John being an ass."

Grey ignored this, waving the letter at his brother.

"What the devil is Charlie Carruthers being court-martialed for? And why on earth am I being summoned as a character witness?"

"Failure to suppress a mutiny," Hal said. "As to why you—he asked for you, apparently. An officer under charges is allowed to call his own witnesses, for whatever purpose. Didn't you know that?"

Grey supposed that he had, in an academic sort of way. But he had never attended a court-martial himself; it wasn't a common proceeding, and he had no real idea of the shape of the proceedings.

He glanced sideways at Hal.

"You say you didn't mean to show it to me?"

Hal shrugged, and blew softly over the top of his daughter's head, making the short blond hairs furrow and rise like wheat in the wind.

"No point. I meant to write back and say that as your commanding officer, I required you here; why should you be dragged off to the wilds of Canada? But given your talent for awkward situations . . . what did it feel like?" he inquired curiously.

"What did—oh, the eel." Grey was accustomed to his brother's lightning shifts of conversation, and made the adjustment easily. "Well, it was rather a shock."

He laughed—if tremulously—at Hal's glower, and Dottie squirmed round in her father's arms, reaching out her own plump little arms appealingly to her uncle.

"Flirt," he told her, taking her from Hal. "No, really, it was remarkable. You know how it feels when you break a bone? That sort of jolt before you feel the pain, that goes right through you, and you go blind for a moment and feel like someone's driven a nail through your belly? It was like that, only much stronger, and it went on for longer. Stopped my breath," he admitted. "Quite literally. And my heart, too, I think. Dr. Hunter—you know, the anatomist?—was there, and pounded on my chest to get it started again."

Hal was listening with close attention, and asked several questions, which Grey answered automatically, his mind occupied with this latest surprising communiqué.

Charlie Carruthers. They'd been young officers together, though from different regiments. Fought beside one another in Scotland, gone round London together for a bit on their next leave. They'd had— well, you couldn't call it an affair. Three or four brief encounters—sweating, breathless quarters of an hour in dark corners that could be conveniently forgotten in daylight, or shrugged off as the result of drunkennness, not spoken of by either party.

That had been in the Bad Time, as he thought of it; those years after Hector's death, when he'd sought oblivion wherever he could find it—and found it often—before slowly recovering himself.

Likely he wouldn't have recalled Carruthers at all, save for the one thing.

Carruthers had been born with an interesting deformity—he had a double hand. While Carruthers's right hand was normal in appearance and worked quite as usual, there was another, dwarf hand that sprang from his wrist and nestled neatly against its larger partner. Dr. Hunter would probably pay hundreds for that hand, Grey thought with a mild lurch of the stomach.

The dwarf hand had only two short fingers and a stubby thumb—but Carruthers could open and close it, though not without also opening and closing the larger one. The shock when Carruthers had closed both of them simultaneously on Grey's prick had been nearly as extraordinary as had the electric eel's.

"Nicholls hasn't been buried yet, has he?" he asked abruptly, the thought of the eel party and Dr. Hunter causing him to interrupt some remark of Hal's.

Hal looked surprised.

"Surely not. Why?" He narrowed his eyes at Grey. "You don't mean to attend the funeral, surely?"

"No, no," Grey said hastily. "I was only thinking of Dr. Hunter. He, um, has a certain reputation . . . and Nicholls did go off with him. After the duel."

"A reputation as what, for God's sake?" Hal demanded impatiently.

"As a body-snatcher," Grey blurted.

There was a sudden silence, awareness dawning in Hal's face. He'd gone pale.

"You don't think—no! How could he?"

"A . . . um . . . hundredweight or so of stones being substituted just prior to the coffin's being nailed shut is the usual method—or so I've heard," Grey said, as well as he could with Dottie's fist being poked up his nose.

Hal swallowed. Grey could see the hairs rise on his wrist.

"I'll ask Harry," Hal said, after a short silence. "The funeral can't have been arranged yet, and if . . ."

Both brothers shuddered reflexively, imagining all too exactly the scene as an agitated family member insisted upon raising the coffin lid, to find . . .

"Maybe better not," Grey said, swallowing. Dottie had left off trying to remove his nose and was patting her tiny hand over his lips as he talked. The feel of it on his skin . . .

He peeled her gently off and gave her back to Hal.

"I don't know what use Charles Carruthers thinks I might be to him—but all right, I'll go." He glanced at Lord Enderby's note, Caroline's crumpled missive. "After all, I suppose there are worse things than being scalped by Red Indians."

Hal nodded, sober.

"I've arranged your sailing. You leave tomorrow." He stood and lifted Dottie. "Here, sweetheart. Kiss your uncle John good-bye."

A month later, Grey found himself, Tom Byrd at his side, climbing off the *Harwood* and into one of the small boats that would land them and the battalion of Louisbourg grenadiers with whom they had been traveling on a large island near the mouth of the St. Lawrence River.

He had never seen anything like it. The river itself was larger than any he had ever seen, nearly half a mile across, running wide and deep, a dark blue-black under the sun. Great cliffs and undulating hills rose on either side of the river, so thickly forested that the underlying stone was nearly invisible. It was hot, and the sky arched brilliant overhead, much brighter and much wider than any sky he had seen before. A loud hum echoed from the lush growth—insects, he supposed, birds, and the rush of the water, though it felt as though the wilderness were singing to itself, in a voice heard only in his blood. Beside him, Tom was fairly vibrating with excitement, his eyes out on stalks, not to miss anything.

"Cor, is that a Red Indian?" he whispered, leaning close to Grey in the boat.

"I don't suppose he can be anything else," Grey replied, as the gentleman loitering by the landing was naked save for a breech-clout, a striped blanket slung over one shoulder, and a coating of what—from the shimmer of his limbs—appeared to be grease of some kind.

"I thought they'd be redder," Tom said, echoing Grey's own thought. The Indian's skin was considerably darker than Grey's own, to be sure, but a rather pleasant soft brown in color, something like dried oak leaves. The Indian appeared to find them nearly as interesting as they had found him; he was eyeing Grey in particular with intent consideration.

"It's your hair, me lord," Tom hissed in Grey's ear. "I told you you ought to have worn a wig."

"Nonsense, Tom." At the same time, Grey experienced an odd frisson up the back of the neck, constricting his scalp. Vain of his hair, which was blond and thick, he didn't commonly wear a wig, choosing instead to bind and powder his own for formal occasions. The present occasion wasn't formal in the least. With the advent of fresh water aboard, Tom had insisted upon washing his hair that morning, and it was still spread loose upon his shoulders, though it had long since dried.

The boat crunched on the shingle, and the Indian flung aside his blanket and came to help the men run it up the shore. Grey found himself next the man, close enough to smell him. He smelled quite unlike anyone Grey had ever encountered; gamy, certainly—he wondered, with a small thrill, whether the grease the man wore might be bear-fat—but with the tang of herbs and a sweat like fresh-sheared copper.

Straightening up from the gunwale, the Indian caught Grey's eye and smiled.

"You be careful, Englishman," he said, in a voice with a noticeable French accent, and reaching out, ran his fingers quite casually through Grey's loose hair. "Your scalp would look good on a Huron's belt."

This made the soldiers from the boat all laugh, and the Indian, still smiling, turned to them.

"They are not so particular, the Abenaki who work

for the French. A scalp is a scalp—and the French pay well for one, no matter what color." He nodded genially to the grenadiers, who had stopped laughing. "You come with me."

There was a small camp on the island already; a detachment of infantry under a Captain Woodford— whose name gave Grey a slight wariness, but who turned out to be no relation, thank God, to Lord Enderby's family.

"We're fairly safe on this side of the island," he told Grey, offering him a flask of brandy outside his own tent after supper. "But the Indians raid the other side regularly—I lost four men last week, three killed and one carried off."

"You have your own scouts, though?" Grey asked, slapping at the mosquitoes that had begun to swarm in the dusk. He had not seen the Indian who had brought them to the camp again, but there were several more in camp, mostly clustered together around their own fire, but one or two squatting among the Louisbourg grenadiers who had crossed with Grey on the *Harwood*, bright-eyed and watchful.

"Yes, and trustworthy for the most part," Woodford said, answering Grey's unasked question. He laughed, though not with any humor. "At least we hope so."

Woodford gave him supper, and they had a hand of cards, Grey exchanging news of home for gossip of the current campaign.

General Wolfe had spent no little time at Montmorency, below the town of Quebec, but had nothing but disappointment from his attempts there, and so had abandoned that post, regathering the main body of his troops some miles upstream from the Citadel of Quebec. A so-far impregnable fortress, perched on sheer cliffs above the river, commanding both the river and the plains to the west with her cannon, obliging English warships to steal past under cover of night—and not always successfully.

"Wolfe'll be champing at the bit, now his grenadiers are come," Woodford predicted. "He puts great store by those fellows, fought with 'em at Louisbourg. Here, Colonel, you're being eaten alive—try a bit of this on your hands and face." He dug about in his campaign chest and came up with a tin of strong-smelling grease, which he pushed across the table.

"Bear-grease and mint," he explained. "The Indians use it—that, or cover themselves with mud."

Grey helped himself liberally; the scent wasn't quite the same as what he had smelled earlier on the scout, but it was very similar, and he felt an odd sense of disturbance in its application. Though it did discourage the biting insects.

He had made no secret of the reason for his presence, and now asked openly about Carruthers.

"Where is he held, do you know?"

Woodford frowned and poured more brandy.

"He's not. He's paroled; has a billet in the town at Gareon, where Wolfe's headquarters are."

"Ah?" Grey was mildly surprised—but then, Carruthers was not charged with mutiny, but rather with failure to suppress one—a rare charge. "Do you know the particulars of the case?"

Woodford opened his mouth, as though to speak, but then drew a deep breath, shook his head, and drank brandy. From which Grey deduced that probably everyone knew the particulars, but that there was something fishy about the affair. Well, time enough. He'd hear about the matter directly from Carruthers.

Conversation became general, and after a time, Grey said good-night. The grenadiers had been busy; a new little city of canvas tents had sprung up at the edge of the existing camp, and the appetizing smells of fresh meat roasting and brewing tea were rising on the air.

Tom had doubtless managed to raise his own tent, somewhere in the mass. He was in no hurry to find it, though; he was enjoying the novel sensations of firm footing and solitude, after weeks of crowded shipboard life. He cut outside the orderly rows of new tents, walking just beyond the glow of the firelight, feeling pleasantly invisible, though still close enough for safety—or at least he hoped so. The forest stood only a few yards beyond, the outlines of trees and bushes still just visible, the dark not quite complete.

A drifting spark of green drew his eye, and he felt delight well up in him. There was another . . . another . . . ten, a dozen, and the air was suddenly full of fireflies, soft green sparks that winked on and off, glowing like tiny distant candles among the dark foliage. He'd seen fireflies once or twice before, in Germany, but never in such abundance. They were simple magic, pure as moonlight.

He could not have said how long he watched them, wandering slowly along the edge of the encampment, but at last he sighed and turned toward the center, full-fed, pleasantly tired, and with no immediate responsibility to do anything. He had no troops under his command, no reports to write . . . nothing, really, to do until he reached Gareon and Charlie Carruthers.

With a sigh of peace, he closed the flap of his tent and shucked his outer clothing.

He was roused abruptly from the edge of sleep by screams and shouts, and sat bolt upright. Tom, who had been asleep on his bedsack at Grey's feet, sprang up like a frog onto hands and knees, scrabbling madly for pistol and shot in the chest.

Not waiting, Grey seized the dagger he had hung on the tent-peg before retiring, and flinging back the flap, peered out. Men were rushing to and fro, colliding with tents, shouting orders, yelling for help. There was a glow in the sky, a reddening of the low-hanging clouds.

"Fire-ships!" someone shouted. Grey shoved his feet into his shoes and joined the throng of men now rushing toward the water.

Out in the center of the broad dark river stood the bulk of the *Harwood*, at anchor. And coming slowly down upon her were one, two, and then three blazing vessels—a raft, stacked with flammable waste, doused with oil and set afire. A small boat, its mast and sail flaming bright against the night. Something else—an

Indian canoe, with a heap of burning grass and leaves? Too far to see, but it was coming closer.

He glanced at the ship and saw movement on deck—too far to make out individual men, but things were happening. The ship couldn't raise anchor and sail away, not in time—but she was lowering her boats, sailors setting out to try to deflect the fire-ships, keep them away from the *Harwood*.

Absorbed in the sight, he had not noticed the shrieks and shouts still coming from the other side of the camp. But now, as the men on the shore fell silent, watching the fire-ships, they began to stir, realizing belatedly that something else was afoot.

"Indians," the man beside Grey said suddenly as a particularly high, ululating screech split the air. "Indians!"

This cry became general, and everyone began to rush in the other direction.

"Stop! Halt!" Grey flung out an arm, catching a man across the throat and knocking him flat. He raised his voice in the vain hope of stopping the rush. "You! You and you—seize your neighbor, come with me!" The man he had knocked down bounced up again, white-eyed in the starlight.

"It may be a trap!" Grey shouted. "Stay here! Stand to your arms!"

"Stand! Stand!" A short gentleman in his night-shirt took up the cry in a cast-iron bellow, adding to its effect by seizing a dead branch from the ground and laying about himself, turning back those trying to get past him to the encampment.

Another spark grew upstream, and another beyond it: more fire-ships. The boats were in the water now, mere dots in the darkness. If they could fend off the fire-ships, the *Harwood* might be saved from immediate destruction; Grey's fear was that whatever was going on in the rear of the encampment was a ruse designed to pull men away from the shore, leaving the ship protected only by her marines, should the French then send down a barge loaded with explosives, or a boarding craft, hoping to elude detection whilst everyone was dazzled or occupied by the blazing fire-ships and the raid.

The first of the fire-ships had drifted harmlessly onto the far shore, and was burning itself out on the sand, brilliant and beautiful against the night. The short gentleman with the remarkable voice—clearly he was a sergeant, Grey thought—had succeeded in rallying a small group of soldiers, whom he now presented to Grey with a brisk salute.

"Will they go and fetch their muskets, all orderly, sir?"

"They will," Grey said. "And hurry. Go with them, Sergeant—it is sergeant?"

"Sergeant Aloysius Cutter, sir," the short gentleman replied with a nod, "and pleased to know an officer what has a brain in his head."

"Thank you, Sergeant. And fetch back as many more men as fall conveniently to hand, if you please. With arms. A rifleman or two, if you can find one."

Matters thus momentarily attended to, he turned his attention once more to the river, where two of the

Harwood's small boats were herding one of the fireships away from the transport, circling it and pushing water with their oars; he caught the splash of their efforts, and the shouts of the sailors.

"Me lord?"

The voice at his elbow nearly made him swallow his tongue. He turned with an attempt at calmness, ready to reproach Tom for venturing out into the chaos, but before he could summon words, his young valet stooped at his feet, holding something.

"I've brought your breeches, me lord," Tom said, voice trembling. "Thought you might need 'em, if there was fighting."

"Very thoughtful of you, Tom," he assured his valet, fighting an urge to laugh. He stepped into the breeches and pulled them up, tucking in his shirt. "What's been happening in the camp, do you know?"

He could hear Tom swallow hard.

"Indians, me lord," Tom said. "They came screaming through the tents, set one or two afire. They killed one man I saw, and . . . and scalped him." His voice was thick, as though he might be about to vomit. "It was nasty."

"I daresay." The night was warm, but Grey felt the hairs rise on arms and neck. The chilling screams had stopped, and while he could still hear considerable hubbub in the camp, it was of a different tone now; no random shouting, just the calls of officers, sergeants, and corporals ordering the men, beginning the process of assembly, of counting noses and reckoning damage.

Tom, bless him, had brought Grey's pistol, shot-bag,

and powder, as well as his coat and stockings. Aware of the dark forest and the long, narrow trail between the shore and the camp, Grey didn't send Tom back, but merely told him to keep out of the way as Sergeant Cutter—who with good military instinct, had also taken time to put his breeches on—came up with his armed recruits.

"All present, sir," Cutter said, saluting. "'Oom 'ave I the honor of h'addressing, sir?"

"I am Lieutenant-Colonel Grey. Set your men to watch the ship, please, Sergeant, with particular attention to dark craft coming downstream, and then come back to report what you know of matters in camp."

Cutter saluted and promptly vanished with a shout of "Come on, you shower o' shit! Look lively, look lively!"

Tom gave a brief strangled scream, and Grey whirled, drawing his dagger by reflex, to find a dark shape directly behind him.

"Don't kill me, Englishman," said the Indian who had led them to the camp earlier. He sounded mildly amused. "*Le capitaine* sent me to find you."

"Why?" Grey asked shortly. His heart was still pounding from the shock. He disliked being taken at a disadvantage, and disliked even more the thought that the man could easily have killed him before Grey knew he was there.

"The Abenaki set your tent on fire; he supposed they might have dragged you and your servant into the forest."

Tom uttered an extremely coarse expletive and

made as though to dive directly into the trees, but Grey stopped him with a hand on his arm.

"Stay, Tom. It doesn't matter."

"The bloody hell you say," Tom replied heatedly, agitation depriving him of his normal manners. "I daresay I can find you more smallclothes, not as that will be easy, but what about your cousin's painting of her and the little 'un she sent for Captain Stubbs? What about your good hat with the gold lace!"

Grey had a brief moment of alarm—his young cousin Olivia had sent a miniature of herself and her newborn son, charging him to deliver this to her husband, Captain Malcolm Stubbs, presently with Wolfe's troops. He clapped a hand to his side, though, and felt with relief the oval shape of the miniature in its wrappings, safe in his pocket.

"That's all right, Tom; I've got it. As to the hat . . . we'll worry about that later, I think. Here—what is your name, sir?" he inquired of the Indian, unwilling to address him simply as *you.*

"Manoke," said the Indian, still sounding amused.

"Quite. Will you take my servant back to the camp?" He saw the small determined figure of Sergeant Cutter appear at the mouth of the trail, and firmly overriding Tom's protests, shooed him off in care of the Indian.

In the event, all five fire-ships either drifted or were steered away from the *Harwood.* Something that might—or might not—have been a boarding craft did appear upstream, but was frightened off by Grey's

impromptu troops on the shore, firing volleys—
though the range was woefully short; there was no
possibility of hitting anything.

Still, the *Harwood* was secure, and the camp had
settled into a state of uneasy watchfulness. Grey had
seen Woodford briefly upon his return, near dawn,
and learned that the raid had resulted in the deaths of
two men and the capture of three more, dragged off
into the forest. Three of the Indian raiders had been
killed, another wounded—Woodford intended to in-
terview this man before he died, but doubted that any
useful information would result.

"They never talk," he'd said, rubbing at his smoke-
reddened eyes. His face was pouchy and gray with
fatigue. "They just close their eyes and start singing
their damned deathsongs. Not a blind bit of difference what you do to 'em—they just keep singing."

Grey had heard it, or thought he had, as he crawled
wearily into his borrowed shelter toward daybreak. A
faint high-pitched chant that rose and fell like the rush
of the wind in the trees overhead. It kept up for a bit,
then stopped abruptly, only to resume again, faint and
interrupted, as he teetered on the edge of sleep.

What was the man saying? he wondered. Did it
matter that none of the men hearing him knew what he
said? Perhaps the scout—Manoke, that was his name—
was there; perhaps he would know.

Tom had found Grey a small tent at the end of a
row. Probably he had ejected some subaltern, but Grey
wasn't inclined to object. It was barely big enough for
the canvas bedsack that lay on the ground and a box

that served as table, on which stood an empty candle-stick, but it was shelter. It had begun to rain lightly as he walked up the trail to camp, and the rain was now pattering busily on the canvas overhead, raising a sweet musty scent. If the deathsong continued, it was no longer audible over the sound of the rain.

Grey turned over once, the grass stuffing of the bedsack rustling softly beneath him, and fell at once into sleep.

He woke abruptly, face-to-face with an Indian. His re-flexive flurry of movement was met with a low chuckle and a slight withdrawal, rather than a knife across the throat, though, and he broke through the fog of sleep in time to avoid doing serious damage to the scout Manoke.

"What?" he muttered, and rubbed the heel of his hand across his eyes. "What is it?" *And why the devil are you lying on my bed?*

In answer to this, the Indian put a hand behind his head, drew him close, and kissed him. The man's tongue ran lightly across his lower lip, darted like a lizard's into his mouth, and then was gone.

So was the Indian.

He rolled over onto his back, blinking. A dream. It was still raining, harder now. He breathed in deeply; he could smell bear-grease, of course, on his own skin, and mint—was there any hint of metal? The light was stronger—it must be day; he heard the drummer pass-ing through the aisles of tents to rouse the men, the rattle of his sticks blending with the rattle of the rain, the shouts of corporals and sergeants—but still faint and gray. He could not have been asleep for more than half an hour, he thought.

"Christ," he muttered, and turning himself stiffly over, pulled his coat over his head and sought sleep once again.

The *Harwood* tacked slowly upriver, with a sharp eye out for French marauders. There were a few alarms, including another raid by hostile Indians while camped on shore. This one ended more happily, with four marauders killed, and only one cook wounded, not seriously. They were obliged to loiter for a time, waiting for a cloudy night, in order to steal past the fortress of Quebec, menacing on its cliffs. They were spotted, in fact, and one or two cannon fired in their direction, but to no effect. And at last came into port at Gareon, the site of General Wolfe's headquarters.

The town itself had been nearly engulfed by the growing military encampment that surrounded it, acres of tents spreading upward from the settlement on the riverbank, the whole presided over by a small French Catholic mission, whose tiny cross was just visible at the top of the hill that lay behind the town. The French inhabitants, with the political indifference of merchants everywhere, had given a Gallic shrug and set about happily overcharging the occupying forces.

The General himself was elsewhere, Grey was informed, fighting inland, but would doubtless return within the month. A lieutenant-colonel without brief or regimental affiliation was simply a nuisance; he was provided with suitable quarters and politely shooed away. With no immediate duties to fulfill, he gave a shrug of his own and set out to discover the whereabouts of Captain Carruthers.

It wasn't difficult to find him. The *patron* of the first tavern Grey visited directed him at once to the habitat of *le Capitaine*, a room in the house of a widow named Lambert, near the mission church. Grey wondered whether he would have received the information as readily from any other tavern-keeper in the village. Charlie had liked to drink when Grey knew him, and evidently still did, judging from the genial attitude of the *patron* when Carruthers's name was mentioned. Not that Grey could blame him, under the circumstances.

The widow—young, chestnut-haired and quite attractive—viewed the English officer at her door with a deep suspicion, but when he followed his request for Captain Carruthers by mentioning that he was an old friend of the Captain's, her face relaxed.

"*Bon,*" she said, swinging the door open abruptly. "He needs friends."

He ascended two flights of narrow stairs to Carruthers's attic, feeling the air about him grow warmer. It was pleasant at this time of day, but must grow stifling by midafternoon. He knocked, and felt a small shock of pleased recognition at hearing Carruthers's voice bid him enter.

Carruthers was seated at a rickety table in shirt

and breeches, writing, an inkwell made from a gourd at one elbow, a pot of beer at the other. He looked at Grey blankly for an instant; then joy washed across his features, and he rose, nearly upsetting both.

"John!"

Before Grey could offer his hand, he found himself embraced—and returned the embrace wholeheartedly, a wash of memory flooding through him as he smelled Carruthers's hair, felt the scrape of his unshaven cheek against Grey's own. Even in the midst of this sensation, though, he felt the slightness of Carruthers's body, the bones that pressed through his clothes.

"I never thought you'd come," Carruthers was repeating, for perhaps the fourth time. He let go and stepped back, smiling as he dashed the back of his hand across his eyes, which were unabashedly wet.

"Well, you have an electric eel to thank for my presence," Grey told him, smiling himself.

"A what?" Carruthers stared at him blankly.

"Long story—tell you later. For the moment, though—what the devil have you been doing, Charlie?"

The happiness faded somewhat from Carruthers's lean face, but didn't disappear altogether. "Ah. Well. That's a long story, too. Let me send Martine for more beer." He waved Grey toward the room's only stool, and went out before Grey could protest. He sat gingerly, lest the stool collapse, but it held his weight. Besides the stool and table, the attic was very plainly furnished; a narrow cot, a chamber pot, and an ancient washstand with an earthenware basin and ewer completed the ensemble. It was very clean, but there was a faint smell of something in the air—something sweet and sickly, which he traced at once to a corked bottle standing at the back of the washstand.

Not that he had needed the smell of laudanum; one look at Carruthers's gaunt face told him enough. Returning to the stool, he glanced at the papers Carruthers had been working on. They appeared to be notes in preparation for the court-martial; the one on top was an account of an expedition undertaken by troops under Carruthers's command, on the orders of a Major Gerald Siverly.

> *"Our orders instructed us to march to a village called Beaulieu, some ten miles to the east of Montmorency, there to ransack and fire the houses, driving off such animals as we encountered. This we did. Some men of the village offered us resistance, armed with scythes and other implements. Two of these were shot, the others fled. We returned with two waggons filled with flour, cheeses, and small household goods, three cows, and two good mules."*

Grey got no further before the door opened.

Carruthers came in and sat on the bed, nodding toward the papers.

"I thought I'd best write everything down. Just in case I don't live long enough for the court-martial." He spoke matter-of-factly, and seeing the look on Grey's face, smiled faintly. "Don't be troubled, John.

I've always known I'd not make old bones. This—"
He turned his right hand upward, letting the droop-
ing cuff of his shirt fall back. "—isn't all of it."

He tapped his chest gently with his left hand.

"More than one doctor's told me I have some gross
defect of the heart. Don't know, quite, if I have two of
those, too—" He grinned at Grey, the sudden charming smile he remembered so well. "—or only half of
one, or what. Used to be, I just went faint now and
then, but it's getting worse. Sometimes I feel it stop
beating and just flutter in my chest, and everything
begins to go all black and breathless. So far, it's always started beating again—but one of these days, it
isn't going to."

Grey's eyes were fixed on Charlie's hand, the small
dwarf hand curled against its larger fellow, looking as
though Charlie held a strange flower cupped in his
palm. As he watched, both hands opened slowly, the
fingers moving in strangely beautiful synchrony.

"All right," he said quietly. "Tell me."

Failure to suppress a mutiny was a rare charge;
difficult to prove, and thus unlikely to be brought,
unless other factors were involved. Which in the present instance, they undoubtedly were.

"Know Siverly, do you?" Carruthers asked, taking
the papers onto his knee.

"Not at all. I gather he's a bastard." Grey gestured
at the papers. "What kind of bastard, though?"

"A corrupt one." Carruthers tapped the pages
square, carefully evening the edges, eyes fixed on them.
"That—what you read—it wasn't Siverly. It's General

Wolfe's directive. I'm not sure whether the point is to deprive the fortress of provisions, in hopes of starving them out eventually, or to put pressure on Montcalm to send out troops to defend the countryside, where Wolfe could get at them—possibly both. But he means deliberately to terrorize the settlements on both sides of the river. No, we did this under the General's orders." His face twisted a little, and he looked up suddenly at Grey. "You remember the Highlands, John?"

"You know that I do." No one involved in Cumberland's cleansing of the Highlands would ever forget. He had seen many Scottish villages like Beaulieu.

Carruthers took a deep breath.

"Yes. Well. The trouble was that Siverly took to appropriating the plunder we took from the countryside— under the pretext of selling it in order to make an equitable distribution among the troops."

"What?" This was contrary to the normal custom of the army, whereby any soldier was entitled to what plunder he took. "Who does he think he is, an admiral?" The navy did divide shares of prize money among the crew, according to formula—but the navy was the navy; crews acted much more as single entities than did army companies, and there were Admiralty courts set up to deal with the sale of captured prize-ships.

Carruthers laughed at the question.

"His brother's a commodore. Perhaps that's where he got the notion. At any rate," he added, sobering, "he never did distribute the funds. Worse—he began withholding the soldiers' pay. Paying later and later, stopping pay for petty offenses, claiming that the paychest hadn't been delivered—when several men had seen it unloaded from the coach with their own eyes.

"Bad enough—but the soldiers were still being fed and clothed adequately. But then he went too far."

Siverly began to steal from the commissary, diverting quantities of supplies and selling them privately.

"I had my suspicions," Carruthers explained, "but no proof. I'd begun to watch him, though—and he knew I was watching him, so he trod carefully for a bit. But he couldn't resist the rifles."

A shipment of a dozen new rifles, vastly superior to the ordinary Brown Bess musket, and very rare in the army.

"I think it must have been a clerical oversight that sent them to us in the first place. We hadn't any riflemen, and there was no real need for them. That's probably what made Siverly think he could get away with it."

But he hadn't. Two private soldiers had unloaded the box, and, curious at the weight, had opened it. Excited word had spread—and excitement had turned to disgruntled surprise when, instead of new rifles, muskets showing considerable wear were later distributed. The talk—already angry—had escalated.

"Egged on by a hogshead of rum we confiscated from a tavern in Levi," Carruthers said with a sigh. "They drank all night—it was January, the nights are damned long in January here—and made up their minds to go and find the rifles. Which they did—under the floor in Siverly's quarters."

"And where was Siverly?"

"In his quarters. He was rather badly used, I'm afraid." A muscle by Carruthers's mouth twitched. "Escaped through a window, though, and made his way through the snow to the next garrison. It was twenty miles. Lost a couple of toes to frostbite, but survived."

"Too bad."

"Yes, it was." The muscle twitched again.

"What happened to the mutineers?"

Carruthers blew out his cheeks, shaking his head.

"Deserted, most of them. Two were caught and hanged pretty promptly; three more rounded up later; they're in prison here."

"And you—"

"And I." Carruthers nodded. "I was Siverly's second-in-command. I didn't know about the mutiny—one of the ensigns ran to fetch me when the men started to move toward Siverly's quarters—but I did arrive before they'd finished."

"Not a great deal you could do under those circumstances, was there?"

"I didn't try," Carruthers said bluntly.

"I see," Grey said.

"Do you?" Carruthers gave him a crooked smile.

"Certainly. I take it Siverly is still in the army, and still holds a command? Yes, of course. He might have been furious enough to prefer the original charge against you, but you know as well as I do that under normal circumstances, the matter would likely have been dropped as soon as the general facts were known.

You insisted on a court-martial, didn't you? So that you can make what you know public." Given Carruthers's state of health, the knowledge that he risked a long imprisonment if convicted apparently didn't trouble him.

The smile straightened, and became genuine.

"I knew I chose the right man," Carruthers said.

"I am exceeding flattered," Grey said dryly. "Why me, though?"

Carruthers had laid aside his papers, and now rocked back a little on the cot, hands linked around one knee.

"Why you, John?" The smile had vanished, and Carruthers's gray eyes were level on his. "You know what we do. Our business is chaos, death, destruction. But you know why we do it, too."

"Oh? Perhaps you'd have the goodness to tell me, then. I've always wondered."

Humor lighted Charlie's eyes, but he spoke seriously.

"Someone has to keep order, John. Soldiers fight for all kinds of reasons, most of them ignoble. You and your brother, though . . ." He broke off, shaking his head.

Grey saw that his hair was streaked with gray, though he knew Carruthers was no older than himself.

"The world is chaos and death and destruction. But people like you—you don't stand for that. If there is any order in the world, any peace—it's because of you, John, and those very few like you."

Grey felt he should say something, but was at a loss as to what that might be. Carruthers rose and came to Grey, putting a hand—the left—on his shoulder, the other gently against his face.

"What is it the Bible says?" Carruthers said quietly. "Blessed are they that hunger and thirst for justice, for they shall be satisfied? I hunger, John," he whispered. "And you thirst. You won't fail me." The fingers of Charlie's secret moved on his skin, a plea, a caress.

> "*The custom of the army is that a court-martial be presided over by a senior officer and such a number of other officers as he shall think fit to serve as council, these being generally four in number, but can be more but not generally less than three. The person accused shall have the right to call witnesses in his support, and the council shall question these, as well as any other persons whom they may wish, and shall thus determine the circumstances, and if conviction ensue, the sentence to be imposed.*"

That rather vague statement was evidently all that existed in terms of written definition and directive regarding the operations of courts-martial—or was all that Hal had turned up for him in the brief period prior to his departure. There were no formal laws governing such courts, nor did the law of the land apply to them. In short, the army was—as always, Grey thought—a law unto itself.

That being so, he might have considerable leeway in accomplishing what Charlie Carruthers wanted—or not, depending upon the personalities and professional alliances of the officers who composed the court. It would behoove him to discover these men as soon as possible.

In the meantime, he had another small duty to discharge.

"Tom," he called, rummaging in his trunk, "have you discovered Captain Stubbs's billet?"

"Yes, me lord. And if you'll give over ruining your shirts, there, I'll tell you." With a censorious look at his master, Tom nudged him deftly aside. "What you a-looking for in there, anyway?"

"The miniature of my cousin and her child." Grey stood back, permitting Tom to bend over the open chest, tenderly patting the abused shirts back into their tidy folds. The chest itself was rather scorched, but the soldiers had succeeded in rescuing it—and Grey's wardrobe, to Tom's relief.

"Here, me lord." Tom withdrew the little packet and handed it gently to Grey. "Give me best to Captain Stubbs. Reckon he'll be glad to get that. The little 'un's got quite the look of him, don't he?"

It took some little time, even with Tom's direction, to discover Malcolm Stubbs's billet. The address—insofar as it could be called one—lay in the poorer section of the town, somewhere down a muddy lane that ended abruptly at the river. Grey was surprised at this; Stubbs was a most sociable sort, and a conscientious officer. Why was he not billeted in an inn, or a good private house, near his troops?

By the time he found the lane, he had an uneasy

feeling; this grew markedly as he poked his way through the ramshackle sheds and the knots of filthy polyglot children that broke from their play, brightening at the novel sight, and followed him, hissing unintelligible speculations to each other, but who stared blankly at him, mouths open, when he asked after Captain Stubbs, pointing at his own uniform by way of illustration, with a questioning wave at their surroundings.

He had made his way down the lane, and his boots were caked with mud, dung, and a thick plastering of the leaves that sifted in a constant rain from the giant trees, before he discovered someone willing to answer him. This was an ancient Indian, sitting peacefully on a rock at the river's edge, wrapped in a striped British trade blanket, fishing. The man spoke a mixture of three or four languages, only two of which Grey understood, but this basis of understanding was adequate.

"*Un, deux, trois*, in back," the ancient told him, pointing a thumb up the lane, then jerking this appendage sideways. Something in an aboriginal tongue followed, in which Grey thought he detected a reference to a woman—doubtless the owner of the house where Stubbs was billeted. A concluding reference to "*le bon Capitaine*" seemed to reinforce this impression, and thanking the gentleman in both French and English, Grey retraced his steps to the third house up the lane, still trailing a line of curious urchins like the ragged tail of a kite.

No one answered his knock, but he went round

the house—followed by the children—and discovered a small hut behind it, smoke coming from its gray stone chimney.

The day was beautiful, with a sky the color of sapphires, and the air was suffused with the tang of early autumn. The door of the hut was ajar, to admit the crisp, fresh air, but he did not push it open. Instead, he drew his dagger from his belt and knocked with the hilt—to admiring gasps from his audience at the appearance of the knife. He repressed the urge to turn round and bow to them.

He heard no footsteps from within, but the door opened suddenly, revealing a young Indian woman whose face blazed with sudden joy at beholding him.

He blinked, startled, and in that blink of an eye, the joy disappeared and the young woman clutched at the door-jamb for support, her other hand fisted into her chest.

"*Batinse!*" she gasped, clearly terrified. "*Qu'est-ce qui s'passe?*"

"*Rien,*" he replied, equally startled. "*Ne t'inquiete pas, madame. Est-ce que Capitaine Stubbs habite ici?*" *Don't perturb yourself, madam. Does Captain Stubbs live here?*

Her eyes, already huge, rolled back in her head, and he seized her arm, fearing lest she faint at his feet. The largest of the urchins following him rushed forward and pushed the door open, and he put an arm round the woman's waist and half dragged, half carried her into the house.

Taking this as invitation, the rest of the children crowded in behind him, murmuring in what appeared to be sympathy, as he lugged the young woman to the bed and deposited her thereon. A small girl, wearing little more than a pair of drawers snugged round her insubstantial waist with a piece of string, pressed in beside him and said something to the young woman. Not receiving an answer, the girl behaved as though she had, turning and racing out of the door.

Grey hesitated, not sure what to do. The woman was breathing, though pale, and her eyelids fluttered.

"Voulez-vous un peu de l'eau?" he inquired, turning about in search of water. He spotted a bucket of water near the hearth, but his attention was distracted from this by an object propped beside it. A cradle-board, with a swaddled infant bound to it, blinking large, curious eyes in his direction.

He knew already, of course, but knelt down before the infant and waggled a tentative forefinger at it. The baby's eyes were big and dark, like its mother's, and the skin a paler shade of her own. The hair, though, was not straight, thick and black. It was the color of cinnamon, and exploded from the child's skull in a nimbus of the same curls that Malcolm Stubbs kept rigorously clipped to his scalp and hidden beneath his wig.

"Wha' happen with *le Capitaine*?" a peremptory voice demanded behind him. He turned on his heels, and, finding a rather large woman looming over him, rose to his feet and bowed.

"Nothing whatever, madam," he assured her. *Not yet, it hasn't.* "I was merely seeking Captain Stubbs, to give him a message."

"Oh." The woman—French, but plainly the younger woman's mother or aunt—left off glowering at him and seemed to deflate somewhat, settling back into a less threatening shape. "Well, then. *D'un urgence*, this message?" She eyed him; clearly other British officers were not in the habit of visiting Stubbs at home. Most likely Stubbs had an official billet elsewhere, where he conducted his regimental business. No wonder they thought he'd come to say that Stubbs was dead or injured. *Not yet*, he added grimly to himself.

"No," he said, feeling the weight of the miniature in his pocket. "Important, but not urgent." He left then. None of the children followed him.

Normally, it was not difficult to discover the whereabouts of a particular soldier, but Malcolm Stubbs seemed to have disappeared into thin air. Over the course of the next week, Grey combed headquarters, the military encampment, and the village, but no trace of his disgraceful cousin-by-marriage could be found. Still odder, no one appeared to have missed the Captain. The men of Stubbs's immediate company merely shrugged in confusion, and his superior officer had evidently gone off upriver to inspect the state of various postings. Frustrated, Grey retired to the riverbank to think.

Two logical possibilities presented themselves—no,

three. One, that Stubbs had heard about Grey's arrival, supposed that Grey would discover exactly what he *had* discovered and had in consequence panicked and deserted. Two, he'd fallen foul of someone in a tavern or back alley, been killed, and was presently decomposing quietly under a layer of leaves in the woods. Or three—he'd been sent somewhere to do something, quietly.

Grey doubted the first exceedingly; Stubbs wasn't prone to panic, and if he had heard of Grey's arrival, Malcolm's first act would have been to come and find him, thus preventing his poking about in the village and finding what he'd found. He dismissed that possibility accordingly.

He dismissed the second still more promptly. Had Stubbs been killed, either deliberately or by accident, the alarm would have been raised. The army did generally know where its soldiers were, and if they weren't where they were meant to be, steps were taken. The same held true for desertion.

Right, then. If Stubbs was gone and no one was looking for him, it naturally followed that the army had sent him to wherever he'd gone. Since no one seemed to know where that was, his mission was presumably secret. And given Wolfe's current position and present obsession, that almost certainly meant that Malcolm Stubbs had gone downriver, searching for some way to attack Quebec. Grey sighed, satisfied with his deductions. Which in turn meant that—barring his being caught by the French, scalped or abducted by hostile Indians or eaten by a bear—Stubbs would be back, eventually. There was nothing to do but wait.

He leaned against a tree, watching a couple of fishing canoes make their way slowly downstream, hugging the bank. The sky was overcast and the air light on his skin, a pleasant change from the summer heat. Cloudy skies were good for fishing; his father's gamekeeper had told him that. He wondered why—were the fish dazzled by sun, and thus sought murky hiding places in the depths, but rose toward the surface in dimmer light?

He thought suddenly of the electric eel, which Suddfield had told him lived in the silt-choked waters of the Amazon. The thing did have remarkably small eyes, and its proprietor had opined that it was able to use its remarkable electrical abilities in some way to discern, as well as to electrocute, its prey.

He couldn't have said what made him raise his head at that precise moment, but he looked up to find one of the canoes hovering in the shallow water a few feet from him. The Indian paddling the canoe gave him a brilliant smile.

"Englishman!" he called. "You want to fish with me?"

A small jolt of electricity ran through him and he straightened up. Manoke's eyes were fixed on his, and he felt in memory the touch of lips and tongue, and the scent of fresh-sheared copper. His heart was racing—go off in company with an Indian he barely knew? It might easily be a trap. He could end up scalped or worse. But electric eels were not the only ones to discern things by means of a sixth sense, he thought.

"Yes!" he called. "Meet you at the landing!"

Two weeks later, he stepped out of Manoke's canoe onto the landing, thin, sunburnt, cheerful, and still in possession of his hair. Tom Byrd would be beside himself, he reflected; he'd left word as to what he was doing, but naturally had been able to give no estimate of his return. Doubtless poor Tom would be thinking he'd been captured and dragged off into slavery or scalped, his hair sold to the French.

In fact, they had drifted slowly downriver, pausing to fish wherever the mood took them, camping on sandbars and small islands, grilling their catch and eating their supper in smoke-scented peace, beneath the leaves of oak and alder. They had seen other craft now and then—not only canoes, but also many French packet boats and brigs, as well as two English warships, tacking slowly up the river, sails bellying, the distant shouts of the sailors foreign to him just then as the tongues of the Iroquois.

And in the late summer dusk of the first day, Manoke had wiped his fingers after eating, stood up, casually untied his breech-clout and let it fall. Then waited, grinning, while Grey fought his way out of shirt and breeches.

They'd swum in the river to refresh themselves

before eating; the Indian was clean, his skin no longer greasy. And yet he seemed to taste of wild game, the rich, uneasy tang of venison. Grey had wondered whether it was the man's race that was responsible, or only his diet?

"What do I taste like?" he'd asked, out of curiosity.

Manoke, absorbed in his business, had said something that might have been, "Cock," but might equally have been some expression of mild disgust, so Grey thought better of pursuing this line of inquiry. Besides, if he *did* taste of beef and biscuit or Yorkshire pudding, would the Indian recognize that? For that matter, did he really want to know, if he did? He did not, he decided, and they enjoyed the rest of the evening without benefit of conversation.

He scratched the small of his back where his breeches rubbed, uncomfortable with mosquito bites and the peel of fading sunburn. He'd tried the native style of dress, seeing its convenience, but had scorched his bum by lying too long in the sun one afternoon, and thereafter resorted to breeches, not wishing to hear any further jocular remarks regarding the whiteness of his arse.

Thinking such pleasant but disjointed thoughts, he'd made his way halfway through the town before noticing that there were many more soldiers in evidence than there had been before. Drums were pattering up and down the sloping, muddy streets, calling men from their billets, the rhythm of the military day making itself felt. His own steps fell naturally into the beat of the drums, he straightened, and felt the army reach out suddenly, seizing him, shaking him out of his sunburnt bliss.

He glanced involuntarily up the hill and saw the flags fluttering above the large inn that served as field headquarters. Wolfe had returned.

Grey found his own quarters, reassured Tom as to his well-being, submitted to having his hair forcibly untangled, combed, perfumed, and tightly bound up in a formal queue, and with his clean uniform chafing his sunburnt skin, went to present himself to the general, as courtesy demanded. He knew James Wolfe by sight; Wolfe was his own age, had fought at Culloden, been a junior officer under Cumberland during the Highland campaign—but did not know him personally. He'd heard a great deal about him, though.

"Grey, is it? Pardloe's brother, are you?" Wolfe lifted his long nose in Grey's direction, as though sniffing at him, in the manner of one dog inspecting another's backside.

Grey trusted he would not be required to reciprocate, and instead bowed politely.

"My brother's compliments, sir."

Actually, what his brother had had to say had been far from complimentary.

"Melodramatic ass," was what Hal had said, hastily briefing him before his departure. "Showy, bad judgment, terrible strategist. Has the Devil's own luck, though, I'll give him that. *Don't* follow him into any-thing stupid."

Wolfe nodded amiably enough.

"And you've come as a witness for, who is it—Captain Carruthers?"

"Yes, sir. Has a date been set for the court-martial?"

"Dunno. Has it?" Wolfe asked his adjutant, a tall, spindly creature with a beady eye.

"No, sir. Now that His Lordship is here, though, we can proceed. I'll tell Brigadier Lethbridge-Stewart; he's to chair the proceeding."

Wolfe waved a hand.

"No, wait a bit. The Brigadier will have other things on his mind. 'Til after . . ."

The adjutant nodded and made a note.

"Yes, sir."

Wolfe was eyeing Grey, in the manner of a small boy bursting to share some secret.

"D'you understand Highlanders, Colonel?"

Grey blinked, surprised.

"Insofar as such a thing is possible, sir," he replied politely, and Wolfe brayed with laughter.

"Good man." The General turned his head to one side and eyed Grey some more, appraising him. "I've got a hundred or so of the creatures; been thinking what use they might be. I think I've found one—a small adventure."

The adjutant smiled, despite himself, then quickly erased the smile.

"Indeed, sir?" Grey said cautiously.

"Somewhat dangerous," Wolfe went on carelessly.

"But then, it's the Highlanders . . . no great mischief should they fall. Would you care to join us?"

Don't follow him into anything stupid. Right, Hal, he thought. Any suggestions on how to decline an offer like that from one's titular commander?

"I should be pleased, sir," he said, feeling a brief ripple of unease down his spine. "When?"

"In two weeks—at the dark of the moon." Wolfe was all but wagging his tail in enthusiasm.

"Am I permitted to know the nature of the . . . er . . . expedition?"

Wolfe exchanged a look of anticipation with his adjutant, then turned eyes shiny with excitement on Grey.

"We're going to take Quebec, Colonel."

So Wolfe thought he had found his point *d'appui*. Or rather, his trusted scout, Malcolm Stubbs, had found it for him. Grey returned briefly to his quarters, put the miniature of Olivia and little Cromwell in his pocket, and went to find Stubbs.

He didn't bother thinking what to say to Malcolm. It was as well, he thought, that he hadn't found Stubbs immediately after his discovery of the Indian mistress and her child; he might simply have knocked Stubbs down, without the bother of explanation. But time had elapsed, and his blood was cooler now. He was detached.

Or so he thought, until he entered a prosperous tavern—Malcolm had elevated tastes in wine—and found his cousin-by-marriage at a table, relaxed and jovial among his friends. Stubbs was aptly named, being approximately five foot four in both dimensions, a fair-haired fellow with an inclination to become red in the face when deeply entertained or deep in drink.

At the moment, he appeared to be experiencing both conditions, laughing at something one of his companions had said, waving his empty glass in the barmaid's direction. He turned back, spotted Grey coming across the floor, and lit up like a beacon. He'd been spending a good deal of time out of doors, Grey saw; he was nearly as sunburnt as Grey himself.

"Grey!" he cried. "Why, here's a sight for sore eyes! What the devil brings you to the wilderness?" Then he noticed Grey's expression, and his joviality faded slightly, a puzzled frown growing between his thick brows.

It hadn't time to grow far. Grey lunged across the table, scattering glasses, and seized Stubbs by the shirt-front.

"You come with me, you bloody swine," he whispered, face shoved up against the younger man's, "or I'll kill you right here, I swear it."

He let go then, and stood, blood hammering in his temples.

Stubbs rubbed at his chest, affronted, startled—and afraid. Grey could see it in the wide blue eyes. Slowly, Stubbs got up, motioning to his companions to stay.

"No bother, chaps," he said, making a good attempt at casualness. "My cousin—family emergency, what?"

Grey saw two of the men exchange knowing glances, then look at Grey, wary. They knew, all right.

Stiffly, he gestured for Stubbs to precede him, and they passed out of the door in a pretense of dignity. Once outside, though, he grabbed Stubbs by the arm and dragged him round the corner into a small alleyway. He pushed Stubbs hard, so that he lost his balance and fell against the wall; Grey kicked his legs out from under him, then knelt on his thigh, digging his knee viciously into the thick muscle. Stubbs uttered a strangled noise, not quite a scream.

Grey dug in his pocket, hand trembling with fury, and brought out the miniature, which he showed briefly to Stubbs before grinding it into the man's cheek. Stubbs yelped, grabbed at it, and Grey let him have it, rising unsteadily off the man.

"How dare you?" he said, low-voiced and vicious. "How dare you dishonor your wife, your son?"

Malcolm was breathing hard, one hand clutching his abused thigh, but was regaining his composure.

"It's nothing," he said. "Nothing to do with Olivia at all." He swallowed, wiped a hand across his mouth, and took a cautious glance at the miniature in his hand. "That the sprat, is it? Good . . . good-looking lad. Looks like me, don't he?"

Grey kicked him brutally in the stomach.

"Yes, and so does your *other* son," he hissed. "How could you do such a thing?"

Malcolm's mouth opened, but nothing came out. He struggled for breath like a landed fish. Grey watched without pity. He'd have the man split and grilled over charcoal before he was done. He bent and took the miniature from Stubb's unresisting hand, tucking it back in his pocket.

After a long moment, Stubbs achieved a whining gasp, and the color of his face, which had gone puce, subsided back toward its normal brick color. Saliva had collected at the corners of his mouth; he licked his lips, spat, then sat back, breathing heavily, and looked up at Grey.

"Going to hit me again?"

"Not just yet."

"Good." He stretched out a hand, and Grey took it, grunting as he helped Stubbs to his feet. Malcolm leaned against the wall, still panting, and eyed him.

"So, who made you God, Grey? Who are you, to sit in judgment of me, eh?"

Grey nearly hit him again, but desisted.

"Who am *I*?" he echoed. "Olivia's fucking cousin, that's who! The nearest male relative she's got on this continent! And you, need I remind you—and evidently I do—are her fucking husband. Judgment? What the devil d'you mean by that, you filthy lecher?"

Malcolm coughed, and spat again.

"Yes. Well. I said, it's nothing to do with Olivia— and so it's nothing to do with you." He spoke with apparent calmness, but Grey could see the pulse hammering in his throat, the nervous shiftiness of his eyes. "It's nothing out of the ordinary—it's the bloody custom, for God's sake. Everybody—"

He kneed Stubbs in the balls.

"Try again," he advised Stubbs, who had fallen

down and was curled into a fetal position, moaning. "Take your time; I'm not busy."

Aware of eyes upon him, he turned to see several soldiers gathered at the mouth of the alley, hesitating. He was still wearing his dress uniform, though—somewhat the worse for wear, but still clearly displaying his rank—and when he gave them an evil look, they hastily dispersed.

"I should kill you here and now, you know," he said to Stubbs after a few moments. The rage that had propelled him was draining away, though, as he watched the man retch and heave at his feet, and he spoke wearily. "Better for Olivia to have a dead husband—and whatever property you leave—than a live scoundrel, who will betray her with her friends—likely with her own maid."

Stubbs muttered something indistinguishable, and Grey bent, grasping him by the hair, and pulled his head up.

"What was that?"

"Wasn't . . . like that." Groaning and clutching himself, Malcolm maneuvered himself gingerly into a sitting position, knees drawn up. He gasped for a bit, head on his knees, before being able to go on.

"You don't know, do you?" He spoke low-voiced, not raising his head. "You haven't seen the things I've seen. Not . . . done what I've had to do."

"What do you mean?"

"The . . . the killing. Not . . . battle. Not an honorable thing. Farmers. Women . . ." He saw Stubbs's heavy throat move, swallowing. "I—we—for months now.

Looting the countryside, burning farms, villages." He sighed, broad shoulders slumping. "The men, they don't mind. Half of them are brutes to begin with." He breathed. "Think . . . nothing of shooting a man on his doorstep and taking his wife next to his body." He swallowed. " 'Tisn't only Montcalm who pay for scalps," he said in a low voice. Grey couldn't avoid hearing the rawness in his voice; a pain that wasn't physical.

"Every soldier's seen such things, Malcolm," he said after a short silence, almost gently. "You're an officer. It's your job to keep them in check." *And you know damn well it isn't always possible*, he thought.

"I know," Malcolm said, and began to cry. "I couldn't."

Grey waited while he sobbed, feeling increasingly foolish and uncomfortable. At last, the broad shoulders heaved and subsided.

After a moment, Malcolm said, in a voice that quivered only a little.

"Everybody finds a way, don't they? And there're not that many ways. Drink, cards, or women." He raised his head and shifted a little, grimacing as he eased into a more comfortable position. "But you don't go in much for women, do you?" he added, looking up.

Grey felt the bottom of his stomach drop, but realized in time that Malcolm had spoken matter-of-factly, with no tone of accusation.

"No," he said, and drew a deep breath. "Drink, mostly."

Malcolm nodded, wiping his nose on his sleeve.

"Drink doesn't help me," he said. "I fall asleep, but

I don't forget. I just dream about . . . things. And whores—I—well, I didn't want to get poxed and maybe . . . well, Olivia," he muttered, looking down. "No good at cards," he said, clearing his throat. "But sleeping in a woman's arms—I can sleep, then."

Grey leaned against the wall, feeling nearly as battered as Malcolm Stubbs. Bright leaves drifted through the air, whirling round them, settling in the mud.

"All right," he said eventually. "What do you mean to do?"

"Dunno," Stubbs said in a tone of flat resignation. "Think of something, I suppose."

Grey bent and offered a hand; Stubbs got carefully to his feet and, nodding to Grey, shuffled toward the alley's mouth, bent over and holding himself as though his insides might fall out. Halfway there, though, he stopped and looked back over his shoulder.

There was an anxious look on his face, half-embarrassed.

"Can I—the miniature? They are still mine, Olivia and the . . . my son."

Grey heaved a sigh that went to the marrow of his bones; he felt a thousand years old.

"Yes, they are," he said, and digging the miniature out of his pocket, tucked it carefully into Stubbs's coat. "Remember it, will you?"

Two days later, a convoy of troop ships arrived, under the command of Admiral Holmes. The town was flooded afresh with men hungry for unsalted meat, fresh-baked bread, liquor and women. And a messenger arrived at Grey's quarters, bearing a parcel for him from his brother, with the Admiral's compliments.

It was small, but packaged with care, wrapped in oilcloth and tied about with twine, the knot sealed with his brother's crest. That was unlike Hal, whose usual communiqués consisted of hastily dashed-off notes, generally employing slightly fewer than the minimum number of words necessary to convey his message. They were seldom signed, let alone sealed.

Tom Byrd appeared to think the package slightly ominous, too; he had set it by itself, apart from the other mail, and weighted it down with a large bottle of brandy, apparently to prevent it escaping. That, or he suspected Grey might require the brandy to sustain him in the arduous effort of reading a letter consisting of more than one page.

"Very thoughtful of you, Tom," he murmured, smiling to himself and reaching for his pen-knife.

In fact, the letter within occupied less than a page, bore neither salutation nor signature, and was completely Hal-like.

Minnie wishes to know whether you are starving, though I don't know what she proposes to do about it, should the answer be yes. The boys wish to know whether you have taken any scalps—they are confident that no Red Indian would succeed in taking yours; I share this opinion. You had better bring three tommyhawks when you come home.

Here is your paperweight; the jeweler was most impressed by the quality of the stone. The other thing is a copy of Adams's confession. They hanged him yesterday.

The other contents of the parcel consisted of a small wash-leather pouch and an official-looking document on several sheets of good parchment, this folded and sealed—this time with the seal of George II. Grey left it lying on the table, fetched one of the pewter cups from his campaign chest and filled it to the brim with brandy, wondering anew at his valet's perspicacity.

Thus fortified, he sat down and took up the little pouch, from which he decanted a small, heavy gold paperweight, made in the shape of a half moon set among ocean waves, into his hand. It was set with a faceted—and very large—sapphire, which glowed like the evening star in its setting. Where had James Fraser acquired such a thing? he wondered.

He turned it in his hand, admiring the workmanship, but then set it aside. He sipped his brandy for a bit, watching the official document as though it might explode. He was reasonably sure it would.

He weighed the document in his hand and felt the breeze from his window lift it a little, like the flap of a sail just before it fills and bellies with a snap.

Waiting wouldn't help. And Hal plainly knew what it said, anyway; he'd tell Grey eventually, whether he wanted to know or not. Sighing, he put by his brandy and broke the seal.

I, Bernard Donald Adams, do make this confession of my own free will. . . .

Was it? he wondered. He did not know Adams's handwriting, could not tell whether the document had been written or dictated—no, wait. He flipped over the sheets and examined the signature. Same hand. All right, he had written it himself.

He squinted at the writing. It seemed firm. Probably not extracted under torture, then. Perhaps it was the truth.

"Idiot," he said under his breath. "Read the goddamned thing and have done with it!"

He drank the rest of his brandy at a gulp, flattened the pages upon the stone of the parapet and read, at last, the story of his father's death.

The Duke had suspected the existence of a Jacobite ring for some time, and had identified three men whom he thought involved in it. Still, he made no move to expose them, until the warrant was issued for his own arrest, upon the charge of treason. Hearing of this, he had sent at once to Adams, summoning him to the Duke's country home at Earlingden.

Adams did not know how much the Duke knew of his own involvement, but did not dare to stay away, lest the Duke, under arrest, denounce him. So he armed himself with a pistol, and rode by night to Earlingden, arriving just before dawn.

He had come to the conservatory's outside doors

and been admitted by the Duke. Whereupon "some conversation" had ensued.

I had learned that day of the issuance of a warrant for arrest upon the charge of treason, to be served upon the body of the Duke of Pardloe. I was uneasy at this, for the Duke had questioned both myself and some colleagues previously, in a manner that suggested to me that he suspected the existence of a secret movement to restore the Stuart throne.

I argued against the Duke's arrest, as I did not know the extent of his knowledge or suspicions, and feared that if placed in exigent danger himself, he might be able to point a finger at myself or my principal colleagues, these being Joseph Arbuthnot, Lord Creemore, and Sir Edwin Bellman. Sir Edwin was urgent upon the point, though, saying that it would do no harm; any accusations made by Pardloe could be dismissed as simple attempts to save himself, with no grounding in fact—while the fact of his arrest would naturally cause a widespread assumption of guilt, and would distract any attentions that might at present be directed toward us.

The Duke, hearing of the warrant, sent to my lodgings that evening, and summoned me to call upon him at his country home, immediately. I dared not spurn this summons, not knowing what evidence he might possess, and therefore rode by night to his estate, arriving soon before dawn.

Adams had met the Duke there, in the conservatory. Whatever the form of this conversation, its result had been drastic.

I had brought with me a pistol, which I had loaded outside the house. I meant this only for protection, as I did not know what the Duke's demeanor might be.

Dangerous, evidently. Gerard Grey, Duke of Pardloe, had also come armed to the meeting. According to Adams, the Duke had withdrawn his own pistol from the recesses of his jacket—whether to attack or merely threaten was not clear—whereupon Adams had drawn his own pistol in panic. Both men fired; Adams thought the Duke's pistol had misfired, since the Duke could not have missed, at the distance.

Adams's shot did not misfire, nor did it miss its target, and seeing the blood upon the Duke's bosom, Adams had panicked and run. Looking back, he had seen the Duke, mortally stricken but still upright, seize the branch of the peach tree beside him for support, whereupon the Duke had used the last of his strength to hurl his own useless weapon at Adams before collapsing.

John Grey sat still, slowly rubbing the parchment sheets between his fingers. He wasn't seeing the neat strokes in which Adams had set down his bloodless account. He saw the blood. A dark red, beautiful as a jewel where the sun through the glass of the roof struck it suddenly. His father's hair, tousled as it might be after hunting. And the peach, fallen to those same tiles, its perfection spoilt and ruined.

He set the papers down on the table; the wind stirred them, and by reflex, he reached for his new paperweight to hold them down.

What was it Carruthers had called him? *Someone who keeps order. You and your brother,* he'd said. *You don't stand for it. If the world has peace and order, it's because of men like you.*

Perhaps. He wondered if Carruthers knew the cost of peace and order—but then recalled Charlie's haggard face, its youthful beauty gone, nothing left in it now save the bones and the dogged determination that kept him breathing.

Yes, he knew.

Just after full dark, they boarded the ships. The convoy included Admiral Holmes's flagship, the *Lowestoff*; three men of war, the *Squirrel*, *Sea Horse*, and *Hunter*; a number of armed sloops, others loaded with ordnance, powder and ammunition, and a number of transports for the troops—1,800 men in all. The *Sutherland* had been left below, anchored just out of firing range of the fortress, to keep an eye on the enemy's motions; the river there was littered with floating batteries and prowling small French craft.

He traveled with Wolfe and the Highlanders aboard *Sea Horse*, and spent the journey on deck, too keyed up to bear being below.

His brother's warning kept recurring in the back of

his mind—*Don't follow him into anything stupid*—but it was much too late to think of that, and to block it out, he challenged one of the other officers to a whistling contest—each party to whistle the entirety of "The Roast Beef of Old England," the loser the man who laughed first. He lost, but did not think of his brother again.

Just after midnight, the big ships quietly furled their sails, dropped anchor and lay like slumbering gulls on the dark river. L'Anse au Foulon, the landing spot that Malcolm Stubbs and his scouts had recommended to General Wolfe, lay seven miles downriver, at the foot of sheer and crumbling slate cliffs that led upward to the Heights of Abraham.

"Is it named for the biblical Abraham, do you think?" Grey had asked curiously, hearing the name, but had been informed that, in fact, the clifftop comprised a farmstead belonging to an ex-pilot named Abraham Martin.

On the whole, he thought this prosaic origin just as well. There was likely to be drama enough enacted on that ground, without thought of ancient prophets, conversations with God, or any calculation of how many just men might be contained within the fortress of Quebec.

With a minimum of fuss, the Highlanders and their officers, Wolfe and his chosen troops—Grey among them—debarked into the small *bateaux* that would carry them silently down to the landing point.

The sounds of oars were mostly drowned by the river's rushing, and there was little conversation in the boats. Wolfe sat in the prow of the lead boat, facing his troops, looking now and then over his shoulder at the shore. Quite without warning, he began to speak. He didn't raise his voice, but the night was so still that those in the boat had little trouble in hearing him. To Grey's astonishment, he was reciting "Elegy Written in a Country Churchyard."

Melodramatic ass, Grey thought—and yet could not deny that the recitation was oddly moving. Wolfe made no show of it. It was as though he were simply talking to himself, and a shiver went over Grey as he reached the last verse.

> " 'The boast of heraldry, the pomp of pow'r,
> And all that beauty, all that wealth e'er gave,
> Awaits alike the inexorable hour.

> *The paths of glory lead but to the grave,*' " Wolfe ended, so low-voiced that only the three or four men closest heard him. Grey was close enough to hear him clear his throat with a small *hem* noise, and saw his shoulders lift.

"Gentlemen," Wolfe said, lifting his voice as well, "I should rather have written those lines than have taken Quebec."

There was a faint stir, and a breath of laughter among the men.

So would I, Grey thought. *The poet who wrote them is likely sitting by his cozy fire in Cambridge eating buttered crumpets, not preparing to fall from a great height or get his arse shot off.*

He didn't know whether this was simply more of Wolfe's characteristic drama. Possibly—possibly not, he thought. He'd met Colonel Walsing by the latrines that morning, and Walsing had mentioned that Wolfe had given him a pendant the night before, with instructions to deliver it to Miss Landringham, to whom Wolfe was engaged.

But then, it was nothing out of the ordinary for men to put their personal valuables into the care of a friend before a hot battle. Were you killed or badly injured, your body might be looted before your comrades managed to retrieve you, and not everyone had a trustworthy servant with whom to leave such items. He himself had often carried snuff-boxes, pocket-watches, or rings into battle for friends—he'd had a reputation for luck, prior to Krefeld. No one had asked him to carry anything tonight.

He shifted his weight by instinct, feeling the current change, and Simon Fraser, next him, swayed in the opposite direction, bumping him.

"*Pardon,*" Fraser murmured. Wolfe had made them all recite poetry in French round the dinner table the night before, and it was agreed that Fraser had the most authentic accent, he having fought with the French in Holland some years prior. Should they be hailed by a sentry, it would be his job to reply. Doubtless, Grey thought, Fraser was now thinking frantically in French, trying to saturate his mind with the language, lest any stray bit of English escape in panic.

"*De rien,*" Grey murmured back, and Fraser chuckled, deep in his throat.

It was cloudy, the sky streaked with the shredded remnants of retreating rain clouds. That was good; the surface of the river was broken, patched with faint light, fractured by stones and drifting tree branches. Though even so, a decent sentry could scarcely fail to spot a train of boats.

Cold numbed his face, but his palms were sweating. He touched the dagger at his belt again; he was aware that he touched it every few minutes, as if needing to verify its presence, but couldn't help it, and didn't worry about it. He was straining his eyes, looking for anything—the glow of a careless fire, the shifting of a rock that was not a rock . . . nothing.

How far? he wondered. Two miles, three? He'd not yet seen the cliffs himself, was not sure how far below Gareon they lay.

The rush of water and the easy movement of the boat began to make him sleepy, tension notwithstanding, and he shook his head, yawning exaggeratedly to throw it off.

"Quel est c'est bateau?" What boat is that? The shout from the shore seemed anticlimax when it came, barely more remarkable than a night bird's call. But the next instant, Simon Fraser's hand crushed his, grinding the bones together as Fraser gulped air and shouted, *"Celui de la Reine!"*

Grey clenched his teeth, not to let any blasphemous response escape. If the sentry demanded a password, he'd likely be crippled for life, he thought. An instant later, though, the sentry shouted, *"Passez!"* and Fraser's death-grip relaxed. Simon was breathing like a bellows, but nudged him and whispered *"Pardon,"* again.

"De fucking *rien,"* he muttered, rubbing his hand and tenderly flexing the fingers.

They were getting close. Men were shifting to and fro in anticipation, more than Grey, checking their weapons, straightening coats, coughing, spitting over the side, readying themselves. Still, it was a nerve-wracking quarter hour more before they began to swing toward shore—and another sentry called from the dark.

Grey's heart squeezed like a fist, and he nearly gasped with the twinge of pain from his old wounds.

"Qui etes-vous? Que sont ces bateaux?" a French voice demanded suspiciously. *Who are you? What boats are those?*

This time, he was ready, and seized Fraser's hand himself. Simon held on, and leaning out toward the shore, called hoarsely, *"Des bateaux de provisions! Tasiez-vous—les anglais sont proches!"* *Provision boats! Be quiet—the British are nearby!* Grey felt an insane urge to laugh, but didn't. In fact, the *Sutherland* was nearby, lurking out of cannon shot downstream, and doubtless the frogs knew it. In any case, the guard called, more quietly, *"Passez!"* and the train of boats slid smoothly past and round the final bend.

The bottom of the boat grated on sand, and half the men were over at once, tugging it farther up. Wolfe half leapt, half fell over the side in eagerness, all trace of somberness gone. They'd come aground on a small sandbar, just offshore, and the other boats were beaching now, a swarm of black figures gathering like ants.

Twenty-four of the Highlanders were meant to try the ascent first, finding—and insofar as possible, clearing, for the cliff was defended not only by its steepness but also by abatis, nests of sharpened logs—a trail for the rest. Simon's bulky form faded into the dark, his French accent changing at once into the sibilant Gaelic as he hissed the men into position. Grey rather missed his presence.

He was not sure whether Wolfe had chosen the Highlanders for their skill at climbing, or because he preferred to risk them rather than his other troops. The latter, he thought. Like most English officers, Wolfe regarded the Highlanders with distrust and a certain contempt. Those officers, at least, who'd never fought with them—or against them.

From his spot at the foot of the cliff, he couldn't see them, but he could hear them; the scuffle of feet, now and then a wild scrabble and a clatter of falling small stones, loud grunts of effort and what he recognized as Gaelic invocations of God, His mother and assorted saints. One man near him pulled a string of beads from the neck of his shirt and kissed the tiny cross attached to it, then tucked it back and, seizing a small sapling that grew out of the rock-face, leapt upward, kilt swinging, broadsword swaying from his belt in brief silhouette, before the darkness took him. Grey touched his dagger's hilt again, his own talisman against evil.

It was a long wait in the darkness; to some extent,

he envied the Highlanders, who, whatever else they might be encountering—and the scrabbling noises and half-strangled whoops as a foot slipped and a comrade grabbed a hand or arm suggested that the climb was just as impossible as it seemed—were not dealing with boredom.

A sudden rumble and crashing came from above, and the shore-party scattered in panic as several sharpened logs plunged out of the dark above, dislodged from an abatis. One of them had struck point down no more than six feet from Grey, and stood quivering in the sand. With no discussion, the shore-party retreated to the sandbar.

The scrabblings and gruntings grew fainter, and suddenly ceased. Wolfe, who had been sitting on a boulder, stood up, straining his eyes upward.

"They've made it," he whispered, and his fists curled in an excitement that Grey shared. "God, they've made it!"

Well enough, and the men at the foot of the cliff held their breaths; there was a guard post at the top of the cliff. Silence, bar the everlasting noise of tree and river. And then a shot.

Just one. The men below shifted, touching their weapons, ready, not knowing for what.

Were there sounds above? He could not tell, and out of sheer nervousness, turned aside to urinate against the side of the cliff. He was fastening his flies when he heard Simon Fraser's voice above.

"Got 'em, by God!" he said. "Come on, lads—the night's not long enough!"

The next few hours passed in a blur of the most arduous endeavor Grey had seen since he'd crossed the Scottish Highlands with his brother's regiment, bringing cannon to General Cope. No, actually, he thought, as he stood in darkness, one leg wedged between a tree and the rock-face, thirty feet of invisible space below him, and rope burning through his palms with an unseen deadweight of two hundred pounds or so on the end, this was worse.

The Highlanders had surprised the guard, shot their fleeing captain in the heel, and made all of them prisoner. That was the easy part. The next thing was for the rest of the landing party to ascend to the cliff-top, now that the trail—if there was such a thing—had been cleared, where they would make preparations to raise not only the rest of the troops now coming down the river aboard the transports, but also seventeen battering cannon, twelve howitzers, three mortars and all of the necessary encumbrances in terms of shell, powder, planks and limbers necessary to make this artillery effective. At least, Grey reflected, by the time they were done, the vertical trail up the cliffside would likely have been trampled into a simple cow-path.

As the sky lightened, Grey looked up for a moment from his spot at the top of the cliff, where he was now overseeing the last of the artillery as it was heaved over the edge, and saw the *bateaux* coming down again like a flock of swallows, they having crossed the river to collect an additional 1,200 troops that Wolfe had directed to march to Levi on the opposite shore, there to lie hidden in the woods until the Highlanders' expedient should have been proved.

A head, cursing freely, surged up over the edge of the cliff. Its attendant body lunged into view, tripped, and sprawled at Grey's feet.

"Sergeant Cutter!" Grey said, grinning as he bent to yank the little sergeant to his feet. "Come to join the party, have you?"

"Jesus fuck," replied the sergeant, belligerently brushing dirt from his coat. "We'd best win, that's all I can say." And without waiting for reply, turned round to bellow down the cliff, "Come *on*, you bloody rascals! 'Ave you all eaten lead for breakfast, then? Shit it out and step lively! *Climb*, God damn your eyes!"

The net result of this monstrous effort being that as dawn spread its golden glow across the Plains of Abraham, the French sentries on the walls of the Citadel of Quebec gaped in disbelief at the sight of more than four thousand British troops, drawn up in battle array before them.

Through his telescope, Grey could see the sentries. The distance was too great to make out their facial expressions, but their attitudes of alarm and consternation were easy to read, and he grinned, seeing one French officer clutch his head briefly, then wave his arms like one dispelling a flock of chickens, sending his subordinates rushing off in all directions.

Wolfe was standing on a small hillock, long nose lifted as though to sniff the morning air. Grey thought he probably considered his pose noble and commanding; he reminded Grey of a dachshund scenting a badger; the air of alert eagerness was the same.

Wolfe wasn't the only one. Despite the ardors of the night, skinned hands, battered shins, twisted knees and ankles, and a lack of food and sleep, a gleeful excitement ran through the troops like wine. Grey thought they were all giddy with fatigue.

The sound of drums came faintly to him on the wind: the French, beating hastily to quarters. Within minutes, he saw horsemen streaking away from the fortress, and smiled grimly. They were going to rally whatever troops Montcalm had within summoning distance, and he felt a tightening of the belly at the sight.

The matter hadn't really been in doubt; it was September, and winter was coming on. The town and fortress had been unable to provision themselves for a long siege, owing to Wolfe's scorched-earth policies. The French were there, the English before them—and the simple fact, apparent to both sides, was that the French would starve long before the English did. Montcalm would fight; he had no choice.

Many of the men had brought canteens of water, some a little food. They were allowed to relax sufficiently to eat, to ease their muscles—though none of them ever took their attention from the gathering French, massing before the fortress. Employing his telescope further, Grey could see that while the mass of milling men was growing, they were by no means all trained troops; Montcalm had called his militias from the countryside—farmers, fishermen, and *coureurs du bois*, by the look of them—and his Indians. Grey eyed the painted faces and oiled topknots warily, but his acquaintance with Manoke had deprived the Indians of much of their terrifying aspect—and they would not be nearly so effective on open ground, against cannon, as they were sneaking through the forest.

It took surprisingly little time for Montcalm to ready his troops, impromptu as they might be. The sun was no more than halfway up the sky when the French lines began their advance.

"*Hold* your fucking fire, you villains! Fire before you're ordered, and I'll give your fuckin' heads to the artillery to use for cannonballs!" He heard the unmistakable voice of Sergeant Aloysius Cutter, some distance back but clearly audible. The same order was being echoed, if less picturesquely, through the British lines, and if every officer on the field had one eye firmly on the French, the other was fixed on General Wolfe, standing on his hillock, aflame with anticipation.

Grey felt his blood twitch, and moved restlessly from foot to foot, trying to ease a cramp in one leg. The advancing French line stopped, knelt, and fired a volley. Another from the line standing behind them. Too far, much too far to have any effect. A deep rumble came from the British troops—something visceral and hungry.

Grey's hand had been on his dagger for so long that the wire-wrapped hilt had left its imprint on his fingers. His other hand was clenched upon a saber. He had no command here, but the urge to raise his sword, gather the eyes of his men, hold them, focus them, was overwhelming. He shook his shoulders to loosen them and glanced at Wolfe.

Another volley, close enough this time that several British soldiers in the front lines fell, knocked down by musket fire.

"Hold, hold!" The order rattled down the lines like gunfire. The brimstone smell of slow match was thick, pungent above the scent of powder-smoke; the artillerymen held their fire as well.

French cannon fired, and balls bounced murderously across the field, but they seemed puny, ineffectual despite the damage they did. How many French? he wondered. Perhaps twice as many, but it didn't matter. It wouldn't matter.

Sweat ran down his face, and he rubbed a sleeve across to clear his eyes.

"Hold!"

Closer, closer. Many of the Indians were on horseback; he could see them in a knot on the left, milling. Those would bear watching. . . .

"Hold!"

Wolfe's arm rose slowly, sword in hand, and the army breathed deep. His beloved grenadiers were next him, solid in their companies, wrapped in sulfurous smoke from the matchtubes at their belts.

"Come on, you buggers," the man next to Grey was muttering. "Come on, come on!"

Smoke was drifting over the field, low white clouds. Forty paces. Effective range.

"Don't fire, don't fire, don't fire . . ." Someone was chanting to himself, struggling against panic.

Through the British lines, sun glinted on the rising swords, the officers echoing Wolfe's order.

"Hold . . . hold . . ."

The swords fell as one.

"Fire!" And the ground shook.

A shout rose in his throat, part of the roar of the army, and he was charging with the men near him, swinging his saber with all his might, finding flesh.

The volley had been devastating; bodies littered the ground. He leaped over a fallen Frenchman, brought his saber down upon another caught halfway in the act of loading, took him in the cleft between neck and shoulder, yanked his saber free of the falling man and went on.

The British artillery was firing as fast as the guns could be served. Each boom shook his flesh. He gritted his teeth, squirmed aside from the point of a half-seen bayonet, and found himself panting, eyes watering from the smoke, standing alone.

Chest heaving, he turned round in a circle, disoriented. There was so much smoke around him that he could not for a moment tell where he was. It didn't matter.

An enormous blur of something passed him, shrieking, and he dodged by instinct and fell to the ground as the horse's feet churned past, hearing as an echo the Indian's grunt, the rush of the tomahawk blow that had missed his head.

"Shit," he muttered, and scrambled to his feet.

The grenadiers were hard at work nearby; he heard their officers' shouts, the bang and pop of their explosions as they worked their way stolidly through the French like the small mobile batteries they were.

A grenade struck the ground a few feet away, and he felt a sharp pain in his thigh; a metal fragment had sliced through his breeches, drawing blood.

"Christ," he said, belatedly becoming aware that being in the vicinity of a company of grenadiers was not a good idea. He shook his head to clear it and made his way away from them.

He heard a familiar sound, which made him recoil for an instant from the force of memory—wild Highland screams, filled with rage and berserk glee. The Highlanders were hard at work with their broadswords—he saw two of them appear from the smoke, bare legs churning beneath their kilts, pursuing a pack of fleeing Frenchmen, and felt laughter bubble up through his heaving chest.

He didn't see the man in the smoke. His foot struck something heavy and he fell, sprawling across the body. The man screamed, and Grey scrambled hastily off him.

"Sorry. Are you—Christ, Malcolm!"

He was on his knees, bending low to avoid the smoke. Stubbs was gasping, grasping desperately at his coat.

"Jesus." Malcolm's right leg was gone below the

knee, flesh shredded and the white bone splintered, butcher-stained with spurting blood. Or . . . no. It wasn't gone. It—the foot, at least—was lying a little way away, still clad in shoe and tattered stocking.

Grey turned his head and threw up.

Bile stinging the back of his nose, he choked and spat, turned back, and grappled with his belt, wrenching it free.

"Don't . . ." Stubbs gasped, putting out a hand as Grey began wrapping the belt round his thigh. His face was whiter than the bone of his leg. "Don't. Better . . . Better if I die."

"The devil you will," Grey replied briefly.

His hands were shaking, slippery with blood. It took three tries to get the end of the belt through the buckle, but it went, at last, and he jerked it tight, eliciting a yell from Stubbs.

"Here," said an unfamiliar voice by his ear. "Let's get him off. I'll—shit!" He looked up, startled, to see a tall British officer lunge upward, blocking the musket butt that would have brained Grey. Without thinking, he drew his dagger and stabbed the Frenchman in the leg. The man screamed, his leg buckling, and the strange officer pushed him over, kicked him in the face and stamped on his throat, crushing it.

"I'll help," the man said calmly, bending to take hold of Malcolm's arm, pulling him up. "Take the other side; we'll get him to the back." They got Malcolm up, his arms round their shoulders, and dragged him, paying no heed to the Frenchman thrashing and gurgling on the ground behind them.

Malcolm lived, long enough to make it to the rear of the lines, where the army surgeons were already at work. By the time Grey and the other officer had turned him over to the surgeons, it was over.

Grey turned to see the French scattered and demoralized, fleeing toward the fortress. British troops were flooding across the trampled field, cheering, overrunning the abandoned French cannon.

The entire battle had lasted less than a quarter of an hour.

He found himself sitting on the ground, his mind quite blank, with no notion how long he had been there, though he supposed it couldn't have been much time at all.

He noticed an officer standing near him, and thought vaguely that the man seemed familiar. Who . . . Oh, yes. Wolfe's adjutant. He'd never learned the man's name.

He stood up slowly, stiff as a nine-day pudding.

The adjutant was simply standing there. His eyes were turned in the direction of the fortress and the fleeing French, but Grey could tell that he wasn't really seeing either. Grey glanced over his shoulder, toward the hillock where Wolfe had stood earlier, but the General was nowhere in sight.

"General Wolfe—?" he said.

"The General . . . ," the adjutant said, and swallowed thickly. "He was struck."

Of course he was, silly ass, Grey thought uncharitably. *Standing up there like a bloody target, what could he expect?* But then he saw the tears standing in the adjutant's eyes, and understood.

"Dead, then?" he asked, stupidly, and the adjutant—why had he never thought to ask the man's name?—nodded, rubbing a smoke-stained sleeve across a smoke-stained countenance.

"He . . . in the wrist, first. Then in the body. He fell, and crawled—then he fell again. I turned him over . . . told him the battle was won; the French were scattered."

"He understood?"

The adjutant nodded and took a deep breath that rattled in his throat. "He said—" He stopped and coughed, then went on, more firmly. "He said that in knowing he had conquered, he was content to die."

"Did he?" Grey said blankly. He'd seen men die, often, and imagined it much more likely that if James Wolfe had managed anything beyond an inarticulate groan, his final word had likely been either "Shit," or "Oh, God," depending upon the general's religious leanings, of which Grey had no notion.

"Yes, good," he said meaninglessly, and turned toward the fortress himself. Ant-trails of men were streaming toward it, and in the midst of one such stream, he saw Montcalm's colors, fluttering in the wind. Below the colors, small in the distance, a man in general's uniform rode his horse, hatless, hunched and swaying in the saddle, his officers bunched close on either side, anxious lest he fall.

The British lines were reorganizing, though it was clear no further fighting would be required. Not today. Nearby, he saw the tall officer who had saved his life and helped him to drag Malcolm Stubbs to safety, limping back toward his troops.

"The major over there," he said, nudging the adjutant and nodding. "Do you know his name?"

The adjutant blinked, then firmed his shoulders.

"Yes, of course. That's Major Siverly."

"Oh. Well, it would be, wouldn't it?"

Admiral Holmes, third in command after Wolfe, accepted the surrender of Quebec three days later, Wolfe and his second, Brigadier Monckton, having perished in battle. Montcalm was dead, too; had died the morning following the battle. There was no way out for the French save surrender; winter was coming on, and the fortress and its city would starve long before its besiegers.

Two weeks after the battle, John Grey returned to Gareon, and found that smallpox had swept through the village like an autumn wind. The mother of Malcolm Stubbs's son was dead; her mother offered to sell him the child. He asked her politely to wait.

Charlie Carruthers had perished, too, the smallpox not waiting for the weakness of his body to overcome him. Grey had the body burned, not wishing Carruthers's hand to be stolen, for both the Indians and the local habitants regarded such things superstitiously. He took a canoe by himself, and on a deserted island in the St. Lawrence, scattered his friend's ashes to the wind.

He returned from this expedition to discover a letter, forwarded by Hal, from Mr. John Hunter, surgeon. He checked the level of brandy in the decanter, and opened it with a sigh.

My dear Lord John,

I have heard some recent conversation regarding the unfortunate death of Mr. Nicholls last spring, including comments indicating a public perception that you were responsible for his death. In case you shared this perception, I thought it might ease your mind to know that in fact you were not.

Grey sank slowly onto a stool, eyes glued to the sheet.

It is true that your ball did strike Mr. Nicholls, but this accident contributed little or nothing to his demise. I saw you fire upward into the air—I said as much, to those present at the time, though most of them did not appear to take much notice. The ball apparently went up at a slight angle, and then fell upon Mr. Nicholls from above. At this point, its power was quite spent, and the missile itself being negligible in size and weight, it barely penetrated the skin above his collarbone, where it lodged against the bone, doing no further damage.

The true cause of his collapse and death was an aortic aneurysm, a weakness in the wall of one of the great vessels emergent from the heart; such weaknesses are often congenital. The stress of the

*electric shock and the emotion of the duello that
followed apparently caused this aneurysm to rup-
ture. Such an occurrence is untreatable, and in-
variably fatal, I am afraid. There is nothing that
could have saved him.*

*Your Servant,
John Hunter, Surgeon*

Grey was conscious of a most extraordinary array
of sensations. Relief, yes, there was a sense of profound relief, as of one waking from a nightmare. There
was also a sense of injustice, colored by the beginnings
of indignation; by God, he had nearly been married!
He might, of course, also have been maimed or killed
as a result of the imbroglio, but that seemed relatively
inconsequent; he was a soldier, after all—such things
happened.

His hand trembled slightly as he set the note down.
Beneath relief, gratitude and indignation was a growing sense of horror.

I thought it might ease your mind. . . . He could
see Hunter's face, saying this; sympathetic, intelligent,
and cheerful. It was a straightforward remark, but
one fully cognizant of its own irony.

Yes, he was pleased to know he had not caused
Edwin Nicholls's death. But the means of that knowledge . . . gooseflesh rose on his arms and he shuddered involuntarily, imagining . . .

"Oh, God," he said. He'd been once to Hunter's
house—to a poetry reading, held under the auspices of

Mrs. Hunter, whose salons were famous. Dr. Hunter did not attend these, but sometimes would come down from his part of the house to greet guests. On this occasion, he had done so, and falling into conversation with Grey and a couple of other scientifically minded gentlemen, had invited them up to see some of the more interesting items of his famous collection: the rooster with a transplanted human tooth growing in its comb, the child with two heads, the fetus with a foot protruding from its stomach.

Hunter had made no mention of the walls of jars, these filled with eyeballs, fingers, sections of livers ... or of the two or three complete human skeletons that hung from the ceiling, fully articulated and fixed by a bolt through the tops of their skulls. It had not occurred to Grey at the time to wonder where—or how— Hunter had acquired these.

Nicholls had had an eyetooth missing, the front tooth beside the empty space badly chipped. If he ever visited Hunter's house again, might he come face-to-face with a skull with a missing tooth?

He seized the brandy decanter, uncorked it, and drank directly from it, swallowing slowly and repeatedly, until the vision disappeared.

His small table was littered with papers. Among them, under his sapphire paperweight, was the tidy packet that the widow Lambert had handed him, her face blotched with weeping. He put a hand on it, feeling Charlie's doubled touch, gentle on his face, soft around his heart.

You won't fail me.
"No," he said softly. "No, Charlie, I won't."

With Manoke's help as translator, he bought the child, after prolonged negotiation, for two golden guineas, a brightly colored blanket, a pound of sugar, and a small keg of rum. The grandmother's face was sunken, not with grief, he thought, but with dissatisfaction and weariness. With her daughter dead of the smallpox, her life would be harder. The English, she conveyed to Grey through Manoke, were cheap bastards; the French were much more generous. He resisted the impulse to give her another guinea.

It was full autumn now, and the leaves had all fallen. The bare branches of the trees spread black ironwork flat against a pale blue sky as he made his way upward through the town to the small French mission. There were several small buildings surrounding the tiny church, with children playing outside; some of them paused to look at him, but most of them ignored him—British soldiers were nothing new.

Father LeCarré took the bundle gently from him, turning back the blanket to look at the child's face. The boy was awake; he pawed at the air, and the priest put out a finger for him to grasp.

"Ah," he said, seeing the clear signs of mixed blood, and Grey knew the priest thought the child was his. He started to explain, but after all, what did it matter?

"We will baptize him as a Catholic, of course,"

Father LeCarré said, looking up at him. The priest was a young man, rather plump, dark and clean-shaven, but with a gentle face. "You do not mind that?"

"No." Grey drew out a purse. "Here—for his maintenance. I will send an additional five pounds each year, if you will advise me once a year of his continued welfare. Here—the address to which to write." A sudden inspiration struck him—not that he did not trust the good father, he assured himself—only . . . "Send me a lock of his hair," he said. "Every year."

He was turning to go when the priest called him back, smiling.

"Has the infant a name, sir?"

"A—" He stopped dead. His mother had surely called him something, but Malcolm Stubbs hadn't thought to tell him what it was before being shipped back to England. What should he call the child? Malcolm, for the father who had abandoned him? Hardly.

Charles, maybe, in memory of Carruthers . . .

. . . *one of these days, it isn't going to.*

"His name is John," he said abruptly, and cleared his throat. "John Cinnamon."

"*Mais oui,*" the priest said, nodding. "*Bon voyage, monsieur—et voyez avec le Bon Dieu.*"

"Thank you," he said politely, and went away, not looking back, down to the riverbank where Manoke waited to bid him farewell.